Deadly Shoals

Also by Joan Druett

IN THE WIKI COFFIN SERIES

Run Afoul
Shark Island
A Watery Grave

OTHER FICTION

Abigail
A Promise of Gold
Murder at the Brian Boru

NONFICTION

Island of the Lost
In the Wake of Madness
Rough Medicine
She Captains
Hen Frigates
The Sailing Circle (with Mary Anne Wallace)
Captain's Daughter, Coasterman's Wife
"She Was a Sister Sailor" (editor)
Petticoat Whalers
Fulbright in New Zealand
Exotic Intruders

Joan Druett

Deadly Shoals

ST. MARTIN'S MINOTAUR NEW YORK

This is a work of fiction. All of the characters, organizations, and events portrayed in this novel are either products of the author's imagination or are used fictitiously.

 For information, address St. Martin's Press, 175 Fifth Avenue, New York, N.Y. 10010.

www.minotaurbooks.com

Library of Congress Cataloging-in-Publication Data

Druett, Joan.

Deadly shoals / Joan Druett.—1st ed.

p. cm.

ISBN-13: 978-0-312-35337-7

ISBN-10: 0-312-35337-5

1. Coffin, Wiki (Fictitious character)—Fiction. 2. United States Exploring Expedition (1838–1842)—Fiction. 3. Americans—Foreign countries—Fiction. 4. Linguists—Fiction. 5. Scientific expeditions—Fiction. 6. Patagonia (Argentina and Chile)—Fiction. I. Title.

PR9639.3.D68D43 2007

823'.914—dc22 2007032239

First Edition: December 2007

10 9 8 7 6 5 4 3 2 1

For Laura Langlie, loyal agent,
faithful friend, and Wiki's first fan

Author's Note

On Sunday, August 18, 1838, the six ships of the first, great United States South Seas Exploring Expedition, commanded by Lieutenant Charles Wilkes, set sail from Norfolk, Virginia, headed for the far side of the world. The goal was the Pacific, but over the next four months the fleet surveyed the Atlantic Ocean, various calls being paid at Madeira, Cape Verde Islands, the northeast coast of Brazil, and Rio de Janeiro. The final Atlantic landfall was at Patagonia, for a survey of the shifting shoals of the Río Negro. This is the setting of the fourth Wiki Coffin mystery.

While the background is based on true events, the real people in the following list of dramatis personae are treated novelistically, while other characters are imagined, some of them being the crew of the equally fictional seventh ship of the fleet, the U.S. brig *Swallow*.

List of Several of the Officers and Men
Attached to
The United States Exploring Expedition

UNITED STATES SHIP *VINCENNES*

Charles Wilkes, Esq.	Commanding Exploring Expedition
Thomas T. Craven	Lieutenant
Lawrence J. Smith	Lieutenant
Christian Forsythe	Lieutenant
Edward Gilchrist	Surgeon
John Fox	Assistant Surgeon
Robert R. Waldron	Purser
Joseph P. Couthouy	Naturalist

UNITED STATES SHIP *PEACOCK*

William L. Hudson, Esq.	Commanding
Oliver Hazard Perry	Lieutenant
Silas Holmes	Surgeon
James Dwight Dana	Mineralogist
Titian Ramsey Peale	Naturalist
Horatio Hale	Philologist

UNITED STATES SHIP *RELIEF*

Andrew K. Long	Lieutenant-Commandant

UNITED STATES BRIG *PORPOISE*

Cadwallader Ringgold	Lieutenant-Commandant transferred to *Sea Gull* for the Río Negro survey

UNITED STATES BRIG *SWALLOW*

George Rochester	Passed Midshipman, Commandant
Constant Keith	Junior Midshipman
William "Wiki" Coffin	Linguister
James Stoker	Steward
Robert Festin	Cook
Dave Meagher	Gunner
Sua, "Jack Polo"	Seaman
Tana, "Jack Savvy"	Seaman

TENDER *SEA GULL*

James W. E. Reid	Passed Midshipman, Commandant

TENDER *FLYING FISH*

Samuel R. Knox	Commandant

Deadly Shoals

One

Off the coast of Patagonia, January 24, 1839

Wiki Coffin was in the saloon of the U.S. brig *Swallow* when he heard the man at the masthead call out for a sail. The *Swallow* was flying south on the breast of a favorable nor'west wind, so he assumed the sighting was of a homeward-bound ship passing on the opposite course. However, it was the first sign of company on the seas for the past eight days, and so he ran up the companionway to the deck and then climbed the mainmast to see what it was all about.

It proved to be a whaleship, about five miles away but coming down fast from the east, with all sails set but flying no flags. Her four boats were triced up in davits on the outside of the vessel, ready to be lowered at an instant's notice if whales were sighted, but her canvas was pristine white, unmarked by tryworks smoke, an indication that she hadn't done any whaling of late. Even from this distance, Wiki could discern a glint of copper under her foot as she crested the top of a wave, so knew that this was no northbound whaler deeply laden with oil.

Instead, she was racing to come up with them. Looking about the empty sea from his lofty vantage point, Wiki frowned, touched with uneasiness. They were off the Patagonian coast, with the shoal-ridden estuary of the Río Negro on the western horizon. It was notorious as a hotbed of revolutionaries, having been deliberately impoverished by General de Rosas, the tyrant of Buenos Aires. Wiki also knew that de Rosas was currently waging war with the French over his territorial ambitions in Uruguay—and had heard rumors in Rio that the French were issuing letters of marque to their merchant vessels on this coast, which included a number of whalers. He swung down a backstay to the quarterdeck.

Captain Rochester was standing on the weather side, one fist gripping the starboard shrouds. He was scowling, too. The instant he sighted Wiki he said, "What do you reckon, old chap?"

"Her captain seems determined to intercept us, but he isn't flying any signals—not even his ensign."

"Do you recognize her?"

Wiki grimaced. For the past seven years he had drifted from one American whaleship to another, deserting at exotic landfalls whenever he had become heartily tired of whaling, or fed up with the captain and officers, or simply wanted to get back to the Bay of Islands to pay a call on his *whanau*—his folks in New Zealand. However, this made him no authority on the identity of individual whalers.

He said, "It's infamously hard to tell one whaleship from another, George."

The trouble was, they were all built for the same purpose, with no variety in the pattern. There had been one captain of his acquaintance who had painted his command in a myriad of colors just to make himself different, but most of his crew had promptly jumped ship, declaring that their garish appearance frightened off the whales. Accordingly, the old spouter master had returned his typically beamy old tub to her former livery of black, interrupted with one white streak painted with black squares to fool innocent savages into thinking she had gunports with cannon behind them. And, with that, she had returned to being indistinguishable from the rest of the whaling fleet.

"So how do we know she's American?"

Wiki, who'd had the same thought, said flatly, "We don't. She could be French. If she is, she could be a privateer—which seems likely, as she looks far too clean to be a working whaler."

"Then let's make sure that her master knows beyond doubt that we're a United States Navy brig," Rochester decided. "Bo'sun," he hollered. "Get the biggest ensign aloft."

It took just a moment to comply, and events followed fast. No sooner had the bright flag been run up to flicker from the gaff of the *Swallow*, than smoke puffed up from the stranger's foredeck, and a cannonball screamed across the rapidly diminishing gap between the two ships. "He's fired a shot across our bows!" George exclaimed in shocked disbelief. "Beat to quarters, by God—*beat to quarters*!"

The stunned silence fore and aft turned into commotion. Sua, the brig's Samoan drummer, rushed into the forecastle for his drum—a length of log—and set to hammering out a primitive, blood-stirring rhythm even before he arrived back on deck. Rochester's youthful second-in-command, Midshipman Keith, raced up from below, the off-duty watch tumbling hard on his heels. As usual in any emergency, Wiki, who was the best helmsman in the ship, took over the wheel.

Every man was at his station; every head turned to watch the captain. "Wear ship, Mr. Keith, if you please," instructed Rochester. Not only would this bring the brig around so that the two chaser cannon on the deck at the stern would come to bear on the stranger, but the *Swallow* would present a much smaller target.

"Sta-a-a-*tions*!" Keith yelled, and hands clapped on to the weather braces and the spanker sheets. Men tailed onto lines, orders were shouted, and the spanker was hauled in with muscular jerks. Wiki heaved the wheel to leeward, and the *Swallow*'s fine bow turned away from the wind. His broad back suddenly chilled as a splash lifted over the taffrail and wetted his shirt.

"Brace round foresails!" *Down* went the helm as Wiki shoved on the spokes, and *round* the brig came. When he looked over his shoulder the whaleship was firmly in their sights. Crews hauled manfully at train tackles to drag the guns inboard, and powder and shot were rammed home. Then, with the cannon run out again, they were ready for action.

It had been a matter of mere moments. "Let's return the compliment, and fire a shot across *his* bows," Rochester suggested to the gunner, Dave. "Let's see how *he* likes being brought to," he added, and received a broad grin.

There was a huge explosion, the gun carriage screeched backward across the planks, and the cannonball whistled across the bows of the whaleman with wonderful precision. The result was both dramatic and effective—to Rochester's immense gratification, the spouter captain came up into the wind and backed his fore and mizzen topsails in a panic-stricken hurry, slowing to a near standstill.

His blood being thoroughly up, however, George Rochester was determined to teach the impudent stranger yet another lesson. In response to his orders the brig luffed up, rounded to with a flourish, hastened up the wind, and bore down on the whaleship with all sails set. Moments rushed by in the creaking of rigging and the swish of water, and then Wiki could see the expressions on the faces of the men who were standing at the rails of the whaler. They were staring paralyzed with horror as the brig tore down upon them.

Just as impact seemed inevitable, "Ready about!" George bellowed, and around the *Swallow* came. Losing speed fast, the brig sheered past the whaleship's stern, while the sailors who could read called out the name on the sternboard—"*Trojan* of New London, Connecticut"—to those who could not. Their voices were incredulous. A fellow national had fired at them—a countryman! Oaths echoed from all about the decks, and the boatswain hollered for quiet.

Like most American whalers, the *Trojan* had a hurricane house built over the stern, which was designed to shelter the helmsman, and contain such amenities as the sail locker. The master was standing on the flat roof of this, his fists propped on his belt, and his wide-brimmed leather hat crammed well down on his head. He was a middle-aged, deeply tanned, extremely wrinkled character, wearing a New Bedford beard—a fringe of short whiskers around the edges of his cheeks and chin—and a deeply wounded expression.

Such had been the precision of Rochester's maneuver, the captains were able to converse without speaking trumpets as the brig slid slowly past the whaleship's stern. According to protocol, this chat should have been an exchange of formal details, such as names of ship, captain, and last port, but instead the spouter skipper inquired in unmistakably aggrieved tones, "Why the hell did you fire a gun at me, sir?"

"I could say the same to you, sir," Rochester replied.

"Well, ain't you a United States Navy ship?"

"U.S. brig *Swallow*—and I'm uncommon glad you recognized me as such," Captain Rochester said dryly.

"So why didn't you respond to my flag of distress?" the other demanded. "You carried on without giving me a chance to run down and speak! All you did was send up a bloody big ensign—as if you wished to taunt me! What choice did I have but to fire a gun to make you pay attention?"

There was a moment of utter silence, disturbed only by the swish of the sea. Then George queried gently, "*What* flag of distress?"

The spouter master visibly started, then stared up and about his own rigging. Wiki, still at the helm, saw him push back his hat to scratch his head, and distinctly saw his lips move in the words, "Well, goddamn it." Someone on board the *Trojan* who had neglected to follow orders was going to be in big trouble, obviously—once the encounter was over.

The gap between the two ships was widening. Rochester lifted his voice, yelling, "Come on board and explain yourself, sir!" and then they had sailed on past.

The *Swallow* stilled a half-mile downwind from the whaleship, her mainyard brought aback so that the sails worked against each other, keeping her in more or less the same spot as she waited for her visitor. Then, everyone on deck watched the whaleboat cross the sparkling stretch of water, a process that evidently took long enough for the master to remember his manners, because when the boat touched the side of the brig, he stood up and hailed, "Ship ahoy!"

George arrived at the rail. "U.S. Exploring Brig *Swallow*, Rochester, five months from Norfolk, Virginia, last port Rio de Janeiro."

"Whaleship *Trojan* of New London, Stackpole, twenty-five months out, last port Montevideo, eight hundred barrels," said the other. His expression was dour as he rattled off the information, and Wiki grimaced in understanding. After a two-year voyage eight hundred barrels was a truly miserable report, indicative of long months with no glimpse of whales. No wonder, he thought, the *Trojan*'s sails were so clean.

The whaling master went on, "Permission to come aboard?"

George Rochester cast an all-comprehensive look at the boat and the ship beyond. Apart from the usual knives sheathed in their belts, the oarsmen were unarmed. Their ship floated quietly in plain view, the sun shining on her pale canvas. However, he decided to keep his crew at battle stations, so said to the boatswain, "Tell the men to stand fast." Then he nodded, and stepped back from the rail.

Stackpole reached out, grabbed a dangling rope, and walked his way up the side of the brig. Close up, he didn't appear any less confrontational. Like all seamen, he first cast a comprehensive, professional look at the sails and rigging. Then, after glancing suspiciously about the decks where men waited alertly with their pistols and cutlasses, he challenged, "What do you mean, *exploring* brig?"

George was studying him with his head tipped a little on one side, his hands linked loosely behind the seat of his white trousers, his muscular calves pushing out the legs at the back. He said, "We're part of the United States Exploring Expedition."

"The—what?" Stackpole's face was quite blank.

"The U.S. Exploring Expedition," George repeated, eyebrows high. "I'm surprised you haven't heard of it."

"Well, I haven't," confirmed the other, as hostile as ever.

"But that's amazing," said Rochester, obviously wondering where this chap had been all these years. "It took a whole decade of heated discussion in clubs, salons, and conference chambers to get the mission going, and then, when the seven ships finally departed from Norfolk, Virginia, back in August, it was a national sensation."

"Well, I wasn't there, was I? Seven ships?" Stackpole repeated, and whistled. "That's quite a fleet. Who's the commodore?"

"Lieutenant Charles Wilkes."

"A *lieutenant*?"

"It's complicated," said George. Wiki, listening from the helm, thought it was more than that—even though Charles Wilkes was called "captain" out of respect for the position he held, the fleet commander was understandably aggrieved that the Navy Department had not thought fit to endow him with a rank to suit the demanding job. Furthermore, it made the situation devilishly difficult at times, what with having to hand down orders to men who were actually higher than he was on the Navy List, which had a bad effect both on his temper and on general shipboard morale.

"But I do assure you that the mission is a grand one," Rochester assured his listener. "We have instructions to explore and survey the Atlantic and Pacific, promote the honor and dignity of our nation, forward the interests of science, further American commerce, and protect American whaling adventures."

Stackpole did not look impressed. Indeed, Wiki thought that his expression had become more suspicious than ever. He repeated, "*Seven* ships?"

"Seven," repeated George, whose patience was starting to fray. "The flagship is the sloop of war *Vincennes,* and the other six ships are—"

"So how come there's only one of you here?"

George said stiffly, "The others aren't far away, I assure you."

"But why ain't you sailing as a squadron?"

"There was an unfortunate incident as we were leaving the harbor of Rio de Janeiro, involving both the *Vincennes* and the second-in-command, the sloop *Peacock*, and—"

"You mean they got into a *war*, or something?"

"Absolutely not. They merely ran afoul of a merchant brigantine."

"What? *Both* of them?"

"The *Vincennes* blundered into the merchantman first. Unfortunately, the *Peacock*, which was following close behind, didn't have time to take evasive action."

"In full view of the whole of Rio?"

Stackpole snorted rudely, Rochester kept a dignified silence, and Wiki winced. The merchant brigantine had been his father's Salem trader *Osprey*, and it had been not the first, but the *second* time, that she had got into a collision with expedition ships. While Wiki had not been on board the *Vincennes* to see the confrontation with Wilkes that had followed this latest episode, he had been assured by those who had been there that Captain Coffin's fury had been truly awe-inspiring.

The whaling master jibed, "I hope they made a real lubberly job of it, and sent the brigantine to the bottom."

"On the contrary, it was a trivial matter," Rochester snapped. "There were a few repairs to be done, and the matter of compensation to be discussed with the master of the merchantman, but that should delay them only a couple of days."

"So what about the other four vessels? Did they get into collisions, too?"

"The gun brig *Porpoise* was instructed to send a party into the city in search of a few deserters, with squads from the schooners *Flying Fish* and *Sea Gull* to assist. The storeship *Relief* was sent ahead some days before, as she's a slow sailer, and impedes the fleet sadly."

Wiki concealed a grin at this. He had been on board the *Vincennes* when Captain Wilkes had given the captain of the *Relief* his marching orders, and so he knew better—that Wilkes had sent the storeship off early *not* because of her undeniably slow sailing qualities, but because rumors had been running about the fleet that the captain and officers of the *Relief* had been invited to a merry spree on shore.

Then he heard the whaling master say, "And you were sent ahead, too?"

"*Not* because the *Swallow* is a slow sailer," George said, very firmly indeed.

"I reckon not," Stackpole agreed without hesitation, taking another admiring look at the brig's vast sails and taut rigging. "But why were you in such a hurry?"

"Our orders are to get to the mouth of the Río Negro—where the other ships will join us—and commence a survey of the shoals."

"But what the hell for? They change with every tide!"

Wiki silently agreed. Indeed, he considered the assignment insane. Though it was supposed to be a secret as deep as the grave, every member of the expedition was perfectly aware that Captain Wilkes was determined to embark on a search for the fabled Antarctic continent as soon as the fleet had doubled Cape Horn—but if that was ever to be undertaken, it had to be accomplished before the end of the southern summer, and it was the third week of January already.

"And the taxpayers are *paying* for this useless expedition?"

"Over the past five months we've accomplished a great deal," George Rochester returned with offended dignity. "Unknown tracts of the ocean have been charted—making the sea safer for people like you! Important gravitational measurements were carried out in Rio—mountains were surveyed, along with an immense lot of jungle. Great loads of specimens will be forwarded to the States. By the time the mission is over, the government will be well rewarded for their investment, I assure you!"

"Well, I most surely do hope so," said the whaling master, sotto voce, and then, with an abrupt change of topic, inquired, "Do you have any marines on board?"

"Marines? No, we do not. Why do you ask?"

"Because I'm in dire need of a well-armed squad."

"What the devil for?"

"You said that part of the mission is to protect American whaling adventures, and that's exactly what I need—protection!"

George Rochester cast an all-comprehensive look about the innocently sparkling sea. "Protection from what, pray?"

"I need help to apprehend a thief."

"A thief? You need a sheriff, Captain, not a squad of marines!"

"Well, there ain't no sheriff about here—and I don't actually care how you do it, sir, just so long as I get my money back."

"You've been robbed?"

"Of a significant sum—by a man by the name of Adams, who's American, which I reckon makes all the difference. He's an American trader who has a store in the village of El Carmen, up the Río Negro," Stackpole went on, jabbing a finger at the landward horizon. "I gave him a thousand dollars—and he absconded with it!"

Wiki, at the helm, had trouble not shaking his head in disbelief at such credulous trust in an undoubted adventurer, and George, obviously, felt the same, demanding, "What in God's name did you give him all that money for?"

Stackpole shifted from one boot to another, giving the sails another look to conceal his embarrassed expression. "The whaling hasn't been going well," he muttered. "So I thought I'd invest in sealing."

"Sealing?"

"And why not?" queried the whaling master, back to delivering George an antagonistic stare. "The sealing trade ain't finished, yet. There's plenty of rookeries what ain't been discovered, with hordes of seals just waiting to be taken."

Wiki and George exchanged a startled glance, having already heard this kind of claptrap from a bunch of old sealers they had picked up at Shark Island, off the coast of Brazil, a couple of months earlier in the voyage. There had been a time when men could make a fortune out of a sealing venture, when an eight-man gang could take twenty thousand skins in one four-month season, but since then the rookeries—the breeding beaches—had been devastated, the seal herds wiped out to the very last pup by the hunters' cruel greed. Despite all the grim evidence, however, a certain type of sealing man still clung obstinately to the mad belief that there were some more lucrative beaches to be found, if only one kept up the hunt. An experienced whaling master, in Wiki's silent estimation, should have had more sense.

Rochester said, "But why Patagonia?"

"There's plenty of seals about these parts, believe me. Patagonia has been considered too dangerous till just lately, but only six years ago the *Penguin* sailed into Stonington with fourteen hundred pelts from round these parts, and since then there's been a lot of interest in the coast. Just one month ago, I heard that the New York brig *Athenian* did very well indeed over the past coupla seasons, and so I thought I might as well try a venture of my own. The season don't finish till March, you know! But I need a tender to do it. Adams had a schooner for sale, so I agreed to buy her, even if she were a bit pricey."

"But that's a devil of a lot of money to hand over to a Río Negro trader, American or not!"

"Adams has never cheated me before," the whaling master protested. "And I've been buying his stores for the past three years. All the whalers use him when they recruit for salt beef on this part of the coast—he's built up a good little business."

"And he just *happened* to have a schooner for sale?"

"It wasn't his vessel," Stackpole said defensively. "He told me he was acting as the agent for the captain of the *Athenian*. The brig's holds are full, so they are heading home. Naturally, they wanted to sell their tender first—a solid little schooner, ideal for me. I gave Adams the wherewithal to buy her, and then told him to provision her, load her with salt for curing the skins, and hire a gang of Indians for sealing hands. I'd be back before long, I said, to take over the craft and settle up accounts. But when I arrived up the river with three spare hands to collect the schooner and sail her downriver, it was to find he'd vanished, along with my cash!"

Wiki asked curiously, "Did you really pay him in cash?"

Stackpole turned and looked him up and down, from wild black ringlets to bare brown feet. Then he turned away again, saying contemptuously, "Say *sir* when you speak to me, boy."

George flushed. "I'm sorry, *sir,* I should have introduced you before," he snapped. "This is Mr. Coffin, the expedition linguister."

"He's—*what?*"

"Wiki Coffin is a member of the scientific corps."

The whaling master looked at Wiki again, eyebrows high as he surveyed his muscular, dungaree-clad frame again. "But how can a Pacific Islander—a *kernacker!*—be a scientist, for God's sake?"

"Not only is Wiki Coffin a scientist, but he could be exactly the man you need," Rochester loftily informed him. "He's the representative of U.S. law and order with the expedition, authorized by the sheriff's department of Portsmouth, Virginia."

"What the *hell* are you talking about?"

George said to Wiki in tones of sorely tried patience, "Could I trouble you to fetch your warrant, old chap? It seems we have to prove our point."

Wiki paused, interested enough by the contradictions of this strangely blatant theft to repeat his question to Stackpole. "Did you really give him the thousand dollars in cash?" he asked.

The whaling master frowned, but admitted, "I gave him a draft on my Connecticut bank, payable to bearer."

Wiki's lips pursed up in a silent whistle as he contemplated the interesting implications of this. "And the schooner has disappeared, too?"

"Of course," said Stackpole sourly.

Two

January 25, 1839

At eight bells—four the next morning—the *Trojan* whaleboat arrived at the starboard rail of the *Swallow*. Wiki, who was ready and waiting as arranged, jumped into it. The six men of the boat's crew looked at him, and he nodded in return. Two of them, he noticed with interest, were Pacific Islanders—*kanaka*, a word that Stackpole pronounced "kernacker," Yankee fashion. Remembering how the whaling master had disdainfully addressed him as "boy," he wondered how they were treated on board the *Trojan*. However, there was no opportunity to ask them questions, or even to learn their names.

Once Wiki was settled in the stern sheets Captain Stackpole barked an order, and a sail was set. Then they sailed with the sureness of past experience toward the unseen shoals of the Río Negro. The onshore wind was with them, and the *Trojan* and the *Swallow* were soon out of sight. An hour later the sun nudged the seaward horizon, setting the tips of the little waves to dancing orange and gold, and lighting up a tall reddish cliff at the edge of a high headland. At the top of this, the silhouette of a bare flagpole poked a narrow finger at the paling sky.

This, evidently, was the landmark they were aiming to fetch. At a word from their captain, the sail was taken in, the mast unshipped, and the tiller exchanged for a steering oar. The oarsmen set their shoulders into pulling through the broad band of wild surf that crashed on the beach below the flagstaff, while the headsman, standing in the stern, leaned hard on the big sweep, his eyes slitted. The boat danced madly at first, but a moment later they were through the breakers. The boat grounded with a crashing of gravel and sand.

Wiki waded ashore, then sat down on a rock and brushed off his feet before putting on his boots and rolling down the legs of his trousers. Two of the men had already turned the boat around for the return trip to the *Trojan*, while Stackpole stood in the surf, giving orders. Listening to the shouted conversation, Wiki gathered that the *Trojan* was to go out on a short cruise after whales with the first mate in command, while their captain attended to his business here. Then, with a helping shove from Stackpole, the boat pulled off through the waves.

When Stackpole arrived on the beach he sat down to put on his own boots, and then led the way up the face of the cliff, which was so steep that the narrow track tagged back and forth along rocky terraces. Stones rolled away as they climbed. Wiki paused to catch his breath when they reached the top, finding that there was a more extensive view than he had expected, the beach being over one hundred feet below his feet. He could see the estuary of the Río Negro immediately to the south of the headland, the black waters heavily braided with shoals which gleamed in streaks of green and russet. On the far side of the river sandhills bulged up and down, pink and gray in the early sun.

Stackpole had kept on moving across the promontory, heading toward a sere thicket, and as Wiki watched he disappeared into the scrub. When Wiki caught up with him, he was trudging down a narrow track, heading for a long, low, barnlike building which proved to be the pilothouse. Once inside, the whaling master engaged in conversation with two frowsty, weather-beaten river pilots who looked as alike as brothers, though one turned out to be French, while the other was English. They lived comfortably enough, in a kind of cozy squalor, the single room being furnished with a table and benches, and bunks piled high with blankets. Tins, boxes, bags of provisions, and bottles of grog were stacked along wide shelves that ran around two of the walls, while cutlasses and pistols dangled from pegs.

As Wiki stepped inside, Stackpole was asking the pilots about the hireage of horses for the trek to El Carmen de Patagones, eighteen miles upriver. Neither of them looked very happy about this, there being no commission for sending a party upriver on horseback, but the Englishman consented to give them directions to a nearby *estancia,* along with a dour warning that it was a twenty-minute walk away. Undeterred, Stackpole nodded thanks, and then headed back through the scrub to the stony headland, where the short, hard grass was turning gold-colored with the rays of the lifting sun.

Striding along behind him, Wiki looked about with interest, comparing this sere Patagonian steppe with the lush Argentinian pampas of his memories. Just over a year ago, back in October 1837, when his ship had dropped anchor in Callao he had heard talk that the bark of war George Rochester was serving on was lying at Montevideo, so Wiki had jumped ship to head about the Horn as the second mate of a Peruvian trader, in the hope of seeing his old comrade. Arriving in the Uruguayan port, he had found to his delight that the talk was true—George's ship, the *Acasta,* was there, and would be there for some time, too, being in the middle of refitting for the West Indies station.

Equally elated, George had immediately requested leave, and after this had been granted the two friends had hired two tough ponies, and galloped off into the hinterland, where they had joined a band of gauchos, and had learned to use the *lazo* and hunt with the bolas—*les tres Marías*. At night, they had sipped the green tea called maté from a common gourd, while they traded yarns of the sea for tales of the pampas. Their new friends had told them that here, at the Río Negro, the great grass plains evolved into a stony semidesert that stretched all the way to Cape Horn, and what Wiki saw now confirmed it.

The dirt between the clumps of tussock was thin, and dust rose with every step, while mirages shimmered in the inland distance. It was a break in the arid monotony when Stackpole found a path that straggled off to the left, leading past a weather-silvered fence to a clump of big trees and a house with barns perched halfway down the slope. It took another five minutes to rouse the *estanciero* from his breakfast. Then Wiki dickered in Spanish while the rancher's wife and children watched him raptly with huge brown eyes, and Stackpole, though he could understand scarcely a word, kept on urging him to get the price still lower. Evidently the loss of the thousand-dollar bond had cost the whaleman dearly, because when they came to an agreement he opened his purse so reluctantly that Wiki fully expected the ranch owner to cheat them. Instead, however, the *estanciero* produced a strong gray mare for Wiki himself, and an experienced pinto for Stackpole, both equipped with capacious sheepskin saddles and proper European stirrups, though dangling long in the gaucho fashion. There was even a plaited rawhide *lazo* provided—presumably, thought Wiki, to lasso the horses if they tried to escape.

Clambering heavily onto his mount, Stackpole trotted down the rest of the slope to a winding riverside trail, rimmed by rushing water on one side, and by tall banks on the other. Following him, Wiki meditated with some amusement that the whaling master rode in the stolid manner of a farmer, the reins held short and his boots jammed into the stirrups. Personally, he kept a long rein and didn't bother with the stirrups, at times riding with his feet dangling, and at other times with one foot tucked up under the other thigh, native fashion. It was the way he had ridden bareback as a child—a style that was so relaxed and easy that he could keep it up for scores of miles without tiring.

The world was filled with the rippling sounds of water, the distant cries of birds, and the clatter of hooves—and then Stackpole's gruff voice. Evidently he had been impressed by Wiki's handling of the rancher, because he asked over his shoulder, "You been about these parts often, boy?"

Wiki glanced at him with no friendliness at all, greatly disliking that word *boy*. He said briefly, "Not exactly."

"What do you mean, *not exactly*?"

"I once spent a few weeks riding the pampas, but it was north'ard of here, on the Río de la Plata."

"Well, you sure do seem well acquainted with the local customs."

Wiki nodded. The terrain might be very different, but the people were the same. He glimpsed men passing by on the heights above, seated upright on their huge sheepskin saddles—*recaos*—and swinging their whips over their heads as they drove small herds of cattle or horses before them. The long silver-hilted knives thrust slantwise into their belts at the back stuck out on either side like the upper yards of lateen sails. The steeds' long manes and the men's long black hair flew out in the wind, parallel with the ragged fringes of their ponchos.

He looked back at Stackpole. "Do you come here often?"

"Often enough. Adams's salt beef is cheaper than what I can get in Montevideo, and keeps better, too."

That was because of the saltpeter in the local salt; Wiki had heard about that, too. The sealers liked it because it preserved the pelts so well. Instead of commenting, he reined in to look around. They had arrived at a valley where several small streams joined the river. A cluster of white ranchhouses had been built on the sandy confluence, partly shaded by pergolas and groves of peach trees, pegged-out hides making rectangular shadows on the ground in front of them. Children ran out to offer them fruit and water, while their sparkling-eyed sisters giggled demurely behind their palms, and their mothers teased Wiki to see his creased-up grin, and told him to go away before he seduced their daughters. Then, with an impatient grunt, Stackpole hassled them on.

Farther along the trail, a burned-out ruin presented a grim contrast to this lively scene. The buildings were so collapsed that it was evident the place had been ravaged years ago, but no one had bothered to rebuild. When Wiki asked about it, Stackpole said that it was one of the many relics of the war between the settlers and the local Indians—which the Indians, of course, had lost.

"So where are the Indians now?"

"The Tehuiliche tribe have their *toldos*—tents—staked on the plain opposite the fort. The governor sends 'em clapped-out military horses to eat, and they make some kind of living by working the hides into leather, and the legs into gaucho boots. They usually look pretty poverty-stricken, but when I last called the young bloods were strutting about very rich, flaunting pretty new clothes. Then I found they'd been away for the past two years, working as sealing hands on the schooner that was tender for the *Athenian*, and had only just got back."

"I see," said Wiki. Obviously, when Stackpole had found that the young Tehuiliches had done so well, he had made up his mind that sealing was the way to repair his fortunes. "And that's when you decided to give Adams the draft for the *Athenian*'s schooner—the one that's gone missing?"

"The *Grim Reaper*," Stackpole agreed.

"I beg your pardon?"

"*Grim Reaper*. That's the schooner's name."

And an apt one, too, considering the brutal nature of the sealing trade, Wiki mused, but was still surprised. He said, "You inspected her before you handed over the money?"

"Of course I did! Do you think I'm a complete bloody fool? She was lying at anchor off the pueblo, and I went on board, looked at her holds, tested her pumps, and rowed around her in a boat. She was oily as hell, and stank like hell, too, but she was as sound as a nut. There were even some furs still stowed in her holds, ready for collection later."

That sounded odd, Wiki thought. He said, "Were any of the *Athenian* crew on board?"

"Nope. Just Adams and me."

Odder still, considering the valuable pelts. "The captain of the *Athenian* hadn't hired a shipkeeper?"

"It was broad of day. I guess someone kept watch at night."

Wiki was prepared to bet that it was Adams himself who had been paid to keep watch. He said, "It sounds as if the *Athenian* came back for the schooner, not just the pelts—that Adams made up the story that the captain intended to sell her, and pocketed the money himself." It was easy to imagine the storekeeper seizing the chance to "sell" the vessel he was looking after to the first credulous customer who happened along, and smiling complacently as the *Grim Reaper* was sailed away by her rightful owners, leaving him a thousand dollars richer.

Captain Stackpole scowled. "I had no reason not to believe Caleb Adams—I've dealt with him often, and know him well enough to take him at his word. Nope," he said, his tone definite. "I would've known if he was lying."

"But did anyone confirm that the vessel was up for sale?"

Dead silence. Then Stackpole admitted, "Adams's clerk didn't know nothing about it."

"Clerk?" This was the first Wiki had heard of a clerk. However, he didn't have a chance to ask further, because they came around a bend in the path to find a man waiting on the track ahead.

This fellow was holding a horse by the bridle, and looked as if he had been standing there for quite a while, though he had an air of being too important to be the type to be kept hanging around. He was also quite a dandy. With his pointed black beard, his wide-brimmed black hat, his embroidered boots, ruffled shirt, short jacket, and tight black trousers, he could have stepped out of old Spain.

Stackpole muttered, "Goddamn it." Then he said to Wiki, "Tell him that my ship is off on a cruise for whales; that I'm here on personal business, and don't intend to do any trading. He'll try to persuade you different, but don't listen."

"Why?"

"Because he's determined to charge me customs duty."

So this gentleman, Wiki deduced, was the collector of customs.

He proved to be as courtly as he looked, once he got over his surprise that a South Seas native should speak intelligent Spanish, listening politely, though very regretfully, to the message that Wiki passed on. As he proceeded to convey in delicate phrases, His Excellency Juán José Hernández, the governor of El Carmen de Patagones, was greatly in need of money. Because General de Rosas, the tyrant of Buenos Aires, was deliberately impoverishing the people of the Río Negro, the exportation of salt and beef was very difficult, and the importation of goods impossible, and so the tax basket was empty. For lack of public funds, the government had not been paid a salary for the past eighteen months.

Then he apologized about being obliged to ask an impertinent question, adding, "We are forced to be cautious, because of the war with the French, you understand."

Wiki listened, and then turned to Stackpole and said, "He wants to know what we're up to, since we're not conducting any business here."

"Tell him we wish to arrest an American thief by the name of Caleb Adams."

"He'll want to know the details."

"Just tell him you're an officer of the American law."

Wiki conveyed this. "Undoubtedly you have proof of your office," the customs official remarked, with yet another apologetic smile.

Wiki produced his letter of authority from the sheriff's department of Portsmouth, Virginia. He had unfolded this grand document several times already during the voyage, but this was the first time it had been spread out on the back of a horse.

The officer was marvelously impressed by the crest, the ribbons, the seal, and the flourishing signatures, even if he couldn't comprehend the flowing English script. "But you must pay your respects to His Excellency the Governor-general before attempting any kind of investigation," he objected, however. "He, you understand, is in charge of law and order here."

Wiki translated this for Stackpole, who merely jerked his head. "Tomorrow," he said curtly, and galloped off without another word.

It was just noon when they arrived at El Carmen. Here, the river widened even further, and started to become dotted with little islets thickly clothed in drooping willow trees. The town was laid out like a chessboard on an embayment, sloping all the way up to the buttress of the cliff. The space was so limited that some of the rearmost houses were hunched as tightly into the sandstone as if they had been hewn out of the rock. Various small craft lay on the surface of the water, the current tugging at their anchors.

A palisade curved around the western fringe of the village and climbed up the long slope to the clifftop, where a walled fort with a single tall tower bulked against the sky. Wiki pointed to it and said, "Is that the barracks?"

"Aye. About two hundred ex-felons what call themselves soldiers live there."

"What about the governor?"

"He has quarters there, too, along with his staff."

"We really should go up and report."

"What the hell for? Can't you see it's just the start of siesta? We won't raise a living soul for hours." Without troubling to argue further, Stackpole set his horse into a canter, clattering up a flight of shallow stone steps into the heart of the town.

Wiki followed, heading up an alley that was lined with single-storied, flat-roofed buildings. Made of whitewashed adobe, they stood out sharply against the reddish sandstone cliffs and the bright blue sky, throwing short black shadows onto the baked mud street. Beyond, the streets intersected each other in squares, trapping heat and light. In many ways, Wiki thought, El Carmen looked like paintings he had seen of towns in the Arabian desert. The church had a tower like a minaret, and a domed roof like a mosque, and there was a plaza with a well. Even the horses, with their arched necks and sloping shoulders, looked Arabian. Every building had a hitching rail outside, where at least one pony stamped and whisked its tail at the flies. An abundance of yellow dogs slunk about, too, but the human populace was invisible, though a smell of burning charcoal and cooking food pervaded the warm, still air.

Stackpole drew to a halt outside a rectangular building that stood out from the rest because it was made of red brick instead of adobe. Iron gratings over the windows indicated that this was a trading post, with goods inside that thieves might consider worth stealing, and a small, weathered sign confirmed that this was Adams's store. The door was wide open. Wiki tied his horse to the rail, and walked across the echoing boards of the verandah to follow Stackpole inside.

The dim interior was shaped like an inverted L, being a lot wider at the back than at the front. The narrow leg of the L was the place where sales were made, being furnished with a counter. Opposite this was a door bearing a notice attesting in Spanish that it led to a surgery, which Wiki judged must be quite a large room. Beyond, the wide back part of the store was used both for storage and for receiving and discharging goods, because a double door, shut and stoutly bolted and barred, was set into the wall of the farthest left-hand end.

Right now, though, this area was a yawning, empty space. Where bags and barrels had been recently stacked, there were only outlines in the dust on the floor, surrounded by the scuffles of many feet. All that remained was a smell of tobacco, dusty corn, old brine, and vinegar. Shelves hung on the wall between the dispensary door and the front entrance, but, save for a few boxes of figs and sardines, a couple of square bottles of gin, and a cask of *aguardiente,* these were equally bare.

Puzzled, Wiki said to Stackpole, "The provisions have all gone."

"I gave Adams instructions to supply the schooner, didn't I?" the whaling master growled. "Obviously, the string-shanked bastard did just that before he run off with the vessel and my money."

The long, broad counter did carry a few goods, but nothing more substantial than a few red-striped shirts, a small pile of wool ponchos, and a box of red silk bandannas. Behind this, a wizened old man was perched on a stool, pretending that he hadn't heard them come in. He was reading a Portuguese book, so Wiki used that language when he addressed him.

"I am the clerk of Senhor Adams," the fellow grudgingly replied, without the slightest hint of surprise at being questioned in his mother tongue. He kept a finger in his book to mark his place, and refused to meet Wiki's gaze, focusing on the wall by the surgery door instead.

"Where is your employer?"

At this, the clerk did look at Wiki. "Why do you ask?"

"Captain Stackpole is anxious to speak to him."

"As I told the captain one week ago, Senhor Adams is not available."

"He has not returned?"

"He has not."

"How long is it since you saw him last?"

There was a long pause as the little, hostile eyes looked everywhere except at Wiki's face, and then the clerk grunted, "I have told Captain Stackpole this already."

"But you have not told me," Wiki pointed out.

"Indeed, I have not," the clerk agreed, and prepared to return to his book.

Wiki produced his sheriff's certificate. The inspection the Portuguese gave the document was insultingly brief. "What has this to do with Senhor Adams?"

"Senhor Adams is a citizen of America, and subject to United States law—of which I am an agent, as this paper certifies."

The clerk remained unimpressed. "I can say nothing of use to you."

"Let me be the judge of that," Wiki advised him. "Just tell me exactly what you told Captain Stackpole."

This elicited a martyred sigh. Then the Portuguese recited, "On January fifteenth—ten days ago, now—I arrived here as is my usual habit, but Senhor Adams, he was not here, so I let myself in with my own key. Alone, I attended the counter until the evening. Then I locked up and went home. The next day, Captain Stackpole arrived to see Senhor Adams, but he was not here. Still, he has not returned. Myself, I have looked after the store as usual."

"Did Senhor Adams leave a note for you?"

"A note was not necessary."

"This has happened before?"

"Many times."

"But where does Senhor Adams go?"

"I would never inquire." As the clerk haughtily intimated, he had been Senhor Adams's trusted employee for several years, and was not the type to ask his employer impertinent questions.

"Your job is just to look after the store?"

"And to help keep the books, too," the clerk said, unable to stop himself from bragging, and Wiki instantly demanded to see them.

Very reluctantly, two ledgers were produced from a cubbyhole in the back of the counter. Wiki took them both, while the clerk's eyes suspiciously followed every movement. Ignoring this, Wiki settled down to read, half listening as Stackpole started a halting exchange in English with the clerk, and then losing interest as it became obvious that the whaleman was simply covering the ground he had gone over during his last visit, with as little result as before.

The first book was one of those usually kept as a ship's logbook, its ruled columns for position and weather assigned to lists of purchases, sales, and customers' names instead. Everything was written in English, the script very neat. The catalogue was initially a very long one, and there had been a great deal of trade in both dry and salt provisions for ships. Captain Stackpole's name featured many times, mostly in connection with the purchase of large quantities of salt beef, much of it carrying the notation that it had come from a ranch owned by a man named Ducatel. Stackpole had been a trader as well, however, having sold Adams rather a lot of tobacco, and Wiki wondered if the collector of customs knew about this.

Back in October 1836 there had been a big sale of provisions and salt to a man by the name of Rowland Hallett. Since then, trade had fallen off so drastically that the store was probably on the verge of collapse, which provided a good reason for Wiki's guess that Adams had grasped the chance to "sell" the schooner he'd been hired to look after, and pocket the money before handing her back to her rightful owners.

That left the puzzle of the disappearing goods, however, because there was no record of a recent sale of that magnitude. Was Stackpole right, and Adams had stocked the schooner before absconding with her? Wiki looked about the empty storage space again, noting the marks in the dust where barrels and boxes had recently stood, and said to the clerk, "On the fifteenth, when you came to find Senhor Adams gone, was the store empty like this?"

The clerk drew himself up. "Of what crime do you accuse Senhor Adams?"

"I'm accusing him of nothing. I asked you a question."

"Because of an illness in the family, I was away for a week. On the fifteenth I returned to find Senhor Adams gone and the store empty. Yet still I remained at my post, and did my work."

"And you have no way of telling when the goods were removed?"

"It is not in the account book, so how can I tell?"

"I see," said Wiki. He was deep in thought, meditating that the storekeeper would have had to equip the *Grim Reaper* with more than provisions before setting out for the open sea.

He said, "Are there seamen for hire in this village?"

The clerk didn't answer, looking around evasively instead, and Stackpole said, "What did you ask him?"

Wiki repeated the question in English, and watched the whaling master's brows bristle upward as he realized its significance. "I've never once had a Río Negro man apply to me for a berth on board my ship, not in all the times I've been here. They're horsemen, not sailors," he said. "So how did Adams find a crew?"

"What about the Indians?"

"They're sealers, not seamen, and have to be trained, at that."

"Deserters? Maybe some men jumped from the *Athenian* while she was here, and were hanging about the waterfront, looking for another berth."

"The *Athenian*?" Stackpole shook his head. "She did uncommon well, so why would any of her crew walk away at the end of a profitable voyage? They'll get a nice packet of money after dropping anchor in New York."

"There might have been other ships," Wiki said, because he had never known a ship without potential deserters in the crew. "There's a number of men set to jump ship and leave the expedition at the first opportunity," he added wryly, thinking that if Adams had delayed the theft of the schooner until the fleet arrived, he would have had no trouble filling his berths. Though the morale of the expedition seamen was slowly improving from its parlous state when they had left Norfolk, Virginia, back in August, the unpredictable and ascerbic nature of their commander didn't help.

Stackpole said derisively, "Life ain't all that great in the navy?"

"Seven men in particular would run first chance," Wiki assured him. "If there was a sealing voyage in the offing, they'd probably kill to join it. But," he added, "they aren't navy men."

"They're sealers?" guessed Stackpole, looking very interested.

"A gang of sealers we rescued from their sinking ship at an island off northeast Brazil," Wiki said, then turned to the other ledger, which looked very different from the first, being tall and narrow.

To his surprise, it was an apothecary's account book. He turned the pages curiously, finding that Adams had sold everything from absinthe to zinc, plus patent medicines with names like "Turlington's Balsam of Life," and "Carter's Spanish Mixture." It ended eighteen months earlier, with a black line ruled underneath the last entry, which read, "Last of stock sold to Dr. Ducatel."

When he asked the clerk about it, the old man proved a lot more amenable, evidently possessing none of the loyalty to Ducatel that he held for his employer. Dr. Ducatel, he revealed, had rented the side room for a surgery, but in the months since that last sale he had gone out of business. No medicines could be obtained now, as the brutal administration of Buenos Aires did not allow drugs of any kind to be exported from that city. Even if they were available, no one in El Carmen could afford a doctor, as no one had been paid for many months. Accordingly, Ducatel was now running a ranch—he was *estanciero*, having married the daughter of a local landholder—and the surgery was locked and out of use.

Ducatel—ranch. The two words seemed linked. Wiki frowned, and turned back to the first ledger, the one that recorded ordinary trade. A little gust came in the front door as he riffled through the pages, and a paper fluttered out of the back.

"What's that?" said Stackpole.

Wiki bent to retrieve the document, which had fallen to the floor. Then he unfolded it, and spread it out on the top of the counter. Stackpole breathed heavily from behind his shoulder as he read it.

The paper was a standard printed form, with gaps that had been filled in with inked names, a date, and a sum of money, and had been signed by Adams and a man who wrote in an illegible scrawl. Wiki scanned the copperplate script with growing stupefaction: "*. . . whereas said schooner and outfits as she now lies at El Carmen de Patagones is this day sold by Rowland Hallett to Caleb Adams on behalf of S. R. Stackpole for the sum of one thousand . . .*"

He looked up at Stackpole and exclaimed, "It's the deed of sale for the *Grim Reaper*!"

The whaling master's eyes widened for an instant, but then he grimly nodded. To have it confirmed that Caleb Adams had bought the schooner with his money and then sailed off with his property did not surprise Captain Stackpole at all.

Three

When Wiki crossed the verandah of the store and went out into the afternoon sunshine, to his great surprise he found that a dozen gauchos on angular, unshod horses were waiting in the street, though he hadn't heard them arrive. They were sitting sideways on their great fleece-covered saddles, brushing back their ferocious black mustachios to puff judiciously at skinny cigars of flaked tobacco wrapped in scraps of paper, and gave every appearance of having been there quite a while.

Wiki studied them, and the cowboys studied him back with narrowed eyes. A gust lifted their ponchos and ruffled the hairs on the back of Wiki's neck. Then, as the striped fabric fell back against their lean bodies, one of them lifted a yellow-stained finger, and in the accent of the *arribeño* of the upper provinces stated, "We believe you have lost an article of value."

Stackpole asked, "What did he say?"

"They know you've been robbed," Wiki told him.

"They're probably the men who helped Adams sail off with my schooner," the whaleman growled. "Now they've come to claim a fee for pretending to hunt for it."

"Be careful what you say—they often understand some English. They're *rastreadores*, professional trackers, and very proud men. They make their living by finding strayed animals, and hunting down thieves."

"How do you know that?"

"Because I've ridden with men like them before."

"So how do they know I've been robbed?"

"By magic," said Wiki dryly. It was well known in the Río de la Plata that if the owner of a *ranchería* woke up one morning to find horses or cattle gone, a *rastreador* would magically arrive at his door. "If there's a chance of getting your schooner back, these are the men who'll do it."

Meantime, he was studying the *rastreadores'* spokesman very thoughtfully. Walking up to him, he asked permission, and then inspected his steed. It was a good horse, with one white forefoot and one white hindfoot, which according to gaucho lore guaranteed it to be fast. As further testament to its quality, it bore several marks on its flanks, evidence that it had been bought and sold several times. When a man acquired a new mount, he put his personal brand on it, and then when he sold it he repeated the brand, doubling it to show that the horse was no longer his property.

Wiki tapped a double brand made up of four stars in the shape of the Southern Cross, and said, "I knew the man who owned this mark."

"My brother," said the rider.

"Your brother?" Wiki echoed, astonished, and said, "May I ask your name?"

"Bernantio," said the other. "Manuel."

Wiki lifted his brows, amazed at the coincidence, though he knew from personal experience how wide and far the gauchos wandered—and how many brothers they had, some by birth, others adopted. "I believe your brother is Juán," he said after identifying himself. "A year ago, I rode with him."

"He spoke of you," said Bernantio without a trace of surprise. Then he added, "He also said that your comrade was a tall man with yellow hair whose face resembled that of a sheep."

Wiki ducked his head, partly to hide his grin at this apt description of George Rochester, and partly to show his respect for the gossip of the pampas, which apparently was as accurate as shipboard scuttlebutt.

"He is well?" the gaucho inquired. Wiki, who had almost forgotten the elaborate courtesies of the region, assured him of George's health, and asked equally politely about the welfare of Bernantio's brother Juán. That ritual over, Bernantio remarked, "I was reliably informed that you had long hair like our own. Something has happened?"

Typically, these gauchos had hair that fell past their shoulders, and were inordinately proud of the black tresses that flew in the wind as they galloped. Wiki's own hair had indeed been as long as theirs, but was now reduced to six-inch ringlets springing ferociously about his face.

"It was cut," he admitted.

"May I ask the reason?"

"For a woman. As a sentimental gift for her to remember me by."

Bernantio nodded judiciously. "Without doubt she had an elegant ankle."

"A most elegant ankle," Wiki reminiscently agreed, then returned to business. "You can help us find the schooner that Captain Stackpole has lost?"

"Perhaps if you accompanied me to the back of the store, it would assist."

Bernantio slid down from his horse, handed the rein to a companion, and then led the way around the corner with a great clattering of dragging spurs. He opened a big double gate in a wooden fence, revealing a spacious yard at the back of Adams's store. There was a privy in one corner, a dusty bougainvillea growing in another, a pile of empty sacks where a cat was raising a family of kittens, and a large, broken-down cart. A ramp led up to a wide set of two doors, confirming that this was the way goods were received and discharged. Alongside it was a single, narrow door, and though it didn't have a notice Wiki judged it led to the disused surgery.

He looked back at Bernantio, and waited. The gaucho blew a stream of tobacco smoke out of the side of his mouth, took out his thin, misshapen cigar, and used it to gesture about the trampled dried mud of the yard. "There were horses here," he said. "Many horses. They were loaded, and then driven away. Another rider followed later."

So this was how the missing goods had been carried, Wiki thought—to be stowed on board the schooner. It looked increasingly as if Stackpole were right, and Adams had paid for the *Grim Reaper* with the draft, waited until the *Athenian* men had finished their business and gone, and then placed his own goods on board to provision the voyage before taking the schooner downriver to the sea.

But why the horses? Presumably, they had been used for carrying the provisions down the streets to the riverside, to be ferried on board the *Grim Reaper*—perhaps because the cart was broken. Wiki hunkered down, but could see nothing but shuffles in the dust. He looked up and said, "By what magic can you discern all this?"

Bernantio smiled. "Can't you, yourself, see how the packhorses were always the same space apart—which means that they were roped together? The mount of the man who followed favored its left hindfoot—see how the mark is uneven? And see how its prints overlay all the others?"

Wiki peered, but could discern nothing to match what the *rastreador* said. He stood up, shaking his head in wonder, and said, "Can you tell how many days have passed since the packhorses were driven out of here?"

"Some day since the last rain," the gaucho said, and shrugged, looking up at the bright blue sky. Obviously, it didn't rain often in the summer.

"Can you follow these tracks?" The lane that ran past the gate on the way down to the river was unpaved.

"I believe they will lead upriver."

Wiki only just stopped himself from exclaiming out loud in disbelief. According to the bill of sale, the schooner had been lying off the pueblo at the time—and it was logical for the contents of the store to be stowed in her holds as soon as the *Athenian* men had left. Yet, as Bernantio stalked to the front of the store and remounted his steed, his demeanor was remarkably confident.

Wiki went inside, where Stackpole was back to trying to pry information out of the clerk, and conveyed this puzzling news. The whaling master didn't look particularly surprised, remarking, "The schooner must've been up at the dunes."

"Dunes?"

"Salt dunes. They're at the edge of the river where it runs closest to the *salinas*."

Wiki was none the wiser. *"Salinas?"*

"The great salt lake. It's about five miles inland. The salt is dug there, carted to the riverbank, and piled up in dunes, ready for loading."

Stackpole had told Adams to load the schooner with salt as well as provisions, Wiki remembered, so it looked as if the storekeeper had been following the whaling master's instructions right up to the moment of the robbery. But why pack the provisions to the dunes, instead of waiting until the schooner had been sailed back to El Carmen, where it would have been so much easier to stow them on board?

Stackpole interrupted his meditations, saying impatiently, "Come on, let's go."

"Don't you think we should be asking more questions while

we're here in El Carmen?" They should notify the governor, too, Wiki thought.

"About what?" the whaling master demanded.

"About Rowland Hallett, for instance. Is he the master of the *Athenian*?"

"Nope. The captain of the *Athenian* is a fellow called Nash."

So who was Hallett? An officer who belonged to the *Athenian*—the sealing master, perhaps? Or had he been an agent, like Adams, acting as Nash's representative?

Wiki said, "Have you ever heard of this man Hallett before?"

"Nope. All I know," said Stackpole bitterly, "is that he's got my money, but I don't have a schooner."

"Do you know Captain Nash?"

"Never clapped eyes on neither him nor the *Athenian*. I heard lots of gossip that they did uncommon well in the sealing line, and that's it."

"What about Dr. Ducatel? Do you know him?"

"Aye." Stackpole grinned contemptuously. "He's a joke. Three or four Americans live here, trying to make their fortune up the Río Negro. Caleb Adams is one of them, and Ducatel another. But at least Adams behaves like a regular Yankee. Ducatel acts like a comedian."

"What kind of comedian?"

"He pretends to be a real live gaucho, wears their fancy gear, rattles away in some kind of Spanish. The governor encourages him because he finds it so comical."

Reminded of the governor, Wiki said, "We should pay our respects to His Excellency."

"Damn it, no. By the time we got through with all the ceremonious nonsense these trackers would've given up and gone home."

This was a good point, Wiki thought, but objected, "It's late. We'll probably be out overnight."

"What difference does that make?"

Wiki shrugged, and headed into the store. Inside, he chose a brown-striped poncho, pleasantly surprised at the weight and quality of the wool, and paid over some coins to the clerk, who didn't look at all excited about making a sale. Back at the door, he had another thought, and returned to the counter to sort through the red bandannas. When he rejoined the whaling master, he was wearing one of these tied about his head at forehead level, gaucho-style, taming most of his ringlets, while the folded poncho lay over his left shoulder.

Stackpole studied the effect with open contempt, but said, "Out all night?"

"Aye."

"Then perhaps I should get one of those ponchos."

"Good idea," said Wiki.

Instead of waiting for Stackpole to make the purchase, he mounted and cantered after the gauchos, who had already headed off down the street. The whaleman seemed to take a long time, because when he rejoined them they had arrived on the path that led upriver, and were waiting impatiently to go. Bernantio was in the lead, leaning down from his saddle at such a steep angle that he could have dragged his knuckles on the ground, but keeping his seat with miraculous agility. Once, he pointed at a mark in the sandy embankment, and even Wiki could see the print of a horse that had favored one foot.

Soon, however, the baked mud of the track turned into stones and gravel, furrowed with old wagon wheel ruts that were encrusted with some kind of chalky mineral deposit. Bernantio stopped, and slid to the ground stealthily, as if the hoofprints Wiki could barely distinguish would take flight if disturbed. They all waited as he cast back and forth. Then, with an abrupt movement, he sprung back onto his horse, beckoning his companions from over his shoulder as he went.

"They went that way," he said, and pointed up the trail.

As the troop rode inland, always heading west, the valley widened into a plain of gravel, pumice, and sunbaked mud. The pink and gray rampart of the sandstone cliffs, which had been so close to the river before, was now about three miles away. The scant growth that struggled to survive in the flatness the cliffs had left behind was studded with small thorn bushes, and trampled with ruts and dried wallows, which straggled off to the side of the trail. These old tracks had been made by parties who were traveling back and forth between scattered ranches and the river, Wiki supposed. Then, however, Bernantio pointed a finger at the distant cliffs, and said significantly, "Men who plot rebellion against de Rosas have their hideouts there."

Wiki, feeling interested, would have liked to rein in and have a better look, but the *rastreadores* kept on, and he was forced to gallop after them. As they progressed, the cliffs receded even further, so that the expanse of the plain became immense. Then the flatness of the vista was interrupted by strange pale pyramids that stood up out of the hammered clay. As Wiki cantered closer, they proved to be heaps of salt piled up on the bank of the Río Negro, blindingly white against the background of the black water. They had been pushed into the curved shapes of dunes by the wind, so that Wiki was yet again reminded of Arabia. A rough pier extended out into the water, but no vessel was moored there. Nor were there any craft at anchor, the only feature disturbing the rushing water being the willow-swathed islets dotting the way upriver.

Here by the dunes, the wagon wheel ruts became denser than ever, their furrows, both old and recent, interspersed with the hoofmarks left by the bullocks that had drawn the carts. It was impossible to distinguish one mark from another in the dusty muddle, Wiki thought. He watched as Manuel Bernantio walked his horse back and forth, leaning precipitiously from his saddle again, and was not at all surprised when the *rastreador* straightened, reined in, and said regretfully, "The trail is lost."

When Wiki translated, however, Stackpole exclaimed, "No!"

The *rastreador* contemplated him with the disdain of a man looking at someone who refuses to see the obvious—that they had reached a dead end, that the prints were irretrievably confused with the tracks of many wagons, many bullocks, and many horses. Instead of troubling to reply, he lifted his shoulders in an eloquent shrug. Then he set to scraping a plug of tobacco with his huge knife, and delicately prodding the shreds onto a thin piece of paper, which he rolled into yet another skinny cigar.

Stackpole said to Wiki, "The schooner must have been moored at the wharf when they loaded her—so where has she gone now?"

Out to sea with whatever crew Adams had been able to scrape together, Wiki thought, but, instead of saying so, he asked, "How long would it take to stow the provisions and load salt?"

"Days! How much salt do you think a sealing voyage requires?"

The whaling master knew what he was talking about, Wiki supposed, but still thought he'd been wildly overoptimistic to hope to find the schooner here. He slid down from his horse, at the same time keeping a firm hold of the rein, because if the mare ran away it was a long walk back to the village. Then he went over to a trench that had been dug out of the side of the nearest dune, and hunkered down to study its shape. The edges were crumbling and falling in, making it evident that the digging had been done some days ago. He scooped up a handful of salt and let it run through his fingers, surprised at the size and squareness of the crystals, rather like the brine that crystallized on the surface of old salt meat, only pure white instead of brown.

The gauchos sat on their saddles and watched him. Most were smoking, and none of them spoke. Instead, they watched and waited. Wiki had the strong impression that the leadership of the group had moved from Bernantio to him, and they were waiting for him to make the decision about what to do next. Brushing his palm against his thigh to dislodge the last of the salt, he looked around, disturbed by the empty desolation of the scene. Where there had been bullocks, horses, and men, there was no one, and he wondered where the salt harvesters had gone.

And the packhorses—where had they been driven after the *Grim Reaper* had taken on the provisions, and finished loading with salt? He was very conscious of the strong tang of dried brine overriding the warm sweat scent of the mare and the musty wool smell of his saddle fleece. When he looked up at the sky, the scudding clouds were spreading out toward the horizon, their edges shining gold and pink with the late afternoon sun.

Then Wiki's quick eyes spied black specks high in the sky, revolving over an unseen spot that could be as far as several miles away.

Vultures. Their slow, circling, apparently motionless mode of flight was unmistakable. He pointed them out to Bernantio, saying, "They're waiting for something to die."

Manuel Bernantio turned in his saddle, and shaded his eyes with a thin brown palm. "No," he said. "Some animal is dead already."

Wiki wondered how he knew that. Surely, if there was a corpse, the vultures would have been on the ground, indulging in their ghastly banquet? Then Bernantio added, "If something drowns in the *laguna salada,* the vultures cannot scent it. They know there has been death, as they saw the last throes, but because of the salt they cannot locate the body. It often happens."

Laguna salada—lake of brine. "Is that where they collect the salt for these dunes?" Wiki asked. He could see many ancient wagon-wheel ruts leading in that direction, and salt-rimmed potholes made by the hooves of many cattle and horses.

The *rastreador* didn't answer. Instead, as he looked that way, too, his bearing became alert, as if he had suddenly discerned something he had missed before. Dismounting, he gave his bridle to a comrade to hold, and then cast back and forth about the ruts and potholes for what seemed a long time. Then he returned, and said, "The man who rode the horse that favored its hindfoot traveled on to the *salinas.*"

"Alone?"

Manuel shrugged. "It is impossible to tell."

The sun was lowering, turning the distant heights to purple, and a breeze came up off the river. The short hairs on the back of Wiki's neck lifted in a shiver, and he abruptly didn't want to go anywhere near where the vultures circled. However, though Bernantio's mouth, beneath the flourishing mustachios, was as straight as ever, Wiki knew that the *rastreador* was deeply chagrined that he had taken so long to see what was now obvious to him.

Back in the Bay of Islands, loss of face was an important issue, so Wiki understood how he felt. To allow Bernantio to regain *mana*—prestige—he said, "Would you think it was possible for you to do us the great favor of tracing those prints, even as it grows dark?"

Still, the *rastreador* was expressionless. However, Bernantio inclined his head in acknowledgment as he agreed, "I believe I can do it."

Without another word, he remounted his horse and set off, with the others following in a line, as before. This time, Wiki was in the rear. As they progressed over a semibarren plain, where the short, scrubby bushes were armed with increasingly long thorns, the wagon ruts became deeper, having run through mud that had later baked dry in the sun. The horseman, obviously, had avoided these, though Wiki could not pick his tracks out of the general muddle. In places the furrows were crusted with salt, where puddles had become brackish and then dried out.

Abruptly, he became aware of a shocking smell, like putrefying eggs. His stomach clenched, and he expected to see the legs of some poor dead beast sticking up ahead. Instead, a flat shimmer appeared in the dun of the plain. It was like a vast plate, white and almost featureless, a reflection of the paling sky. The vultures still circled in the far reaches of the clouds, with a long line of pink flamingos arrowing south below them, but were yet some distance off.

Then Wiki understood that the great white shimmer was the *salinas*—a lake of solidified salt. The little cavalcade had stopped where the plain ended and the *laguna salada* began. As he joined them, they were sitting still in their saddles, staring over the wide lagoon, which was whiter than ice and eerily still, frozen in space and time. It was possible to see where there had been ripples in the original brine, which had set so fast the movement had been caught forever.

At his mare's feet there was a thick ribbon of black mud, studded with giant crystals that gleamed in shades of yellow and green. "*Padre del sal,*" said Manuel Bernantio, pointing at the strange prisms. The band of mud marked the boundary of the salt lake. There was a reddish effect just below the surface of the *salinas,* which seemed to creep, very slowly, as if some incredible life-form lurked there, in the form of animalcula, perhaps. It emanated a greenish froth, which scudded toward them with a frisk of the breeze, and was the source of the terrible stench. When the wind died down the smell became so strong that it seemed to have physical force.

"The horseman traveled farther," said Bernantio, who had dismounted to study the ground again, and gestured toward the west, where the vultures still patrolled the sky. "And," he added, "I can see now that one other rider went the same way." He climbed back into the saddle, and spurred his mount into moving again. Like the others, Wiki silently followed.

Just as the sun began to dip below the horizon a strange landmark bobbed into view, standing out black against the sky. It was on the top of a rise, and proved to be a huge thorn tree, its trunk about a yard around at the base. Its horizontal branches extended out for several feet, seeming quite luxuriant though very stunted in height. The sun was setting in a garish display of red and purple behind it.

As they came close it was apparent that the tree's branches were dense with foliage—peculiar foliage, which turned out not to be leaves at all, but objects tied to twigs and impaled on the spines. Wiki counted broken bridles, bolas, animal skins, and pieces taken from old ponchos. Even more eerily, this strange tree was surrounded by scores of horse skeletons, some still complete, others widely scattered. A great heap of salt lay directly at the foot of the eminence where it grew, blown into the typical dunelike shape.

A vulture, colored dirty white so that it blended into the stony soil, hopped away as they came close. One of the horses snorted, and the bird spread black-tipped wings and clumsily flapped into the air, emitting a vile stench of decay as it went. Directly above, its brethren circled on and on in the paling sky.

Captain Stackpole pointed at the tree, and said, "What's all that junk?"

Wiki asked Bernantio about it. "This is the Gualichú tree," the *rastreador* explained. "It is revered by the Indians. Those objects are offerings. One must not tether one's horse to this tree, or use any of its branches for firewood."

"Why the horse bones?"

"Some say they sacrifice old horses here to make the young horses strong and fast, but I think maybe the real reason is that this is where they hold their feasts. The Indians like to eat the flesh of mares. I have seen them eat it raw, with the blood pouring down their chins." Glancing up at the birds that hovered high in the sky, he observed, "They wait for yet another sacrifice."

But Wiki had stopped listening. His whole attention was taken up by what he had suddenly glimpsed poking out of the salt—a human skull, with tiny scraps of flesh still adhering to it despite the attentions of the vultures. It was obviously still attached to a body that was buried in the dune, like the head of a man who had been lying on the sand, and buried up to his neck as part of some seaside game, then forgotten and left to die.

Wiki slid off his mare, keeping a convulsive grip on her bridle. For a moment, there was a jerk of nausea in his throat. When he crouched down, the skull grinned up at him, misshapen where the hard beaks of the vultures had hacked at the bone, the eye sockets vacant. There was a hole in the front of the skull where a bullet had penetrated the forehead, which looked like a third eye.

Hearing a step, he looked up. Captain Stackpole was standing close by, holding on to his own horse.

Wiki asked, "Do you have any idea who it was?"

"No, of course not." Whaling was a hard trade that made hard men, but Stackpole looked and sounded shaken. "It's just a skull," he mumbled.

"We'll see what the rest of the body looks like, shall we?" Enough time had elapsed for the *kehua*—the man's earthly ghost—to have fled to the underworld, *te pou*, and so it was reasonably easy for Wiki to make his tone practical.

Without waiting for an answer, he stood up, looked around, and handed the mare's bridle to one of the gauchos. Then he picked up a horse's shoulder-blade bone, and used it as a spade. After a moment, Stackpole did the same, and gradually they uncovered the body of a slightly built man, clothed in a checkered shirt and rough duck trousers held up by an elaborately tooled leather belt, and lying on his back. Every fold of his clothes was full of white crystals, which sifted away with an audible rustling. The torso, arms, and legs were almost entire, having been preserved by the salt from both putrefaction and the carrion eaters. This was why the vultures circled and waited, Wiki thought—they knew there was more to the feast than one well-scoured skull, but because of the salt they couldn't locate it.

He put aside his spade and crouched down again, studying the body where it lay in the opened trench. The unbuttoned neck of the shirt exposed a tarnished gold medal hanging from a braided string. Below the metal disk the cloth was flooded by a stain that had spread all the way to the fancy leather belt. The great blot had been bleached to a pale rusty color by the salt, but undoubtedly had been blood, because it had flowed out of the wound left by a big knife that had been shoved into this man's chest and then yanked away. He had been frozen by death into a position where the shoulders were hunched higher than the waist, as if he had curled himself over the agony of the thrust that had killed him . . . and yet there was that bullet hole in the middle of the skull's forehead.

It was ghoulishly easy to picture what had happened. Wiki straightened, and said, "Whoever stabbed him thought he was dead, and buried him, but then he came to life and lunged up in a last spasm, jerking his head out of the salt. The murderer must have been thoroughly spooked—he shot him to finish him off, but instead of burying him properly again he ran off, leaving him so that the skull was exposed to the vultures."

Stackpole's throat pulsed as he swallowed hard. He said in a low voice, "It sure does look that way."

"Do you recognize him now?"

Instead of replying, Stackpole unfolded a jackknife, hunkered down, and cut the medal away from the string. He inspected it, and looked for a sick moment as if he wanted to throw it away. Instead, he closed his fist on it, and said briefly, "Aye."

Wiki had a preternatural feeling that he knew the answer already. He said, "Adams?"

"Aye. That man was Caleb Adams."

Four

January 26, 1839

When Wiki woke up, wrapped in his poncho and lying on his saddle blanket with his saddle fleece as a pillow, it was dawn, and he was covered with a heavy layer of dew. He was thirsty, because they had carried too little water for a decent draft of maté the previous night, but when he skimmed a palmful of droplets off his poncho they were too brackish to swallow. His skin and hair must be impregnated with salt as well as his clothing, he realized, for when he yawned his face felt stiff enough to crack.

The fire the gauchos had made out of horse bones had almost died down, and there was no water left and nothing to cook, so they put it out by throwing salt on it, setting up a little cloud of vivid blue sparks. Their steeds, thought Wiki, looked as hungry and thirsty as the men. They bucked angrily as the reassembled saddles were put on their backs and tightly cinched, and his gray mare was just as uncooperative.

Once he was finally mounted, he paused to study Caleb Adams's grave. Perhaps, he mused, they should have dug the body out, and taken it to El Carmen to hand over to the authorities. However, the *rastreadores* did not have a spare mount, so someone would have been forced to walk, and over the long, hot trek the corpse would have become disgusting. He and Stackpole were already sickened by the ghastly pecked skull, which had suddenly become detached, and had rolled around grinning at them while they searched the dead man's pockets to make certain they were empty. The decision to leave the corpse in the trench had been easy, and it had been a huge relief to pile the salt back, though not without making very sure that the skull was packed down with the body.

Stackpole had gone to some trouble to make Adams's last resting place look like a proper grave. By firelight, he had whittled away at a broad piece of scapula, etching the words: *"Caleb Adams, American trader, murdered by person or persons unknown, discovered 25 January 1839,"* and this morning he had made a cross, with the scapula as the traverse and another horse bone for the upright, and had shoved it into the head of the grave.

Wiki turned to Manuel Bernantio, who was smoking as he, too, contemplated the grave. "You still cannot tell what happened here?"

Again, Bernantio shook his head. The light of day had made no difference. Any traces Adams and his killer or killers might have left of their struggle—if there had been a struggle here—had been destroyed by the vultures' flapping and copious defecations.

Wiki deliberated, and then asked, "Do you think he might have been knifed somewhere else, and strapped to his horse for the journey?"

The *rastreador* pursed his mouth. "Perhaps," he allowed. Then he gestured with his cigar at the horse skeletons, and said, "The victim's steed may yet be here."

That was a point, Wiki thought. The vultures would have made such short work of the exposed body of the dead horse that its bones would be indistinguishable from the rest. Then he wondered again what had happened to the packhorses after they had been unloaded of the provisions, down by the salt dunes at the side of the river. When he asked Bernantio about it, the *rastreador* paused, but finally shook his head. With a decisive movement, he spurred his mount, gesturing at his comrades to commence the journey back to the Río Negro.

The party took the much shorter direct route, bypassing the *salinas* by several miles, to find the salt dunes as deserted as before. When they reached the water the horses drank thirstily, the gauchos built a fire and made maté, and Wiki scouted around the hills of salt, but without finding anything to indicate a struggle.

Captain Stackpole was standing apart from the rest, staring out over the water. Wiki said to him, "We have to get back to the pueblo."

"But what about my schooner?" the whaling master protested. "The gauchos promised to find her."

"No, they did not," Wiki contradicted. "And they've found Adams, which is more than you expected. Now, you have to pay them."

Stackpole grimaced. "In money?"

"Chilean dollars would be best."

Unfortunately, Wiki's earlier suspicions about Stackpole's financial state proved to be correct, and he had to help him out with a handful of the silver coins. Stackpole didn't bother to thank him, fixing him with a cynical eye, instead. "Men who've whaled in the Pacific have assured me that kernackers are incurable thieves," he observed. "I guess you're the exception what proves the rule."

"You might be surprised," said Wiki wryly. In his home village it was very hard for anyone to hang on to personal possessions. Not only was hospitality lavish, and generosity a much admired virtue, but shared ownership was the rule, along with *muru,* a kind of ritual plundering that was an intrinsic part of most ceremonials, and which *pakeha*—foreigners—misinterpreted as theft. Once again, too, he refrained from pointing out that he was Maori, which was a different kind of Polynesian, and not a *kanaka,* which was the whaleman's catch-all term for a Pacific Islander.

When the gauchos, having received their cash, bowed in acknowledgment of the role he had played in this sudden rush of riches, he nodded. One of them stowed the empty maté gourd behind his saddle, and they touched their spurs to their steeds. To Wiki's surprise, they headed upriver, and he wondered where they were going. Why inland? And why with such an air of decision?

They were heading for the horizon in their usual flamboyant fashion, and it was far too late to ask, so he dismissed it from his mind, saying to Stackpole, "We'd better get going, too. We have to report the discovery of Adams's body—and we should try to find Hallett."

"The man who took my money," Stackpole grimly agreed.

"Aye," said Wiki, thinking they knew far too little about the mysterious Hallett, and that it was time they learned a lot more. He went on, "I wondered if he belonged to the *Athenian*. Back in October 1836 he bought a lot of provisions from Adams, and was in and out after that, making a few more purchases, and it could have been on behalf of the sealing brig. The clerk should be able to tell us something to confirm that. There's also the possibility that he's a ship's agent, like Adams—which means he might be a local."

"Or he could be at sea on my schooner."

"True," said Wiki. "But we have to try—it's no use giving up just yet." Decisively, he mounted his mare, listening to the grunts and groans as the whaling master stiffly followed suit, and set her into a trot along the well-worn path to El Carmen.

A couple of hours later, he heard Stackpole say in puzzled tones, "What's up?"

Wiki, who had been deep in speculation, raised his head to see a great cloud of dust billowing over the trail. He reined in, and a herd of cattle came out of the haze, driven by women and children on horses. Behind them, more cattle dragged carts laden high with household goods. It looked as if the whole of the pueblo and surrounding countryside was in panic-stricken retreat—except for the men, it seemed.

As the crowd approached, warning cries rose up: "The French are coming!"

Wiki restrained his mare, who was dancing in nervous circles, having caught the atmosphere of alarm. He shouted, "The French? What do you mean?"

"They are coming to attack the pueblo and seize the countryside!"

The war between Buenos Aires and the French has spread to engulf the Río Negro, Wiki thought with alarm. It was what he had first feared when the lookout on the *Swallow* had spied the strange whaleship. The vessel had turned out to be Stackpole's *Trojan,* but the danger had been real.

He cried, "Where *are* the French?"

"Their squadron is already off the mouth of the Río Negro!" a woman shrieked, and flailed a lash over the cattle she drove, setting up a commotion of hoofbeats and lowing.

Dear God, thought Wiki, *the* Swallow*!* The woman passed by with her cows, and another great cloud of dust was flooding toward them. This time, it was a flock of sheep, so long-legged and shaggy they looked like goats. Wiki and Stackpole drew their horses over to the edge of the river, and when the herders—who were all women, again—came abreast, Wiki shouted, "Where are all the men?"

The cry came back faintly: "Getting ready to fire the countryside!"

As Wiki was relaying this to Stackpole, they were overtaken from behind by Manuel Bernantio and his gaucho band, traveling at full gallop. They had heard the news of the invasion, and now, filled with bloodlust and the prospect of loot, were off to join the fight. Swinging their ponchos, they thundered by, hollering as they went.

Gradually the commotion diminished, as the women, children, and cattle disappeared in one direction, and the gauchos in the other. Wiki and Stackpole hurried in the wake of Bernantio's party, with Wiki worrying about the *Swallow,* and reassuring himself that the

United States was not at war with France. Men at the foot of the sandstone cliffs, which were much closer now, could be seen gathering up brush for fuel, preparing to set fire to the scrub. He could now guess where the salt harvesters had gone.

They arrived in El Carmen in a clatter of hooves, to find the streets silent and deserted. Adams's store was firmly locked, with the shutters up over the windows, and there was no answer when they hammered at the door. Wiki remounted his horse and sat in the saddle looking around, and then said, "The fort's empty, too. The governor will be at the estuary with his troops."

Stackpole was looking saddle-sore, and very much the worse for wear. His clothes were smeared with salt and extremely dusty, and his eyes were bloodshot and red-rimmed.

He said, "So what next?"

"I'm heading back to the river mouth to learn what's happening." And make sure the *Swallow* was not under attack. "And then I'll find the governor and report the murder."

"Well, I'm staying."

"What about the *Trojan*? Aren't you worried about the French squadron?"

Stackpole snorted. "Why should I worry? My mate will have her well out to sea, cruising for whales the way I told him. It's a lot more important to find Rowland Hallett and shake my money out of him, the cheating bastard. There's that closemouthed clerk, too. He won't get away with silence so easy this time."

"But what about the French? What if they take El Carmen?"

"I'm American, aren't I? And I ain't worth robbing, anyway."

Wiki hesitated, torn between his sense of responsibility to the victim of Adams's theft and his fears for the brig *Swallow*. The weather was deteriorating fast, and the older loyalty won. He wheeled his horse, crying, "I'll be back as soon as I can!"

If I can, he thought, but still didn't change his mind. Slapping the reins, he dashed down the shallow steps that led to the river, turned onto the riverside path, and hurried in the direction of the sea, where a great bank of black clouds was forming. Twice, in the distance, he saw the quick flicker of lightning.

It wasn't until he was a half mile away that the horrid thought occurred to him—that Hallett might not be just a thief. The man who had cheated Stackpole of his money could also be the man who'd killed Adams.

It was mid-afternoon before Wiki reached the sidetrack that led past the ranch where he had hired the horses and on up to the headland. It looked more treacherous than he remembered, winding steeply upward through scrub and sliding screes of gravel. Most horses would have been too tired after the trek to attempt the climb, but his mare was a hardy gaucho steed, and after a bit of kicking on Wiki's part she obliged, finally lunging over the top with a snort and a shake that shivered sweat off her shoulders.

Wiki sat up straight in his saddle to scan the promontory for any sign of soldiers—either the governor's troops or the invading French. However, the scene was empty, apart from birds and a few scurrying small animals, and he wondered where the gauchos had gone. Encouragingly, however, he could just discern a flagstaff lifting out of what seemed to be thick fog in the distance, and recognized it as the one that stood above the beach and the pilothouse.

A wind whisked up, sending the fringes of his poncho flying, and heavy spots of rain smacked against his face, forcing him to duck his head. For a while, though he cantered briskly through thickening weather, the flagpole did not seem to come closer. It wasn't until the sun was low in the sky, penetrating the fog and silvering the edges of the black-bellied clouds, that he abruptly arrived at the edge, to look down on the beach where he and Stackpole had landed the morning before.

Wiki immediately spied the squadron, because the ships were just a mile off, floating between rolling banks of mist. Seagulls patrolled the sky above the masts, their screeching faint with distance. For a transient moment the vessels were sharply delineated in a column of misty light slanting down to the sea from a hole in the roiling clouds. Wiki could see every detail, and count the ships, too—a couple of large sloops of war, a gun brig, a smaller brig, and two schooners . . . *The so-called enemy French squadron was the United States Exploring Expedition!*

He laughed out loud, because it was so easy to guess what had happened. The fleet had emerged from the fog, and the local populace, being in a state of terrified expectation already, had jumped to the wrong conclusion.

Then Wiki saw that the expedition was accompanied by a flamboyantly overcanvased brigantine. Like the other ships, she was vividly familiar—being none other than Captain William Coffin's Salem trader *Osprey*! What the devil, Wiki thought, was his father up to? The last time he had talked with him it had been in Rio, a couple of days before they had all weighed anchor, and the last time he had seen the brigantine *Osprey* was when the *Vincennes* and then the *Peacock* had run afoul of her. The damage had been relatively minor, or so Wiki had been assured, and Captain Coffin should be homeward bound. So what had happened since?

Just as the fog closed in again, Wiki saw that one of the expedition schooners was beating her way into the mouth of the Río Negro, and recognized the *Sea Gull*. She was making a pretty mess of it, too, as she was heading unerringly for the shoals. If she kept on the same course she'd be stranded on a bar within an hour, he calculated, easy prey for whatever unseen ambush was lying in wait on the banks of the river. However, he could not see what happened next. Frustratingly, the clouds came down, accompanied by squalls of rain. Surely her captain had ordered a retreat, he thought, and kicked his mare into moving again.

Scenting grass and water, she readily obliged, cantering down the narrow track that meandered through bushes, and arriving at the open door of the pilothouse just as dark fell. Wiki jumped down, and tied her to the hitching rail. He called out, but got no answer, and when he went inside and lit a lamp, it was to find that the two pilots had absconded, which was not particularly surprising, considering that one of them was French. Otherwise, the cabin looked just as it had the day before. Strangely, the weapons were still hanging on the wall—cutlasses, carbines, and pikes, all burnished and in excellent condition, which made Wiki wonder what arms the pilots were carrying.

They had abandoned their stores as well, taking the liquor instead, which didn't worry Wiki a jot, because like most of his people he had no taste for spirits. To his delight, there was a wheaten loaf of the durable kind that was usually sold in *pulperías*. He split this, daubed it generously with good butter scooped from the cowhide bag in which it had been churned by being towed behind a horse, and then sprinkled it with coarse brown sugar that he found in a little sack, usually kept for sweetening maté. It went down well, because he was very hungry, not having eaten since the night before.

After finishing off his meal, Wiki filled a basin for his mare from the rainwater cask outside the door. The night was clammy, filled with swirling mist, and the slurping noises as she drank seemed unnaturally loud. Then he frowned as he heard distant shouts echoing over the water. *My God*, he thought, the schooner *Sea Gull* had kept on course, blindly heading for the estuary! His sight had adjusted to the dark, so he didn't go inside for the lamp, instead heading down the path to warn them about the waiting troops.

When he arrived on the riverbank the sounds were louder, lookouts calling urgently as the bottom became treacherous, but no soldiers rushed out of the scrub. Wiki heard many thumps and rattles as long sweeps were put out, and swishing sounds as the crew rowed hard, making great efforts to clear the shoals. Inevitably, however, the schooner grounded. The misty night was rent by a great deal of loud

American cursing as the crew tried without avail to get her off. Clanking of chains followed, and a couple of splashes as the anchors were dropped.

Silence—and then with a hiss and a roar a rocket ripped up through the fog and exploded in a blinding blue glare. Wiki stood up in the reflected light and shouted, "Ahoy, a boat, if you please!"

Instead, a rifle shot slammed out. It was the flat, dull clap of a gun aimed directly at him. Wiki dived headlong into the bushes.

He hugged the ground, his heart hammering with fright, keeping very still as he listened to the sounds of the schooner lowering a boat, and that boat being rowed to shore. It seemed to take them a long time to make up their minds to jump out and wade to the bank. Even after they finally clambered onto high ground, asking each other where the mysterious voice had come from, he remained in hiding, having no intention of being shot at again, particularly from such close quarters.

Finally, the boat party gave up looking, and blundered along the path, one of them shouting that he'd seen a light—the lantern Wiki had left on the table. He clambered to his feet and followed at a wary distance. He could hear the men calling out to each other that they had found a horse hitched to the post outside the pilothouse, and after that sounds of rummaging inside the cabin.

Judging that they were all safely inside, he yelled again, "Ahoy!"

Silhouettes appeared in the lit rectangle of the doorway. There were at least six men, all aiming guns, and Wiki instantly dropped flat again. "I'm unarmed!" he shouted from the ground.

"Who goes there?" a panicky voice hollered, and then, without waiting for an answer, "Come out with your hands up!"

Wiki slowly stood, his spread palms raised. No one moved, but the weapons were still leveled. Very cautiously indeed, his stomach clamped with expectant dread, he took a pace into the shaft of light that fell out of the doorway.

No one, thankfully, pulled a trigger, but even when the party could see his face, the reception didn't get any friendlier. Instead, the foremost demanded with his pistol lifted menacingly, "Have you come to parley?"

"Parley?" echoed Wiki, astonished.

"You're one of them suspicious gauchos, ain't you?"

Wiki said blankly, *"Me?"* Then he remembered the poncho and red silk bandanna, and hastily said, "I'm Wiki Coffin."

"Who?"

"I belong to the brig *Swallow.*"

"What?"

Oh, for God's sake, thought Wiki. Then, to his vast relief, a man at the back of the group said, "Isn't he Captain Wilkes's native translator?"

"That's me," said Wiki emphatically. Oddly, however, he didn't know the speaker, even when he stepped forward into the lamplight. The fellow was distinctive enough, being a middle-aged man with deep-set, intelligent eyes, fluffy russet side-whiskers, and a leonine head of reddish-brown hair, but Wiki couldn't remember ever having seen him before.

"Titian Peale," the other said helpfully.

The name meant nothing. Wiki said, "You're one of the artists?"

He saw the other smile slightly. "Naturalist, based on the *Peacock.*"

"I see," said Wiki, though he was none the wiser. "What are you doing on the *Sea Gull*?"

"I'm one of the scientifics chosen to accompany Captain Ringgold on shore."

"But Captain Ringgold's in command of the *Porpoise,* not the *Sea Gull*!"

At this display of privileged knowledge the weapons were lowered, and Wiki was able to drop his hands. He asked, "Why did you shoot at me?"

A seaman exclaimed, "Because you was one of them devils a-lyin' in ambush, of course!"

"You know about the ambush?" Wiki said, astonished.

"Of course we know about the ambush! We spied a posse of more than thirty gauchos suspiciously reconnoitering us from the flagstaff on the top of the hill. Cap'n Wilkes sent off the *Sea Gull* to investigate, with Cap'n Ringgold in command, but the chart what he gave Cap'n Ringgold was wrong, and we got into the shoals, and then we got stuck on a sandbar. Night closed in and there we was a sitting duck, but though we fired a rocket for assistance, no one come to help! Then we heard you holler out for a boat, but how were we to guess that you was one of us? And why is the locals a-warring with us, anyways?"

"They think you're a French squadron come to rape and pillage," Wiki told him, wondering what had happened to the gauchos. "And are even more scared than you are," he added with a private grin.

The party bridled indignantly at this, but protest was forestalled by the two river pilots, who materialized smelling highly of liquor. At once, Wiki said, "What happened to the troops? And the gauchos?"

The French pilot executed a Gallic shrug, leaving the English one to say, "The sentries heard these fellows cursing in Yankee, so the gov'nor called 'em all off."

"So where is he?" Wiki felt anxious to report the discovery of Adams's corpse and ask a few questions about the identity of Rowland Hallett, but before he could get a sensible answer Mr. Peale interrupted, saying to the Englishman, "Can you navigate the schooner out of the shoals?"

"Of course, sir, once we have daylight."

"And pilot us up the river?"

"Of course," said the pilot promptly, and repeated the word, "Sir," at the prospect of such a lucrative commission. Then he invited them all to partake of liquid hospitality, but much to the regret of the seamen Mr. Peale firmly but politely turned the offer down, and after making arrangements for the pilot to come on board in the morning, he led the way out of the cabin.

It was a lot easier for the boat's crew to find the schooner than it had been for them to locate the landing place, because someone on the *Sea Gull* had been brave enough to hang lanterns in the rigging. Then, with a hail and a click, the bow of the boat touched the side of the schooner, and with a single jump Wiki arrived on deck. He had never called on the 110-ton craft before, but he had visited her sister ship, the schooner *Flying Fish,* and stepping on board was just as easy. Not only was the little craft only a fraction higher out of the water than the boat but she had hardly any bulwarks.

It was even easier to recognize the tall figure of Captain Ringgold, with his flop of fine, fair hair, and patrician, clean-shaven features. One of the older members of the expedition at the age of thirty-seven, he was also one of the most popular, known for running a taut and happy ship. However, he looked irate enough as he bellowed at the boat's crew, "What the devil do you mean by bringing one of those goddamned desperadoes on board?"

"It's Wiki Coffin," Mr. Peale informed him, arriving on board.

"Wiki Coffin?" echoed Ringgold, and swung round and had another look. "Wiki, why the hell are you rigged up as a gaucho?" he demanded, losing none of his aggression. "Is it on account of the war? Are you pretending to be some sort of spy?"

"Not at all," said Wiki. "And there isn't any war—it was just a comical mistake. As for me, I was simply investigating a robbery, only it turned out to be a murder. Tell me," he went on, "did you happen to raise a sealer when you were on the way into the coast?"

"What the devil are you talking about?"

And Wiki proceeded to explain.

Five

January 27, 1839

"Forget this murder," Captain Ringgold crisply instructed in the morning.

Wiki frowned. "Just like that?" He and Ringgold were standing on the diminutive deck of the schooner, watching the boat being put overboard ready for a return to shore. The early wind was chilly, and Wiki pulled his poncho closer.

"Even a blind fool could see what happened. Adams stole the schooner after he bought her from Hallett, sent her upriver to load with salt, packed goods from his own store to provision her, and then was murdered by some local ruffian who dumped his corpse in the desert and sailed off with the prize. It's a matter for the governor's attention, not ours. Report it to him, and put it out of your mind. Do you hear me?"

"Aye, sir," said Wiki, though he wondered what Stackpole would say about it, and wondered, too, if the whaling master had had any luck in tracking down either Hallett—who might not be as innocent as Captain Ringgold suggested—or the clerk. He also thought that if Ringgold had been the one to find the half-buried corpse, he would not be nearly so dismissive of the matter.

"And you should've reported to the governor the moment you arrived in El Carmen," Ringgold continued, quite unaware of this. "Even a blithering idiot could see that informing him the expedition was on the way would've prevented all this panic and confusion. And why the devil did you cut your hair?" he demanded with a disconcerting change of subject. "At least it was *tidy* when you tied it back, even though it made you look like an out-of-work opera singer, but now it's a bloody disgrace."

"I thought the bandanna would keep it neat," protested Wiki, who had no intention whatsoever of revealing the romantic reason for cutting his hair.

"It's mostly on account of that red rag that you look like a rascal of a gaucho. You're damned lucky you weren't shot as a spy during the fright about the French," opined Ringgold, who appeared to have spies on the brain. "Or hanged," he went on meditatively. "Did you know that the great Connecticut patriot Nathan Hale, the first American spy of the Glorious Revolution, was hanged by the British?"

"Good heavens, was he?" murmured Wiki.

"He was," Ringgold assured him. "And where the hell is the pilot? Mr. Peale was positive he'd be here by dawn to get us up the river."

Wiki looked around. Mr. Peale—like the pilot—was nowhere to be seen. "It seems we have to fetch the pilot from the pilothouse," he said, and followed Ringgold into the boat, where a boat's crew was ready to pull them ashore.

To their consternation and dismay, as they arrived on the riverbank a guard of lancers galloped around a bend, hauled their steeds to a stop, and jumped down with leveled weapons. The boat's crew and Captain Ringgold beat a hasty retreat to the safety of the boat, while Wiki explained the situation to the man who was in charge of the squad. Finally, to his relief, the pikes and cutlasses were lowered, and

Ringgold bravely stepped ashore. Then the chief guard revealed that though they were still very jumpy about the rumored French invasion, their real mission was to arrest the pilots and carry them off to the fort.

"For God's sake, why?" Ringgold demanded, after Wiki had conveyed this.

"It seems that agreeing to pilot a foreign vessel without getting permission from the governor first is a heinous offense." The crime, Wiki thought, was trivial enough, but the state of the two pilots when they were dragged out of their cabin was pitiable. As they were hauled off in shackles they begged Captain Ringgold to intercede for them, vowing their lives were at stake.

Ringgold scarcely listened. Instead, as the lancers cantered off down the riverside path with the pilots in tow, he fell into a fit of swearing. He had good reason, Wiki admitted. Since she had grounded, the *Sea Gull* had been sitting relatively still, but now, as they could all see from the riverbank, with the ebb tide she was starting to thump up and down.

Then Ringgold's flow of invective was abruptly interrupted. A man stepped out of the scrub, glanced around in a surreptitious fashion to make sure that the troopers had left, and then offered his piloting services in good American English.

He was a weathered man in his thirties, with a short beard that was redder than his brown hair. Though not large in stature, he carried such a strong impression of an electric abundance of energy that he seemed bigger than his size. He also had wonderful self-confidence. Everyone stared in silence, completely confounded by this sudden apparition, but this didn't faze him in the slightest. Stepping up to Captain Ringgold with his hand outstretched, he announced in hearty Yankee tones, "Benjamin Harden, junior, at your service."

Instead of shaking hands, Ringgold took a quick pace backward, saying with disgust, "You're an *American*?"

"Was left behind by my ship in Buenos Aires quite some years ago," said this fellow, not put out in the slightest. "Came here to make my pile, sir—an ambition that has remained unrealized, unfortunately."

Ringgold stared him up and down, and then observed to Wiki, without bothering to lower his voice, "He's nothing but a confounded adventurer!"

"There's two or three of them around here, sir, or so Captain Stackpole told me," Wiki told him.

"Good God. What's our great nation coming to?"

Wiki was saved from finding an answer by Harden himself, who abruptly improved his position by revealing, "I have my Protection, sir."

Ringgold's brows shot up, and Wiki was equally surprised. The Seaman's Protection was a slip of paper testifying that the bearer was a citizen of the United States, with the right to apply to a U.S. consul for help if he was sick, marooned, or shipwrecked. Any American seaman who failed to go to the local customshouse and get this certificate before he sailed was foolish, as it was valuable evidence of his identity. However, if Harden had been adrift in South America for years, as he claimed, it was amazing that he'd managed to retain it.

While they all watched, Harden felt around in the interior of his shirt, and hauled it out. The captain stared at him for a long moment before taking it, and then gave it only a brief look. "You're a Rhode Islander?"

"Born in Providence thirty-five years ago, sir, just the way it says there."

"And you reckon you can pilot our schooner off the sandbar?"

"And back out to the fleet, sir."

"Not up the river to El Carmen?"

"Ain't possible, sir, not with the tide against us." Harden licked a finger, wetting it, and then held it up in the air, reminding them all that there was no breeze at all, let alone one that would help waft the *Sea Gull* upriver.

Another pause. Then Ringgold nodded, and handed the paper back. "All right," he grunted. "Come on board and navigate her off the sandbank and into deeper water, so we can get her a hundred or so fathoms upstream with the sweeps. Then we'll discuss what happens next." He turned to Wiki, and said abruptly, "Since we're going to El Carmen by land, I need horses."

"How many horses?"

"Lieutenant Perry will come, and I'll take Mr. Waldron, and Mr. Hale, too—so we need four, quick as you can."

Wiki had heard of all three men before, though the only one he had met personally was Mr. Waldron, the purser of the *Vincennes* and one of Captain Wilkes's particular cronies. Wiki had noticed Mr. Waldron on board the *Sea Gull* the night before, but had not paid much attention to anyone else. The schooner had been extremely crowded, having two surgeon-scientists on board as well as Mr. Peale and the crew of fifteen men, and Wiki's major goal had been to find a place to sleep—which had turned out to be within the folds of a spare sail stowed on the foredeck, where he had reposed quite comfortably, wrapped securely in his poncho.

Now, realizing that the crowd must have included Mr. Hale, who was the expedition philologist, he wondered why the oddly named Titian Peale was not taking part in the jaunt to El Carmen. And what about the two surgeon-scientifics? Wiki knew only one, Dr. Fox, by sight—not just because he lived on the *Vincennes*, but also because he was a native of Salem, Massachusetts, Captain Coffin's hometown. John Fox was only three years older than Wiki himself, and during Wiki's first year or so in Salem, he had often seen him walking in and out of the prestigious Salem Latin School, where he was a noted scholar. The other surgeon looked equally high-toned and intelligent, so why had the pair been excluded?

Wiki wasn't foolish enough to ask. Instead, as soon as the boat had pushed off for the *Sea Gull* with the new pilot on board, he went back to the pilots' cabin. His mare, thankfully, was still tethered to the hitching post, the lancers having forgotten to steal her. She shied madly when she saw him, greatly disliking the prospect of another jaunt, and it took several minutes to get the saddle cinched. Then she bucked and kicked viciously when Wiki grabbed a hank of mane, set a bare toe on her knee, and jumped on board.

Curbing her with difficulty, Wiki set off along the top of the headland for the *estancia* where he and Stackpole had hired the horses. So much had happened in the meantime that when the silvery fence and then the cluster of buildings came into sight, it seemed much more than two days since he'd been here last. The *estanciero* had no trouble remembering him, though. Another bout of bargaining commenced, and then, after signing a paper on behalf of Captain Ringgold, Wiki led a string of four ponies back, to find the schooner a half-mile farther upstream, well out of the shoals and bobbing serenely at her anchors. Obviously, Harden had made good his boast that he could pilot her to safety.

However, another crisis had arisen. To Wiki's consternation, when he got to the landing place on the riverbank, he found the six men of the boat's crew holding a posse of gauchos at bay with pistols and rifles, while Ringgold and three companions watched from the safety of the boat.

"They're friends," Wiki hastily said.

The gauchos were, in fact, Manuel Bernantio and his men. They sat at ease in their great sheep-fleece saddles, not even deigning to notice the seamen, who looked scared to death despite their armament. Bernantio was smoking, while others scraped at tobacco plugs with the enormous cut-down swords they used as knives, the little squares of paper they used for making their cigars gripped between their bare toes.

"*Friends?* They look even more rascally than you do, Wiki," Ringgold declared, stepping from boat to shore. "What the devil do they want?"

Wiki asked Bernantio, tactfully rephrasing what Ringgold had said. Then he turned back and said, "They say you need an armed escort to El Carmen, the countryside being in a ferment, still. For a sum, they are willing to provide it."

"H'm!" said Ringgold, thinking this over. "How much?"

Wiki told him, noticing at the same time that Bernantio watched him with the fond expression of a man contemplating a continued source of wealth.

"Do any of them speak English?"

Wiki shook his head.

"Then you will have to come to translate."

And to report to the governor, Wiki silently added, and see if Stackpole had managed to track down the clerk and Hallett in the meantime. He was surprised, though, that Horatio Hale, the philologist—who was supposed to be expert in the science of languages—was not expected to interpret.

As it happened, when the three other men stepped out of the boat, he was not at all sure which of the two younger ones was Mr. Hale, because both were wearing lieutenant's undress uniform of dark blue trousers and claw-hammer coat, and a round hat with a beak. One, according to what Ringgold had said, was Lieutenant Perry, while the other was the twenty-one-year-old philologist. But which was Perry, and which was Hale? And why was a scientific wearing lieutenant's dress?

The party soon became strung out, with the gauchos in the lead, and Ringgold and the officers following in pairs, leaving Wiki to bring up the rear. An hour later, when one of the two young gentlemen fell back to engage him in conversation, Wiki nodded without speaking, being none the wiser.

"You are a New Zealand native," this fellow stated without preamble.

"I am," said Wiki, neglecting to mention that he was also half American. It was growing hot, so he paused to draw off his poncho, fold it, and lay it over the front of his saddle.

"And your name is Wiki," the other went on. Beneath his peaked hat he had short, brown hair drawn back from a pale, high forehead, and his expression was studious and earnest.

Wiki admitted that, too.

"Tell me, what does the word *Wiki* mean?"

Wiki blinked in surprise, then said, "In the Hawaiian language it means *swift*."

"And very appropriate, I am sure," commented the other, casting an envious sideways glance at Wiki's athletic form. "But what does *Wiki* mean in your own dialect?"

"You mean in *te reo Maori*?"

"If that is what you call your form of Polynesian, yes."

"It means nothing at all."

"Nothing? As in null?"

"It has no meaning," Wiki repeated. "It's just a name—like yours, no doubt."

"Horatio?"

So this was Mr. Hale, Wiki realized. He nodded.

"And the word *Maori* that you used just now—I think I have heard it before, though I have always heard your people referred to as 'New Zealanders.' Is *Maori* what you call yourself when people ask you about your race?"

"I call myself *Ngapuhi*—the name of my *iwi*, my tribe."

Mr. Hale opened his eyes wide. "Is it usual with your people to identify themselves by the name of the tribe?"

Again, Wiki nodded.

"So the word you used, *Maori*—what does it mean?"

"It means *normal*."

The philologist seemed quite taken aback, and said cautiously, "So, your word for white men like me—*pakeha*—does it mean *abnormal*?"

Wiki quenched a grin. "No, it means *foreign*—and you don't have to be white to be *pakeha*."

Horatio Hale fell silent awhile, mulling over this last revelation. Then he rallied, saying, "Did you know that small children can speak the sounds of all known languages, and that they employ these when they make up their own words?"

"No, I did not," Wiki confessed.

"Well, that is how languages were originally formed, the Polynesian language being no different from the rest."

"There are several Polynesian languages," Wiki corrected. "Samoan, for instance, is quite a lot different from *te reo Maori*." He remembered the first time he had heard Samoan spoken, and how intrigued he had been by its energy, the odd clicks, and sharp consonants. Compared to the sealike resonance of *te reo Maori*, it had sounded to him like the birds in the trees. Then he had recognized familiar words and concepts, and so he had learned Samoan, which he now talked like a native. In fact, he spoke in that language much more often than he did in Maori, on voyage, because two of his closest friends on the *Swallow*, Tana and Sua, were Samoan.

"But alas, you are wrong," the other informed him. "Being an illiterate islander, it's probably very hard for you to realize that the languages of the Pacific are all forms of the same tongue."

Wiki said coldly, "I am not illiterate."

Mr. Hale blinked. "You can read?"

"That's what I said."

"Taught by the missionaries, no doubt."

As it happened, Wiki had originally learned to enjoy books because a drunken Yankee beachcomber—a man who, once upon a time, had been a respectable Edgartown captain—had taught him how to read and write. However, he kept silent.

"Valuable men, the missionaries," Mr. Hale declared. "In addition to their traditional tasks, many of those great laborers in the foreign field have written down lengthy vocabularies of the people with whom they work, and a detailed study of these lexicons leaves no doubt whatsoever that the tribes belong to a single nation, and have a common language that varies only as dialects differ."

Remembering how difficult it had been to make himself understood at some of the island landfalls he had made in the past, Wiki kept silent.

"For illustration, give me the various Polynesian words for canoe."

Wiki shrugged. "In Samoa and Tahiti, the word for canoe is *va'a*, in Tonga and Rarotonga, *vaka*, in Maui and Oahu, *wa'a*, and in *te reo Maori*, *waka*."

"Can't you see how the great similarity of the words proves my point?" exclaimed Mr. Hale, delighted with himself that he had chosen such an apt example. "In each great area of the earth—or, in the case of the Pacific Ocean, the sea—there was a single original language, which evolved as people moved from one place to another. It is by means of tracing these changes that we can chart the past migrations."

"Is this why you have come on the expedition?" Wiki queried. "To make lists of words?"

"Precisely! My mission is to collect a sample vocabulary of each language, and compare the resultant lexicons to see how the tongues have evolved as the tribes moved farther apart, then to publish my findings in a volume of ethnology."

"I see," said Wiki, thinking that he now understood why he, and not Horatio Hale, was the expedition translator. Right from early childhood, he had derived immense pleasure from his gift for absorbing new languages whole passages at a time, complete with their depth and emotion. Didn't Mr. Hale understand that words lost most of their meaning when ripped singly from their context? Apparently not.

Then the philologist pronounced, "I am convinced that once I have collated my information, I will be able to prove beyond academic doubt that the Polynesian tribes originated in Malaya, and that islands like New Zealand were populated as these people sailed from one island group to another, moving from the west to the east and spreading out as they went."

Involuntarily, Wiki exclaimed, *"That's just not so!"*

Mr. Hale looked surprised. "Why are you so angry?"

Wiki was silent. Normally, he was able to ignore *pakeha* misconceptions, but Hale had blundered onto sacred ground. Every New

Zealander knew beyond doubt that the ancestors had come from a fabled island that lay far to the east—that they were the descendants of the greatest seamen the world had ever known, who had navigated their way across an immense tract of unknown waters, *from the east to the west.* The tribal knowledge that their forefathers had sailed to New Zealand from the direction of the rising sun had great spiritual significance—houses were built with their doorways facing east, and people sang *karakia* prayers to greet the dawn.

However, Mr. Hale simply waited, so finally Wiki pointed out, "The prevailing winds blow from the east."

"Not at all times of the year," the other corrected. "You must have heard of islanders who were blown great distances by unexpected storms—and this is most probably how the migrations took place. And, if not by an accident of nature," Mr. Hale amended, noticing Wiki's involuntary gesture of rejection, "then the great outward movement was achieved by waiting for the seasonal reversal of winds, which would have carried the canoes east. Thus, the Fijis were colonized first, then Samoa, then Tahiti, and finally the Marquesas Islands. The missionaries have already gone a long way to prove this with their observation that in the west the Polynesian tribes have a simple mythology and spiritual worship, while in the east this has been debased to a cruel idolatry."

Wiki retreated into cold silence again. After waiting another moment Mr. Hale decided that he'd won the argument, because he changed the subject, saying, "It surprises me greatly that you do not have a tattooed face. Why do you not?"

"I was carried to America when I was just twelve years old."

"That makes a difference?"

"Twelve isn't old enough to have a *moko.*"

"*Moko?* Is that your word for tattoo?"

"Aye."

"That's strange! Why do New Zealand Maori use that word for tattoo when the rest of Polynesia has a different word?"

"I don't know," said Wiki, rather pleased that he had produced something, even if inadvertently, that rattled Mr. Hale's superiority. However, he had to admit that it was indeed odd. The generally accepted word for tattoo was the Tahitian one, *tatau.* Only in New Zealand had he heard it called *moko.*

Finally, he said, "*Moko* is also our word for lizard. Maybe the curves of the lizard inspired the curved lines of the *moko.*"

"That's clever!" said Mr. Hale. Wiki had the impression that if he'd had a notebook, it would have been written down. "Do you ever think you will get tattooed?"

Wiki didn't want to tell him that he already had spiral tattoos on his buttocks, as he had a nasty feeling that his listener would demand to see them—in the cause of science, of course. Instead, he asked, "Why are you surprised I don't have a *moko?*"

"Because the other New Zealander with the expedition has a tattooed face."

"*Other* New Zealander?" exclaimed Wiki, astounded.

"Didn't you know? A New Zealand chief is on board the *Peacock*—the same ship where I live. For the past nine or ten years he has exhibited himself all over the States," Mr. Hale informed him, going on in enthusiastic tones, "We often have him to dance and sing after the manner of your people—'tis as good as a play! When we get to New Zealand we're to leave him at his home, where no doubt he will revert to his old primitive habits." He suddenly smiled, his face becoming round and angelic. "You must feel so delighted to learn that there is a countryman with the fleet! What a joy it will be for you to talk over the endearing scenes of home!"

Wiki said cautiously, "I don't suppose you know his name?"

"But of course I do. It's Jack Sac."

That, Wiki knew, would be the name given to the Maori seaman by his first American captain, probably because he'd been so highly delighted when someone on board had given him an old coat, or sacque.

He said, "I meant his Maori name."

"In the crew list, he is also put down as Tuatti."

Te Aute, Wiki thought. Even more warily, he asked, "Do you know the name of his home village in New Zealand?"

"He said a name that sounded like *Maketu*, and told me that it is on the east coast of your northern island."

Wiki said nothing, but his face had given him away, because Mr. Hale said with disappointment, "You aren't pleased?"

That was a gross understatement, but Wiki merely said, "His tribe is different to mine. He is Ngati Porou; I am Ngapuhi."

"So he will not be overjoyed to meet you?"

He's much more likely to kill me, Wiki thought.

They cantered around the next bend to find that the party had stopped in an untidy huddle, because a man was standing in the middle of the path. This time, it was not the courtly customs man, but instead a portly fellow wearing the complete costume of a gaucho. His shirt was red-striped, and there was a red sash about his rotund waist, which held up his *calzoncillos*—long white drawers. Scarlet *chiripá* Turkish trousers were draped about the underpants, drawn up between his legs and lashed fore and aft to the sash, which was reinforced by a traditional broad leather belt. One of the huge facóns that the gauchos made by snapping a sword short and then sharpening it to a wicked point was thrust slantwise into the back of his belt. A folded poncho hung over one shoulder.

The apparition called out heartily, "*¡Che!*"

Captain Ringgold turned in his saddle, and beckoned. Wiki cantered to the front of the crowd, summed up the fellow in one comprehensive glance, and said in English, "How do you do?"

"Dr. Ducatel, at your service," replied the other in a broad Yankee accent, not a whit abashed.

"You're *another* American?" exclaimed Captain Ringgold.

"I am indeed—and proud of it, too."

"My God, how many of the rascals are there?" muttered Ringgold.

"He's a surgeon," Wiki informed him, seeing Ducatel's brows shoot up at the news that he was known to this brown stranger.

Ringgold, however, looked even less impressed. "A *doctor*?" he expostulated. "How long have you been living in this hole, for God's sake?"

The surgeon transferred his gaze to the sky, evidently counting, because he finally said, "Five years? Perhaps as few as four."

"Doing *what*?"

"A variety of things, sir—a medley of accomplishments! To put it in a nutshell," Ducatel elaborated freely, "I graduated from the New York College of Physicians and Surgeons in 1832, but while the degree was substantial, my funds were slight. Accordingly, I signed articles as a ship's surgeon, but then made the unfortunate choice of leaving the ship at Montevideo. I'd heard that *médicos* were in short supply up the Río Negro, the most southern outpost of civilization in the Americas, and so I journeyed here. And, believe it or not, sir, I actually did quite well for a while! However, the tyrant of Buenos Aires has put an end to that, so you see me making my money any way I can. Is your business urgent?" he inquired. "I've good beef to sell, if you need it in a hurry."

So this was why he'd lain in wait, Wiki deduced—when the ex-surgeon had heard rumors that the so-called French squadron was really an American fleet, he'd scented profitable trade. When Ringgold said nothing, evidently having lost track sometime during the monologue, Wiki said quickly to Ducatel, "Tell me, when did you last see Caleb Adams?"

"Why do you ask?" the surgeon said, puzzled. "I've been away for the past ten days, upcountry, and didn't see much of him even before that."

"Wiki," said Ringgold warningly.

Wiki ignored him. "How about a man by the name of Rowland Hallett?"

"You mean Captain Hallett?"

"Captain?" Wiki echoed, surprised.

"Captain of the New York brig *Athenian*. When he first arrived, a couple of years back—about October 1836, I think, because it was the beginning of the sealing season—he acquired a schooner, to be used as a . . . tender? Is that the correct word for a small vessel that works alongside a big one?"

"It is," said Wiki, all attention.

"The schooner was called the *Grim Reaper*," said the physician, and let out a womanish giggle. Then he sobered and went on, "He hired a gang of Indians to do the killing and skinning, and did very well, I believe. In the sealing way, that is," Ducatel amended, and then added, "The schooner came back about three weeks ago. The arrangement with the Indians was that they were to be returned to El Carmen de Patagones, and he was also anxious to consult with me professionally."

"He was sick? Or did he want beef?"

"He'd been bitten in the hand by a bull seal—a common hazard with sealers, I believe—and gangrene had set in. I was forced to cut off his arm," the surgeon went on, adding pridefully, "Though I have been forced to abandon my profession, I have retained my amputating instruments, along with the appropriate skills."

"So where is he now?" Wiki urgently asked.

"The operation was a complete success," the surgeon complacently said. "Unfortunately, the patient died."

Six

When they got into the pueblo of El Carmen de Patagones, Ringgold and his party were greeted with terrified screams, then a commotion of loud slams as doors were swiftly barricaded. Within instants the alleys were empty, and the yellow dogs were back in control. Captain Ringgold reined in, looking around in astonishment, and the rest straggled to a halt.

A figure appeared at the end of the street, and ran stumblingly toward them—Stackpole, looking extremely dusty and disheveled. Wiki touched his mare with his heel, cantered up to him, and said, "Did you find the clerk?"

"What?" Stackpole blinked bloodshot eyes, and then said with complete lack of enthusiasm, "Oh, it's you."

"Who did you think it was?"

"Everybody here thought it was the French arriving at last."

Wiki said sarcastically, "Didn't that worry you?"

"I've got no personal quarrel with the French, and any official presence whatsoever would be a blessing, believe me. The governor couldn't care less about the state of law and order in this province, and his troops are a bloody disgrace. I need men with guts and discipline, not a bunch of ex-felons pretending to be soldiers! Who's that?" said the whaling master, and jerked his chin at Ringgold, who had jumped off his horse and was stalking their way on foot.

"A captain with the U.S. expedition fleet," said Wiki.

"Well, thank God for that," said Stackpole. He stepped out to meet Ringgold, declaiming in ringing tones, "As an American citizen, I demand the protection of my nation!"

The captain bristled. "Who the hell are you?"

Wiki carried out introductions.

Ringgold removed his cocked hat, but neglected to shake hands. Instead, he said dangerously, "So you're the man who requisitioned Wiki Coffin from the *Swallow*?"

"That's me," Stackpole agreed with spirit. "For the very good reason that I was robbed by a Yankee trader in these parts!"

"Your money was used to buy a schooner, I believe, and in your name, at that," Captain Ringgold corrected, proving to Wiki that there was nothing wrong with his memory. "So you can scarcely say you were robbed."

"But the schooner's been stolen, which is just the same thing—and if stealing a ship ain't piracy, then I don't know what piracy is!"

That was a good point, as Ringgold's expression betrayed. He said reluctantly, "Maybe we could help you—if the schooner sails the high seas. But where *does* she sail? Tell me that!"

"I can't bloody well tell you that, because Adams has been murdered!" Stackpole exclaimed. "If I'd got to Rowland Hallett in time, I could've shaken it out of him, but he's dead, too! He was hospitalized with gangrene, and died after that quack Ducatel cut off his bloody arm!"

"So I heard, and God bless his poor soul," Ringgold said piously.

"And as for Adams's murder, I don't intend to have anything to do with it. Murder's a local matter."

"But Adams was American!"

"You can't expect us to go chasing after every Yankee adventurer who gets himself killed on foreign soil—it just ain't practicable. Particularly when they seem to be as thick as fleas on a dog round these parts," Ringgold added moodily, and then asked, "Have you informed the governor?"

"Of course I've informed the bloody governor!" Stackpole cried, almost beside himself. "But it didn't help a bloody jot! When I asked what happened to my thousand-dollar bank draft after Hallett expired, he informed me that Hallett's possessions were handed in as the law required, and there wasn't any draft among them. When I told him that someone in the fort sick bay must've stolen it, he dismissed me in a rage!"

"Well, now that you've put it into his hands, you can't expect me to interfere," Ringgold snapped. "Not only would it be a diplomatic blunder, but Captain Wilkes would be cross. And it was most improper of you to requisition a member of our expedition to do your detective work! So good day to you, sir," he concluded, and slapped on his hat with finality.

Stackpole spluttered, but Ringgold simply ignored him, turning to Wiki and saying, "Well, it looks as if the robbery and the murder have already been reported to the governor, so there's no need for you to involve yourself further. Dr. Ducatel has offered to guide us to the fort, so we don't need you for that, neither."

"So I return to the *Sea Gull*?"

"No, you damn well don't, because I ain't finished with you yet. While Mr. Perry and Mr. Waldron and I are paying our respects to the governor, you'll oblige me by taking Mr. Hale to the Indian camp."

Wiki said in surprise, "The *toldos*?"

"Aye, if that's what you call it. He wants to question the natives relative to their language. I believe they're a confoundedly treacherous lot, so you'd better take your gaucho friends, too."

Mr. Hale looked rather apprehensive at the prospect of being left alone with Wiki and his gaucho band, but he didn't say anything, instead taking a fresh grip of his reins. Then he watched and waited as Wiki consulted with Bernantio about this new mission. By the time they had finished, Dr. Ducatel and the three expedition officers were well off in the distance, trailing up the hill on their way to the fort.

Wiki turned to Stackpole, who was moodily watching Ringgold and his companions retreat, and said, "Where's your horse?"

The whaling master jerked his thumb over his shoulder at a hitching post up the head of the street, and said, "Why?"

"Have you talked to the Indians who went sealing with Rowland Hallett?"

Stackpole lifted his hat and scratched his head.

"Well, you should—so it would be a good idea to come along with us. Mr. Hale wants to make a list of Indian words, and while he's at work you'll have a chance to track down at least one of the men who went on that voyage."

"But the Indian camp is on the other side of the river!" Stackpole exclaimed.

"Shall we hire a boat?" asked Mr. Hale.

Undoubtedly, he was trying to be helpful, but Wiki's eyes crinkled up in a grin, and when he relayed it to Bernantio all the gauchos enjoyed a hearty laugh. "Horses do swim," he said, and saw Stackpole wince, and Mr. Hale swallow hard.

However, they both kept up with the rest as the party cantered down the steps and galloped into the stream with a mighty splash that drenched Wiki to the waist, the gauchos whirling their ponchos over their heads to urge the horses on. It was easier than Stackpole and Hale might have dreaded, the steeds being used to swimming, but then a steep, slippery bank had to be mounted.

At the top, Wiki turned his snorting, shivering mare, and straightened in the saddle to survey the opposite shore, while water streamed down his legs and off her sides. El Carmen looked smaller from this perspective, perhaps because the pueblo was so compactly tucked into the cliff, and dominated so by the fort that sprawled over the heights above. The scenery inland was surprisingly distinct, partly because of the clarity of the air, and also because the sun was so high, he supposed. He could see the path that led along the river to the salt dunes, and the dun of the undulating plain beyond, and even glimpse the white shimmer of the *salinas* reflected in the sky. The sandstone cliffs were pale in the midday light, and to his surprise, he could discern the black mouths of caves. This was where the cliffs stood about three miles from the river, he judged, and supposed he hadn't been able to see them from the riverside path the day before because of the shimmering effect of distance.

Then Wiki was distracted by a babel of yapping and yodeling. When he turned in his saddle it was to see the gauchos galloping upriver toward the *toldería,* with Horatio Hale and Captain Stackpole gamely keeping up with them, so he urged his mare into a trot.

As he neared the Indian camp, he decided that it looked remarkably temporary for something that was such a long-standing institution, the *toldos* being made up of mats, rugs, and hides tossed casually over light wooden frames. Hitching rails dotted the grass everywhere, with rows of half-wild horses tethered to them, startling and bucking, their eyes rolling. Myriads of yellow dogs slunk about, snapping and snarling at each other.

When Wiki came to a stop by a picket line, the gauchos had dismounted already, and were heading for a large, sturdy adobe building set toward the center of the *toldería.* Once there, they stamped inside with a great clanking of iron spurs, Captain Stackpole close behind them. It was the *pulpería,* Wiki deduced, and probably a *botillería*—or bar—as well as a store, which meant it was the place where he was most likely to find the Indians who'd gone sealing with Captain Hallett. However, duty called, along with Mr. Hale, and so he slid down from the mare, secured her to a post, and joined the philologist.

Together, they approached the nearest tent. The eastern side of this was completely open, revealing a healthy-looking set of people who rose to their feet when they saw them coming. The men were tall and stalwart, particularly the younger ones, and though many wore nothing more than the *guillapiz*, a length of cloth draped about the body, they carried it magnificently. The young women were even more eye-catching, swathed in colorful cloth with chaplets of blue beads about their heads, their glossy black hair braided into two thick plaits. Their bright almond eyes sparkled as they contemplated Wiki, and he studied them back equally appreciatively. Then a meaningful cough from Horatio Hale reminded him of business, and he returned his attention to the men.

The more important-looking wore gaucho costume, embellished with a lot of silver in the shape of buckles, spurs, and jewelry, their murderous facóns having particularly large and ornate silver handles. The metal was a signifier of rank, Wiki deduced, because the more lordly the wearer looked, the more silver there was about his person. Accordingly, he approached the man who was most heavily caparisoned, a well-muscled, middle-aged fellow with a flat, cruel face, and soon found he was right in guessing that he was the chief—the *cacique*. Bowing, Wiki greeted him formally and gravely in the form of Spanish that the gauchos used, and to his relief the chief understood him quite well, probably the result of years of trading. After that, it was rather like being back in the Bay of Islands, because of the dignified precision with which they traded names and other personal details, the *cacique* betraying no surprise that Wiki hailed from a South Seas archipelago he'd probably never heard of before.

Though acutely aware that Mr. Hale was shifting impatiently from boot to boot, Wiki seized his chance to ask about the sealing voyage. He was in luck, as the chief admitted that his son had been the *capataz*—the foreman—of the sealing gang. Where was he? In the *pulpería*, perhaps. Asking more details only resulted in a series of shrugs, so finally Wiki turned to Mr. Hale, and said, "This is Huinchan, one of the chiefs of his tribe."

"Tell him that when I point at something, I want him or one of his subjects to tell me the name of that object in his native tongue."

Wiki relayed this in more diplomatic terms, and the older Indians cooperated, though looking somewhat baffled, and a to-and-fro recitation commenced, while Mr. Hale wrote in a book. He soon lost the attention of all the rest. The pretty, red-cheeked girls were much more interested in teasing Wiki with flirtatious glances, giggling behind their fingers when he winked. Meantime, the young bloods had resumed their seats on the ground, and were carrying on a conversation that was evidently hilarious, being punctuated with shouts of laughter.

After a few moments of this Hale, looking extremely irritated, asked, "What are they talking about?"

Straightfaced, Wiki said, "I haven't a notion." The Indians' language was the strangest he had ever heard, being composed of clicks, grunts, and a harsh sound made by clenching the throat. However, his knack for picking up repeated phrases, allied to the abundant clues given by gesture, expression, and posture, was serving him well, so he had a very good idea indeed what was happening—the young men were discussing the American, and comparing his pale, soft-featured looks somewhat unfavorably to their own.

"It's very distracting," Mr. Hale complained.

"I'm sure it is," agreed Wiki amiably.

"And I think that you are the cause of it. You seem to attract a lot of attention. I really do believe I would do better on my own."

There was nothing Wiki wanted more than to leave, but he couldn't resist saying, "You're sure you can manage?"

"Of course I can manage!" Horatio Hale snapped, and Wiki took himself off to the *pulpería*.

The interior of the adobe building was large, dim, and crowded with both men and goods. The wall by the doorway where Wiki had come in was studded with pegs, from which hung horse gear of all kinds—bridles, stirrups, spurs, and pieces of saddle. He saw sheepskins heaped in a corner of the baked mud floor, great piles of bagged maize and jerked beef, and shelves piled with ponchos and lengths of bright cloth. Barrels of molasses, ship's bread, and salt beef and pork were stacked along another wall, along with hogsheads of tobacco—a telling contrast to the ransacked state of Adams's store.

Wiki found that his guess that this store was a *botillería* was a correct one, too, because at the far end of the room the proprietor stood behind a wooden palisade, presiding over Dutch gin and Spanish wine, *aguardiente* from the Azores, and Brazilian *caña*. There was a strong, all-pervading smell of sweat, leather, wool, aniseed, and horses, and the noise was deafening. Gauchos and Indians hammered on the counter with the flat blades of their knives, saluted each other at the tops of their voices as they passed cups of harsh red wine around, and shouted while they argued about revolutions and horse brands. A drunken musician strummed a guitar just inside the doorway, setting dogs to howling outside.

Captain Stackpole was standing brace-legged in a corner, an empty heavy-bottomed tumbler in his hand, looking all the better for having swallowed whatever had been inside it. Wiki eased over to him, and asked if he had found any of the Indian sealers. When the whaleman glumly shook his head, Wiki lifted his voice, shouting for Ramón, Ramón being the Spanish name the Indian *cacique,* Huinchan, had given his son. Five men answered, but only one was Indian.

Ramón, son of Huinchan, had the same flat, cruel face as his father. He was also half drunk, evidently still celebrating his good fortune on the sealing ground. Luckily, he was in an amenable mood, and ready to chat—in a remarkably polyglot kind of way, as over the sealing voyage he had picked up quite a lot of English to add to his gaucho-style Spanish.

"I liked to go a-sealing," he informed them. Not only had the adventure yielded wonderful riches, but he'd found he had a natural talent for killing and skinning seals. Also, Captain Hallett had been a fair and just *caudillo,* who worked as hard as his men.

Wiki said curiously, "How many skins did you get?"

"Five thousand," said the Indian, and puffed his chest out.

It didn't sound terribly many to Wiki. Though he'd be the first to admit that he knew nothing about the sealing trade, he'd read of ventures that yielded twenty thousand pelts or more. However, Ramón was clearly pleased with the number, so Wiki observed, "It must have been tempting to sail with the schooner again."

"The opportunity, señor, was not there."

"Because of Captain Hallett's injury?"

"He died," the Indian told him. "He went to Dr. Ducatel's ranch and when the doctor cut off his arm his life leaked out of the end."

Stackpole shifted abruptly, exclaiming, "He went to Ducatel's *ranch*?"

"Captain Hallett died at Dr. Ducatel's ranch," the Indian confirmed, adding solemnly, "He died on the Sabbath."

"My *God*!" The whaleman sounded on the verge of exploding.

Wiki waited, but Stackpole didn't elaborate, so he carried on with the cross-examination, saying to the Indian in Spanish, "The schooner was bought from Captain Hallett for another captain, who was taking the schooner a-sealing again. Would he not want to use the same gang that had done so well with you as *capataz*?"

"Another captain?" Ramón let out a derisive sound, and then said in English, "Ah, who could that be?"

Wiki had been thinking of Stackpole, but instead he said tentatively, "Señor Adams?"

"Adams?" Another contemptuous snort. "What kind of man would allow himself to be shipped by a *pulpero*?"

"A *pulpero* who is missing," Wiki remarked meaningfully, and waited.

Silence. The Indian looked away, glancing all about the crowded store.

Giving up, Wiki said in English, "What about the schooner?"

"Ah, she sailed away."

Stackpole exclaimed, "Where?"

"Up the river."

Stackpole and Wiki looked at each other. Then the whaleman demanded, "When did she come back?"

"I did not see her come back," said Ramón indifferently.

"So who was it who sailed her up the river?" Wiki asked.

"Peter and Dick, they sailed her," said Ramón.

"*Who?*" said Stackpole, thunderstruck.

"Our seamen," said the Indian, and then added in Spanish to Wiki, "My men and I, you understand, were the sealers, not the sailors. We did not sail the schooner. Peter and Dick did the sailing work."

So Peter and Dick were members of the *Athenian* crew—men who had been seconded to the schooner. Wiki wondered if they had been opportunistic enough to pirate the *Grim Reaper* after Adams had failed to come back from the *salinas*. More likely still, he suddenly realized, they could have been recruited by the killer after he'd returned from burying the corpse. Or were they murderers themselves?

He said, "Did she not have a captain when she sailed up the river?"

"No captain of the schooner I saw, just a common *pulpero* who held the tiller while Peter and Dick worked the sails," Ramón said with disdain, and lifted his glass and drank.

Wiki stared at him. While this confirmed that Adams had stolen the schooner and sailed her upriver, it simply deepened the mystery of the men who had driven the packhorses to the salt dunes, and the horseman who had pursued them. Then, while he was phrasing another question, all hell let loose in the *toldería* outside.

Threatening shouts in the Indian tongue were punctuated with bloodcurdling screams, and the insane yapping of dozens of dogs. When Wiki shouldered his way through the crowd and out of the *pulpería*, it was to see Horatio Hale backing off rapidly from the tent

where he had been collecting words. A young Indian man was jabbing menacingly with his long knife as he advanced on the philologist.

Wiki found himself shoved aside as Bernantio and his gauchos rushed with enthusiasm to the rescue. Their ponchos had been wound around their left arms, which were held across their stomachs to protect their vital organs; their facóns were gripped in their right hands, and their lean, high-cheeked faces were hungry for battle. The Indian stared at them aggressively, but his knife was lifted to jab the philologist.

Wiki raced obliquely toward Hale, dived, and wrestled him to one side just as the Indian's knife started its downward plunge. The young scientist thumped to the ground with a startled yell. Wiki rolled, staggered to his feet, and yanked him up again. Then he propelled him into a headlong dash with a palm planted between his shoulder blades.

When they were well clear, he said, "What the devil happened?"

"I was merely about my work." The philologist was looking back at the developing fight with a bewildered air. "After eliciting the words for horse, house, knife, and writing them down, I was then trying out the adjuncts, *your* horse, *his* house, *my* knife—and he took fire, supposing some awful insult."

"Oh, Lord," said Wiki, instantly seeing what had happened. "He thought you were challenging his ownership of these things—that you were calling him a liar."

"But we were doing so *well* until the misunderstanding. Even the *dogs* were friendly. In fact, they gave me fleas. Can't you *explain* it to him, so we can go back to work?"

"God, no," said Wiki, casting a comprehensive glance at the scene. "*You're* the cause of the trouble, I'm afraid. The sooner we remove you, the better."

He shoved Hale toward his horse, saw him mount, leaped on board his own mare, and looked about for Stackpole. The whaleman, as alert to trouble as all of his kind, had found his own steed in the

confusion, and the three of them galloped down the steep slope to the river, hooves kicking and sliding in the rush. Into the water they plunged, and labored briskly toward the other side, getting ashore a couple of hundred yards downstream from the pueblo.

When they arrived back at the steps that led up to the village, Dr. Ducatel was standing in the middle of the path, just as if he expected them.

"Mr. Coffin," he said with a formal little bow. "Mr. Hale. Captain Stackpole."

Stackpole roared, *"Ducatel!"*

Everyone jumped with fright, including the surgeon, who spluttered, "I have merely come to deliver a message from—"

"I heard just now that Rowland Hallett died at your ranch, not up at the barracks the way that I thought!"

Ducatel licked his lips, visibly gathered rags of dignity about him, and muttered, "Like any rational man who was lucky enough to be able to afford the cost, Captain Hallett preferred not to be sent to the hole they call a sick bay at the fort."

"Afford the cost?" Stackpole echoed with thunderous fury. "Of course he could afford the bloody cost—and do you know why? Because he had my money!"

"What m-money?" the surgeon stuttered, backing off a step.

Wiki interrupted, "How much did Hallett have on him when he died?"

"Enough," Ducatel answered, his look becoming evasive.

Stackpole thundered, "What do you mean, *enough*?"

"Enough for my fee! Once I'd subtracted the amount of that, I put all the deceased's possessions into official hands. If you don't believe me, you can ask the governor! I handed over Captain Hallett's sea chest the very same day that he died, even before I buried him—in my

own burying ground on the ranch," he said with an air of wounded virtue. "After filling out the death certificate, naturally," he added.

Wiki scowled, thinking that it had all happened in rather a rush, and said, "When did this happen?"

Ducatel didn't need to stop to think, saying at once, "He passed away on January thirteenth. The Sabbath," he added, in the same solemn tone the Indian had used.

"Was Captain Hallett at your house all the time he was ill?"

"Right from the hour he came to consult—which he did the first possible moment after the *Grim Reaper* arrived off the pueblo."

"What date was that?"

"January sixth."

So Hallett had been under the surgeon's care for a week before he died. Thinking that the fee Ducatel charged must have been a substantial one, Wiki looked at Stackpole, and asked, "Did Adams have the money on the sixth?"

Stackpole shook his head. "I gave it to him on the eighth, the same day I inspected the schooner. I handed it over, got a receipt, and that's the last I saw of it, because I headed back to my ship."

"And he didn't mention that Captain Hallett was on shore?"

"Didn't say a bloody word," said Stackpole moodily. "He was too busy planning to steal the schooner, I reckon."

The whaling master was probably right, Wiki thought, but then wondered when the transaction had taken place. He asked the surgeon, "When did Caleb Adams come to the ranch?"

"I've already told you I haven't seen Adams for weeks!"

So how had Adams managed to buy the schooner? Wiki was silent a moment, abstractedly restraining his mare as she shifted restlessly from one hoof to another, and wishing he could remember the details of the deed of sale.

He said, "And when you subtracted the amount of your fee from the money in the dead man's pockets, you didn't see a bank draft?"

"What draft?" the surgeon cried. "I don't know anything about any draft!"

Stackpole snapped, "We're talking about a draft to the amount of one thousand dollars that Adams paid Hallett for that goddamned schooner!"

Ducatel's eyes popped. "One *thousand* dollars?"

"That's what I said—and I want to know what happened to it after Hallett died!"

The surgeon cried, "I didn't even know that the schooner was sold! And you're trying to accuse me of stealing one thousand dollars from Captain Hallett? On what grounds, pray? No one has whispered a single word about any sale—the schooner was here, and then she was gone, and that's all I know about it! Do you have any proof? I bet you don't! And Adams never came to the ranch, I swear! If anyone stole any draft, it was him!"

Struck with inspiration, Wiki interrupted, "You still hold a key to the outside door of the surgery in Adams's store?"

"How did you know I had a key?" Ducatel demanded.

Wiki didn't admit that he'd been guessing, saying instead, "You have it now?"

"Yes, I do, but why—"

"Because the proof you want that the sale really happened is there," Wiki said, and without waiting for any more argument he slapped his reins, urging the mare up the steps into El Carmen. When Stackpole called out his name he didn't pay attention. Instead, he listened to Ducatel's steps as he hurried after him on foot, followed by the other two men on their horses.

The front door of Adams's store was still firmly shut and locked, the windows shuttered tight. Wiki dismounted, secured the mare to the rail, and headed after Ducatel, who had walked around the corner and into the yard. Stackpole and Mr. Hale were a couple of dozen yards behind.

First, Wiki checked the double doors, finding them solidly shut. As he remembered, there was no way of opening them from the outside, once they were bolted and barred on the inside. The only way into the store from the yard was through the outer surgery door. He looked at Dr. Ducatel, and lifted his brows.

The surgeon fished the key out of a pocket in his coat. Judging by the way he braced himself, he expected the lock to be stiff with disuse, but instead the key turned smoothly. The door swung silently back on its hinges, revealing a large consulting room with a desk, a chair, and a long couch that had evidently served as a sickbed, because it was rigged out with neatly folded blankets.

It was as if the surgery were ready to be put to use again at a moment's notice, and Wiki's neck crept with a sense of human presence. Then Stackpole let out a startled curse, accompanied by a ghoulish rattle. He had blundered into a skeleton hanging from a hook that had been screwed into one of the ceiling beams.

"My property," said Dr. Ducatel. His giggle sounded forced. No one else laughed.

Papers on the desk lifted and rustled as Wiki opened the inner door, letting in a draft of dry, stale air, and flies rose and buzzed. The store looked exactly the same as the last time he had seen it, but the hairs on the back of his neck were creeping. He stood just clear of the doorway of the surgery, staring around as the others pushed past him, and warily sniffing the musty air.

Then he heard Horatio Hale's whine of utter horror.

Wiki jerked around, to find the white-faced philologist pointing a shaking finger at the floor behind the counter. Four hurried strides, and he could see what had gripped Hale's shocked attention—the distorted corpse of the Portuguese clerk.

Seven

The old man was lying on his back with the fallen stool between his legs, frozen by death into a sitting-down position. His eyes were wide open, staring up from between his knees. Judging by the expression of stupefaction on the dead face, he had been taken completely by surprise. The big ledger was lying open on the counter, as if he had been absorbed in noting down the details of a sale when his killer had walked in the door.

Wiki looked down at the body. The attack had been violent as well as sudden and unexpected, because the clerk had been struck with a very large knife so hard that the hilt had left imprints on his shirt before it was hauled out and taken away. The stain of blood about the wound in his chest had dried many hours ago. It was ghoulishly reminiscent of Caleb Adams's corpse, except that the body was entire.

He said to Ducatel, "How long has he been dead?"

The surgeon was staring down at the ungainly remains, his expression withdrawn and brooding. Now he roused himself, glanced at Wiki, and said, "I need to have a better look. Give me a hand to haul him out of there."

Because of the cramped space behind the counter, it took three of them to drag the stiff, resistant form out into the open, Stackpole lending a hand to pull at the legs. Even though they did their best to straighten him out, the knees remained rigidly bent toward the chest, frozen by rigor mortis into the way the body had landed when it had tumbled off the stool, and the hands still grasped at the air.

Ducatel crouched down by the corpse, and pulled back the shirt to expose the great gash in the ribs. When he stood again, his face was expressionless. "He was killed at least thirty-six hours ago."

Wiki said, "How can you tell?"

"There are maggots in the lips of the wound."

For the first time, Wiki felt a snatch of nausea. He swallowed, and said, "What about the stiffness?"

"It takes three to four days for rigor mortis to relax, so he'll be petrified in that position for quite a while yet."

So, Wiki mused, the clerk had been dead when he and Stackpole had checked the store—he had been killed not long after their departure for the salt dunes. He wondered why he had not sensed the shocked spirit—the *kehua*—when they had tried the door after coming back from the *salinas*, and thought wryly that he was becoming more American by the moment. The flies were circling lower, and he saw two settle on the glazed eyes. Turning to the box of red silk bandannas on the counter, he plucked one up, and dropped it over the dead man's face. It landed neatly, covering the entire head. This made the sight of the contorted body even more grotesque, but to have those staring eyes hidden was a distinct relief.

Ducatel was glancing around the emptied store. He looked at Wiki and remarked, "The thieves must have been a cold-blooded lot—they took their time after killing the old man. Just about everything's been cleared out."

"No, it's the way we saw it last," contradicted Stackpole. His voice was low and hoarse.

"Nothing's gone?" Mr. Hale blurted out. "But they must have killed him for *something*. What about the cash drawer?"

Wiki went around the back of the counter to check. When he pulled the drawer open, it rattled emptily. However, the coins he had paid for the bandanna and the poncho, plus some extra cash that Stackpole, presumably, had paid after coming back into the store for a poncho for himself, were in a little purse at the back.

"The killer must have been after the deed of sale," he said. He was so sure of it that he felt no surprise when no paper fell out as he picked up the ledger by the spine and shook it. Riffling the pages had the same lack of result. The deed was definitely gone. When he looked at Stackpole, the whaleman's face was pale and withdrawn.

"But why did they steal it?" objected Ducatel.

"Because it's proof of ownership of the schooner," Wiki replied. To make sure, he searched the drawer again, and then went through the dead man's clothing, finding nothing but a key and a grubby handkerchief, both of which he placed on the counter. Finally, he turned back to the last written page in the ledger, to see what the clerk might have been noting when he had been surprised by his murderer. The last entry was the sale of the poncho to Stackpole.

Looking up at the whaling master, he observed, "You're probably the last man to have seen him alive."

Stackpole's mouth became more tightly compressed than ever. He bit out, "He was perfectly fine when I left."

"He was sitting on his stool writing in this book?"

Stackpole nodded.

"Did anyone come in while you were going out?"

The whaleman shook his head.

"Was there anyone in the street?" He and the gauchos had gone on ahead, Wiki remembered, and had arrived at the upriver path by the time Stackpole had rejoined them.

Again, Stackpole shook his head.

Wiki turned to Ducatel. "Which one of Hallett's arms did you amputate?"

Ducatel blinked in surprise. "The left. Why?"

"And which hand did he write with?"

"I have no idea. He had no occasion to use the pen while I was watching."

"Did you watch him use his unhurt hand? To lift a mug, for instance?"

"He was clumsy—the water slopped. But what can you expect of a sick man? Why do you ask?"

Wiki shrugged. "Because the signature on the deed was very indistinct."

Ducatel silenced. Wiki picked up the key from the counter, went to the front door, and unlocked and opened it. The bright siesta-time street was deserted. He looked back into the dark store, and said, "We'll have to inform his family. Do they live in the pueblo?"

"I know them well," Ducatel's voice replied at once. "There's a whole tribe of them living in a couple of houses jammed together—in one of the back streets, hard up against the cliff. There are several daughters, and two sons—a shiftless pair, who spend most of their time on the family fishing boat. That is, when they're not busy fathering children," he added with a snigger.

It sounded as if the clerk had been the main source of family income. Wiki said, "What was the clerk's name, anyway?"

It had been Gomes. As he followed Ducatel through the deserted alleys, Wiki wondered how many tribes of that name were scattered about South America.

The hot sun was just past the meridian, and the hard shadow of the cliff fell upon them as they made their way to the rearmost street of El Carmen. The sprawling adobe house where the Gomes clan lived was in the form of a U, enclosing a big yard ruled by a spectacular cockerel with a large harem of cowed hens. Inside, the baked-mud floor was half-hidden with a few mats, and the furniture was rough and scanty. As Ducatel had indicated, at least three generations lived there, including several matronly women and many children. However, it was very quiet, the atmosphere somnolent. The family had eaten their midday meal, and were snoozing out siesta.

Despite the overcrowding, they seemed remarkably well set up. While Dr. Ducatel communicated the awful tidings in experienced tones, Wiki thoughtfully noted bulging sacks of corn, and barrels of oil, salt meat, and molasses, both inside the house and out in the yard. Then his attention was taken up by the reaction to the news. It was almost as if the clerk's death had been anticipated, because the women collapsed with grief before the last words had left Ducatel's mouth. Mothers and daughters threw their aprons over their heads and rocked as they wailed, and small children screamed half comprehendingly.

Finally, however, one of the older women recovered enough to answer questions. Yes, they had all felt great concern for her father-in-law when he had failed to come home two nights previously. The children had been sent to the store, and had reported that the *pulpería* was shut and shuttered. When the woman's husband and her brother-in-law had returned from their fishing they had gone to check, but there had been no response when they had hammered at the door. There was no spare key, and it was impossible, of course, to break in. They had tried again the next day, but with equal lack of result.

Realizing that the grandfather had been lying there dead all the time, she collapsed again—though not so completely that she didn't find the breath to ask Dr. Ducatel if he would be kind enough to attend to her youngest son, obviously calculating that he wouldn't be callous enough to ask for payment from a household that was so recently bereaved. The son, who looked about ten years old, was indeed in a bad way, having broken his leg two weeks before. Judging by the smell in the small, close room where he tossed in delirium, it would not be long at all before he joined Captain Hallett in the graveyard.

So the clerk had been telling the truth when he mentioned the family illness, Wiki meditated. However, as he quickly learned from the other women while Ducatel was passing on advice to the sick boy's mother, Gomes had lied when he claimed to be away from the store. They all insisted that he had gone to work for Adams as usual. They had not actually seen him behind the counter during that time, but he had left for the store at the usual hour, and returned at the usual hour, too.

When Wiki stepped back into the street, it was to find that Stackpole and Hale were standing in a patch of sun and turning themselves from side to side, to finish off drying their trousers, which were still damp from the river crossing. He conveyed what he had learned, and the whaling master asked, "So what are you going to do?"

Wiki turned and surveyed the palisade curving up to the fort, which bulked on the cliff far above his head, and was invisible from this perspective. He felt no desire whatsoever to go up there and report to Ringgold, as the captain would merely repeat his order to forget about the murder. The discovery of a second body would make no difference, as the clerk had not even been English. Captain Wilkes, on the other hand, might be sufficiently scandalized by the piracy of an American-owned schooner to send the *Swallow* out in search.

He said, "I think we should report to Captain Wilkes, and ask him to start up a hunt for the *Grim Reaper*."

"Now you're talking!" exclaimed Stackpole.

They were interrupted as Dr. Ducatel joined them, rubbing his hands together as if to get rid of the last traces of his examination of the sick boy. The physician said briskly, "We must hurry to the fort. They'll be waiting."

"Nope," said Stackpole at once. "We don't have time for that."

Wiki nodded emphatically. "It's more important to get out to the *Vincennes*."

Ducatel flushed, and protested, "But the governor sent me with a pressing invitation—for you and Mr. Hale to join his party for a banquet this evening. That's why I was waiting on the path—and he'll be most offended if you don't come."

So Ducatel survived in this place by kowtowing to the governor, Wiki mused. Undoubtedly His Excellency would be angry with Ducatel, his messenger boy, for having failed in his mission. "Mr. Hale will be glad to attend," he callously said. "Just convey apologies from Captain Stackpole and myself."

"But you should report the murder!"

"As the man who discovered the corpse, Mr. Hale's best qualified for that."

"Me?" Horatio Hale exclaimed. His face was a picture of horror.

"You," confirmed Wiki. "And you're the best man to inform Captain Ringgold what has happened, too. Tell him I'm heading for the estuary to report to Captain Wilkes."

And with that, he briskly turned on his heel, before Hale and Ducatel could start arguing again.

Two hours later they had almost reached the boat-landing place on the estuary, when Stackpole looked over his shoulder, and said, "What's happening back there?"

Wiki reined in, and looked around, too. Sounds of fast galloping echoed from behind them. In a crescendo of hoofbeats, Bernantio and his gauchos arrived pell-mell from around a bend, hollering happily as they sighted Wiki. Horatio Hale was with them, looking flushed but gamely keeping up. Wiki gave him an ironic salute as he hurtled by.

Then, after the philologist had managed to rein in and come back, Wiki queried with his brows arched, "Aren't you supposed to be at the governor's feast?"

Mr. Hale shook his head. When he'd regained his breath, he said, "Captain Ringgold sent me with an urgent message."

Wiki said warily, "For me?"

"Yes. He wanted me to pass on his most strict instructions that you are *not* to take this investigation any further. He said it is none of your business, and that you are *not* to bother Captain Wilkes with it."

"You did tell him about discovering the clerk's body?"

"Of course. He vowed it did not make a shred of difference—that it is still a matter for the local authorities."

Wiki made no comment, though he was privately determined to go on board the *Vincennes* and make a full report. After all, Captain Wilkes, not Ringgold, was the commodore of the expedition. "Well," he said, "I'm sorry it cost you a fine meal. Why are the gauchos with you?"

"Captain Ringgold decided I needed an escort, since the governor's people informed him that the mood of the province is still one of high excitement. By great good luck Señor Bernantio and his friends arrived at that very moment, as Captain Ringgold wanted to retain Dr. Ducatel as a guide for his own party."

"Where are they going?"

"Nowhere—not tonight, anyway. Captain Ringgold, Mr. Waldron, and Lieutenant Perry will all attend the banquet, and then stop the night at the fort before returning in the morning. Which leads me to my second message," Hale added.

"Another message? For me?"

"No, not for you, but for Mr. Peale, Dr. Fox, and Dr. Holmes, informing them that we are all to be on the riverbank landing at nine in the morning, ready to go off to the *Sea Gull*."

"Why, where are they?" asked Wiki, feeling puzzled, because when he had left that morning, Titian Peale and the two surgeon-scientists had been on board the *Sea Gull*, and he'd had the impression they would have a boat at their disposal for the day, so that they could explore the estuary at leisure.

At that moment Titian Peale himself appeared from the seaward end of the path, trailed by Doctors Fox and Holmes. All three were on foot. They looked hot, dusty, disheveled, and extremely aggrieved, and Mr. Hale's message didn't improve their tempers in the slightest.

"So we'll have to spend the night at the pilothouse," griped Dr. Fox.

"And it's nothing better than a filthy *hovel*," Dr. Holmes declared.

"There's only one word for it," Titian Peale decided. "We've been *marooned*. And not only is it inconvenient, but it's *humiliating*."

Then the trio competed to grumble loudly to Mr. Hale about the horrible day they'd passed. After Ringgold's party had ridden off that morning, the boat had collected them from the *Sea Gull*, and dropped them on shore. The three scientists had explored the terrain contentedly for a while, collecting samples of shells, grass, thorny bushes, and aromatic plants, and shooting a number of birds. However, when they had returned to the riverbank, and made signs requesting to be taken off, they had been completely disregarded. Finally, in belated response to their shouted pleas, one of the surveying boats had deigned to approach the bank—but only to convey the message that Captain Ringgold had left orders that no boat was to be sent for the scientifics until it was time for the *Sea Gull* to leave the river.

"And since then they've ignored us *completely*," exclaimed Dr. Holmes. "The boats have all steered in other directions, and anyone who has emerged onto deck has *very carefully* looked the other way."

Wiki looked at the *Sea Gull*, which was bobbing quietly at her anchors. There was no activity whatsoever on her deck, and there were no boats to be seen. They were off surveying, he supposed.

"As I've told you time and time again throughout our voyage on the *Peacock*, the attitude of the officers to the scientifics has been unacceptable," Mr. Peale said to Mr. Hale.

Dr. Holmes (who also lived on the *Peacock*) nodded emphatically. "But this is utterly beyond words!" he expostulated.

"I'm going to post a strong complaint with Captain Wilkes when I get back to the fleet," decided Mr. Peale. "If ever I do," he added broodingly.

Then Manuel Bernantio interrupted this to-and-fro grumble by riding up to Wiki and jerking his head downstream. When Wiki looked in that direction he saw a great cloud of gulls dipping and diving about an unseen spot on the bank of the river, and could hear their strident screeching.

"Something is dead," the gaucho remarked.

With an abrupt chill, Wiki was reminded of the vultures. When he kept silent Titian Peale answered. Evidently he understood some Spanish, though he used English when he explained, "That's what's left of my specimens."

Wiki said, "What specimens?"

"Birds, mostly. I got an excellent bag."

"Mr. Peale is a very fine shot," Mr. Hale proudly elaborated. "I've personally seen him kill two turkeys simultaneously with one bullet, and I am told that he has been known to dispatch two deer with one shot, too."

"The bag today did include a fine buck," Mr. Peale admitted, not at all embarrassed by this callow display of hero worship. "Dr. Fox and I carried the carcass for several miles in the heat, thinking it would make a fine present for the officers' supper, but after one hour and a half of waiting *in vain* for them to notice us from the ship, we dumped it."

"You let it go to *waste*?" Wiki exclaimed.

"It was exactly what their uncivil behavior deserved," said Dr. Fox.

"Just to make a *point*?" Wiki was shocked, because he had learned thrift from a very early age. Though his father had taken him away from his *iwi* in the Bay of Islands at the age of twelve, he vividly remembered the long, damp winters when the village *pataka*—the long, low, elaborately carved storehouse that was on stilts to guard the precious contents from rats and thieves—had been their bulwark against starvation. Throughout the summers and autumns the young bloods carried in great nets of birds they had snared, which were cooked and then preserved in gourds in their own fat, and the older men contributed great loads of fish and eels, which were hung to dry on racks. All this, stored in the *pataka,* ensured the survival of the tribe over the dark months when food was scarce.

"They can watch it rot, and good luck to them," Mr. Peale sniffed.

When Wiki conveyed this to Manuel Bernantio, the *rastreador* agreed that it was quite incomprehensible. The other gauchos clustered around to offer their own opinions, and then became very animated at the prospect of game. "Where did you find this buck?" Mr. Peale was asked, through Wiki, and when he waved an arm toward the headland at the top of the cliff, Bernantio cried, *"¡Vamos!"*

"¡Vámonos!" the rest yelled, and spurred their steeds up the sliding gravel.

When Wiki arrived at the top himself, it was to find that the gauchos were rapidly vanishing into the dusty distance, looking oddly like small craft disappearing over the horizon at sea, their horses fading first, then their bodies, and lastly their heads. He didn't try to pursue them, as he was more interested in riding to the flagstaff and hoisting a signal. Obviously, he couldn't rely on a boat coming from the *Sea Gull,* and so his best hope was that someone on the *Swallow* was keeping a watch, and would send a boat to fetch him.

When he arrived there, it was to find that the scene from the headland was quite a contrast to the day before. The sun sparkled bravely on the dipping waves. All the expedition ships, save the schooner *Sea Gull,* were anchored well beyond the surf with their boats down. Wiki could plainly see the *Osprey* tacking slowly back and forth on smoother water a mile farther out to sea, and again he wondered what his father was doing here. Just to seaward of the bar the shoals were dotted with surveying boats, presumably including those that belonged to the *Sea Gull.* Closer still, the sky over the river was full of gulls drawn by the carcasses Mr. Peale had dumped, and their screeching seemed to ring as high as the scudding clouds.

Then Wiki abruptly became aware not only that Stackpole had joined him at the foot of the flagpost but that the whaleman was in a state of high excitement. "Look!" he shouted, and pointed. "See that! I do reckon she's the *Trojan*—and trying out blubber, by heaven! Tell me, boy—do you think she's the *Trojan*?"

Squinting in the same direction, Wiki saw a puff of black smoke issuing from a ship that was gradually plowing toward the fleet—a nasty puff of smoke with hellish tints of red and orange on its bottom edges. He did not have a notion whether she was the *Trojan* or not, but certainly agreed that the foul, black cloud was a sign of a whaleship boiling whale blubber into oil. He knew that because it was something he had experienced firsthand—often, much more often than he liked.

However, he didn't answer, instead watching Stackpole with hidden amusement. Ever since he had first shipped on a whaler at the age of just seventeen, when Captain Coffin's wife had rid herself of his embarrassing presence by signing him onto her brother's elderly Nantucket whaleship *Paths of Duty*, it had amazed him how revitalizing the taking of a whale could be for a career whaleman. Wiki had seen gray-bearded captains who were depressed to the point of suicide prance about like young colts when whales were raised, and even the most ill-paid seamen dance for joy as blubber was hoisted on board. Now Stackpole, who a moment before had looked depressed, defeated, and exhausted, had dropped at least ten years from his age.

"Get a signal up that spar, young man," he ordered, as if Wiki were one of his hands. "I need to be on board my ship—signal for a boat, for God's sake! She has to be the *Trojan*! Oh, my Lord, I'd trade my mother-in-law for a spyglass! My mother-in-law? By God, I'd give away my wife!"

However, when Wiki looked around, the usual box of signals wasn't there at the foot of the pole. Evidently, they were stored back in the pilothouse. "The crew wouldn't notice a flag, anyway," he commented. "You know what it's like when they're trying out—they'll be far too busy to pay attention."

"Trying out—yes, trying out!" Stackpole repeated in an ecstasy of delight.

Wiki's attention was distracted by faint shouts and the sounds of galloping that echoed from the distance, gradually drawing closer. Then he glimpsed busy clouds of dust. With shrill cries the gauchos loomed from several points of the compass, their whirled ponchos and long hair appearing first, floating out with the wind of their progress, and then their lean, taut frames. When they thundered into sight, gradually converging, Wiki saw that they were driving a panicked buck before them.

Nearer they came, nearer. Wiki became aware that Stackpole had hastily dismounted and was dragging his horse out of the way, but he remained steadfast, bolt upright in his saddle, eyes narrowed as he watched the oncoming rush, calculating that the deer would burst past twenty feet to his right. As if of its own volition, his hand sought out the thin plait of the lariat that was coiled at the side of his saddle. He shook it out, adjusting the iron ring at the end to make a noose before taking the loose loops in his left hand, watching the oncoming buck with slitted eyes, gauging pace and distance. It was a whole year since he had last cast the *lazo*, but the thrill of the hunt was pulsing through his veins.

His wrist pivoted, and the noose curved out, smoothly gleaming as it caught the sun. His throw looked perfect—and then it all went cataclysmically wrong. The lariat tapped the ground, bounced, writhed like a snake, and flickered back to curl viciously about his horse's legs.

She lurched, stumbled, and crashed to the ground. If Wiki had the European habit of keeping his feet home in the stirrups, he would have gone with her, to meet a quick, brutal end beneath her threshing weight. Instead, he jumped free, arms whirling as he spun through the air. His ears were full of the mare's scream of surprise and rage, the thunder as the chase pounded past, and the shouting of the scientifics, who had arrived to witness the drama.

Wiki hit the ground running, miraculously keeping his feet. The thump as his soles struck the dirt jolted the breath out of his chest. However, not only had he kept his balance but he was safe yards from the kicking horse. He kept his wits, too, spinning at once to jump on the end of the trailing rein as the mare struggled unhurt to her feet, bringing her up short before she even thought of bolting away.

Grasping the bridle in his hand, he approached her warily, because she had her back arched and her tail bunched up like a cat in a fight. As he shortened his grip she stretched out her neck and did her damnedest to bite him, and when he dodged clear she reared, trying to rip the rein out of his fist. This gave him the chance he needed—Wiki took a running jump as she dropped from the plunge, and launched himself into the saddle with the touch of a toe on her knee.

No sooner had he landed than she whirled round and round. The plain revolved dizzily around him, while the gauchos thundered past again, still in hot pursuit of the deer, which was now running in the opposite direction. The beast's end was near, though. When at last Wiki had the mare under control, it was to find that the buck was roped, and Manuel Bernantio had dismounted, drawing his facón. At a word, the gaucho's horse set its feet, and leaned powerfully back. The buck crashed to the ground, and the *rastreador* cut its extended throat.

After cleaning the blade by wiping it on the animal's hide, Bernantio stalked over in a clattering of iron spurs. He looked Wiki up and down, and then said sternly, "Why did you do that?"

"I wanted to be the man who brought down the buck," Wiki confessed. His voice came out more of an abashed mutter than he had intended, and he couldn't quite meet Bernantio's disapproving stare. He felt a complete fool.

There was a long silence, and then the gaucho's severe expression relaxed. Perhaps, thought Wiki, Bernantio remembered that he had helped him save face after losing the tracks at the salt dunes, because he said, "My brother must have taught you that it is not only necessary for a gaucho to ride well, but that he must fall well, too. I will congratulate him, when I see him."

"I thank you," said Wiki humbly.

"But was he really the one who taught you the art of the *lazo*? That, I cannot believe, though it is truly said that only he who is born to the lariat can use it well."

Wiki said nothing, feeling more sheepish than ever. Bernantio contemplated this philosophical tidbit for a meditative moment, and then went back to his horse. To Wiki's surprise, he came back with a bolas in his hands, and handed it up to him. "For you, *las boleadoras* is much easier to learn," he said. "Keep this one. A man never knows when again he will meet up with a buck."

Wiki smiled in appreciation of his dry humor, but received the gift with due reverence. Unique to the south of South America, the three balls of stone had felled thousands of horses, and killed hundreds of the men who rode them. Every Indian warrior had carried several sets, as did the gauchos later. Manuel was right—using the bolas was much easier to learn than working the lasso, but the creation of a set wasn't quick and easy.

Each of the three stones—two as big as a half-grown child's fist, and the third the size and shape of an egg—had to be hammered into shape, wrapped in hide that was shrunk, then fastened to a three-foot length of thin, tough, greasy rawhide cord. Then, with the lashing of the free ends of the three cords together, the bolas was complete. A year ago, on the grassy pampas, Wiki and George had practiced for hours with bolas like these, under the close eye of Juán Bernantio, Manuel's brother, gripping the egg-shaped hand ball tight as they whirled *las boleadoras* around their heads. Then with a jerk, it was released. If the strings hit the legs of the target, entangling was instant. Accuracy was the tricky part.

Back on the pampas, Wiki thought he'd done quite well. Now, he was keen to see if his eye and hand had retained any skill, but he didn't dare try them out in front of Manuel Bernantio's critical eye. Instead, he inspected the weapon, making admiring comments about the fine workmanship and the evenly weighted balls.

"But you must take immense care not to ensnare the legs of your mount," Manuel advised at the end of this polite recital.

"I shall," Wiki most sincerely assured him.

The four scientifics had taken the pilothouse over, the pilots not having returned, presumably still being in prison. As Wiki dismounted outside the cabin, he could hear their low, angry voices as they went over and over this business of being *marooned* by Captain Ringgold's highhanded actions.

He was still keen to hoist a rendezvous flag, but didn't go into the cabin to find one for a while. Instead, feeling guilty that he had misused the mare so, he picketed her where she could get at the best of the scant herbage, and then devoted twenty minutes to watering and grooming her. She didn't seem particularly grateful, instead stretching her neck and baring her huge yellow teeth in another try at a bite. Wiki backed off in a hurry, gave up trying to be kind, and walked into the cabin.

The scientifics were so preoccupied with their grumbling that they didn't notice his arrival. Mr. Hale and Doctors Fox and Holmes were crowded along one side of the table, watching Mr. Peale sketch while they talked. Wiki eased over behind the surgeons to have a look, and was instantly fascinated. Titian Peale was very talented indeed. The scene, executed in rapid black scribbles, was the lassoing of the buck, and the drawing leaped from the paper so vividly that Wiki could almost hear the last struggles of the deer.

What he did hear was the scientifics gossiping about Captain Wilkes. "Mind you," Dr. Holmes was saying, "he *had* been overdoing it with those pendulum observations in Rio."

"That's very true," said Dr. Fox. "And taking a warm bath, followed by the exertion of dressing, triggered a natural syncopy. He fell into his servant's arms in a dead faint—not that I witnessed it myself, as by the time Gilchrist and I arrived he was conscious again."

"Dr. Gilchrist told me that Wilkes was incapable of speech when he regained his senses," confided Mr. Hale.

"Gilchrist told a *lot* of people that," Dr. Fox answered tartly. "But his prognostication of a mental and nervous breakdown is quite unjustified. He even talked of sending Captain Wilkes back home, and replacing him with another commander! I simply recommended rest, and Captain Wilkes took my advice. After a good night's sleep he was as energetic and eloquent as ever."

"Then it's little wonder he now considers *you* his personal surgeon, and spurns poor Gilchrist," said Dr. Holmes, with some malice in his tone.

"Captain Wilkes is getting the best of medical care from me, I assure you," Dr. Fox countered at once, adding defensively, "And no one likes Gilchrist, anyway."

At the back of the group, Wiki lifted his brows, as this was news to him. Up until this moment he had been under the impression that Dr. Gilchrist, a portly, dignified man who was the chief surgeon of the expedition (though now, apparently, the ex-chief surgeon), had been respected by all. He was also feeling very troubled. As captain's clerk and translator, he had worked with Captain Wilkes for hours on end while the fleet was in Rio, and knew better than most what stresses afflicted the commander of the expedition. Not only was Wilkes faced with a constant struggle to satisfy the demands of a scientific corps, most of whom had no idea what the job of a shipmaster involved, but because of that strangely savage Navy Department decision not to give him the rank of captain to match that job, his temper was quick and uncertain. While it was becoming more and more apparent that the scientifics resented Captain Wilkes's manner, which they considered capricious and overbearing, and many expedition officers were expressing dismay at his increasing attacks of hysteria, Wiki understood the reason for the nervous outbreaks, and still held great respect for the man.

Wiki also thought that this was getting embarrassing, and it was high time he made his presence known. However, Dr. Holmes was saying insinuatingly to Fox, "I know a number of officers who are very unhappy that you scotched the idea of sending Captain Wilkes back to the States and replacing him with someone much less committed to the scientific aims of the expedition."

"How could *anyone* be less committed to the scientific aims of the expedition?" Mr. Peale demanded in sarcastic tones. "Before we sailed Wilkes promised me most faithfully I would find the sailors ready and willing to do anything I asked, but instead I have to do everything myself—dissect, preserve, draw, write, and explain to the uninitiated! *All* the sailors are required for ship duties, and they're not willing to do anything extra to help. I boarded the *Peacock* with high expectations, only to find it is nothing but humbug! *I* can't think of anyone who could be less responsive to the ambitions of the scientific corps than Captain Wilkes!"

Then Wiki was distracted. Quite involuntarily, he leaned forward and pointed at two horsemen right at the back of the gaucho band, who were taking shadowy shape under Mr. Peale's pencil.

He said, "They shouldn't be carrying rifles—gauchos never carry guns."

All four heads turned; all four men stared. Their expressions shifted from startled realization that they had been overheard to icy outrage at his temerity.

Titian Peale said frigidly, "I beg your pardon?"

"You told me you're not an artist," Wiki said, his own tone slightly reproving.

There was a short pause. Then, with the same faint smile Wiki had seen before, Peale said, "I have a brother named Rembrandt and another named Rubens."

And parents with eccentric tastes in naming their offspring, Wiki deduced. The other scientifics were still staring at him with cold disapproval, but he didn't bother to excuse himself, because he thought he had just as much right to be in the pilots' cabin as they did. Instead, he nodded, and turned to locate the box of signals. Taking his time, he sorted out the flag he wanted, acutely aware of them all watching and waiting for him to go. He was barely out the door when the rush of muttered comments began.

Outside, the atmosphere was a lot more convivial. The buck was roasting over a fire, and a gourd of freshly brewed maté was being passed around. The horses, crammed in a row along the hitching post, stamped and flicked their long tails at flies, and snorted as they cropped. One of the gauchos called out an invitation to join them, but Wiki merely waved and headed up the path to the headland.

Captain Stackpole was still on watch at the foot of the flagpole, squinting alertly out to sea. Wiki noticed that the whaleship, still spouting a cloud of red-tinged smoke, was perceptibly closer. She was definitely sailing this way, he saw. Then his quick eyes glimpsed the tiny triangle of the sail of a whaleboat heading toward the shore.

Wondering if Captain Stackpole had seen it, too, he threaded the blue and white checkered rendezvous flag onto the signal lanyard, and hauled it up. Standing back, he surveyed it with satisfaction as it stood out boldly from the flagstaff, then looked at the sea again, and said, "That's a big whale they're trying out."

"Sixty barrels at least," Stackpole agreed. He was now so disgracefully stubbled that it was hard to tell where the fringes of his beard stopped and began. His weathered face had gone round in shape with his delirious grin.

"The mate is keen to have you back on board," Wiki observed.

"What?"

"He's sent a boat, which should be at the beach within the hour."

"You say so? My God, boy!" Captain Stackpole peered at the scene with his hand held alongside his cheek to shade the setting sun, which streamed over his shoulder, and then let out an oath, and cried, "You're right!"

Without hesitation, he abandoned his horse, which cropped at the sparse grass at the foot of the flagpole where it was tethered, strode to the top of the path which led down the precipice, and headed down the narrow terraced track. As he bobbed downward, he called over his shoulder to Wiki, "My God, boy, I surely could use a man with sight like yours in the t'gallant crosstrees when we're on whaling ground!"

Then he was gone. The whaleboat was perceptibly closer, the onshore wind and the running tide helping its headlong progress. On impulse, Wiki followed, jumping onto the path and then running to keep his balance, one hand held out to push against the cliff face. It was exhilarating to leap from one terrace to another with the steady salt-laden wind in his face.

Considering what an unrelenting job it had been to climb the path, the descent seemed amazingly fast. Within ten minutes they were both standing on the gritty gray sand with surf foaming toward their feet, staring past the rolling breakers. At sea level the whaleboat seemed much farther off, the hull disappearing in the troughs of the waves, and only the top of the mast and a triangle of canvas showing up against the paling sky and the first dim stars.

She was going to be a little while yet. Stackpole visibly relaxed. He looked around, spied a big rock, used it as a seat, and hauled out his pipe. When he finally had it lit, he shook out the match, and puffed contentedly. Then Wiki, who was standing nearby with his feet braced and his thumbs hooked into his belt, found himself the subject of a very shrewd look.

Stackpole said, "You know something about whaling, young man."

Wiki grinned, realizing that he had given himself away with that observation about the size of the whale. He walked over to the rock where he had perched while putting on his boots earlier, and sat down. He could feel the residue of the day's warmth through the seat of his pants, but knew it would soon be cold.

He said, "Shipped first on the Nantucketer *Paths of Duty*, seven years ago."

"That old box?" Stackpole snorted. "You must've been a green boy."

"Just passed my seventeenth birthday," said Wiki, and they settled down to a cozy exchange of ships and captains and voyages. Their paths had never crossed, as Wiki had sailed the Pacific, and Stackpole the Atlantic, but they knew a surprising number of men in common. Even more oddly, after a while Wiki realized he was enjoying trading yarns with Stackpole. Not only was it like being back on home territory but it was a refreshing change from the scientifics.

"What was your last berth?" the whaling master finally asked.

"*Mandarin*, second mate," Wiki answered, without mentioning that the *Mandarin* was the ship he had jumped from in Callao, a couple of months before he had met up with George Rochester in Montevideo and they had embarked on the pampas adventure. When he'd got back to Boston, as the mate of a coffee-laden trader, George had been waiting for him with the offer of a post with the exploring expedition, and so he'd not been a-whaling since.

"*Mandarin?* That old devil Israel Starbuck was in command?"

Wiki laughed, and said, "Aye."

"You got along with him?"

"First-rate, as it happens." Starbuck was a farthest limit skipper with strong ideas of discipline and order, but he also had a good sense of humor.

Stackpole looked very thoughtful, and then said, "I could offer you the same berth on the *Trojan*."

Wiki smiled and shook his head, a decision that came easily because he disliked whaling so much. Judging it was a good time to change the subject, he said, "When the gauchos arrived in hot pursuit of that deer, did you see any of them carrying rifles?"

"Not that I remember. Why?"

"That naturalist—Titian Peale—was drawing a picture of the gauchos when I called into the pilothouse for a flag, and in his sketch two of them had guns."

"Artistic license," the whaling master said wisely. "He sketches?"

"Very well indeed. To tell the truth, I mistook him for an artist at first—because of his name, though he's certainly talented enough to be one. Then he informed me he has brothers named Rubens and Rembrandt."

Stackpole's eyebrows were as high as his hat. He was silent a moment, staring far out to sea, where the evening mists gathered. A cloud above the *Trojan* reflected the orange-red of the tryworks.

Then he said meditatively, "I once shipped a hand by the name of Peale—Linnaeus Peale, another odd name. He used to sketch a bit, too. Shiftless lad, about as much use about decks as a bishop in a whorehouse. When he jumped ship in Brazil, I didn't bother to go looking for him."

"Long ago?"

"About the time of the war for free trade and sailors' rights, so aye, it was quite a tidy time ago. His father ran a museum, he said—in Philadelphia."

"Museum?" said Wiki. "How odd! But it does sound like the same family."

"You should ask that naturalist about it."

"I don't think so." Wiki shook his head, certain that any such familiarity would meet with a very cold reception.

"Well, it's up to you—but aren't you supposed to be a detective of some sort?"

Wiki laughed instead of answering this, and then jumped up on top of his rock as he glimpsed movement on the far side of the surf. He was just in time to see the boat's crew take in the sail and unstep the mast. A heave on the heavy oars, and the boat took on even more momentum, riding the crest of a billow with foam boiling at her bow.

For a breath-held moment it seemed as if she would charge the strand full speed and arrive with a crash, but at the very last moment the mate at the steering oar hollered, "Stern all!" As one, the men pulled in reverse, so powerfully that their oars visibly bent with the tremendous pressure. The boat stopped dead, and Wiki and Stackpole hopped out of the way of the wash that boiled up the sand. Another few seconds, and the *Trojan* boat had been steadied by four muscular whalers who had jumped out into the shallows.

Wiki was grinning broadly, dramatically reminded of the well-known fact that American whalemen were the best in the world in small boats. Captain Stackpole waded into the surf, and set to firing questions at his men, the answers to which sent him into a state of high excitement. Wiki heard him shouting at the top of his considerable lungs, "*Ninety* barrels? *Ninety?*"

Then he came plunging back, shouting at Wiki, "They took a buster whale! *A ninety-barrel spermaceti!*"

Wiki was suitably amazed. A whale that yielded that much oil was a record buster indeed, being nearly a hundred feet long, as long as the ship. It was a great rarity, something for everyone on the *Trojan* to brag about for the rest of their lives.

He asked, "What does sperm oil fetch on the market these days?"

Stackpole's exultant grin stretched his face sideways to an incredible extent. "The last I heard, over a dollar a gallon. Ninety barrels will fetch three thousand dollars—*three thousand dollars at a minimum*!"

Wiki whistled, thinking that it almost made up for the loss of the thousand-dollar bond.

"Ship with us," Stackpole urged. "You won't regret it, not now our luck has changed. And I could sure use a sharp-eyed second mate. The one I've got is as blind as a bat."

Again, Wiki shook his head without hesitation. While the prospect of spending the night in the company of the four scientifics was unattractive, the thought of working on the oil-soaked, blood-stained, stinking decks of a whaleship in the throes of trying out was vastly worse. "I've signed a contract," he said, but then added, "You'll report to Captain Wilkes?"

To his surprise, Stackpole's face closed up, abruptly becoming expressionless. When he didn't answer, Wiki urged, "You're the one who should ask him to stage a search for the *Grim Reaper*. I'll talk to him as soon as possible after the *Sea Gull* rejoins the fleet in the morning, of course, but he'll take a lot more notice of you than he will of me."

"We'll be a mite too busy for quite a while," the whaling master objected. "It's likely you'll get on board the *Vincennes* before me."

Wiki frowned at the evasiveness in his tone. When they had left El Carmen that afternoon Stackpole had been on fire to report to Wilkes and get a search under way, he remembered, and he wondered why he had changed his mind in the meantime. Thinking back, Wiki realized that the whaleman had been unusually silent on the ride to the estuary. At the time he had thought he was simply brooding, but now he wondered if he had been turning something over in his mind.

Instead of explaining, Stackpole said, "The horses? You'll return them?"

"Aye," said Wiki wryly, for this was going to cost him money.

"Well, then," said Stackpole. He cleared his throat, and waded back into the surf. Just as he was about to clamber into the *Trojan*'s boat, however, he hesitated, turned around, and splashed back to the beach, hauling his poncho over his head as he came.

When he arrived he handed it to Wiki, saying rather awkwardly, "I don't need this anymore, I reckon—so you might as well have it. You've been a good lad, withal, even though you ain't got my money back, nor my schooner, and don't you forget that offer. If you change your mind, you're welcome to ship on the old *Trojan*."

"Well," said Wiki, trying not to laugh, "I thank you."

"Think nothing of it." And, with that, and a brisk nod, Captain Stackpole plunged back to his boat. Seizing the steering oar, he barked commands, the boat was turned around, the oarsmen jumped in, and off she went. Birds called, and the breakers swished, but the world seemed quiet after they had gone.

The sun set as Wiki arrived back at the top of the cliff, leaving a broad red band on the horizon where the dark plain met the black sky.

Stackpole's pinto was still nibbling at the short, unappetizing tussock, and for some moments Wiki stood rubbing the horse's warm, bristly neck and watching the familiar southern constellations appear, reluctant to go back to the pilothouse where the hostile scientifics awaited. Then he heard one of the gauchos lift his voice in a song, a plaintive air that sounded thin and unearthly in the night, and roused himself to unhitch the bridle. When he led the horse down the path the aroma of roasting meat rose to meet him, along with shouts from the gauchos. He was only just in time, they informed him as he arrived.

Wiki tethered the pinto next to the gray mare, who appeared a lot more pleased to see her stablemate than she was to see Wiki. After filling a bowl of water for them both, he joined the gauchos at the fire, trailed by the four scientifics, who seemed rather overawed by the exotic company. Joints were being torn apart and handed around, while one of the gauchos turned out some large loaves of coarse bread, and another brewed more maté.

Within thirty minutes the last bones were smoking in the flames. The scientifics retired to the cabin with an air of relief, lighting their pipes as they went, but Wiki stopped by the fire. As the stars dragged across the sky a tin mug of rough red wine was passed around. The gaucho who sang broke into melody again, Wiki sipped maté through a grass-stem straw, and four of the *rastreadores* argued about politics and revolution.

The name of the tyrant of the Río de la Plata featured prominently in the discussion, Wiki noticed. He thought it was understandable. The gauchos had fathers and uncles who had helped de Rosas conquer the Indians, but since then the tyrant had kept up an iron rule by the time-honored method of imprisoning and murdering any man who stood against him, not sparing those who had fought on his side in the past. Like all dictators, his time would come, they said; revolution was as inevitable as the turning of the seasons.

Wiki sought out Bernantio, who was smoking meditatively. He sat on the grass beside him, and asked, "Do you know of the clerk whose name was Gomes?"

"The clerk of Señor Adams's store?"

Wiki nodded. "He has two sons."

"I believe they fish," said the *rastreador,* confirming what Ducatel had said. "Though that is not a living. Too, they steal horses, and sell them to men who will pay. Just some days ago, we saw them taking a *tropilla* to the caves where the rebels live. There, the money would be good."

A *tropilla* was a small herd of horses. Wiki remembered the dark mouths of caves he had glimpsed from the bluff on the other side of the river, and realized that these were the hideouts Bernantio had indicated on the ride to the dunes.

He said, "Perhaps the Gomes brothers did not ask for money—perhaps they sympathize with the rebel cause."

"That would not be unusual," Manuel admitted.

"Is there a chance that the clerk was killed because of their politics?"

The *rastreador* let out a sound of utter contempt. "His sons might wear the *chiripá* and the poncho, but they are rough Portuguese fishermen. Such men would never fight for Argentina."

Wiki lifted his brows, thinking that the tribes of South America were as apt to be disdainful of each other as the tribes of the South Pacific. He said, "Do you believe the rebels of the caves of the Río Negro will ever fight for Argentina?"

Bernantio spat to one side, and said, "Not until a leader presents himself who is better than the one they have now."

Wiki said, "You know this man?"

Bernantio shook his head, but then changed his mind and said mysteriously, "It is not good when outsiders intrude on local affairs."

Wiki paused, wondering what the *rastreador* was hinting at, and hazarded, "Some foreigner in this place has been trying to organize a revolution?"

"So runs the gossip. They say he has provided arms."

"But who would it be—and why would he do it?"

"I believe he is American."

Wiki said quickly, "Dr. Ducatel?"

Again, Bernantio grunted with derision. "The doctor who pretends to be a gaucho? Have you seen that one on a horse? No, this one was a seaman who joined the army of de Rosas during the war with Brazil, but soon rebelled, and incited a mutiny. He killed two men, so was condemned to death. Instead, however, he was flogged twelve hundred lashes over three different times. Now, he strives to overthrow his sworn enemy, General de Rosas, which is the reason he supports the rebels. Undoubtedly, he will end up on the gallows."

Wiki grimaced. Twelve hundred lashes was an extreme punishment, even when divided into three sessions. He felt skeptical that anyone would survive it.

"Perhaps he is dead already," he suggested.

Bernantio shook his head. "He works on the river as a pilot, and at other times he disappears, sometimes for months on end—or so they say."

Wiki said quickly, "A pilot? Do you know his name?"

"I believe I have heard it," Manuel allowed. He pursed his lips as he drew in smoke from his thin cigar, and then blew it out reflectively. "Could it be Harden?"

"It could indeed," said Wiki softly.

Eight

January 28, 1839

Wiki slept soundly, one more human spoke in the wheel of gauchos about the fire, wrapped in his poncho with his boots pointing to the heat, and woke feeling magnificent. As he washed away his travel stains in the river, *"E te hihi o te ra,"* he sang, to greet the first rays of the sun and celebrate the ancestors who had voyaged from the direction of the dawn:

E kokiri kei runga e
Tarahau, e, pikipiki ake ra, e
Nga moutere tahore tia mai te moana!
Kaore iara, pikipiki ao, pikipiki ao,
Ka puta iara kei tua e!
Sail out all over, O rays of the sun,
Sail over the islands, spread over the sea!
Spread your greatness all over, all over
Sail to the far side of the world!

When he arrived back at the fire, shaking the water out of his springing ringlets ready to bind the bandanna round them again, it was to find the gauchos saddling up their horses. Hale, Peale, and the two doctors were standing around, complaining about the uncomfortable night they had passed in the cabin. To Wiki's hidden amusement, they were also grouching about Horatio Hale's fleas, which apparently he had generously shared with them all. At the same time, they were watching intently as the gauchos carried out their morning routine. The scientists' expressions were distant and objective, yet oddly greedy, as if they were mentally noting the details of this exotic sight for future dissertations and lectures.

After taking this in, Wiki walked over to Mr. Peale. "Because of Bernantio and his gauchos, you ate well last night," he remarked.

The middle-aged naturalist frowned. "What do you mean?"

"You should recompense them in some way. Life is hard on the steppe, but they willingly shared all they had. Courtesy is important here; it can make all the difference between survival and death."

"But Captain Ringgold paid them well, I believe." Titian Peale looked at Horatio Hale, who emphatically nodded. The two doctors were listening; their faces had gone quite blank.

Wiki said obdurately, "Tobacco is a suitable gift."

Silence. For long seconds the four scientists didn't move. Then they glanced at each other before turning out their pockets. Bernantio, who had a very good idea of what had happened though he hadn't understood a word, gave Wiki a fond look before sharing the bounty with his *compadres*, taking punctilious care that no one had less than the rest.

Then he announced that it was time to go. Wiki, who had saddled both horses meantime, mounted the mare, took the pinto's bridle, and accompanied them as far as the headland, where the rendezvous flag still fluttered. The *Trojan* was now at anchor, Wiki noticed, and still smoking hellishly. She was a good two miles downwind from the *Vincennes*, which was well advised, considering how she was fouling the air, but he wondered if Stackpole had changed his mind, and hastened to contact Wilkes. Remembering the whaling master's evasive, sheepish expression, he somehow didn't think so, and felt puzzled again.

"I shall have much to relate to my brother," said Bernantio.

Wiki smiled. "Give him my best wishes for good health, and for that of his friends and family. Tell him I am working hard on growing my hair, and shall soon be the long-haired rascal he remembers."

The *rastreador*'s deeply tanned face creased up as he nodded, and passed on similar polite good wishes for George Rochester. "Perhaps we will meet again," he said, and touched his steed with one heel. With a loud yell and a whirling of ponchos, the gauchos spurred their mounts into a gallop, and then they were off.

Would he ever see them again? Wiki watched until the dust they kicked up had settled. It was not until after they were gone that he realized they had taken Mr. Hale's horse with them.

When he finally looked back at the river, the lack of activity was in distinct contrast to the energy of the gauchos' departure. The *Sea Gull* was still floating in the same place, making no discernible move toward raising the anchors. He looked at the sun, thinking that he would have to return the horses now if he was to make the nine o'clock rendezvous on the riverbank—but then, just as he was about to turn away, he saw the whaleboat that was heading briskly shoreward from the direction of the fleet.

Even though it was within a mile of the beach, Wiki was certain it had come from the *Swallow*. Looking up at the flapping rendezvous flag, he found it easy to make up his mind that the lookout on the brig had seen it, and George Rochester had sent the boat for him. Tethering the two horses to the post, he headed pell-mell down the cliff track again, landing on the beach with an athletic, exultant leap.

The boat was approaching the breakers already, and it was possible to see that there was a man wearing uniform in the stern sheets—an officer, because there was a glint of gold in the dark blue. George? And why the uniform? Did he plan to go to El Carmen?

With a swish and a grate of gravel, the boat came to a landing, and to his surprise Wiki realized that it wasn't a *Swallow* boat at all, but belonged to the *Osprey*, his father's brigantine. The six men of the boat's crew weren't even men—they were mere boys, his father's cadets! However, they looked competent enough, as rough and ready as the seamen back on the *Osprey* who were training them to be sailors. One, Wiki noticed, bore the signs of recent battle, and he assumed they had got into a ruckus, as proud, high-spirited, young sailors were often apt to do.

Then he forgot it, beaming delightedly at the uniformed officer, who was most certainly George. His old comrade sprang over the bulwarks with his shiny half-boots in his left hand, waded through the surf, and shook hands heartily with his right. "My God, old man, you're the complete gaucho," he said. "What the devil have you been up to? Have you met Mr. Seward?"

Mr. Seward was Captain Coffin's first mate, who had been working the steering oar. A lean, athletic-looking character, he walked the length of the boat, then took a leap from the bow that almost cleared the ebb of a wave. His handshake was firm and brief, his hand bony and strong, and he nodded curtly instead of speaking. Wiki had seen him in passing in Rio, and had got the impression of an energetic, impatient character, and Mr. Seward's busy expression and sharp pale green eyes confirmed it.

"When I heard that Mr. Seward was bringing the boys to the beach on a liberty jaunt, I asked the favor of a ride," George went on. "All our boats are surveying the shoals and tides, according to Wilkes's instructions, and so I had none of my own at my disposal." Then he added mysteriously, "I couldn't wait to see you."

Wiki waited, but instead of explaining George waited, too, his expression expectant. Even more perplexingly, Mr. Seward seemed amused at Wiki's open puzzlement. A knowing smile crossed his high-cheekboned, rather good-looking face, before he turned to organize his band of boys into hauling the boat well up the beach and getting out their fishing gear.

When Wiki returned his inquiring gaze to his friend, still no explanation was forthcoming. Instead, George sat down on a rock, brushed his feet and shins, and pulled on his boots. Losing patience, Wiki said, "I can't stay. I have to deliver two horses to a ranch and be down at the river landing by nine."

Rochester looked up. "Nine? Why so?"

Wiki told him about the *Sea Gull,* and Ringgold's instructions.

George said, "You can come back to the fleet with us, on the *Osprey* boat. Alf Seward and the boys will be here for a few hours yet."

Wiki was tempted. Surely Captain Stackpole had seen sense, and reported the piracy of the schooner, which meant there was no urgency about seeing Captain Wilkes. When George followed him up the cliff path, announcing that he would help deliver the horses, he made no objection, saying over his shoulder instead, "You've left Midshipman Keith in charge of the brig?"

"Nope." George sounded rather breathless. Being a captain who spent most of his time in the cabin and on the quarterdeck, and seldom aloft in the rigging, he was not as fit as Wiki.

He said, "We've had a few changes while you've been away."

"Changes?" Wiki was abruptly full of misgiving, because the word *change* was an ominous one in the expedition fleet, Captain Wilkes being prone to impulsive shiftings about of personnel.

"We have a new first officer," George said.

On the face of it, this was a very good move. Constant Keith had been a particularly weird choice for second-in-command of the *Swallow,* being a junior mid who'd not even sat his examinations yet, let alone passed them. Though a cheerful, obliging shipboard companion, he was in constant need of Wiki's discreet advice and supervision. It had turned out quite comfortably, as it happened, but was not the most desirable situation, because all hell would let loose if Captain Wilkes ever found out that it was really Wiki who did the mate's job. Accordingly, having a better qualified second-in-command promised to be a big improvement.

However, Wiki's tone was very cautious as he asked, "Who is it?"

"Forsythe."

Wiki stopped dead with one foot in the air, too shocked for speech. He had personally benefited from Lieutenant Forsythe's stalwart qualities—not only was he a remarkably good shot, but he was a magnificent mariner, too—but the burly, tough Virginian was notorious for his unpredictability, brutality, and foul tongue. During a disastrous couple of weeks, earlier in the voyage, he had replaced Rochester as captain of the *Swallow*, and while all the hands had admired his death-defying seamanship, he had been universally feared.

Wiki demanded, "How the devil did *that* happen?"

Rochester was holding on to a jutting rock for balance. He grinned wryly, and said, "It was one of our dear commodore's sudden decisions."

"I'd guessed that already—but what was his excuse for landing you with *Forsythe*, of all men?"

"After that American river pilot signed up with the fleet, Wilkes wanted to make use of his local knowledge, and so all the boats have been sent out surveying, with Harden in the role of general instructor. Young Keith was put in charge of one of them, and when I protested about not having a second-in-command on board Wilkes kindly sent Lieutenant Forsythe to take over the job."

"Harden's signed up with the fleet?" said Wiki in alarm. This was change with a vengeance. Everything that Manuel Bernantino had told him about the troublemaking Harden flooded into his mind.

"A boat from the *Porpoise* called on the *Sea Gull* to see if they needed assistance, and whoever talked to Harden was highly impressed by the way he'd navigated the *Sea Gull* out of the shoals. When they got back to the *Vin* and told Wilkes, Harden was summoned to the flagship for an interview. It's obvious to everyone else that the man's just a common adventurer, but Lieutenant Lawrence J. Smith, who was toadying around Wilkes as usual, talked him into signing him up."

Wiki thought, *He's more than a common adventurer—he's a deserter, an inciter of mutiny, and a killer, according to Río Negro gossip.* Shaking his head, he started climbing again, saying over his shoulder, "So Keith has been shifted back to the *Vin*?"

"Nope, he's still with us, but in the more suitable station of junior officer." Rochester paused as he negotiated a tricky hairpin turn in the track, and then said apologetically, "Which means that you're both shifted to the other stateroom, I'm afraid."

Wiki shrugged. "I expected no less." Over the past couple of months he had been sharing the first mate's stateroom with the young midshipman, to make it easier to pass on the benefit of his seafaring experience. Wiki had commandeered the top berth, and made himself very cozy with a bookshelf and a lamp, but it was only natural for Forsythe to demand the stateroom that was his by right.

He hauled himself over the top of the cliff, rose to his feet, and turned to look out over the sea. The bigger ships of the fleet lay quietly, surrounded by the busy small craft, though he noticed that the whaleship *Trojan* had raised anchor and was slowly heading seaward. The dirty smoke of her tryworks furnace rose in clouds about her white sails as they were set one by one, like wings. When he looked down at the river, the *Sea Gull* was still anchored in the same place, with no discernible movement on her decks.

He looked back at George, who had arrived on the headland, too, and was standing with his hands clasped behind his back in a typical pose, his flat bottom tucked in and his muscular calves pushing out the back of his white trousers. He was smiling placidly as he gazed about the scenery, his eyes creased up with the glare of the early sun.

Wiki said, "I'm amazed you're so serene."

"Because Forsythe is my first officer, now? But he's well fitted to the station—he's a strict disciplinarian, and an energetic man. And what's even more important in an officer, he speaks prompt, loud, and to the point."

"Prompt and loud to the point of mortal insult," agreed Wiki dryly. "But what about the problem of rank?" Though George Rochester had command of a ship, he was only a passed midshipman, which meant that Forsythe, being a lieutenant, was higher in the ranking order, and took precedence when Rochester was away from the *Swallow*.

"What problem?" inquired George. With fastidious gestures, he brushed down the sleeves of his uniform coat.

It was reminiscent of a cockerel preening itself. Wiki also noticed that his friend was wearing a complacent smirk.

He said flatly, "Tell me."

"What?"

"*E hoa*—my friend—you can't expect me to guess. I'm ignorant of the ways of the navy, remember."

"My left shoulder," said George pointedly, and jerked with his chin.

Wiki looked. The smartly squared left shoulder of Rochester's blue coat bore a gold epaulette that sparkled grandly in the sun, but for the life of him he couldn't remember whether it was a new addition or not. As far as he was concerned, it had always been there.

"And you call yourself a sleuth," George chided. "The swab was on the *right* shoulder before."

"And the fact that it is now on your left means something?"

"It does," said George complacently.

Light dawned. With a huge grin, Wiki exclaimed, "You've been promoted!"

"You behold *Lieutenant* George Rochester."

"My God! Turn around—let's look at you in all your glory, from back as well as front! When did you find out?"

"When your father raised the *Swallow* he lowered a boat, and arrived on board with newspapers he'd taken off an incoming Yankee as he was leaving Rio. The top paper was folded to the page with the navy promotions of October. The old devil said nothing, just smiled as he handed it over, and then watched me as I found *my own name* in the list!"

Wiki was silent, greatly marveling. As he knew very well indeed, George Rochester had worked out his seagoing apprenticeship as an officer in the U.S. Navy with grit, determination, and unflagging enthusiasm—all three years, ten months, fourteen days, and sixteen hours of it. Then he had reported to the Gosport Navy Yard for eight months of instruction in the technical and theoretical aspects of seafaring, before keeping an appointment in Baltimore for the grueling oral examination in front of a board of senior officers. He had come through the ordeal at the top of his class, which was the reason he'd been given the command of the *Swallow*—but this was the most remarkable achievement of all. He had been proclaimed a passed midshipman only twenty months earlier, and in times of peace, promotion from passed midshipman to lieutenant happened at a snail-like pace.

Rochester said happily, "I didn't look forward to being a lieutenant until I was a gray-haired chap past thirty—it seemed as distant as the Day of Judgment!"

"It's only what you deserve," Wiki said, though he privately thought it probably had a lot to do with George's grandfather, who had raised George after both parents had died. Both power and wealth had been necessary to get George a junior midshipman's commission in the first place, only the sons of lofty individuals like great navy captains, important merchants, and U.S. senators being eligible, but George's grandfather was both rich and influential.

Then a thought struck him, and he said, "Wilkes's name wasn't in the list? They haven't made him a proper captain, yet?"

George shook his head, and Wiki winced. He asked, "Does he know you've been promoted?"

"I haven't announced it—though you should have heard me exclaim for joy when I finally understood what I was reading, Wiki! But you know how scuttlebutt gets around the fleet, old chap."

There was going to be hell to pay, Wiki thought—Wilkes would be both jealous and vindictive. However, he wasn't going to spoil George's mood by pointing this out, so instead he said, "And you couldn't wait to come and show off your new glory to me—I'm flattered, George."

"I thank you," said George, very complacently indeed. "Mind you," he added, "I will have to change the swab around once we get back on board the dear *Swallow*."

"I beg your pardon?"

"Because I'm in *command*, you see."

"I don't understand."

"A man below the rank of captain who is a commanding officer wears one epaulette on the *right* shoulder."

Wiki blinked, and then said cautiously, "That's why you've been wearing that swab—as you call it—on your right shoulder all along?"

"Exactly."

"So, if you hadn't come on shore with a left-shoulder epaulette, I wouldn't have had a notion that anything had changed?"

"Exactly," said George.

"Good God," said Wiki, completely flummoxed. Then he said, "Why is my father sailing with the fleet?"

"Surely Ringgold told you, old chap? Carpenters, Wiki, carpenters! Your father demanded a gang after the *Vin* and then the *Peacock* run afoul of him on the way out of Rio and spoiled the looks of his pretty brigantine. Wilkes handed a couple over, it seemed, but with the stipulation that the *Osprey*, being perfectly seaworthy, if somewhat untidy, kept pace with the fleet while the repairs were carried out."

"And my father agreed to that? I can't believe he caved in so easily! Mind you," Wiki went on with a grin, "he was probably relieved that the *Vin* and the *Peacock* didn't do the same good job of stoving him as you did on the way into Rio."

"Cruel, Wiki, cruel!" George cried. Two months earlier, when the fleet had been entering the great harbor of Rio de Janeiro, George's brig *Swallow* had been involved in a nasty collision with

Captain Coffin's *Osprey*, one that had sent the *Osprey* to the shipyard for the next four weeks. "It wasn't my fault, and you know it!"

Wiki merely laughed, and George said thoughtfully, "What do you think of your father's mate—that Alf Seward?"

Wiki pursed his lips, surprised at the change of subject, and said, "I can't say I know anything about him. I glimpsed him herding the six cadets around while the *Osprey* was being fixed in the shipyard at Rio, and thought he looked like some sort of schoolmaster, and saw him once on board my father's ship, when she was starting to be restowed. He was informing my father exactly how it should be done, and taking no ifs or buts or arguments. I got the impression that he bosses him around unmercifully."

"With amazing good results," George told him. "I've never seen a vessel kept so shipshape, not even in the navy. I'd swear there's not a ropeyarn out of place, and the standing rigging is as taut as a Baptist pastor—and yet the crew is as happy a bunch as ever I saw. Those six cadets seem to idolize him, for all that he treats them so strict. But when I tried to compliment him on his housekeeping, he looked me up and down and stalked away."

"A good first mate doesn't have to be a gentleman—and in my experience very often isn't," Wiki said.

"It's more than that. For a while I wondered if he bore a grudge because it was my ship that knocked that great hole in the *Osprey*, but then I got the strange impression that he's jealous of my friendship with your father."

Wiki was silent, because he understood how Seward felt, if so, as he felt a little jealous of the warm friendship his friend and his father had struck up, himself. After the two vessels had collided, the *Osprey* had been so near to sinking that most captains in Rochester's position would have taken the crew of the crippled ship on board, and then left her to founder. Instead, George and his men had struggled to get a patch over the hole in the hull, and then tow the *Osprey* to the shipyard. Naturally, Captain Coffin had been profoundly grateful—but the friendship was based on a mutual respect and liking, too. They had so much in common and got along so well that when Wiki was in their company he almost felt excluded.

"Perhaps Seward's the possessive type," he said at last. Then he was distracted by a glimpse of movement on the far side of the braided shoals—a party of horsemen on the opposite bank, with the tall figure of Ringgold in their midst. It seemed that they had crossed the river at El Carmen by boat, because they were riding different animals. Wiki wondered what had happened to the mounts he had hired on their behalf, and whether the *ranchero* would tax him about them when he delivered the two horses. Ringgold and his companions weren't going to make that nine o'clock appointment, obviously, which wouldn't do anything to improve the tempers of the four scientifics, he thought.

Then he saw that George was studying his outfit meditatively, from the red silk bandanna that half tamed his wild black curls to the two folded ponchos draped over one shoulder. His friend said, "Is that a set of bolas round your middle?"

"Aye." As was usual with gauchos when away from their steeds, Wiki had wrapped the cords of the bolas around his waist. He said, "Do you remember Juán Bernantio?"

"I do indeed. The hardest taskmaster on the pampas. He taught us both *las boleadoras* and the *lazo*."

"I've become well acquainted with his brother Manuel."

"Here?" George was astonished, and looked around the headland as if he expected the gaucho to gallop into sight.

"Aye. Apparently he and his friends spend the summer months ranging about the Río Negro, and go back north in the fall. They were very useful to me."

Wiki reached up the flagpole, released the lanyard, brought down the rendezvous flag, and folded it. Then he unhitched the bridles of the two horses, who were companionably cropping the tussock.

George said, "The mare is yours?"

"How did you guess?"

"One can't mistake the look of deep loathing she casts in your direction, old chap. I'll take the other horse," said George with great animation. "Let's have a lassoing contest."

Wiki, amused, was greatly enticed. It would be like being a sixteen-year-old student again, when he and George had prowled the forests of New Hampshire with the local Abnaki huntsmen. It was a testament, as well, to how much more relaxed Rochester felt now that he had a competent and experienced second-in-command on board the brig, he thought.

However, he objected, "I should be getting the horses back to the ranch."

"Nonsense, old chap. We have plenty of time. Seward and his boys will be happily fishing and crabbing for hours. Hand me the bolas, and let's see if I'm still better at throwing 'em than you are."

Wiki laughed, and stopped arguing. "Wear this poncho Stackpole kindly handed on to me," he said. "You don't want to spoil your beautiful swab."

He pulled on his own poncho after unwinding the bolas, and for the next hour the two friends galloped back and forth about the headland, poncho fringes flying as they took turns to relearn the exhilaration of throwing *las boleadoras*. The hand ball was firmly gripped as the rest was whirled about the head, the two larger balls flying out side by side at the far end of their strings, which were firmly secured to the end of the hand-ball cord, so that the whistling bolas was a total of six feet in length.

A wild shout as the hand ball was released and the bolas was cast, and then suspense as it flew on and on for fifty or more yards, the three balls spinning about the knot that tied the three strings together, out to their fullest extent. It looked like a three-legged symbol of violence as it blurred through the air, to collapse with a slap as it connected. If well aimed, the three strings wrapped around the target, driven by the momentum of the stones. It was the most effective long-distance grapple imaginable.

"Dismantling shot," Rochester remarked once, as he handed the bolas back to Wiki. He was panting and sweating, and flushed with high enjoyment.

"What?"

"It's used to destroy enemy rigging, old chap. Just like the bolas, but made of lengths of chain secured together at a common end. They're rolled into a ball, and fired from a cannon. Once in the air, the chains spread out and revolve. Any rigging they hit is smashed to smithereens. That is," George added smugly, "if the gun captain has *my* knack for accuracy. Admit it, old chap, I'm better than you are."

"Fiddlesticks," said Wiki, and an argument commenced. Finally, George suggested another bout to prove his point, but it was too late for that, being high time to return the hired horses, and so they galloped for the track and the silvered fence.

After they arrived at the ranch, Wiki thought wryly that the *estanciero* must certainly be charging him for the four other horses, all of which were still among the missing, because the bill that was presented was even more hefty than he'd feared. However, George helped him out with the necessary coins, and Wiki said goodbye to the mare, who bared her teeth and stretched out her neck for a last try at a bite. Then the two companions climbed back to the headland, and trekked on foot to the flagpole, their folded ponchos draped over their shoulders, their heads down as they talked and trudged.

George had evidently been thinking in the meantime, because he said, "Why did you say that Bernantio and his gauchos were useful? Is it something to do with the theft of Captain Stackpole's money?"

"They are *rastreadores*—trackers—who offered to find the missing schooner. Manuel Bernantio picked out the tracks of a train of packhorses that had been driven from Adams's store, and we followed them to the *salinas*, and from there to the place where we found Adams's corpse."

George said, astonished, "He's dead?"

"Very dead. His corpse was seven days old at the very least." And

Wiki described the discovery of the skull under the Gualichú tree, and the body buried beneath it.

George's brow wrinkled. "He was killed in a spot that's sacred to the Indians?"

"He might have been killed at the *salinas*." Wiki remembered the shocking stench, and the sense of something moving slowly and malignantly inside the solid salt. "The killer could have tied his body to the saddle and led the horse to the Gualichú tree to bury him in the salt."

"But why the Gualichú tree?"

"Why?" echoed Wiki. He kicked out at a rolling ball of furze, sending it scudding as it picked up the breeze. He shook his head, and said, "I don't know."

"Is it the custom here on the Río Negro to bury people in salt?"

Wiki grimaced, remembering the vultures, and said again, "I don't know." On the Río de la Plata pampas, as in Arabia, people were buried in open ground, and as quickly as possible—graveyards were only found on ranches like the one that belonged to Ducatel. Men who were lost in the great grassy waste, forced to walk because of a dead or runaway horse, often traveled in mindless circles, to collapse, die, and fertilize the ground where they lay. Twice, he and George had stumbled across a patch where the grass was taller and greener, and found a naked skull rolled in the midst of it, mute evidence of some past crisis.

"So you set out to uncover a thief, and found a murdered man," George meditated aloud. "And you have no idea about the killer?"

"None," Wiki admitted. "It looks as if it was the same man who stole the schooner, but for all we know it could have been part of some long-standing feud. To be frank, I don't have a notion what really happened."

"It's not like you to have to leave a place with the murder unsolved, old man."

"Well, it's all too likely in this case," said Wiki, moodily, too depressed to confess that there was a second murder, equally unsolved. "Not only did Captain Ringgold order me to forget about it, as he reckons it's a local matter, but Captain Stackpole seems to have lost all interest."

"I heard scuttlebutt that the whale the *Trojan* is boiling out is a buster."

"That's so," Wiki admitted. But did it account for Stackpole's strange reversal of attitude? Remembering the whaleman's anger and mortification at the barefaced robbery, it seemed unlikely.

Then he was distracted by George, who pointed ahead, and said, "Is that someone trying to get our attention?"

It was Dr. John Fox, waving from the flagpole, and looking more dusty and disheveled than ever. Wiki often wondered if Fox remembered him from the time of their youth in Salem, but thought not, because he never acknowledged him by name. Now, when he introduced Rochester, instead of embarking on polite pleasantries the doctor expostulated, "They've *marooned* us again. And what the hell happened to *you*?" he demanded.

Wiki frowned. "I've been delivering the horses," he said stiffly, and didn't feel as if he owed the arrogant scientific any more than that. Instead, he asked, "Why aren't you on the riverbank, according to orders? You were supposed to be there at nine, ready to be picked up."

"We did! We were!" John Fox exclaimed. "We waited for hours, and then saw Ringgold's party *on the other side of the river*! We waved, but they didn't pay attention. We made a signal for a boat, and that, too, was ignored. We're camped here for the rest of our poor lives, apparently! It's just as Mr. Peale says—the officers consider the scientific corps nothing more than a confounded *nuisance*! They foil us at each and every opportunity! It's a bloody *scandal*, and we are all going to post a strong complaint to Captain Wilkes."

Rochester, with perfect propriety, made no comment on this, instead asking, "So what are you doing up here?"

"We talked it over, and decided to fly a signal for someone in the fleet to save us. I volunteered, and saw you coming."

"Then the problem is fixed, old chap," Rochester assured him. "I'm sure Mr. Seward—who is a most obliging fellow, I've found—will have you on board the schooner in a trice." And, with that, he led the way down the cliff to the beach.

Getting to the bottom was a slow business, the surgeon being not nearly as lively on his feet as a sailor who was accustomed to heights, but eventually they arrived on the beach, to find Mr. Seward leaning against a rock smoking a tiny clay pipe with a very long stem, indulgently watching the cadets paddle about in rock pools. When the problem was communicated, he nodded, and the surgeon was heaved into the boat by two strong lads. Wiki, Rochester, and Seward jumped inside, and the boys shoved the craft into the waves before scrambling in and taking up the oars.

No sooner were they floating, than Rochester and Seward had a battle of wills. George wanted Wiki to be the steersman—probably because he was so accustomed to asking him to take over the helm in emergencies, Wiki thought. He felt most embarrassed, and wished that the argument wasn't happening, especially as the six boys listened with such lively interest, and knew it would be reported to his father. In the end Mr. Seward nodded, though he watched with a look of brooding resentment as Wiki negotiated the length of the boat toward him.

Arriving in the stern, Wiki took over the heavy length of ash, and Alf Seward shifted out of the way. A peglike grip projected about a foot from the head of the oar, and Wiki gripped this with his left hand, the oar turned so that the shaft led backward through the crook of his left elbow, and his forearm was laid along it. When he leaned on this arm, the blade dug about in their wake, while the oarsmen looked up at him as they rowed, watching his face for a hint of what dangers lay ahead.

The surf was breasted with a few sickening plunges and surges, and then they were back on the smoother open sea. There was quite a lot of company out here, just as George had described. The *Flying Fish* was sailing on short tacks back and forth across the seaward end of the estuary, dragging a logline. A man was out on the bow heaving a sounding lead, evidently to determine the depth of the water. Dinghies from various expedition ships were dipping up and down at anchor off the mouth of the river, men standing precariously inside them to drop shot-laden tide-staffs into the treacherous shoals, measuring the rise and fall of the tide. One of the cutters was working from one anchored dinghy to another with a man standing in the bows shouting orders. Wiki thought he recognized the slight, wiry form of Benjamin Harden, the river pilot with the murky past.

Giving the cutter a wide berth, he brought the boat around for the entrance of the Río Negro. Here, he faced breakers again—even bigger breakers, forced high by the pressure of the outflowing river, smashing over rocks, hiding sandbars, and setting the boat to jumping and banging. Three vertiginous plunges, and they entered the dark, gleaming rush of the river, where the unbroken crests of the waves were streaked with russet and yellow.

Thrusting the long blade deep into the water to keep the bow pointing forward, Wiki ordered the boys to still the boat, and then stared over their heads as he searched for a passage. For a long moment, they fought to stay in the same spot, with the boat tossing and plunging beneath them. Then, just as Dr. Fox was beginning to turn green and gulp, Wiki spied a snake of deeper blackness in the dark waters. He heaved down on the oar, telling the boys on one side to pull forward and those on the other to pull sternward, thus swiveling the lively boat to enter the narrow, winding passage.

Twenty hard strokes, a stream of quick orders that set them twisting from one side to another, and all at once they were floating in smooth, mirrorlike water, with only the current against them. To Wiki's further embarrassment, George Rochester led the boys in a round of hearty cheers. Alf Seward simply cupped his pipe to relight it, his lean face quite expressionless.

Ten minutes more, and they had pulled over to the northern bank, taken three highly relieved scientifics on board, and were rowing for the *Sea Gull,* which was still lying at anchor. When they arrived alongside, one of the boys put out a hand and grabbed a hanging rope, and then the overloaded whaleboat stilled. There was no one at all on the decks.

Rochester stood up, and shouted, "Ship ahoy!"

Silence. Then a head poked out of the forward hatch that led to the forecastle, followed by the unfolding body of a seaman. He took one look at the magnificent sight of an officer in uniform, scurried to the hatch that led to the aftercabin, and hollered for Captain Ringgold.

The patrician figure emerged at leisure, strolled over to the rail, and cast a casual glance at the complement in the crowded boat. All at once his eyes widened, and his brows shot up. "Congratulations are in order, George!" he exclaimed. "Or did your looking glass deceive you when you pinned on your swab this morn'?"

"Congratulations are indeed in order," Rochester complacently agreed, and stepped out of the boat and onto the deck. An explanation of how he'd found out about the blessed elevation in rank was demanded and given, and the two captains warmly shook hands, while the four scientifics, still in the boat, watched blankly, with no comprehension at all of what was going on.

Then Titian Peale abruptly regained his wits, stood up, bounded onto the deck with remarkable agility, and advanced on Ringgold like an avenging nemesis. "What the *hell* did you mean by leaving orders to abandon us on shore while you were off on your jaunt to El Carmen?" he shouted, and, when Ringgold lifted a haughty eyebrow instead of deigning to answer, promised to report the *whole disgraceful affair* to Captain Wilkes at the first opportunity.

"And where was the boat at nine this morning, that's what I would like to know!" chimed in Dr. Fox, clambering up beside him. "We were left without anything—no provisions, no word, no communication, not even tobacco!"

Ringgold still didn't bother to respond, instead fixing Wiki with a very cold eye. "I want a word with you, Wiki Coffin," he said grimly, and crooked a finger.

Wiki, still standing at the steering oar, protested, "But Mr. Seward has agreed to take me to the brig *Swallow*—"

"The *hell* he will! Captain Wilkes wants a meeting with all the scientifics in the morning—and that includes you, sir! So you will spend the night aboard the *Sea Gull*—and that's an order you will obey for once, confound it!"

Wiki winced. Surely, he thought, no one had told Ringgold that he had deliberately disobeyed orders, and cross-examined Dr. Ducatel about the death of Captain Hallett and the loss of Captain Stackpole's money. Then a movement caught his attention. As he watched with disbelief, the flamboyant figure of the surgeon stepped out of the cabin and onto the deck.

George Rochester did his best for his friend, arguing that Wiki's presence was urgently needed on board the brig *Swallow*. They were setting up preventer stays to brace the masts ready for the doubling of Cape Horn, and Mr. Coffin's expertise was essential, he said. Ringgold didn't believe him for a minute. All that resulted was a lively technical discussion, along with Ringgold pointing out that Wiki Coffin had been shipped to perform scientific duties, not to help out with the work of the ship.

At that stage, much to Wiki's astonishment, Titian Peale backed him up as well, arguing that if Wiki were a scientist, he couldn't be ordered around like a seaman. However, Ringgold remained adamant, with the result that the *Osprey* boat pulled away with Alf Seward back in charge of the steering oar, leaving Wiki braced for a lecture. Once they got down into the cabin, however, the scolding was surprisingly brief, perhaps because pursuing the mystery had been justified by the discovery of the clerk's corpse. Then Wiki found out Ringgold's real reason for wanting him to spend the night on board—to interview Dr. Ducatel about the economy of the Río Negro, and write up a report for Captain Wilkes.

The next hours were spent in eating supper, and quizzing the Río Negro surgeon about the tariff of duties, what inducements there were for merchant vessels to visit the port, the productions of the place, the climate, the principal articles of trade, the condition of the government, the restrictive policies of de Rosas, and relations with the Indians. Writing down the answers resulted in a dozen neatly written pages. Stacking them into a tidy pile, Wiki mused that Captain Wilkes would be quite impressed when the document was delivered in the morning.

After Ducatel was finally released from the cross-examination, and had left the cramped little captain's cabin, Wiki sat back and contemplated Ringgold, shrewdly guessing that it was Ringgold himself who had been commanded to produce the report. The banquet had distracted him from following Wilkes's orders, no doubt, along with the novelty of the sights of the Río Negro.

Very innocently, he said, "Would you like me to sign it?"

Ringgold cleared his throat, and shook his head.

"I can give it to Captain Wilkes, if you like."

"No, no—I'll do that."

Straight-faced, Wiki folded the report and handed it over. As he watched Ringgold stow it safely away in an inside jacket pocket, he finished off the mug of coffee at his elbow—which was remarkably good, most unlike the bitter brew he was usually served when visiting other ships of the fleet.

Then he said, "Did you know that Captain Wilkes has requisitioned Harden for the survey?"

Ringgold's expression became dour. "So I was told—which leaves me without a pilot to navigate me out, unless the governor releases the regular pilots before morning."

"Harden has the reputation of a troublemaker. He was in the de Rosas army for a while, and then was cashiered for inciting mutiny—a mutiny during which he killed a couple of men. Now, he's involved with the local revolutionaries."

"Mutiny?" Ringgold frowned deeply, *mutiny* being a dire word in a navy officer's lexicon. "Are you certain of that?"

Wiki hesitated, then admitted that it was hearsay, but still Captain Ringgold looked grim. "I didn't like the look of the cove in the slightest," he confessed. "If I hadn't been desperate for someone to navigate us off that confounded sandbar, I wouldn't have countenanced him for a single moment." Then he added, "That he had his Protection Paper made a difference, too."

"Didn't you think it was strange?"

"What do you mean?"

"I was surprised he still had it," said Wiki. "Even if he managed to keep it from being stolen when he was in prison, it's amazing that the army didn't confiscate it to make sure he couldn't escape their clutches."

"He must have hidden it well."

"It seems odd, too, that he didn't ship out with the first Yankee captain to call."

"Maybe there's some reason he doesn't want to go home to Rhode Island."

That was very possible, Wiki thought. He said, "George Rochester told me that Harden's been requisitioned for more than the survey—he's been signed on for the entire voyage."

"*What?* We're always in need of seamen, but I didn't know we were *that* bloody desperate!"

"So you'll have a word with Captain Wilkes?"

"God, no," Ringgold said hastily. "Navy discipline will fix him."

So, thought Wiki resignedly, that was something else he would need to talk over with Captain Wilkes. As he left the cabin to search out a place to sleep, he ruminated that the conference promised to be very tricky indeed.

Nine

January 29, 1839

As before, dawn arrived with no sign of a pilot to get them out of the river. Instead, two of the governor's nephews came trotting along the riverside path. First, they announced that they had returned the horses Captain Ringgold, Mr. Waldron, and Lieutenant Perry had hired to the *estanciero* who had rented them out. Then, they begged an invitation on board.

The entire complement of the schooner thought them interestingly exotic, with the result that they were made very welcome. They were fine, active-looking young men in gaucho dress, who wanted to know everything about the schooner and the expedition, which everyone found flattering. However, they spoke no English, and so Wiki was forced to translate. Back and forth the lively conversation went, while all the time he wondered about the state of Captain Wilkes's temper, which was bound to be deteriorating as he waited for the *Sea Gull* to arrive with its burden of scientifics. It was near noon before the nephews finally made a reluctant departure, taking Dr. Ducatel with them.

As they galloped off, they shouted great promises that they would persuade their uncle, the governor, to release the pilots and send them along. Captain Ringgold was not prepared to wait for such a vague eventuality, however, instead allotting the job to Wiki. "You found your way upriver in the boat, didn't you?" he barked. "Well, then, you can find your way back out to sea again."

Wiki himself didn't feel nearly so confident, and was certain, besides, that there would be hell to pay if Captain Wilkes ever learned that his clerk had conned the schooner out of the river. However, Ringgold didn't stop to listen to any argument, even when Mr. Peale tried again to interfere by pointing out that Wiki was supposed to be a scientific, not a pilot. Instead, the strong-minded captain hollered orders to raise the sails and get ready to weigh anchor.

Hands assembled at the windlass, right in the bows at the inboard end of the bowsprit, while at the same time seamen prodded uncomprehending scientifics out of the way so they could take hold of their respective halyards. The mainsail was set first, followed by the foresail, the men who hauled at the ropes chanting "Ho—ha! Ho—ha! Up—ha! Down—ha!" to keep rhythm as the gaffs from which the great sheets of canvas hung creaked slowly up the masts. They were racing to get sail set before the windlass hands, heaving smartly on the windlass brakes, got the hook off the bottom. Then the jib was also swiftly set, because it was essential for the schooner to pay off as soon as she was free, as without steerage way she would drift broadside to the current.

The hands seemed experienced, but Wiki, standing in the bow to study the water patterns unfolding before the bowsprit, remembered that this schooner had been grounded once already, and felt very tense indeed. As it was, no sooner was the anchor weighed and the canvas slapped full than the *Sea Gull* yawed horribly, which caused Wiki to look anxiously over his shoulder at the helmsman.

The fellow worked too hard at the tiller, swinging it too far one way and then the other, while the schooner, responding fast because of her sharp lines and light displacement, frantically dipped and swung. Canvas flogged as it alternately gained and lost the wind. To complicate matters still further, the tide was on the ebb, vying with the current of the river to carry them pell-mell out to sea.

Within seconds the rippling paleness of shallow water lay almost under their bow. "Hard-a-starboard!" Wiki urgently hollered. Under the helmsman's heavy hand, the schooner staggered back and forth across the current like a drunkard, while Wiki shouted out frantically for corrections. The half-drowned seaman with the sounding lead, hanging over the plunging bow, called out readings that varied as wildly as their erratic course.

The wind suddenly gusted from dead ahead, blowing spiteful sand in their faces and chopping up the water into nasty lumps so that it was impossible to see below the surface. The breakers at the mouth of the estuary surged and roared in Wiki's ears. An angry wave rushed upon them, picked the schooner up on its crest, and then slammed the *Sea Gull* deep into the following trough. As her bowsprit rose high and her foredeck seethed with shed water, her stern dropped with a jerk, and her keel touched mud. The water about her sides foamed yellow.

"What the hell d'you think you're doing, mister?" Ringgold yelled at Wiki.

Without bothering to reply, Wiki sprang up the foremast to the crosstrees, where he stood braced with his back against the naked upper mast, hanging on to a stay. Seventy feet above the tumbled surface of the water was no great height after having been aloft on the mighty 700-ton *Vincennes*, but it felt a lot higher because the mast lashed back and forth like a coach whip, swinging in spirals so that the deck revolved beneath him. But at last Wiki could see the bottom—and there was the black snake of the channel, the start of it fine on the starboard bow.

After the briefest possible of pauses to memorize its course, Wiki jumped onto the spring stay—a great tarred rope that led from one of the two masts to the other—and swung his way sternward like a monkey. Dropping onto the afterdeck, he elbowed the helmsman to one side, and firmly took over the tiller.

The schooner immediately responded to his much surer touch. Into the deeper water of the channel she nosed, and the yellow wash died down. Then the *Sea Gull* was easing safely through the shoals with her sails extended to each side like wings. Wiki was steering by instinct, helped only by the shouted soundings and the memorized track, but somehow, tense moments later, they were out of the shoals, through the breakers, and out at sea. With huge relief, he handed back the tiller, noting at the same time that Ringgold didn't bother to congratulate him on the achievement.

The conditions were even more uncomfortable, however. The schooner bucketed and pitched, and took huge quantities of water over her decks, giving Wiki a great deal of respect for the men who were making the long voyage in her. What would it be like for them off dreaded Cape Horn? He didn't like the feel of the deck beneath his feet at all, and wondered what strains the groundings and thumpings had put on the fabric of the wooden hull.

The temperature was plummeting with the change in the direction of the wind, as if the blizzards of Cape Horn were beckoning. Wiki was glad of his poncho, huddling it closely around him as he stood at the rail with the wind in his teeth, watching the foreboding weather as the schooner laboriously beat toward the flagship, which was plunging at her anchors a mile off the shore. Mountains of black cloud gathered to landward, while the breakers at the mouth of the river crashed higher still, thundering loud in his ears despite the increasing distance.

The *Vincennes* fired a gun, evidently a signal, because Wiki could see the small expedition boats hastily raising anchor, dumping shot, strapping tide-staffs across the thwarts, and heading for the nearest ship, which was the *Porpoise*. Then a great wave rushed upon the *Sea*

Gull and the boats dropped out of sight as she fell into the trough with a sickening plunge.

At last the starboard side of the *Vincennes* was towering above them, a tall black wall interrupted by one white streak marked out with black squares. Because the flagship was broadside on to the wind and tide, she was rolling away and back again, but at least they were in her lee, and so were in comparatively calm water. Rain was starting to lash down. The four scientifics were shoved up first, each one launched upward by a powerful seaman as the *Vincennes* rolled and the ladder loomed over the schooner, and then Wiki followed.

When he scrambled over the gangway rail, he looked back to see the *Sea Gull* brace up and tack away. Ringgold was obviously anxious to beat farther upwind for a better offing before dropping anchor. The scientifics, meantime, were running for the shelter of the big afterhouse. With a wave of the hand, Wiki headed there, too.

The marine corporal standing sentry in the portico snapped a salute so smartly that he lost his balance as the ship pitched her head, and had to take a couple of quick sidesteps. "Mr. Coffin," he exclaimed with obvious relief. "Cap'n Wilkes has been wonderin' where the devil you'd got to, and gettin' right angry about it."

"Oh dear," said Wiki. As he and the four scientifics followed the corporal up the wide passage that led to the big chartroom at the sternward end, infuriated shouting echoed from beyond the shut double doors. The corporal cast an unmistakably sympathetic glance over his shoulder before he knocked.

When the doors opened, Captain Wilkes was exclaiming, "As I have said time and time again, Mr. Couthouy, this is not your private goddamned yacht! You have no right to order an expedition artist around, and abuse him when he works for others instead of rushing to obey your every command! His employment is under *my* control, not yours!"

Once Wiki, with the others, had squeezed into the back, the big room was so full of men that it was almost impossible to see the shelves of books and racks of specimens that lined the walls. When the ship executed a smart roll toward weather the crowd hardly moved at all, everyone being braced against everyone else. However, the expedition artist was easily distinguished from the rest because of his uncomfortably self-conscious expression. Naturalist Couthouy's huge russet beard was jutting out with fury. The only person who was smiling was Captain Wilkes's crony, the tubby and self-satisfied Lawrence J. Smith. Though he was a lieutenant, he was there, Wiki presumed, because he was considered to be a scientific as well as an officer.

Captain Wilkes was standing behind one of the chart desks, giving his customary impression of keeping a barrier between himself and his audience. He was in an evident state of rage, with sweat on his brow and a flush across his high cheekbones as he stared furiously at Joseph Couthouy, who glared back equally aggressively. Wiki winced, knowing Couthouy's temper well, having once lived with him in the afterhouse of the *Vincennes*. A shipmaster out of Boston and a highly intelligent man, Couthouy had crossed swords with the volatile commodore of the expedition often before, but this battle of wills promised to be the nastiest yet.

However, while Couthouy was still sucking in an infuriated breath, a handsome young man with a leonine mop of hair spoke up. "Captain Wilkes," he said, his tone eminently reasonable. "I was under the impression that this meeting was called to sort out disagreements between the scientific corps and the officers, not to berate particular individuals."

"I do understand that the scientifics are experiencing some degree of dissatisfaction with the officers, Mr. Dana," Captain Wilkes stiffly answered.

"Only *some* of the officers, Captain Wilkes," the other corrected. He seemed amazingly calm and composed, considering that he looked just a year or so older than Wiki's own age of twenty-four. "*Some* of the officers are quite accurate in the observations that we ask them to make. Others, unfortunately, are less punctilious. When I ask them to carry thermometers to the masthead, for instance, the readings they take are tantamount to useless, because half the time the thermometer is in the sun, and the rest of the time in the shade."

"The problem must lie with your instructions, Mr. Dana."

"I'm careful to be precise, Captain Wilkes. Unfortunately, they do not listen. While I'd hesitate to condemn all and sundry, there are certain officers who display little interest in the scientific aims of the expedition."

Dead silence. Everyone was holding his breath in suspense, waiting for the explosion. Then Captain Wilkes astounded one and all by sighing, "Unfortunately, I have to agree with you, Mr. Dana."

There was a blank pause. Then Mr. Dana said cautiously, "Yes?"

"In my own department of astronomy I have found officers who are sadly listless in their attitude, being markedly unwilling to carry out the scientific duties I assign them. I believe there was a great deal of muttering about the round-the-clock pendulum observations that I required the officers to carry out in Rio de Janeiro. Some, quite frankly, were so astoundingly ignorant of the science that they had not even heard of using a torsion balance to detect gravitational attraction between metal spheres! Hopefully, this situation will be mended by the passage of time, with patient instructions from you all, and strict attention to discipline from myself. In the meantime, we must all make allowances."

"What allowances?" Couthouy echoed in dangerous tones.

"Mr. Couthouy, I would have expected you, of all people, to understand the cold, hard fact that while it would be ideal for *all* the expedition officers to take the liveliest interest in scientific work, their *own* work must come first," Wilkes snapped, the flush rising high in his cheeks. "Even naval scientists—like myself, and Lieutenant Smith, here—must give priority to the everyday demands of the ships."

They all looked at Lawrence J. Smith, who smirked and said,

"You should count your blessings, gentlemen—you have unlimited leisure to follow your hobbies in the name of science, a luxury not allowed to the officers, who are responsible for the safety of your seagoing homes."

"Hobbies?" someone echoed, outraged.

"It's much more than the prior call of proper duty," Titian Peale objected. "Even when the conditions are ideal, the officers regard us with contempt. Our treatment on the Río Negro is a miserable illustration of this. We were dumped on shore and quite forgotten—for the *next twenty-four hours* our signals were ignored. Yet the weather was hot, and we had no gear and no provisions; all we could find was brackish water to drink, and we had to hunt our own game. As it was, the two surgeons were overcome by the heat. When I brought my specimens to the riverbank, I was informed that Captain Ringgold had issued orders to the boats to hold no communication with the gentlemen of the scientific corps after landing them! It is incomprehensible! My specimens had to be abandoned to shrivel and rot in the sun, along with the carcass of a fine buck I had shot for the officers' dinner. Even as dark fell, we received no sign that our presence was remembered, until Mr. Hale came from the pueblo with a message from Captain Ringgold that we were to attend the landing place on the riverbank at nine. That was yesterday morning, sir—but did the boat from the *Sea Gull* arrive? *No, sir, it did not!*"

This had no discernible effect on Lieutenant Smith's impervious self-satisfaction, but Wiki saw that the skin around Captain Wilkes's nostrils had become pinched and white, and that Dr. Fox was watching him with concern. Again, however, Wilkes failed to explode. "Write it down," he said wearily at the finish. "And I'll arrange for Captain Ringgold's court-martial."

"Court-martial?" Mr. Peale exclaimed. All the scientifics looked at each other, horrified at this development. "I didn't intend the matter to go as far as that! I would rather ask to be returned to the United States at the first opportunity—"

"Impossible, Mr. Peale."

"But it would be better for all concerned if I left—"

"Obviously, sir, you have forgotten the terms of the agreement you signed."

"Agreement, Captain?" The naturalist's voice rose. "The way *I* remember it, the agreement was with *you*—an agreement in which *you* gave *us* a reassurance of protection and assistance for all the members of the scientific corps!"

"Mr. Peale, you have *always* had my protection and guaranteed assistance—just so long as it is possible without sacrificing the greater interests of the voyage. I'm sure you'd be the first to complain if your ship sank under you, sir! And the same applies to all my officers—including the officers on board the surveying schooner *Sea Gull*. Obviously, they had a great deal more to do than cater to the whims of civilians."

"That's it!" exclaimed Mr. Peale. "We're *civilians*, and beneath notice! The officers regard us as mere spectators—people who have an irritating habit of making strange demands, and who get in the way of their proper work. We're subject to the etiquette of a man-of-war without any of its privileges!"

"Etiquette?" Captain Wilkes echoed, his voice rising again. "But you've made no attempt to follow the etiquette of a man-of-war!"

The ship dipped and surged again, so abruptly that this time the scientifics lurched against each other, at the same moment looking at each other in a puzzled fashion, mystified to a man by this strange accusation. "We've all done our best to adjust to the circumstances," objected one.

"Have you picked up a looking glass lately?" Captain Wilkes demanded. "If you'd followed orders—orders handed down by the Department of the Navy!—you would have the appearances of men who are worthy of being treated as officers! Instead, you all—save for a few outstanding examples, such as Mr. Dana and Mr. Hale—have insisted on being a horrid example! How can I keep discipline when the *scientific corps*, who are utterly dependent on my goodwill, disregard my strict instructions?"

Silence. The scientifics all stared at Mr. Hale, who had turned bright red with embarrassment, and Mr. Dana, whose good-looking face was quite blank beneath his great mop of waving hair.

Then Dr. Fox bravely spoke up, saying, "I'm sorry, Captain Wilkes, but we don't have the slightest idea what you're talking about."

"I'm talking about the matter of dress! The instruction from the Navy Department to all the scientifics was to obtain lieutenants' undress uniform, and wear it on all public occasions. You mess with the wardroom officers, and have the same rations, and so you should dress accordingly. But only two—Mr. Dana and Mr. Hale—have complied. How can you expect to be treated as anything but civilians, if you insist on wearing civilian clothes?"

Uniform? It was the first Wiki had heard of it, though he now saw the reason why Mr. Hale had been wearing uniform for the jaunt to El Carmen. The rest of the scientific gentlemen were glancing at each other, obviously as ignorant as he was of the ruling. At the same time, they were shuffling uneasily, distancing themselves from Mr. Hale and Mr. Dana, and making a space around them that revealed that both were wearing the complete undress uniform of a lieutenant, though Wiki noticed that they did not have epaulettes.

The other scientific gentlemen, by contrast, were wearing broadcloth suits, some with shawl-collared long jackets, and others with swallowtail coats. Some even carried silk hats. Wiki thought they presented a most respectable appearance, considering the way most of them looked when they worked at their studies. One of the surgeons was infamous for appearing on deck in the old frock coat he'd used as a gown in the operating theater, which was so stiff with blood and pus that it could stand up by itself.

Their silence was uncomfortable in the extreme, and Captain Wilkes's expression was derisive. "Look at you! Look at the bloody lot of you!" he shouted. His infuriated stare shifted from face to face—and, for the first time, focused on Wiki.

"My God!" he breathed. His eyes widened with utter incredulity. For a second, as everyone turned and looked at him, Wiki's mind went blank. Then he abruptly realized that it would have been a good idea to shed his bandanna and poncho before he entered the room.

Ten

At that awful moment Wiki was abruptly saved, by none other than Lieutenant Forsythe. The double doors swung open with a slam, revealing the burly figure of the notorious Virginian, looking even larger than usual because of the shining wet oilskins with which he was swathed. The ship executed a sharp pitch at the same second, and everyone hopped as a wash of dirty water came sweeping down the corridor and into the room.

"Compliments of Lieutenant Craven," Forsythe barked.

"What is it?" said Captain Wilkes impatiently. Craven was the first lieutenant of the flagship, and therefore the most senior of his officers, and, it seemed, was currently in charge of the deck.

"The weather's kicking up and a dense fog is rolling in. Boats from the *Porpoise* and the *Peacock* are waiting alongside, sir, and he advises that if the scientifics want to get back to their ships, they'd better shift right now. And," said Forsythe, his brows lifting high as he took in Wiki's appearance, "a cutter from the *Swallow* is here for Mr. Coffin, as well."

The room emptied with remarkable suddenness. Some of the scientifics even shoved Forsythe to one side in their hurry, despite his fearsome reputation. Within two moments Wiki was alone with Captain Wilkes, while Forsythe waited restively by the door.

"I'd like to talk with you, sir," he said. "I've got a lot to tell you about what happened on shore, and there are questions—"

"Tomorrow," said Captain Wilkes impatiently. "I'll see you at four bells in the forenoon watch, and this time don't be so bloody late."

Wiki hesitated, but was too wise to argue.

"And for God's sake, come looking more civilized!"

"Aye, sir," said Wiki, and hastily followed Forsythe down the corridor.

"You're a beggar for punishment," observed the southerner as the cutter hauled away from the flagship. "Why are you dressed up like one of the local desperadoes? He's right that you look bloody uncivilized! And what the hell do you want to talk to him for, anyway? About that thousand dollars you've been chasing up for a spouterman what was boneheaded enough to get himself sold a disappearin' schooner by a bloody rascal of a storekeeper?"

Wiki said glumly to all of this, "Aye."

"Did you find anything?"

"The storekeeper's corpse."

Forsythe's eyes widened at that. "Murdered by the thief?"

"Apparently."

"And the schooner?"

"Sailed long since."

"What about the thousand dollars? Gone too, you know not where?"

Wiki nodded, and Forsythe let out an irritating guffaw. "What kind of sleuth do you call yourself?"

This was depressingly like the previous day's conversation with Rochester. Instead of honoring the rhetorical question with an answer, Wiki said, "Thanks for the rescue."

"Cap'n Rochester's orders."

Captain Rochester? Wiki was amazed that the word should come so naturally from the Virginian's lips. Never would he have believed that Forsythe would be so easygoing about being second-in-command to George; never would he have credited that switching a gold epaulette from one shoulder to another could make such a difference. Rochester's elevation had much greater significance than he could ever have guessed, he realized, particularly when it was remembered that Forsythe had been a lieutenant for God alone knew how long, while George had just attained that rank. Was it possible that the unlikely combination wasn't so disastrous, after all? Being acutely aware of his vast ignorance of the ways of the navy, Wiki did not have a notion, but was beginning to feel a touch of relief.

He said, "Is that why you made up that story about a fog coming in?"

Though the water was undercut with a nasty swell that pitched the boat in every direction, making Forsythe work hard at the tiller, the waves were no longer breaking, the wind had entirely died away, and the air was pristine. Mists were rising off the river, but certainly not the sea.

"It ain't made up—it's on the way."

"How do you know that?"

"The bloody temperature's dropped, hasn't it? Ten degrees, or I'm a Dutchman."

Wiki wondered why Forsythe thought fogs and drops in temperature were related, but then they arrived on board the *Swallow*. After the harrowing days he had spent on shore, it had all the connotations of arriving back home, complete with the wonderful smells of good food that wafted up from the cozy saloon with its welcoming table as he followed Forsythe down the companionway stairs.

There were two louvered doors on the larboard side of this mess room, leading to the mates' staterooms. Out of sheer habit, Wiki went to the sternmost one, which led to the abode of the first officer. He stopped himself just in time. When he turned round Forsythe was watching, his beefy tattooed arms folded, a malicious grin on his broad, red face.

With a rueful lift of an eyebrow, Wiki went to the second door, to find that though his sea chest was stowed neatly under the double bunk, his books and the broken pieces of his shelf, along with his lamp, had been tossed into a careless heap on the topmost berth. Well, at least it was the upper one, he thought—if Midshipman Keith had snared the top bunk in his absence, he would have had a foot planted in his face every time the young man got in or out of bed.

Carrying the pieces of his shelf, he went out on deck. Dark was falling and it was colder than ever. Rochester, on watch on the quarterdeck, was huddled in Stackpole's poncho. However, the steerage, where the carpenter, boatswain, sailmaker, gunner, cook, and steward lived, was cozy in the extreme. Braving the companionable fug of pipe smoke, Wiki borrowed a hammer and nails, and garnered a little advice in the carpentering way. Then, by the time he had his berth fixed up the way he liked it, and the tools were returned, suppertime was nigh.

As he briskly washed and changed into clean clothes, he could hear voices in the tiny pantry. One was Stoker, the steward, while the other was Robert Festin, their stowaway chef. The latter was easily distinguished because of his vocabulary, which was a weird combination of Abnaki Indian and the antique French of the remotest maritime provinces, plus English vulgarities learned from Forsythe, the rudest of kitchen Portuguese, and Maori phrases taught by Wiki himself. Festin was supposed to have left the fleet at Rio, having been trapped into a marriage arrangement, but he had stolen back on board the day before the wedding, and the crew of the *Swallow* had kept quiet about it because of his famous cooking.

When Wiki rejoined Forsythe in the saloon, Festin himself emerged from the pantry, a short, squat figure poised on spindly legs, his swarthy face stretched wide in a gap-toothed grin of delight. As Wiki knew well, though the cook was undoubtedly pleased to see him back, most of the joy was reserved for Forsythe, whom Festin adored, though the Virginian would have killed him without compunction if he'd suspected it. Having his idol permanently assigned to the *Swallow* was the pinnacle of delight.

Now he showed them the pan he carried, saying smugly, "Bloody good," in English, and repeating it in *te reo Maori* with a resounding, "*Kapai!*"

Kapai indeed, thought Wiki, because the crisply crusted, fragrant dish certainly promised to be scrumptious. He headed for the forward end of the table, where there was a small bench set against the foot of the mainmast, swung a leg over it, and sat down. Forsythe eased his bulk on to the bench to the starboard side, and both men watched with deep attention as Festin filled their plates with his delicious version of the traditional seaman's lobscouse. Because he liked to watch Festin cooking, Wiki knew that the Acadian concocted this particular dish by soaking broken ship's hard bread in fresh water until soft, draining the result, and mixing it with succulent fillets of boneless fresh fish. Piled into the pan and topped with scraps of crisply fried salt pork, it was then baked in the oven until golden on top.

Leaving the half-full pan in the pantry, Festin headed up to the galley on the foredeck, to serve out the same delicacy to the crew, the *Swallow* being a democratic vessel where the men ate the same fare as the officers. In the saloon silence reigned, save for hungry eating noises. Finally Forsythe leaned back, took a huge slurp from his coffee mug, and said with every evidence of lively interest, "So there's a murderer running loose, huh?"

George Rochester clattered down the companionway stairs, sat in the captain's armchair at the sternward end of the table, and surveyed the filled plate the steward carried in with an appreciative eye. Evidently having overheard Forsythe, he observed to Wiki, "You were extraordinarily lucky to find *rastreadores* in your moment of need, old chap."

"Find *what?*" said Forsythe. Wiki explained about the *rastreadores,* while the southerner listened with deep attention. Having helped Wiki with some sleuthing in the past, he had come to pride himself on his astuteness, as Wiki knew to his cost. "Tracks?" he said at the end. "What kinda tracks?"

"Of a train of packhorses, and a horseman who followed them. The tracks led up the Río Negro to where salt from the inland *salinas* is piled in dunes. All the provisions in Adams's store had been taken away, so it's reasonable to guess that the packhorses were carrying them to the schooner, which was anchored there at the time, loading salt."

"But that's bloody stupid!" Forsythe exclaimed. "Why not sail the vessel back to the village after the salt had been loaded, and collect the goods there? That would've made a damn sight more sense!"

Wiki said, "I agree."

"Wa'al, the only sensible explanation is that they must've been in a helluva hurry."

Surprised, Wiki echoed, "Hurry?"

"Yup. They was prime anxious to get her loaded and out to sea afore the spouterman come back for his purchase."

Wiki blinked. "You're right!" he exclaimed. "That's why they forgot the deed!"

"Deed? What deed?"

Wiki described finding the deed of sale for the *Grim Reaper,* then added, "That's why Adams's killer stayed behind when the schooner sailed."

The Virginian stared, and then said, "Stayed behind? But that's bloody insane! What gives you that crazy idea?"

"The same day we found Adams's body—which was at least a week after Adams was killed—someone killed his clerk, and stole the deed of sale."

Dead silence. Rochester was staring at Wiki with the same riveted expression as Forsythe. Then he said, "*Another* murder, old chap?"

"Aye," said Wiki, and told them about the discovery of the body, adding, "Adams and his clerk were both knifed the same way—brutally, in the chest."

"There's a lot of that going on in South America," Forsythe pointed out wisely.

"I'm sure there is," agreed Wiki. "However, it seems a good reason to believe that Adams and his clerk were killed by the same man."

The southerner's tone became derisive. "You reckon the storekeeper's killer missed the boat because he wanted to get hold of that bill of sale, but then hung around for seven or more days before he finally got around to knifing the clerk?"

Wiki winced. "Presumably he realized then that he needed the bill of sale so he could claim legal ownership of the schooner."

"But the bloody schooner was gone!"

Wiki sighed. "I know."

Forsythe's expression became pitying. "And you're goin' to tell Wilkes this in the morning, even though it don't make a single bit of sense?"

"Aye," Wiki admitted, and wondered yet again if Captain Stackpole had changed his mind and approached the expedition commodore. Reminded of the tirade in the chartroom of the *Vincennes*, he changed the subject, saying, "Did you know that the scientifics are supposed to wear lieutenant's undress uniform?"

Forsythe exclaimed, "Bloody *what*?"

"According to Captain Wilkes, since the scientific corps mess with the wardroom officers, they should dress like them, too."

The southerner went red in the face. "I worked for goddamned years for the honor of wearing lieutenant's uniform!" he barked. "And a bunch of bastards what do nothin' but make observations and clutter up ships with smelly specimens get the same privilege? It's a bloody injustice!"

"I couldn't agree more, old chap!" echoed George. "How would they like it if I claimed to be a fellow of one of their prestigious colleges without having earned it? I went to Harvard to look up some legal papers once, but does that qualify me for the mortarboard and gown?"

"Absolutely bloody right!" said Forsythe.

Never had Wiki seen the two men in such accord—and now he could see, too, why the scientifics had looked so uneasy. They, unlike the expedition commander, understood the resentment it would cause among the officers. It was one of the many ill-conceived Navy Department decisions that made Captain Wilkes's job even harder.

George said to him, "I assume that includes you, old chap. Do you even *own* a lieutenant's undress uniform?"

"Of course not," Wiki said, adding, "And I wouldn't wear it if I did."

"Bloody wise," opined Forsythe. "Natives dressed up in white men's ceremonial rig look more like goddamned savages than ever."

Wiki and George cast him equally impatient looks. Wiki said, "That reminds me—have either of you heard that there's another New Zealand Maori with the expedition?"

They both shook their heads.

"The philologist, Horatio Hale, said there's a Maori chief on the *Peacock*."

"Chief?" said Forsythe, and snorted with derisive amusement. "I bet they call him somethin' different back home."

"The trouble," said Wiki very seriously, "is that they call him 'Ngati Porou.' "

He looked at Forsythe, wondering if he would understand. About the year 1828, a couple of years after Wiki had been carried off to New England, the Virginian had hired himself out to a chief of Wiki's own tribe, Ngapuhi, as a mercenary in their ongoing war against the Ngati Porou. While Wiki had not been there at the time, he had heard often from Forsythe how he had marched the forest warpaths and voyaged on *waka taua*—canoes of war—and how his advice had helped the Ngapuhi warriors win the battle. In Wiki's candid opinion, the basic reason the Ngati Porou had lost was not the expertise of men like Forsythe, but because the Ngapuhi had been armed with the guns they had gained through barter with American and English whalers and traders, while the Ngati Porou fought with traditional weapons.

The Virginian did see the implications of the other man's tribal affinity: the Ngati Porou had harbored a deadly grudge against the Ngapuhi ever since, attributing their defeat to treachery, and would grasp any chance for revenge.

He grinned evilly. "What's the name of this bastard what's going to kill you first chance he gets?"

"They call him Jack Sac, but I believe his Maori name is Te Aute."

"How long ago did he leave New Zealand?"

"Horatio Hale said he'd been in America for the past ten years."

"Then there's a chance he witnessed one or other of the battles between your tribe and his," Forsythe decided. "If he's old enough, he might even have taken part."

"Exactly," said Wiki. They both looked up to the wall at the top of the companionway, where Rochester stowed his pistol, musket, and dress sword on hooks. Now, Forsythe's rifle hung there, too. Alongside it was the *taiaha*—a traditional quarterstaff—that Wiki had made, and a greenstone club, a prestigious *mere pounamu* Forsythe had looted from one of the Ngati Porou chiefs he had killed.

"If I was you, I'd steer bloody well wide of the *Peacock*," he said.

"The same thought occurred to me," said Wiki.

This dire conversation was interrupted by a ruckus out on deck as a boat arrived, and then Midshipman Keith scampered noisily down the companionway. He looked extremely chilled, his lanky form huddled in coats and scarves, though his face was burned red by the wind.

"Food!" he exclaimed, snuffing the air like a puppy.

They all looked at the door of the pantry, the domain of Stoker, the *Swallow*'s gem of a steward, who could be relied on to do something about it. When he emerged, however, Stoker said reprovingly, "Mr. Keith, I thought you was messing on the *Porpoise* while the survey is a-going along."

"I was," the lad admitted. He folded himself onto the larboard bench at Rochester's left hand, cast off about a dozen garments, and helped himself to coffee.

"So, if I asked you," went on the steward severely, "would you persist in trying to give us all the strong impression that you haven't eaten supper already?"

"You greedy dog!" George exclaimed, without waiting for whatever answer Constant Keith might fabricate. "And you've been drinking too—admit it! You smell of claret, you wicked young man!"

"Claret?" said Forsythe alertly. "On the *Porpoise*? But it ain't even Saturday."

"All the surveying boats made for the *Porpoise* in the squall, and now they're making merry in both the foc'sle and the cabin. In fact," Keith guilelessly went on, "some of 'em are getting most awful rotten drunk." Then his face brightened as Stoker, having relented, came in with a bowl of lobscouse he'd found, and slapped it down on the table in front of him.

Forsythe said, "So where the hell is Ringgold?"

"In charge of the *Sea Gull*," said Wiki, Keith's mouth being too full to answer.

"What the hell is he doin' there?"

"I was as surprised as you when I found it out."

"How long has this been goin' on?"

Wiki calculated. Today was Tuesday, so he said, "Four days at least. On Saturday I arrived down the river from El Carmen to find that the fleet had arrived, the citizens were all in a panic about it, and the *Sea Gull* was floundering through the shoals in the descending dark. She shot up a blue rocket, and I yelled out for a boat, but their only response was to try to shoot me dead. It was after I finally persuaded them I belonged to the *Swallow* that I learned Captain Ringgold was in command. And then he accused me of being a spy," he concluded rather moodily.

Forsythe snorted, but Constant Keith looked impressed. The lad confided, "I was on board the *Vin* when that blue light went up."

"So why didn't Captain Wilkes do something about it?" Wiki demanded.

"But he did! The whole ship got into a commotion, with orders flying everywhere, because the officers jumped to the conclusion that the natives were attacking. We soon had five boats full of men and cutlasses pulling stoutly for the river, but then Captain Wilkes went after us in the *Flying Fish*, and called us all back. In a few minutes we were again on board the *Vin*, all safe and unstained with blood."

"Called the boats back?" Wiki echoed, astonished.

"And lucky we were, as the night was dark, and we didn't know the way through the breakers. We could've been lost with a vengeance."

"But wasn't Captain Wilkes worried about the poor stranded *Sea Gull*?"

Midshipman Keith thought about it, his brow wrinkled as he chewed, and then shook his head. "I guess he realized she wasn't being attacked. And then the next day was Sunday, so we got divine services instead of the chance to check."

"So what have you been doing since then?"

"Surveying," said the midshipman importantly. "Yesterday I went into the river on the *Flying Fish*, and today I had command of the *Vin*'s smallest cutter, charged with the job of ascertaining the rise and fall of the tide. I had a tedious and uncomfortable time of it, too—was nearly carried out to sea by the current once, and you've no idea how perplexed and worried I felt. How I wished I was exploring on shore instead! While I was on the *Flying Fish*, I saw two gauchos on the headland," he went on in reverent tones.

"Gauchos?" Wiki was puzzled, because Bernantio and his friends had been the only gauchos he had seen on the headland the day before, and they had left very early.

"Aye, yesterday, before noon—two horsemen on the hilltop by the flagstaff. They dashed across the uplands, taking turns to whirl some kind of lariat about their heads. What a dramatic and primitive scene they made with their ponchos flying out behind them, horses and riders in clear relief against the sky! Oh, but they were wild and picturesque as they galloped back and forth! How I wished for the gift of an artist, to sketch their graceful costume, and their Arab-looking steeds!"

Wiki and George stared at each other in abrupt realization, and then simultaneously hid their faces in their coffee mugs. Forsythe, however, hadn't even been listening. After brooding a moment with his lips pursing in and out, he left the table and headed off up the stairs, muttering something about paying a call on the *Porpoise* to see what was a-going on. Then he disappeared, yelling out for the crew of the cutter.

No sooner had the boat cleared away than the bell by the wheel, on the quarterdeck above their heads, rang out eight times, echoing down the skylight.

Wiki said, "Whose watch is it?"

Instead of answering, Rochester said, "The bo'sun took the second dogwatch."

The boatswain was one of the tradesmen of the ship, who kept the same hours as artisans on shore. It was eight in the evening, the start of the first four-hour watch of the night, and he would be seeking his warm berth. Wiki remembered how cold Rochester had looked as he took the first dogwatch, and that young Keith had spent the day in the breakers, surveying. He finished his coffee, eased himself off the bench, and stood up, saying, "I'll take the deck."

When he arrived at the top of the companionway he realized why the sounds of the bell had seemed so loud. The weather was now dead calm as well as cold, so the brig was lying in a pool of strange silence with just the lap of water against her hull to punctuate her slow roll. The atmosphere, he thought, was ominous. He checked the man at the helm, who was keeping the *Swallow* up to her anchors, and then the lookout on the forecastle-head, before climbing up to the main topgallant crosstrees.

There, Wiki passed an arm around the tie of the halyards to steady himself as he scanned the expanse of ocean all around. The sea was glowing with phosphorescence, gleaming eerily. The five other ships of the discovery fleet—the full-rigged sloops *Vincennes* and *Peacock*, the small schooners *Sea Gull* and *Flying Fish*, and the gun brig *Porpoise*—were well spread out, sitting still on the glowing water with their masts upright. Forsythe's cutter was energetically pulling for the gun brig, the closest to the shore. As Keith had intimated, many small boats were clustered about her. The *Trojan* was nowhere to be seen; even the red glow of her tryworks fires had disappeared.

The brigantine *Osprey* was three miles to the southeast of the anchored fleet, lying at a standstill even though she was under full sail. She had been moving recently, evidently making for the *Swallow*, because her fading phosphorescent wake was slanted in this direction, but now she looked like a paper silhouette. There was still no sign of the fog Forsythe had so confidently predicted. Vivid lightning played over the land beyond the estuary, bringing fleeting glimpses of piled, angry clouds. Wiki listened intently, but there was no thunder to be heard. The only sounds that reached him were the slosh of water against the hull, and the distant whisper of surf.

The temperature was dropping further, and he shivered. However, just as he was about to head down to deck to fetch his poncho, he saw a tiny splash of white halfway between the ships and the beach. He wondered what it was.

It was gone. He kept on staring, afraid to blink in case he missed it. Then he glimpsed it again—another white flicker. He called down for a spyglass.

Tana, who was one of the two Samoan seamen, brought it up, his expression inquisitive, and waited while Wiki aimed the telescope and fiddled with the lens. A flick of foam—several flicks at once—and Wiki abruptly realized it was water kicked up by oars. A few more seconds, and the image came clearly into focus—a whaleboat pulling through the eerily phosphorescent night, coming out from the beach. Instead of heading for the *Porpoise*, the closest ship, it was unmistakably steering south for the *Osprey*, though she was the farthest away.

Wiki dropped down a backstay to the deck, and called down to the saloon through the skylight. George Rochester came up at once, followed by Constant Keith. He frowned as he listened, and then said, "From the shore?"

Wiki nodded.

"It's probably one of the expedition boats making for home after having been caught on the beach by the squall."

"That's what I thought, too. But he's steering for the *Osprey*, and not any of the ships of the fleet."

George Rochester paused meditatively, and then asked, "How often does your father call into this coast?"

"Never, as far as I know," replied Wiki, startled. "Salem traders traditionally take the Cape of Good Hope route. Why?"

"I was wondering if he has ever gone in for smuggling."

"How would *I* know?"

"Well, he's your *father*, old chap."

"Which is a good reason why I'd be the last to know," Wiki said tartly. "Anyway, what the devil would he smuggle into Patagonia?"

"Arms? There's always some kind of revolution brewing—or so they tell me."

George was right, Wiki thought, remembering his conversation with Manuel Bernantio, but objected, "What would he get in return? The Patagonians produce nothing but salt and hides!"

"Take a boat and find out."

Wiki blinked. "Why me? I'm on watch, remember."

"This young glutton can take the deck—he's got two suppers to work off. And don't you want to see your father?"

"Well, of course I do—but I thought tomorrow would be soon enough."

"But what if your father really *is* smuggling?"

Wiki wanted to laugh. He was saved by a shout from Tana, who was still in the main hamper: "Hey, the deck, cap'n sir, the *Vin*'s lowering a boat!"

"They've raised the whaleboat, too, and want to know what the devil's afoot," George decided. "Come on, old chap, get a move on! Your father's reputation could be at stake!"

"Oh, for God's sake," said Wiki, and did laugh, but he left.

Because the *Swallow* was closest to the *Osprey*, Wiki arrived alongside his father's brigantine well ahead of the other two boats. The *Osprey* still had all sail set on her two tall masts, but was making no way at all, merely drifting on the northeast current, so he had no trouble snatching a dangling rope and bringing his boat to a standstill. Then he walked up the side of the ship with the aid of the rope, and climbed over the gangway.

Just about the entire crew of the brigantine was on deck, and Captain Coffin was waiting eagerly by the rail. A tall, lean, handsome Yankee with a head of thick, dark, gray-flecked hair, he normally had the world-weary look of a lizard, because a scar on the left side of his face had weakened one eyelid so that it habitually hung at half-mast. At this moment, however, even the half-hidden eye gleamed with animation, and Mr. Seward, standing at his shoulder, looked equally eager.

Captain Coffin exclaimed, "Have you come to get 'em?"

Wiki surveyed his father for a long moment with his hands propped on his belt, but learned nothing from his expression. Finally he confessed, "I've not a notion what you're talking about."

"The carpenters, Wiki! You've come to take the carpenters away?"

Wiki shook his head.

"What the devil have you come for, then? And what the hell have you done to your hair?"

Wounded, Wiki said, "I thought you always wanted me to get it cut."

"Well, I've now decided I didn't."

Wiki sighed, and said, "You do know there's a boat heading this way from shore?"

"Of course we know. We've been watching it. My guess is that one of the expedition boats strayed too far up the Río Negro, and is late coming home."

"So why is he steering for you? There's a boat from the *Vin* on the way, too. Aren't you worried about that?"

"Why the devil should I be?"

"George wondered if you were going in for some smuggling."

"The slanderous young scoundrel!"

Mr. Seward's face went quite blank, and then his lips twitched and he turned hastily away. At the same time, Wiki could have sworn he heard a muffled giggle. When he looked around it was to see that the brigantine's six cadets were openly listening, broad grins on their ruddy round faces. He winked, because not only did he like them but they had labored earnestly at the oars of the boat when he'd steered it into the river the day before, and one of them openly laughed.

The look Wiki's father cast at the boys, by contrast, was ferocious in the extreme. "Mister," he shouted to Mr. Seward. "Send these young rascals aloft to keep lookout—and if you hear 'em laying bets on which boat gets here first, report 'em in the log!"

That delivered, he jerked his head at Wiki and turned for the door in the break of the poop that led to the captain's cabin. Wiki followed with alacrity, for not only was his father's coffee guaranteed to be good but he had some questions to ask.

Beyond the door lay a short flight of steps—shorter than the companionway on the *Swallow*, because the house was half-set into the deck. These led to a corridor with carved mahogany double doors on the starboard side, which opened into a spacious cabin. This served as both sitting room and saloon, as well as the place where his father slept, a curtained berth being tucked into the niche of the starboard quarter. As Captain Coffin liked to say, it was the heart of the ship.

It was also evidence of his eccentricity, because the horseshoe-shaped settee under the flamboyant expanse of tiered stern windows was upholstered in green on the starboard side, and red to port. Wiki chose a green cushion, and then observed, "I heard you marched on board the *Vin* after they ran afoul of you in Rio, and demanded a carpentering gang. Are those the same carpenters you're so anxious to be quit of?"

"Stupidest thing I've ever done," Captain Coffin said moodily, sitting on the red side of the settee, on the far side of an egg-shaped table that was just knee-high, and set in the sofa's curve. "Wilkes blustered, but then agreed," he went on, adding darkly, "With a proviso."

"That you keep pace with the fleet?"

"That, too."

"There was something else?"

Captain Coffin pointed a long finger at the floor, and said, "Down there—in my private hold, goddamn it—sits the entire damn collection of specimens gathered by those maniac squirrels you call *scientifics* ever since the damn voyage began."

"The *whole* collection?"

"The complete damn lot! Eighty boxes, barrels, half barrels, and bundles, holding samples of natural history, botany, and mineralogy collected from Madeira, St. Jago, the Cape Verde Islands, and Rio—which will be supplemented by whatever the squirrels collect on the Río Negro before I'm allowed to leave."

"For Boston?"

"For Philadelphia—for the Peale museum."

"Peale?" Wiki lifted a brow, realizing that the Peale family had more to do with the exploring expedition than he'd realized.

"Aye. They're addressed to Franklin Peale. They were bound, sealed, and nailed shut under the supervision of a commissioned officer. I'm not allowed to open them, under pain of death—and they stink the whole ship out!"

"But you are being well paid for the inconvenience," Wiki guessed with a grin.

"I had to shift my personal trade goods into the steerage!"

"Displacing coffee—which you sold to Captain Wilkes for the use of the fleet," Wiki further deduced, remembering the good coffee on the *Sea Gull.*

"Exactly," Captain Coffin confirmed complacently. "And I also passed some on to Captain Stackpole—exchanged a few sacks for a couple of barrels of oil, which will fetch a dollar per gallon in the market, he told me."

Wiki said quickly, "You've been gamming with Captain Stackpole?"

"I'm always happy to *gam,* as you whalemen call it, and so I paid a call on board his ship while he was beating out of this godforsaken place. And a foul sight it was," Captain Coffin added. "I'd never imagined a whaleship as the lowest levels of hell, but the *Trojan* sure looked it—and stank like it, too."

"Did he tell you if he'd seen Captain Wilkes?"

"All he told me is that he's anxious to head south—after more whales, I expect. He must be five miles or more out to sea by now." Captain Coffin lifted his voice, crying, "Where's that damn coffee, steward?"

An answering shout came not from the pantry, but from above as one of the boats arrived. Quickly, Wiki followed his father to deck, to find it was the strange whaleboat that had come out from shore. When he looked over the gangway rail the man at the steering oar was holding on to a boat fall.

Benjamin Harden. The ex-river pilot looked up at him with his face tipped back so that the light from the cresset lantern glinted on his reddish beard.

Wiki exclaimed, "What are *you* doing here?"

Captain Coffin said curiously, "Do you know this man?"

Wiki didn't answer, having abruptly realized that the five oarsmen were familiar, too. They were all deeply weathered, middle-aged, hard-bitten sailors, scarred by past encounters with angry bull seals; some of the fists clenched on the handles of the oars were missing fingers.

He said to them, "Aren't you the sealers we rescued from Shark Island?"

Silence. All five looked away, their expressions sullen. Wiki remembered their reputation for inciting mutiny on previous ships, and felt another twinge of uneasiness. Frowning deeply, he said to Harden, "What are you doing with *them* as your boat's crew?"

"Captain Wilkes's orders," Harden said, his tone casual. Without bothering with further explanation he jumped up to deck, where he advanced on Captain Coffin with his hand held out. "Benjamin Harden, junior, at your service, sir," he heartily declaimed. "Originally from Providence, Rhode Island, now with the exploring expedition."

"Is that so?" said Captain Coffin. He was glancing from Harden to Wiki and back, and frowning. Like Ringgold earlier, he stepped back instead of shaking hands.

Harden didn't answer this rhetorical question, because at that moment the boat from the *Vincennes* arrived. The red-cheeked midshipman in charge of this was very junior, but his tone was carefully gruff and officious as he demanded of Captain Coffin, "Is all well here, sir?"

"Of course," said Wiki's father, very surprised. "Why shouldn't it be?"

"There's rumors flying round of a drunken frolic in the fleet. Captain Wilkes thought it might be on board of you, sir, and so he sent me to investigate."

"Me?" Captain Coffin exclaimed. "That's infamous, by God! An insult of the grossest kind! Do you see any drunken frolicking here?"

"That I do not, sir," said the young midshipman, not contrite at all.

"I should bloody well think not!"

"You must understand that we had our reasons, sir. When we raised a boat pulling for the *Osprey,* suspicions were voiced that it was to join some kind of jollification."

"I have as little idea why this man has called on me as you do!"

"Carpenters, sir," interrupted Benjamin Harden, exhibiting the same easy confidence Wiki had noticed back by the Río Negro. "That's what we've come for. The two carpenters. To take them back to the *Vincennes,*" he added.

"Carpenters? You've come to take those string-shanked sogers away?" Captain Coffin cried. "Then, by God, you shall have them!" he exclaimed, and hollered for his mate. "Mister, do me the favor of rousing Boyd and Folger, and clearing them and their chests out of our foc'sle!"

Wiki exclaimed, "Captain Wilkes sent *Boyd and Folger* to do the carpentering?"

"Exactly," said his father impatiently. "What of it?"

Boyd and Folger were two more of the mutinous sealers they had rescued at Shark Island, but Wiki didn't wait to explain. Instead, he hurriedly excused himself, jumped down into the *Swallow* boat, and headed back to the brig.

When he arrived, Constant Keith was on watch, red-nosed in the reflected light of the cresset burning in the starboard mainmast shrouds, and huddled into his jacket. To Wiki's surprise, Forsythe was with him, perfectly sober and extremely bad-tempered. As the lieutenant revealed, Wilkes's enraged shouts had come echoing from the *Porpoise* just as the cutter was about to make contact with the gun brig.

While the boat with the junior officer had been checking the *Osprey*, the commodore himself had boarded the *Porpoise*, and discovered the illicit revelry. Naturally, the instant Forsythe had realized what the thunder and fury was all about, the cutter had beaten a diplomatic retreat.

"He was carrying on like a bloody madman," Forsythe went on, sounding scandalized. "I've never in my life heard such unhandsome language. You was bloody lucky you left the *Porpoise* when you did," he informed young Keith, "or you'd be triced up in the rigging with the rest."

"Who was there at the spree?" Wiki asked Keith.

"Just about all the men who'd been surveying in the boats."

"Oh dear, oh dear," said Wiki. "Anyone in charge?"

"Lieutenant Craven."

My God, Wiki thought. He wondered what Captain Wilkes would do about it. While drunkenness was a flogging offense, he thought that surely even the impetuous commodore would hesitate to string his flag lieutenant to the grating.

Then he asked, "Was there any excuse for this party, or did it just happen out of the blue?"

"Harden told them that H.M.S. *Beagle* had already surveyed the shoals, and so they were drowning their sorrows while they enjoyed a first-rate grumble about the waste of energy and effort."

So Harden had spared no time in making trouble in the fleet, Wiki mused, and felt more uneasy than ever. He said, "That Harden worries me badly."

Forsythe asked, "Why?"

"Do you remember the time we rescued that gang of sealers whose ship was sinking, and carried them on the *Swallow* to the *Vin*?"

"Very well indeed," said Keith happily. "Just as I remember their foul plot to take over the brig."

"Take the *Swallow*?" Forsythe exclaimed. "This is the first I've heard of this!"

"One of our men came to Captain Rochester, and revealed that our passengers were plotting to seize the ship."

"Why didn't you report it?"

"Because we *foiled* them, Mr. Forsythe—the pirating never happened! We tricked them into collecting together in the foc'sle, and then we nailed up the hatch, and we didn't allow them to stumble out until we were up with the *Vin*."

Forsythe's eyebrows shot up. "So you didn't tell Wilkes—but weren't you worried the string-shanked buggers would have the sauce to complain?"

"Never even thought of it," Keith confessed. "And they didn't, anyway—which *proves* that their intentions were foul, sir."

"The point of this," interrupted Wiki, losing patience, "is that they've been spread about the fleet ever since Captain Wilkes shipped them, which meant they couldn't plot trouble together. However, they are now back in a group—with Harden at their head. A boat called at the *Osprey* while I was there—with Harden in charge, and five of the sealers as oarsmen. It turned out he'd come to pick up Boyd and Folger—so he's got seven, all in one boat!"

Forsythe said thoughtfully, "What the hell for, I wonder?"

"Very good question," said Wiki. He looked around to make sure they weren't overheard, and then said, "According to the gauchos, after Harden jumped ship in Buenos Aires, he joined the de Rosas army in the war against Brazil. Not long after that, he incited mutiny, starting a riot in which two men were killed, for which he was brutally flogged. He came to the Río Negro, where he has been organizing a revolution to topple General de Rosas, as he now regards him as his mortal enemy."

"Then why the hell did he join the expedition?" Forsythe demanded. "If he's got such a grand mission for revolution, why would he want to leave the Río Negro?"

Wiki hesitated, because this was a very good point. However, he said, "Personally, I'd like to know why he's deliberately gathered up the sealers—who also have a reputation for mutiny."

"And you're planning to talk to Wilkes about this Harden and the sealers?"

"I am," Wiki admitted.

"Then you have to be bloody crazy," Forsythe said flatly. "If I was you, I'd keep my mouth buttoned up tight on the subject, because you've got enough on your plate already, what with that bloody ridiculous theory that the killer stayed behind to steal the deed of sale, even though the bloody schooner was gone. Don't you realize what a load of trouble you're in? Not only did you let yourself be requisitioned by a civilian—and a stinking spouterman, at that!—but I hear that Ringgold's reported you for disobeying orders. And I'd rig up a lot more proper than you was this afternoon, too. Try to look less like a bloody disgrace."

"I'm going to rig out in my absolute best," Wiki obediently assured him.

"And do something about your goddamned hair, too."

"Aye, sir," said Wiki, thinking that Forsythe sounded more like a proper first lieutenant with every word he uttered.

Eleven

January 30, 1839

It was dawn on the brig *Swallow,* and Wiki was sitting cross-legged on the forecastle deck while his Polynesian seaman friend Sua hunkered down behind him. The big Samoan was plying Wiki's ornately carved whalebone comb, straightening out his curls until he had them trapped in one massive hand, ready to draw the ends through a small wooden ring—a tricky job, because Wiki's hair was too short to be easily passed through the hole. The way it tugged and snagged, it felt to Wiki, who was wincing and grunting, as if Sua were doing it one strand at a time.

"*Kaua e tangi,*" soothed Sua in Maori, adding in English, "Poor baby, don't cry. I thought you was a brave and stalwart warrior."

Wiki winced again, and muttered, "It's the Yankee half that's hurting."

Tana, who was leaning on the windlass, watching, laughed.

Wiki said, "What would you say if I told you that there is a scientific with the expedition who reckons that the Pacific was settled by people from Malaya?"

Having a native interest in maps and charts, Tana and Sua had an exact idea of the whereabouts of Malaya. Tana said, "Where did he get that strange idea?"

"He tried to tell me that those Malays sailed from the west to the east, settling the islands one after another. Fiji and Samoa came first, and after that they kept on eastward, spreading out as they went, and are the ancestors of all the Pasifika people."

Sua said in a tone of utter disgust, "*Malays? Our ancestors?*"

Tana laughed again. "Samoans have *always* been in Samoa," he said.

Surprised, Wiki turned his head, even though it hurt when Sua yanked back. "You Samoans don't have traditions of voyaging ancestors?"

"Nope. The great god Tagaloa lived all alone in an empty expanse until a rock jumped up out of nothingness, and he split up this rock into all different kinds of rock, and made the earth and the sea, water, and the sky with its stars and clouds. He made night and day, and created islands for the people. That's where we've lived ever since. Except," Tana added, "for sailing out to conquer. If there were any voyagers at all, they must have *come* from Samoa. They didn't *go* there."

"We have voyager ancestors," said Wiki, adding very firmly, "But they came to New Zealand from the *east*, and definitely not Samoa."

"But this fellow says you're wrong, that Samoans are your ancestors, and he's a scientific, and so he must be right," Sua jocularly decided. He stood up, the job of fixing Wiki's hair finished. "You should show us proper respect," he advised.

"That's right," said Tana, grinning more widely than ever.

Wiki rose to his feet, too, feeling quite light-headed, his hair tightly confined in the little topknot, and jabbed into place with the comb. He also felt miffed, because his Samoan friends had refused to take his concerns seriously, and so he stalked off after the briefest of thanks, while they enjoyed another laugh behind his back.

Wiki's mood was shared by just about everyone else on board the *Swallow*. The rest of the sailors, who were perched around on spare spars and the topgallant foredeck, were wearing thoroughly disgruntled expressions. It was because of today's breakfast, which had turned out to be different from the delicious repast they had so confidently expected. The plain fact of the matter was that the crew of the brig had become spoiled by Robert Festin's cooking. The lobscouse last night had been relished by all, and while they had eaten greedily, they had hoped—indeed, assumed—that there would be enough of it to be served up for breakfast, as well.

Instead, however, Festin had discovered the *Swallow*'s keg of sauerkraut. Placed on board in Norfolk, Virginia, when the brig had been provisioned for the long voyage, the sauerkraut had been intended as a healthy preventive of scurvy, the scourge of seamen far out at sea. Instead, it had been stealthily hidden in the darkest corner of the hold, and moved to an even more secret place whenever a stray ray of daylight threatened to reveal its presence. When Festin had been overhauling some bags of flour, however, he had come across the keg, and now the unmistakable stench of warm pickled cabbage wafted all about the decks.

The sailors, Wiki observed, were staring at their untouched tin plates and nibbling hard bread. By their expressions, they could all think of a better place to put the sauerkraut than within their vitals, but throwing food overboard was a flogging offense, and Forsythe, who was in charge of the deck, was in a flogging mood, having brooded all night about missing out on a spree.

When Wiki descended to the saloon, it was to find a big bowl of sauerkraut in the middle of the table, along with a plate of ship's hard bread. This was just as anticipated, the crew being served exactly the same as their captain and officers. This was something that Rochester was able to ensure, because he paid for much of the ship's provisioning out of his personal funds—though he was unlikely to shell out for pickled cabbage.

Wiki sat down on his bench at the bottom of the table, poured himself a mug of coffee, and contemplated the repast. George Rochester was staring at the basin just as thoughtfully, his plate still empty before him.

He looked up and said, "How are the men taking it?"

"Badly," said Wiki.

Stoker came into the saloon, and said with an eloquent sniff, "The great Captain Cook set great store by sauerkraut, sir."

As the aftergang was already aware, the steward was a great admirer of the famous explorer. Rochester asked, "So how did Cook get his men to eat it?"

"Ah, sir, he was a crafty cove, a master who knew his people well. Captain Cook decreed that sauerkraut should be a privilege reserved for the cabin table alone, and his officers cooperated by eating it with relish. Within a week the people was threatening mutiny if they could not have their regular ration, too."

"I see," said George, taking the hint. With a great sigh, he scooped a couple of spoonsful onto his plate. While he was stirring it around with his fork, building up courage, Midshipman Keith arrived with a crash on the larboard bench.

He looked brightly at the basin of sauerkraut, and said, "What's it like, sir?"

Rochester silently filled his mouth. It was impossible to tell from his expression what he thought. Keith watched him with his head on one side, rather resembling a robin, and then shrugged and helped himself.

There was perfect silence as the young man chewed. Then he swallowed, smiled widely, revealing several yellow shreds stuck in his teeth, and said, "It's good!"

Wiki still felt suspicious. Constant Keith ate anything that didn't have to be nailed down first, and kept hard bread under his pillow. However, he took a forkful—and it *was* good, the taste a vast improvement on its appearance. Miraculously, there was preserved apple in it, and a faint tang of molasses, along with a dash of aromatic vinegar, and a hint of carraway. Festin, as usual, had not let them down.

It was then that they heard a warning cry from aloft, and a thump as a boat touched the side of the brig. Rochester put down his fork, but before he had a chance to get to the companionway their visitor came down the stairs without waiting for an invitation. Buttoned boots appeared in the rectangle of light at the top of the companionway, followed by short legs in stockings and tight breeches, and then a stout body, surmounted by a flushed, smug face.

Rochester leaned back in his chair. "Lawrence J. Smith," he stated without a smile. "To what do we owe the pleasure?"

"I bear a message from Captain Wilkes," Smith pronounced. He rubbed his hands together, beaming, and said, "So I thought I would join you for breakfast."

It was then that he looked at the table. Never had Wiki seen a man's face fall so fast. Lieutenant Smith exclaimed, *"Sauerkraut?"*

"It's actually quite—" Midshipman Keith blurted out, but subsided with a squeak as George kicked him under the table.

Smith hadn't even noticed. Instead, he expostulated, "But pickled cabbage is not supposed to be served to the officers! Sauerkraut should be reserved for the men—to preserve their health, and to—to keep their internal systems in order."

"Like the great Captain Cook, we thought we should lead by example," said George blandly. "You'll have some?"

"I don't think so, thank you." The lieutenant sat down, however, and reached for a mug and the coffeepot. Then he called out for the steward and demanded cake, but to no avail, as Stoker expressionlessly denied having any on board, before obdurately heading back into his pantry.

"This is ridiculous," Smith complained. "According to Captain Wilkes's *strict* instructions, every captain is to extend the *fullest* hospitality to the officers of the other ships of the expedition fleet. He considers it absolutely necessary that every man should feel as much at home on another vessel as he would on his own. The intention is to create and encourage a feeling of harmony in the squadron, as if it were comprised of just a single crew instead of several—but I assure you that on the other ships *no* officer would be offered food that was intended for the common men."

George paused to make sure the pompous little prawn had finished, and then said, "You have a message?"

"Captain Wilkes asked me to remind Wiremu to arrive on time, and he wants to see you, too."

Wiremu. Wiki winced. He had first encountered this pretentious character at the age of twelve, just after his father had carried him to Salem. Lawrence J. Smith had called at the house, as he regarded himself as one of Captain Coffin's friends, and upon being introduced to Wiki, whom he regarded as interestingly exotic, had taken it upon himself to ask many offensively personal questions. Finding out that the Maori version of Wiki's American name, William, was Wiremu, he had insisted on employing it ever since, much to Wiki's irritation.

Now, as usual, Wiki did his best to ignore it. It was Rochester who answered, saying, "Captain Wilkes wants to see me? But why?"

"He wishes to extend felicitations." Smith didn't offer congratulations himself, Wiki noticed. Instead, after delicately sipping fragrant coffee, he became quite animated, saying, "Isn't it wonderful how we find valuable additions to our complement on the most farflung and desolate shores?"

George blinked. "I beg your pardon?"

"Those sealers I rescued at Shark Island, for instance."

"As I remember," George said coldly, "I was the one who rescued them from their sinking ship, and you were the one who ordered me to carry them to the fleet—and that in spite of my strongest protests, which were confirmed when they gave me a great deal of trouble on passage. I quite honestly did not consider them fit recruits for the expedition."

"But they are seamen of vast experience! They will be of inestimable benefit when we sail in high southern latitudes," Smith assured him with a superior air, before lapsing into reflection again. "And then there was that truly outstanding cook, Festin—what a pity he left to get married! And now there is this pilot," he added.

"You mean Harden?"

"Of course I mean the unfortunate Harden!"

Wiki exclaimed, "I'd like to know why he's been given five of the sealers as his boat's crew! When I saw him last night, he was taking on two more—a total of seven! I thought they were supposed to be spread about the fleet?"

"So they were—but now that the last leg of the passage to Cape Horn is nigh, it is only logical that these experts should be assembled as a group. When I talked this over with Captain Wilkes, we were in perfect agreement. And the unfortunate Harden has been given a boat, so that he can lend his expertise to the survey."

George interrupted, "Why did you call him unfortunate?"

"Because it is the appropriate word! General de Rosas treated him with infamous barbarity! Not only did the de Rosas army sweep him out of prison, where he had most unjustly been incarcerated for desertion from his ship, but over the next two years they stationed him at every godforsaken post that exists between Buenos Aires and the Río Negro."

Wiki stared at him, his mug of coffee halted halfway to his lips. Despite what he had said to Forsythe and Keith, he had harbored the hope that what Bernantio had told him about Harden's mutinous and murderous past was mere gossip. At this confirmation that Harden had definitely been in the de Rosas army, he was struck with foreboding again.

"In particular," Lieutenant Smith gushed on unheedingly, "he was assigned to the Bahía Blanca—a most desolate terrain, where the coast is choked with fetid salt marshes, and plagued with mosquitoes and similar ugly reptiles. According to Harden, the garrison there was squalid indeed, manned almost entirely by a ragged mob of the rascally Argentinian gypsies they call *gauchos*—common desperadoes! He eventually escaped, to eke out a living on the Río Negro—but luckily he has a naturally retentive mind for what he viewed while on patrol."

"Why, what did he see?" Rochester asked.

"Amazing curiosities! Gigantic bones embedded in a cliff—bones of creatures virtually unknown to modern science! Great claws, an immense skull, a giant carapace turned entirely to stone!"

This, for Wiki, brought back gossip he had heard in South American ports nearly five years before. While H.M.S. *Beagle* had been charting this coast, there had been a lot of talk about Charles Darwin, the ship's young English naturalist; he was said to have hacked monstrous stone bones out of the cliffs of Bahía Blanca with a little geologist's hammer. The locals had thought him quite mad.

Wiki had had no trouble believing the stories of what Darwin had found, because he'd seen huge bird bones in New Zealand, and heard many stories about the giant birds, called *moa*, too. As a child, he had met old men who claimed to have seen *moa* striding through the forest with their heads in the tops of the trees.

"Fossils?" he said now, summoning the word from memory.

"Fossils," confirmed Smith with an approving little smile. "Tusks, jaws, and skulls, all immense beyond imagination! They are embedded in banks of ancient seashells even though the cliffs are beyond the reach of the sea, so obviously are the remains of animals that were too big to be taken on board Noah's Ark, and accordingly were left to perish in the flood. Imagine, physical proof of a Bible story!"

"Good heavens," said Wiki without expression. He was amazed that anyone who called himself a scientist could be so blinkered. The giant *moa* had disappeared because of relentless hunting and the loss of their forests through fire, and even the missionaries didn't try to pretend that they'd been destroyed by a biblical flood.

"The scientifics listen to his lively descriptions with great attention, and take many notes. Well—" Smith broke off, and groped around in his vest. After consulting a gold Harland watch that was almost as massive as the fossils he'd been describing, he declared, "Time rushes on, and I must away. Don't be late, Wiremu," he warned Wiki, and then, to everyone's huge relief, he disappeared up the stairs.

"Noah's Ark?" said Rochester. "In *South America*? What next?" he asked rhetorically as he stood up from the table. Then, with a great sigh, he went into his cabin to get rigged up for the interview with Wilkes.

The sea was still calm, and the air was even colder. Forsythe's fog hadn't put in an appearance, and so the pull to the flagship was straightforward, but they were both quite frozen by the time they had reached the gangway of the *Vincennes*.

The boatswain's mate shrilled his call more urgently than usual, presumably in recognition of George's elevated status, but the new lieutenant's returning salute was quite remarkably stiff, because of the chilled state of his limbs. Both he and Wiki were slapping their hands together to get the circulation going as they arrived at the portico of the big afterhouse.

The corporal on duty looked as cold as they felt, and seemed relieved to lead the way along the passage to the double doors of the chartroom, and enjoy a little transitory warmth. Instead of simply knocking and then standing aside to let them through, as usual, he went inside to announce their arrival, closing the doors behind him, while they waited, puzzled. There was the sound of muttering, and then the doors opened again.

The marine recited in a monotone, "Captain Wilkes's compliments, Mr. Coffin, and would you mind waiting out on deck until he has finished with Captain Rochester."

"Certainly," said Wiki, surprised, because he had thought they would make a joint report of Captain Stackpole's complaint of theft and piracy of the schooner he had bought from the brig *Athenian*, along with other events up the Río Negro.

Obviously, George thought this was as ominous as he did, because his friend's shoulders were squared as he went in. However, his voice was as hearty as usual. Wiki heard him say, "Uncommon strange weather we've been having of late, don't you think, sir? Young Keith reckons the odd conditions are caused by a gigantic iceberg lurking somewhere out there. Do you suspect there's a chance he's right, sir, and we ought to keep a sharp lookout when we proceed on our voyage?"

The doors shut, and the reply was unintelligible. Wiki went out on deck to watch seamen being kept hard at work by hectoring boatswain's mates, alternately folding his arms and putting his hands in his pockets to try to keep warm. A moment later, to his surprise, he saw his father come alongside in a boat rowed by his six cadets and steered by Mr. Seward, so headed over to the gangway to meet them.

Captain Coffin led the procession on board, leaving the boat bobbing at the end of a rope. The boys lined up and grinned at Wiki, who winked at them, just as he had the night before. He noticed again that one of them had a black eye and bruised jaw, and remembered Mr. Seward's strong, bony handshake. The first mate looked stern enough as he stood with his thumbs tucked into his wide leather belt and supervised his string of boys, and it was easy to imagine him backing up his orders with his fist. However, the lad didn't look too badly damaged, seeming as enchanted as his comrades at being on board the great seven-hundred-ton ship.

Captain Coffin was dressed in the same kind of broadcloth as Wiki himself, and was sporting a silk top hat. However, this respectable and reticent appearance was rather marred by the gold-embroidered silk brocade vest that glinted rakishly beneath his sober jacket. When he nodded at Wiki, his half-closed eye held a glint of warmth, but his tone was matter-of-fact. "Well, that's a damn sight tidier, if more than a little primitive," he said, evidently in mixed approval of the topknot.

"I thank you," said Wiki.

"Granted," said his father, just as dryly, and strode off for the portico of the afterhouse, where he engaged in some sort of conversation with the corporal on sentry duty. Judging by the echoes Wiki overheard, he was demanding an interview with Captain Wilkes, and was highly annoyed at being informed that Captain Wilkes was busy.

While Wiki was wondering what this was all about, the boatswain of the *Vincennes* swaggered up, a splendid figure in a tailcoat and tall hat, his silver call dangling from the finely braided and intricately knotted lanyard that hung about his neck. This minor god was the terrifying character in charge of the open decks and lofty rigging of this entire great ship, infamous for his stentorian voice and the permanently infuriated color of his face, and the cadets' expressions became even more awed.

He stopped with his feet planted well apart and his rattan cane held in both hands behind his back. "And who, sir, might this be?" he asked Wiki, with a jerk of his chin toward Mr. Seward, whose lean face was as expressionless as ever.

Wiki performed introductions.

"And these young gentlemen?" the boatswain inquired, at the same time surveying the youthful line with the expression of someone who has found something unpleasant on the sole of his boot.

"Captain Coffin's cadets," Wiki supplied, while Mr. Seward inclined his head.

"Cadets?"

The boys nodded happily.

"And on what kind of Salem street," the boatswain inquired of Alf Seward, "does one find little laddies like these?"

The mate replied without a quiver, "They're the sons of rich and influential men who want them to become famous seafarers, but don't want them to go into the navy."

"Good Lord," said the boatswain, looking greatly taken aback. "Not the navy?"

"Not the navy," the first mate of the *Osprey* affirmed. "They go to common school and learn navigation and how to keep books, and then at the age of fourteen they head off to do an apprenticeship in some counting house. After a year of that, the most promising lads are sent to sea with a China-trade shipmaster of good reputation to learn seamanship and the ways of trading in foreign ports."

A shipmaster of good reputation? Wiki was having a job not to laugh.

The boatswain said with an air of disbelief, "You're trying to tell me, Mr. Seward, that it's a system that actually *works*?"

"Not only does it work, but it turns boys into famous China traders and captains, without the hell and hassle of four years of being a dog's body of a midshipman." Alf Seward pointed at the lad with the black eye, and said, "It works so well that his grandfather was *secretary* of the navy for a while. And," he added casually, "his great-uncle carried the first live elephant to America."

"Elephant?"

"It was a female elephant, and the sailors taught it a taste for porter and how to steal bread out of people's pockets. After being put on exhibition it was sold for ten thousand dollars."

"Good Lord," said the boatswain rather faintly, and then rallied, demanding, "How long has this lot been on voyage?"

"Tell him," commanded Mr. Seward. This time the bony, imperious finger was leveled at a boy who stood at the forward end of the line.

"We sailed from Salem in November 1837, in a snowstorm," the apprentice readily recited. "Sailed around the Cape of Good Hope and took the Great Circle route to Hobart, then nor'ard through the Tasman Sea to shift gin and Yankee notions at the Bay of Islands. There, we traded our tobacco for sperm-whale teeth with the whaling masters in port—fetched the Fijis in April 1838, traded away our teeth and smoked a load of bêche-de-mer—made Whampoa in August; shifted our sea slugs for lacquerware—went to Manila, traded off our lacquerware, and loaded tortoiseshell for New York. In September we sailed for home, but were run afoul of in Rio—"

"So these boys have been a whole year at sea, huh?" the boatswain interrupted rather hastily, the fact that the *Osprey* had been so badly hammered by ships of the expedition fleet being more than a little embarrassing. "So maybe there's a chance," he mused aloud, "that they know where to find the keelson, and are maybe even cognizant that it ain't part of the bowsprit. What d'you reckon about that, Mr. Seward?"

Mr. Seward merely smiled.

Taking this as acquiescence, the boatswain set to testing the boys' seamanship, barking at one of them, "Do you know how to pass a nipper, boy? Clap on a jigger? Choke a luff? Snake the backstays? Fleet a purchase?"

"All of that," the lad replied brightly. "And to crown a crotch rope, too, sir!"

"You reckon you know all your hitches, bends, clinches, and splices?"

"Aye, sir!"

"Then do me the favor of naming a few."

"There's the clove hitch, the timber hitch, the Blackwall hitch, the rolling hitch, and the two half-hitches. And there's the sheet bend and the curricle bend; the inside clinch and the outside clinch; the carrick bend, the marline hitch, and the cackling, sir. And there's the—"

"Stop, stop!" cried the boatswain of the *Vincennes*, who was starting to laugh. "It looks like you've done a reasonable good job of coaching these scions of the high and mighty, Mr. Seward, and no doubt they're all keen to do a little skylarking while you wait for Captain Coffin's return. You would allow it, if I asked?" Discerning a nod, he turned back to the boys, saying, "Well, my lads, just remember to never let go one rope until you've clapped a good hold of another, and you should all do jes' fine."

No sooner had said lads swarmed up the weather main shrouds with a cheerful disregard of frozen hands, than a marine marched up to Wiki, saluted, and said, "Captain Wilkes begs the pleasure of your company, Mr. Coffin."

Wiki hadn't noticed that his father was included in the invitation, but as he passed through the portico Captain Coffin emerged from the shadows, and stepped up alongside, and they marched up the passage shoulder to shoulder. George Rochester looked his usual placid self as they passed him in the corridor, and his expression betrayed nothing, though his eyebrows rose high at the sight of Wiki's father.

Captain Wilkes, by contrast, looked dreadful. His long face was perfectly white, and it was obvious that he had an appalling headache, because his large eyes were full of pain and he kept on drawing his hand over his forehead. Dr. Fox was there, giving him a potion. When it was drunk he nodded, and left them alone with the commodore, going out with the tumbler in his hand.

"Captain Coffin," said Wilkes wearily. "To what do we owe the pleasure?"

Instead of answering, Captain Coffin looked around, chose a seat at one of the chart desks, set down his top hat, crossed his legs, and said amiably, "Strange weather we've been experiencing of late. Do you think it might be due to icebergs?"

"Captain, I'm sure you have come across sudden calms before."

"That phosphorescence surely did bring back memories," William Coffin benignly agreed. "Such as one time in the South China Sea when my ship was besieged by six-inch balls of blue fire. One of 'em rolled down the mainstay, jumped onto the chain cable, hissed like a cat, and exploded! My old bo'sun was standing with his foot on the chain holding a lantern, and I swear to you that every pane in that lantern sundered into a thousand pieces. As for him, his hair stood on end, and he was stuck to the spot for several moments, while the helmsman fell over sideways, as rigid as a statue—when we carried him to his berth, it was like heaving along a plank. He was still stiff as a board next morning, though alive, thank God. Which reminds me," he concluded, following some peculiar internal logic, "that those two carpenters you sent me are back on board the *Vin,* and glad we were to be rid of them, too. Now, sir, I've come to tell you I'll steer for home with no further delay."

There was dead silence. Captain Wilkes had his eyes tight shut. Then he opened them and said flatly, "Captain Coffin."

Captain Coffin waited, and when the other kept silent, said, "Captain Wilkes?"

"Do you have any *idea* what a strain I am under? What difficulties have presented themselves? Yesterday morning I gave orders for boats from all ships to carry out a survey of the mouth of the roadstead, and would have supervised the operation myself, but was laboring under one of the horrid headaches that afflict me more and more often as this voyage proceeds. However, the orders were explicit, and should have been easily followed. In the afternoon a squall blew up, but still I managed to hold a conference with the scientifics. After that, it was discovered that nearly all the boats had rendezvoused at the *Porpoise,* which was *not* in their program of duties—and when I finally investigated, I found that the officers had seized upon Captain Ringgold's absence to make merry on board his brig. Here I am at my *wits' end* to know how best to express my extreme displeasure, and now you *bother* me with this disinclination to follow our clear agreement."

Captain Coffin thought about it. Then he said judiciously, "Well, sir, you can scarcely place any blame on Captain Ringgold."

"Of course not! He was not even *there.* Unlike Lieutenant Craven—my *flag lieutenant,* for God's sake—who was the officer in charge of the *Vincennes* boats."

"He was on board the *Porpoise?*"

"He took part in the jollification!"

Captain Coffin's brows shot up and his left eye opened wide. "Good God," he said, with every evidence of sympathy for a fellow shipmaster in a pickle.

"So you agree that I have no choice but to suspend him? That his disregard of his proper duty and his failure to preserve discipline is too outrageous to be passed over? That he should be demoted, as an example to the rest?"

"Well, sir, I guess it depends on whether you have a suitable replacement."

"Luckily, I do. The next-oldest lieutenant is a loyal and reliable man. Indeed, I consider him a friend. He and I have shared many years of service, including a survey of the savannah, where he proved himself a loyal and reliable assistant, particularly during gravitational observations—we swung the pendulum together as midshipmen!"

"Then your problem is solved, sir," said Captain Coffin heartily.

"One problem among many!" Captain Wilkes's face hardened again. "So what the *hell* do you mean by taxing me further with this outrageous demand to forgo the terms of our agreement?"

Captain Coffin echoed, "Terms?"

"Aye, Captain—the agreement that you would take the rest of our specimens on board before departing for Philadelphia. Sir, you will wait until we're ready; you will not leave until I say!" Then, with startling suddenness, Captain Wilkes swerved round at Wiki, and demanded, "And what the hell is it that *you* want?"

Wiki only just stopped himself from jumping a foot with shock. Instead, he braced himself, and said, "I thought it was only proper to make a full accounting of my four days up the Río Negro—and ask your advice about how to proceed."

He had chosen his words well, he saw, because Captain Wilkes nodded, and said briskly, "Yes?"

Wiki hesitated, wondering whether Captain Stackpole had changed his mind about reporting to Captain Wilkes, but then started at the beginning, with Captain Stackpole's report of the loss of both money and schooner, and the decision to go to El Carmen to investigate his complaint of piracy. As his story progressed, it became obvious that this was the first the commodore of the expedition had heard of the outcome of the visit to Adams's store, and he wondered again about Stackpole's strange change of attitude. However, the fact that it was news made the telling easier.

"We found the store cleared out of its provisions, and the clerk extremely uncooperative," he continued. "Providentially, some gaucho trackers arrived, and offered to follow the trail of the horse train that had packed the goods out. They said they led upriver, where we hoped to find the schooner loading salt at the dunes."

"But you didn't?"

"No, sir. She was long gone. However, we pursued the tracks further, and found the murdered body of the storekeeper who had stolen the schooner."

Captain Wilkes's fine, large eyes sparked with interest. *"Murdered?"*

"Aye, sir." Wiki gestured, and said, "He'd been stabbed with a large knife in the lower part of the chest."

Both Captain Wilkes and his father were watching him with riveted attention. "Where did you find the corpse?" demanded Captain Wilkes, while his father, more perceptively, said, "What led you to it?"

"Vultures," said Wiki, answering the second question, and described the trek past the *salinas*, the gruesome discovery of the exposed, picked skull at the foot of the Gualichú tree, and the uncovering of the rest of the corpse in the salt beneath.

Captain Wilkes was frowning, but not with pain or anger—indeed, he seemed to have forgotten his headache. He said, "That's a very strange place to bury a murdered man. It's as if the killer wanted him to be found."

"But we would never have found him if Adams hadn't convulsed just before he died so that his head came up out of the salt," Wiki objected.

"Is that what you think happened? That he convulsed?" And, to Wiki's amazement, Captain Wilkes abandoned dignity and stretched his long body on the deck. Lying down, he said, "He was stabbed in the chest—here?"

The commodore's finger pointed at a spot six inches above his middle. Wiki nodded, and Captain Wilkes clenched his fist, brought it down, slammed himself in the rib cage, and reared up his head. For a moment, he brought back the sight of the dead man's arched torso so vividly that gooseflesh chilled on the back of Wiki's neck.

He said rather weakly, "Aye, sir." After a second's thought, he added, "He had also been shot in the head—with a rifle, I think. My impression was that he reared up out of the salt in the last spasm of death just as the killer was turning away, and the murderer was so shocked that he shot him. Then, because he was spooked, he galloped off without reburying the head."

"Really?" Captain Wilkes remained in that position a moment, staring awkwardly at Wiki from above his chest. Then he rose to his feet with more agility than Wiki would have expected, remarking, "Confoundedly uncomfortable." Seating himself in one of the chart chairs, he picked up a pencil and tapped it rhythmically on the top of the desk, deep in thought. A healthy pink had crept into his cheeks.

"How long is it before rigor mortis sets in, do you know?" he asked.

Wiki thought back to his conversation with Dr. Ducatel while they were studying the corpse of the clerk, but only came up with the memory of being told that rigor mortis took three or four days to dissipate. He confessed, "I don't know."

"You don't? What kind of sheriff's deputy are you?" However, Captain Wilkes's tone was relatively mild. He went to the doors, opened one, stuck his head out, and yelled for Dr. Fox, who came at the run. "How soon after death does rigor mortis set in?" he demanded.

The surgeon looked around rather wildly, and then stuttered, "F-five to t-ten hours, sir." Swallowing, he said, "May I inquire why you ask?"

"No, you can't," Captain Wilkes snapped, and Dr. Fox looked around again, took the hint, and went away. As soon as the door clicked shut, Captain Wilkes turned to Wiki and said, "So why didn't the shot knock the head back into the grave?"

Wiki had anticipated the question, so said at once, "The salt had sifted down into the hole, and formed a sort of pillow."

"Hm," said the commodore. "I suppose that makes sense." Then he asked, "What kind of man was this storekeeper?"

"Caleb Adams? Short and wiry." Wiki itemized what the dead man had been wearing, including the amulet about his neck, and then said, "It's really impossible to tell what his face was like before the vultures got at him."

"I meant, what *kind* of man was he?"

"I don't know," Wiki replied, flustered. "I'd never been up the Río Negro before; I'd never met him. Captain Stackpole—"

"Captain Stackpole knew him well?"

"According to the store's books, Captain Stackpole had done a lot of business with him over the past few years. He had no doubt about the identity of the body, even though the face was gone."

"You went through the store's books—to track past transactions?"

"That's how I found the bill of sale for the schooner." Wiki described finding the deed in the back of the ledger, going on to repeat what Dr. Ducatel had told them about the death of the seller, Captain Hallett, at the surgeon's own ranch.

"Then, when Captain Stackpole wanted to know what had happened to his bank draft after Hallett died," he continued, "Dr. Ducatel became angry, and demanded to see the deed as proof that the sale had really happened, so we went back to the store. It was locked, but we used Dr. Ducatel's key to gain entrance—and found the body of Adams's clerk."

"*Another* body?" exclaimed Wilkes, looking very animated indeed.

"Aye, sir. When we found him he'd been dead only about thirty-six hours—or so Dr. Ducatel said. It seems evident that he was killed by the same man who killed the storekeeper up by the *salinas*, though, because the deed of sale had gone—and he'd been stabbed to death, just like Adams."

"But no salty grave—and no shot in the head?"

Captain Wilkes was actually grinning with enjoyment. Wiki wondered if he should smile back, but decided against it, silently shaking his head, instead. The commodore lapsed into thought again, this time rolling the pencil between his fingers. Then he abruptly turned to Captain Coffin. "You called on board the *Trojan* last night, I believe. Where was she headed?"

Captain Coffin looked surprised at the question, but answered readily enough. "Captain Stackpole was heading south—after whales, I thought, though he might be looking for his missing schooner. He wasn't in any particular hurry. She was under easy sail while they finished boiling out their blubber."

Wilkes nodded decisively. "Take Wiki on board the *Osprey* and go after him."

"*What?*" Captain Coffin stared. To Wiki's surprise, he saw consternation in his father's expression. He expostulated, "How do you know I will find him?"

"If you can navigate your way about Fijian lagoons, then surely it will be a simple matter to find a whaling ship. When you speak to Captain Stackpole, tell him to write me an affidavit. Once I have it in hand, I can seize the *Grim Reaper* in his name if we come across her—and assure him that I will be using it to report the piracy to every man-of-war I meet. And *you*, sir," Captain Wilkes barked at Wiki, swinging round on him. "When you talk to Captain Stackpole, find out a damn sight more about Adams than you appear to know right now! What kind of sheriff's deputy do you call yourself, when you know so little about the victim? Surely the first job of any investigation is to find out what enemies he had, and what reason anyone would have to kill him?"

Wiki was silent, feeling extremely hard done by, wondering how Captain Wilkes would have behaved in the same circumstances. However, Wilkes didn't even notice, saying to Captain Coffin, "We'll be working on this survey for another three days, so it'll make good use of the interval while you are waiting for the last specimens to be loaded. But be sure to be back in time, or you'll be forced to pursue us all the way to Cape Horn!"

Wiki's father looked very annoyed at being ordered around in this peremptory fashion, but Captain Wilkes didn't pay attention to that, either. "Well, off you go," he said with satisfaction. Then, on a last thought, he observed to Wiki, "That topknot arrangement is an improvement, but still far from ideal. Did you know that I had a deputation from the men complaining about your hair?"

Wiki said blankly, "Sir?"

"They say that things have started going wrong ever since you had it cut, and applied to me to order you to grow it again, as quickly as possible."

"Good God," said Wiki. He felt so bemused that it wasn't until he was back in the *Swallow* boat that he realized he hadn't had a chance to talk about Harden and the sealers.

Twelve

Back on board the *Swallow*, Wiki asked George, "Did Captain Wilkes congratulate you on your promotion?"

Wiki was again in dungarees, and had pulled down his topknot so his hair was comfortably loose. Having thrown a few things into a kit bag, he was ready to head over to the *Osprey*. As he remembered, George's face had been quite bland when they had passed each other in the corridor of the afterhouse of the *Vincennes*. Now, by contrast, his friend was wearing an evil grin.

"Smith was right, for once," he said. "It was indeed to give me warmest felicitations—but not on account of my promotion. Instead, Wilkes congratulated me because no one from the *Swallow* had joined the jollification on the *Porpoise*!"

"I don't believe it!" Wiki let out a shout of mirth. "How come no one noticed that Constant Keith was there?"

"If anyone did, they neglected to inform our good commodore, old chap."

"I wonder if he realizes his luck." Wiki shook his head, still enjoying his laugh. Then he sobered. "Did Captain Wilkes tell you he's going to demote Craven, and appoint someone else in his place?"

George grimaced. "No, he didn't, but it's predictable, I suppose, considering that Craven was one of those making merry. Also, he's a tarry old sailor who is popular with the men, which has always worked against him. Did Wilkes reveal the name of his replacement?"

"No—just that he is the next-oldest lieutenant, that they've been cronies for years, and that they swung the pendulum together as midshipmen."

George stared. Then he said in frozen tones of horror, "Oh, my God. It sounds a lot like . . ."

Wiki abruptly had the same terrible thought. "Lawrence J. Smith?"

Rochester nodded grimly. "Let's hope we're wrong," he said.

If they were not, it was an appalling prospect. As Wiki headed for deck with his kit bag over his shoulder, he wondered what state the fleet would be in when he arrived back from his jaunt on the *Osprey*. There'd been changes enough over the days he'd been up the Río Negro, but this promised to be far worse.

He could see boats plying between the *Vincennes*, the *Peacock*, the *Flying Fish*, the *Sea Gull*, and the beach, presumably part of the afternoon's surveying. The *Porpoise* was lying a long way off, he noticed, undoubtedly with officers on board who were regretting their impulsive hospitality, and nursing their headaches. Though Forsythe's fog had still not materialized, the weather was more ominous than ever. On the way over to the *Osprey*, which was now lying at anchor a couple of miles to the southeast of the fleet, Wiki watched the oily roll of the waves, and became absorbed in the low light of the sky, and the dank feel of the chilly air. The clouds were turning from white to dull gray, with a purple glint running along the horizon to the southwest, while the swell was increasing. There was still no wind, but the instinct from years of whaling in treacherous seas told him that a gale was on the way.

Then the *Swallow* boat came within hailing distance of the *Osprey*, and his attention was taken up in admiration of the 200-ton brigantine. Painted gleaming white, with a lot more shiny brass about her than was usually considered modest, she was a very pretty sight. The figurehead—of a fish hawk, naturally—glinted with gilt. The long, tapered spars on the tall foremast were absolutely square, so precisely aligned that it looked as if Mr. Seward had measured them off with his sextant.

Though her hull was as dainty and fine-lined as a yacht, the brigantine was rigged to withstand China Sea monsoons, with both masts stayed and back-stayed into more than ordinary strength; every inch of her running gear was the best that money could buy. The deep rectangular sails on the foremast—course, topsail, topgallant, and royal, in ascending order—were snowy white, without a single patch in evidence, and the huge fore-and-aft mainsail on the mainmast—the biggest and heaviest sail on the ship, spread between its upper spar, the gaff, and lashed to the boom at its foot—was equally immaculate. As the boat came around the quarter, the low light glinted off the polished tiers of windows in the square stern. Mr. Seward, as George Rochester had described, was more house-proud than the usual first officer of a trader.

Captain Coffin met Wiki at the rail, looking preoccupied and busy. Instead of introducing him to any of the crew, he led the way to the break of the poop, and opened the door to the companionway. At the bottom, he indicated one of the staterooms that lined the larboard side of the afterhouse corridor, and then, with scarcely a word, he headed back up to deck. It was as if he were in a big hurry. As Wiki stood looking around, he could hear him hollering for Mr. Seward and then issuing orders to make sail.

The stateroom didn't offer much in the way of hospitality, either, being small to start with, and cramped even further by bolts of Chinese silk stowed along the bulkheads. Wiki eased past the dunnage to the one piece of furniture, which was a rank of lockers and drawers lipped at the top to make a bed, furnished with a thin mattress, and put down his kit bag, frowning as he wondered about his father's unwelcoming attitude. He could understand why he might be angry with Captain Wilkes's peremptory order, but had expected him to have relaxed into his usual jovial and talkative self by the time his son came aboard.

Watery light glimmered through the square sidelight above the berth, sending reflections rippling over the whitewashed bulkheads as the *Osprey* wallowed in the heavy swell. Wiki could hear the cadets calling out to each other as they hauled on lines and laid aloft—familiar sounds, though it was nine years since he had last sailed on the *Osprey*. At the time, he had been just fifteen, and it had been a short voyage to the West Indies, after a freight of sugar and fruit. Within weeks of that last cruise, his father had sailed off on a voyage to the Orient, expecting to come back a year later to find Wiki still at home with his stepmother—Captain Coffin's legal, childless, Nantucket-bred wife. However, the instant the *Osprey* had disappeared over the horizon, Mrs. Coffin had packed Wiki off to a college for missionaries in New Hampshire, in an attempt to reform what she considered his wicked native ways. There, he had met George, and after a few months of skipping classes together to hunt the forest with the local Indians, they had absconded entirely, paddling off down the Connecticut River in a birchbark canoe they had built themselves. When Wiki had reappeared in Salem, Mrs. Coffin's next move had been to send him off to sea on her brother's whaleship, so that by the time her husband got back home, his illegitimate son was back in the Pacific where she reckoned he belonged.

Since then, their paths had crossed only occasionally, mostly by accident, and usually in some farflung port. They were always glad to see each other . . . but, as Wiki mused now, his father had never invited him to join the crew of the *Osprey,* even when he was currently without a berth. Wiki hadn't thought much about it in the past, but now he found it odd. For some reason, it seemed, Captain Coffin didn't want his son on board his ship.

Then Wiki was distracted by the realization that instead of making way, the *Osprey* was still sagging uneasily up and over the swells. A rolling thud rang out in the distance—the *Vincennes* firing a gun to call in her boats. Obviously, Forsythe's fog was upon them at last. It was impossible to stop himself from heading up the companionway to check on the state of affairs, and so he arrived at the rail just in time to see the ships of the fleet disappear one after another in the flowing mist.

The far-off *Porpoise* vanished first. Then the *Vincennes* faded like a ghost, the *Peacock* turned into a wraith, and finally the *Swallow* was lost to view. After that, it was as if the *Osprey* were floating alone in a shifting gray cloud. Dank moisture clung to the rigging. All the sails were spread, but there was no wind to fill them. Instead, the canvas sheets flopped against the tall masts with the slow pulse of the swell.

When Wiki leaned back against the rail and craned his neck he could just glimpse the royal sail dangling at the very top of the foremast hamper. Birds swirled and screamed around it, and then flew off, heading toward the land. Every instinct told him that a gale was in the offing—one of the vicious southwesterlies the Argentinians called *pampero*. The expedition ships, like the *Swallow,* had used the respite to get their heavy foul-weather sails bent, in preparation for awful weather on the way to Cape Horn and beyond, but he saw with disquiet that while the forecourse, topsail, and mainsail of the brigantine were made of stout foul-weather canvas, the topgallant and royal were light ones, as if the *Osprey* were halfway through being readied for the subequatorial trades. Also, if Wilkes should issue an order for the fleet to claw upwind, away from the dangerous lee shore, the brigantine was not far off the path of the expedition ships. The air was as still as death, right now, but Wiki headed anxiously for the quarterdeck.

Captain Coffin was on the weather side, keeping his balance with one upraised hand in the starboard shrouds, deep in conversation with Mr. Seward. Studying them curiously, Wiki was struck again by the mate's good looks. With his curly blond hair, high cheekbones, light green eyes, and square, thin-boned jaw, the fellow was rather Scandinavian in appearance, he thought. In his mid-thirties, he was young enough to have some gaiety of spirit, Wiki thought, and remembered that he had an engaging half-grin. However, when Alf Seward heard Wiki's step and looked up, he certainly didn't smile. Instead, his expression hardened into hostility.

Remembering what George had said about Mr. Seward's possessive, jealous attitude, Wiki wondered if his first mate was the reason his father was so reluctant to have his son on board his ship. Because of the suspicion, his voice was abrupt as he said, "I think a *pampero* is in the offing."

His father frowned. "It's the wrong time of the year."

"I don't like the weather mix—the drop in temperature, the fog, the heavy swell."

Again, the flagship fired a cannon, which echoed flatly in the clinging mist. In the silence that followed, Wiki saw that Mr. Seward was glancing from his face to Captain Coffin's and back, looking for similarities and differences, no doubt, like everyone else who knew that they were father and son. If he did see a resemblance, he wasn't happy about it, that was plain. The slender pipestem clenched between his white teeth puffed aggressive little clouds of smoke.

Then, all at once, the first mate did grin—but it was not a nice smile, at all. "A *pampero*, you reckon? So d'you think we should take in all sail?" he sardonically asked. "Perhaps, Mr. Coffin, we should house in the jibboom?"

Wiki flinched at the open sarcasm. It was as plain as if the mate had said it out loud that he'd been presumptuous to offer advice on his father's ship.

He said doggedly, "It's just a suggestion—and I would also like to say that I'd be happy to help out on deck and in the rigging while I'm on board. I'd be very glad to be considered just another member of the crew."

"Why, Mr. Coffin, what could you do to help?"

Wiki shrugged, thinking that even if Mr. Seward knew he was one of the expedition scientifics, surely his father had mentioned that his son was an experienced whaleman. The trade might be a despised one, but whalemen were famous seamen, both on deck and in the whaleboats, because the toughened officers knew how to pass on their remarkable skills both quickly and efficiently. Within a week of shipping on the *Paths of Duty,* Wiki had learned how to haul out an earring in a howling gale, and furl the main royal by himself. Within three months, not only could he heave a harpoon and command a whaleboat, but if his ship were gale-bound on a dangerous lee shore, he knew how to bring the square sails hard aback, strike the after sails, and boxhaul her out of trouble—he could sail a ship backward just as easily as he could steer her going forward.

For God's sake, he thought, Alf Seward had seen him at the steering oar! He said in a stiff tone of voice, "I'm considered a good hand at the helm."

"I'm sure you are very talented, Mr. Coffin, but we have apprentices for that, thank you very much," said the mate, and turned his attention to relighting his pipe, which had gone out.

Wiki stared, stung by the studied insult. He had not meant to brag, even if it had sounded like it, because what he'd said was nothing but the truth. He had a natural instinct for the wind on his cheek, the shiver in the weather clews of the uppermost sail, and the heel of the deck beneath his feet. He used the minimum of helm, knowing intuitively the exact distance the wheel had to be turned to check the swing of the ship. He liked to think it was a skill that had come down to him from his voyaging ancestors.

And what about his father? Over the years, they had exchanged many tales of deeds done at sea. Wiki looked at him challengingly, wondering if he would express any confidence at all in his seafaring skills. However, Captain Coffin said nothing to ease the situation. Instead, he cleared his throat, and looked away to study the sagging sails.

Furious to the point of indiscretion, and too angry to remember the fog, Wiki opened his mouth to demand a boat to take him back to the *Swallow*. However, he was forestalled. The tense silence was broken in the most unexpected manner—by the splash of oars, and a disembodied hail from the water.

A whaleboat emerged from the mist, so phantomlike that the loud click as the bow touched the side came as a surprise. Heading over to the rail to see who was clambering aboard, Wiki got even more of a shock when Captain Stackpole's head hove into sight, and the whaling master was equally stunned to see him.

"Wiki Coffin!" he exclaimed, and hauled himself over the gangway, bringing a nauseating smell of blood, oil, and tryworks smoke with him. He had taken the time to shave his cheeks and upper lip, so that his New Bedford beard was back in shape, but he looked as exhausted as Wiki remembered, and his little eyes were as bloodshot as ever. Obviously, he'd taken little or no rest since rejoining his ship.

He looked around, appearing confused. "Ain't this the *Osprey*?"

"It certainly isn't the *Swallow*," Wiki dryly agreed.

"What the devil are you doing here?"

"We were trying to sail in search of you, as it happens."

"You were?" Stackpole sniggered, looking at the impotent sails, and said, "Well, you ain't getting very far. Why were you looking for me?"

"When I reported the pirating of the *Grim Reaper* to Captain Wilkes, he gave me orders to collect an affidavit from you, to give him the legal right to hunt for the schooner, and to report the theft to any American men-of-war we encounter."

Instead of expressing gratification at this good news, Stackpole grimaced, shifted his feet uncomfortably, glanced about the decks where men and boys were openly listening, and appeared relieved when Captain Coffin arrived beside them.

"Stackpole!" he exclaimed. "I thought you were making an offing?"

"The ship was fifteen miles out when we lowered, and the mate has orders to keep south—not that he would've got far, on account of the wind died within thirty minutes of us leaving the *Trojan*," Stackpole replied in gloomy tones. "We were forced to strike our own sail, and just when we'd rowed far enough to raise the masts of the squadron, the bloody fog descended."

"You must have been confoundedly glad to find us." Captain Coffin's voice was amiable, as if the unpleasant little altercation between his son and his mate were quite forgotten. "Bring your men on board and make yourselves at home. We keep a set of davits on the larboard quarter for visitors, and you're most welcome to hoist your boat."

"Coffee and a bite to eat would go down first-rate," Stackpole confessed.

Captain Coffin shook his head, contemplating the thick fog yet again. "You'll be on board for more than that," he prophesied. "You're here for the night."

As the six men of his boat's crew assembled on the waist deck, Wiki was interested and pleased to see that it was the same crew that had originally carried him to the beach of the Río Negro, including the two Polynesians. They grinned at him amiably, but it was impossible to tell what island they hailed from until they spoke, or at least exchanged names, and before he could get into conversation, Mr. Seward materialized, looking as affable as his captain. Wiki performed introductions, and the mate of the *Osprey* led the whalemen toward the hospitality of the steerage and the forecastle, while Captain Coffin ushered Stackpole down the companionway to his cabin.

It became immediately apparent that Stackpole had never been on board the brigantine before. His bristling eyebrows shot up when he saw the horseshoe-shaped settee with the green cushions to starboard, and the red padding to port, and hoisted even higher as he looked about at the shining glass and gleaming mahogany. As well as the curved settee that was set under the sweep of many-paned windows, and had its own knee-high table, there was a dining suite with wonderfully carved legs sited farther forward. Above this, an ornate lamp hung down from a long skylight, flanked by two swinging castor racks of cut-glass decanters and matching crystal glasses, which made the slightest of tinkling noises as the brigantine rolled. As Wiki remembered from his youthful voyages on the *Osprey*, when the sun shone they cast little rainbows on the paneled walls as they caught stray sparks of light. Captain Coffin's massive chart desk was right up against the forward bulkhead and next to the pantry door, so that he could look up and see the compass in the binnacle when seated in the chair. There was an ornate chronometer case on the desk, and the barometer and thermometer hung on the wall above, framed in shining brass.

Captain Coffin waved a hospitable arm at the settee, and Captain Stackpole perched his rump on a red cushion, still looking around with an expression of disbelief. A large cat made an appearance, a handsome black and white animal who pushed open the pantry door, paused to sum the company up, undulated forward, sniffed Captain Stackpole's boot, decided his aroma was absolutely wonderful, and leaped up onto his knee.

Captain Coffin sat down on a green cushion. "You're greatly honored," he observed.

"Honored?" his guest echoed. When the steward, a gray-haired, hard-done-by-looking fellow, came in with a tray of coffee, Stackpole grasped a mug gratefully.

"That animal is the most disgusting snob. If a captain and his mate pay a call on board, she will unfailingly choose the captain for her attentions. She *will* consent to visit the bo'sun every now and then," Captain Coffin ruminated. "Particularly if she has noticed that he was in charge of the deck the previous watch. But as much as the boys do to entice her, she won't deign to put her nose into the foc'sle. Up until this moment," he added, "I didn't know how she felt about whalemen."

There was a pause, and then Stackpole said blankly, "It's a she-cat?"

"Indeed. She belongs to Mr. Seward, who strongly believes that every ship needs a female of some sort on board. It's a kind of superstition, with him."

"Good God," said the whaling master, sotto voce. He cautiously stroked the cat's cooperatively arched neck, and then queried, "But don't you get kittens?"

"Kittens aplenty," Captain Coffin admitted. "We keep the ship off-limits to tomcats, but she has different ideas. The instant we drop anchor off some busy waterfront, she vanishes like magic, reappears days later looking confoundedly smug, and produces a litter somewhere mid-sea. Alf Seward," he added, "is the midwife."

Stackpole looked around, but no other cats made their presence known, so he said, "How do you dispose of them?"

Captain Coffin's expression became vague. "The boys sell 'em, I think."

"*Sell* them? *Where?*"

"Oh, sometimes to other ships, and sometimes in port."

"They eat them in China," Wiki helpfully contributed.

Both shipmasters stared. "What the devil gives you that idea?" his father demanded.

"A shipmate who'd dropped anchor once in Hong Kong told me that the sampans come around the ship selling delicious dishes called 'cats and dogs.' "

Mr. Seward's cat was an extremely perceptive specimen, Wiki saw then, because he became the object of a coldly disapproving emerald-green stare. He delivered her a wicked grin, while his father snorted, "Whatever your shipmate ate in Hong Kong, it was something else, I assure you."

"What was it, then?"

"You're being difficult, my son. And don't ever breathe a word of it to Mr. Seward."

With remarkably bad timing, the steward came back with a tray of hot meat pies. However, everyone helped themselves with appetite, and took more coffee, too. Wiping his mouth with one of the monogrammed linen napkins that was another of his father's eccentricities, Wiki observed, "When I was a lad your mate was a different man—a long Yankee, as thin as a whalebone whip."

"Evans? You remember him?" Oddly, his father seemed pleased.

"I certainly do—a gloomy fellow who complained all the time, mostly about the un-American way the locals behaved in South America. He blamed the sun, as I remember—reckoned that it made the inhabitants lazy and gave them too many vacations."

"You remember him well." Captain Coffin was amused.

"So what happened to him?"

"Captured by cannibals."

Captain Stackpole's mouth fell open, releasing a lot of crumbs into his beard, and Wiki exclaimed, *"What!"*

"They plucked him out of a boat while we were collecting bêche-de-mer in Fiji. However, they threw him back, on account of there wasn't enough flesh on his bones to be worth the trouble of lighting a fire. Delivered him to the beach completely unharmed, but the fright knocked the stuffing out of him. Took his discharge the instant we moored up to Derby Wharf, and hasn't put a foot on board a vessel since."

Wiki said, "So you shipped Mr. Seward?"

"Nope. I shipped a Salem worthy who promenaded the town in a silk hat and gloves, an ivory cane in one hand, and a Testament in the other—a man who attended church every day of his life. A highly respectable fellow, you would think? I started to suspect the truth when his private trade goods included three half-gallon jars, which he hid where no one could find them, no matter how hard we searched."

"Holding wine?"

"Brandy," said Captain Coffin. Reminded of liquor, he stood, went over to one of the castors in the skylight, and reached up for a decanter and two tumblers. "There was hardly a day when he wasn't drunk," he went on, pouring liberally for himself and Stackpole. "He'd vanish belowdecks, and come back breathing fire. By the time we were two months out he was wearing a green eye patch to try to correct his double vision. Then he started seeing phantoms and hollering about it, which got the hands so upset they began to see ghosts themselves. The matter came to a head when he blundered up to deck in pursuit of some invisible demon with a loaded pistol in each hand. The entire crew took to the rigging, and I was forced to sort it out myself."

Captain Stackpole reached out for a proffered glass with an air of great need, engulfed a reviving slurp of liquor, and said, "How?"

"Tricked him into going down to his stateroom by telling him I'd left a bottle there. Down the whole confounded companionway he went, in just one step. When I got to him he was stretched out snoring and senseless at the bottom. So I clapped him in irons and discharged him at the next port we touched—which happened to be Batavia, but that was just his bad luck. Providentially, Mr. Seward was on the beach and out of money, and took a pierhead jump onto the *Osprey* the day before we left."

"Why, what was he running from?" Captain Stackpole asked.

"I've never inquired," said Captain Coffin. The hand he waved was casual, but there was an evasive glint beneath his lowered eyelid. "How could I make difficulties with a man who cherishes my ship the way the *Osprey* deserves?"

Stackpole looked around the magnificent cabin again, still with an air of wonder. "In the housekeeping way?"

"Exactly," Captain Coffin heartily affirmed, then lowered his voice. "In Rio he came to me because he wanted some money for gilt decoration on the figurehead—to give the bird a gold beak, for God's sake! And when I refused he paid for gold leaf out of his own pocket, and painted the beak himself! He treats the *Osprey* as if she were his own, but how can I make any objections when he loves her so well?"

"Good God," said Captain Stackpole, and wagged his head. As Wiki knew well, whaling masters made great demands of their officers in the seamanship and whaling way, but a mate who wanted to fancy up the ship would have been considered insane. In fact, most whaling captains and officers of his acquaintance lived in a state of comfortable squalor. Wiki had once served as third mate on a ship where the settee in the aftercabin was in such an embarrassing state that the captain covered it up with the big ensign whenever visitors called, which was amusing when the more patriotic ones were squeamish about sitting on the Stars and Stripes.

Setting his empty plate aside, he remarked, "Maybe that's why Mr. Seward so strongly resents the captain's son being on board of his pride and joy."

Stackpole's stare shifted to Wiki's face, while his expression became knowing. Captains' sons tended to be an arrogant lot, with a high opinion of their status and abilities, because of their privileged place in the cabin, so were universally disliked by their fathers' officers, and despised by the rest of the crew.

"Nonsense," Captain Coffin snapped. "He'll soon get over it. It just that he's used to ruling the roost around here, and doesn't like his position being threatened."

Wiki asked curiously, "How does the second mate feel about that?"

There was a pause, while Captain Coffin cleared his throat. Then he said, "We don't carry a second mate."

"*What?*" Involuntarily, Wiki looked at Stackpole, whose eyes had widened in equal disbelief. Whaleships carried at least three mates, for the simple reason that there had to be an officer for each whaleboat, to take charge of the boat in the chase. However, the mates were useful on board as well—between them, they kept the crew in order, supervised the stowing and issuing of stores, and looked after the ship's gear and rigging. Not only was it economical, because it meant that the captain didn't have to ship a boatswain, but it gave the captain the freedom to concentrate on navigation, plotting the voyage, and entertaining visitors, as whalemen were often apt to do, mid-sea.

Masters of freight-carrying traders might be derisive about this, reckoning that whaleships were as extravagantly overmanned as men-of-war, and overfond of gamming, too. However, it was unheard-of for a blue water vessel, even a relatively small two-hundred-ton ship like the *Osprey,* not to have a second mate. Without a second officer to back him up, the captain would be forced to take charge of every second watch, meaning that he had to take over the quarterdeck for eight hours every second night, and four hours the next.

Wiki observed, "I thought you were too fond of your bunk to rouse up for midnight watches."

His father exclaimed, "You saucy young whelp!"

He was staring at Wiki with such affront that he scarcely noticed Captain Stackpole clear his throat in an embarrassed fashion and then, with the muttered excuse that he wanted to check the fog and his men, retreat hurriedly to deck.

"You're not getting any younger, you know," Wiki pointed out.

"I'm as fit as a fiddle, and have all my faculties, including an excellent memory. Have you ever heard me tell the same story twice? And anyway," Captain Coffin said, "Mr. Seward keeps both ship and crew in good order, and doesn't need help."

Remembering the boy with the bruised jaw, Wiki observed sardonically, "He seems to enjoy keeping the cadets in good shape."

His father saw the implicit meaning at once, and took umbrage. "Apart from the occasional swat with a cane across the backside, Alf has never laid a hand on any one of my cadets! They all revere him!"

"But one of them has certainly been in a fight. Are you trying to tell me that he got into a scuffle with his shipmates?"

"I'm not *trying* to tell you anything—and the boys know better than to get into scuffles. Any bout of fisticuffs would definitely earn a swat across the butt. If you really want to know what happened, he got into a scuffle with one of those goddamned string-shanked carpenters!"

Surprised, Wiki asked, "Boyd, or Folger?"

"The younger one, Boyd—but the older one, Folger, always backed him up, just like he was his father, or something."

"Folger is his uncle," Wiki said. "He raised him as his own after his sister died, or so he testified to me."

"You sound as if you know them well." Captain Coffin's tone was accusing.

"They are two of the sealers we rescued from their sinking ship, three months back, and I had to cross-examine them during a murder investigation."

"Murder?"

"Aye."

"Did you catch the killer?"

"Aye. Did Boyd make a habit of smacking the cadets about?" Wiki asked, because it would explain why his father had been so anxious to get rid of the two men.

To Wiki's surprise, his father blushed. He mumbled, "Boyd pestered them all the time—in an unnatural kind of way. He seemed fascinated by their youth. The boys—they're healthy young scoundrels, and they laughed at him, I think. Then he cornered the lad while he was working in the hold by himself, and a fight developed. Mr. Seward heard the ruckus, went down, and settled it."

"With a belaying pin?"

"He felled Boyd with a punch to the jaw."

"Knocked him *out*?"

"Stretched him senseless on the deck."

So the mate had been in a towering rage—a passion that had lent him unnatural strength, Wiki thought. While Mr. Seward looked athletic enough, he was much more lightly built than Boyd.

Again, he was reminded of George's remark about Alf Seward's strange possessiveness, and said slowly, "I think the real reason you don't carry a second mate is that Mr. Seward doesn't want to share the ship with another officer. And that's the reason he doesn't like me on board, too."

His father flushed again, this time with anger. "I've already told you that he rules the roost around here. You make it obvious that you don't like it, Wiki, but it isn't any of your business. You're here because Wilkes ordered you to get that affidavit from Stackpole, and the sooner you do it, the sooner you can get back to the fleet. So why don't you do your job, instead of trying to tell me how to run my ship?"

"You're right," said Wiki, and stood up and left the cabin.

Thirteen

The fog was thicker than ever, hanging in great gray billows about the masts and rigging, and it was impossible to see the bowsprit from the poop. Wiki paused as the bell by the wheel rang four times for the end of the first dogwatch—just six in the evening, but because of the gloom cast by the fog it seemed dusk already. On the *Swallow*, the second tot of rum of the day would have been issued. Here, Wiki thought, it might be the same, as he heard sounds of jollity from the foredeck, along with the merry scraping of a fiddle and the chorus of a hearty song. Obviously, the visiting whalemen were being well entertained.

Mr. Seward was on the starboard side of the quarterdeck, his oilskins glistening in the light of the cresset lantern, which also shone on his damp blond hair, but he paid Wiki no attention. Stackpole was standing at the rail amidships, looking seaward, and glaring at the billowing mists. As soon as Wiki came up alongside, he grabbed his arm, and hissed in his ear, "William Coffin is your *father*?"

Wiki was surprised. "Didn't you know?"

"Never guessed. Not that there ain't a resemblance," the whaleman added.

"Is there? Good heavens," said Wiki without expression.

"And this ship is a floating antique!"

"Launched in 1813, but looked antique even then, I imagine," Wiki agreed. "She was built according to my father's instructions. He had romantic ideas and almost unlimited funds."

Stackpole paused, but obviously couldn't resist asking, "Family funds?"

"Personally acquired riches. At the start of the war for free trade and sailors' rights he was given the command of the fastest American ship afloat, and within a few months had accumulated enough prize money to have the *Osprey* built."

"He was a *privateer*?"

"And a lucky one, too. The ship he commanded could make thirteen knots with a crew of one hundred and fifty and all her stores, cannon, boats, and bulwarks aboard, and because of her speed he could outrun British frigates with ease. Not only did he capture a large consignment of military supplies intended for Cornwallis, and deliver them to Washington with a flourish, but he took six prizes worth one hundred and sixty thousand dollars, in total. Not bad for a man who was not quite twenty-two years old at the time, don't you think? You should ask him about it."

"Not me," said Stackpole, and shook his head for emphasis.

Obviously, he'd heard enough tales spun for one day. Wiki laughed, and then sobered. He said, "Do you know a Río Negro river pilot by the name of Harden?"

"The only river pilots I know are the Englishman and the Frenchman who live in that pilothouse. Why?"

"This one is American, and he's joined the exploring expedition."

There was a pause while the fog swirled slowly, and then Stackpole said, "Well, you can't blame any American for seizing an excuse to escape from trying to make a living out of piloting the Río Negro."

Escape? Wiki remembered what Forsythe had said: *If he's got such a grand mission for revolution, why would he want to leave the Río Negro?*

He said, "Manuel Bernantio told me he's a revolutionary."

"Oh, you mean *that* Harden," said Stackpole, enlightened. "I've surely heard of *him*. I didn't know he was a pilot. I thought he was just a goddamned rascal of a desperado."

"Have you met him?"

"Never, to my knowledge."

"But you've obviously heard sensational things."

"According to the governor of El Carmen, he supplies arms to the rebels."

"So why doesn't the governor do something about it?" Wiki queried. "He's got plenty of troops."

"Why the hell should he? He owes no debt to the de Rosas government. Truth be told, he probably hates de Rosas as much as the rebels do. Is that why Wilkes sent you in search of me? To tell you what I know about Harden?"

"As I've already told you, Captain Wilkes wants you to write an affidavit."

Stackpole looked away, his expression evasive again. Instead of answering, he demanded, "So why are you asking about Harden?"

"Because I'm curious about Benjamin Harden. Captain Wilkes, by contrast, is curious about Caleb Adams."

"*Adams?* Why?"

"He wants to know what kind of man Adams was."

"You saw the corpse, just as I did."

"That skull was too bare to tell me much," Wiki pointed out.

"But you saw the body, right? A tough, sinewy, slender man—though I guess you couldn't tell that he was a lot stronger than he looked. Many a time I watched him heave up a great sack of grain, swing it onto his back, and then carry it into the store as if it were filled with nothin' more than feathers. I doubt I could have lifted one of those sacks alone."

Wiki paused, finding this interesting. Then he said, "Captain Wilkes wondered what the deceased's nature was like."

"His *what?*"

"His character. What kind of man he was."

Looking thoughtful, the whaling master groped about in a pocket and hauled out his pipe. He took his time about lighting it, while Wiki waited. Finally, he let out a judicious puff, and said, "Angry."

"Angry at what?"

"Everything and everybody, just about. Caleb Adams was chewed up with anger, as if it ate at his insides. He wasn't too bad when I first got to know him, on account of trade was going so well. Then it fell off, and his temper got foul. The only thing that cheered him up," Stackpole said bitterly, "was selling me that bloody schooner."

He puffed so furiously that Wiki took a long step backward to get away from the stinging cloud of tobacco smoke, which mingled revoltingly with the mixed aroma of whale oil, trysmoke, and brandy that surrounded Stackpole already.

Then he observed, "But at least Adams was honest about that."

"Honest?" Stackpole cried.

"The deed of sale proved that the transaction really did take place."

"Are you sure of that?"

Wiki frowned. "What do you mean?"

Stackpole silenced. Captain Coffin had come on deck, his figure so insubstantial that Wiki realized that the fog had got even more dense. Through the mist he saw his father go to Mr. Seward, and engage in talk. Both men were looking curiously at him and Stackpole, he noticed, but after the conversation was over Captain Coffin merely went to the wheel, checked the compass, looked up at the dripping sails, said a few words to the helmsman, and then returned below.

The instant his tall figure vanished, Stackpole muttered, "You don't need that affidavit."

Wiki looked at him. "What?"

"I've got it."

Silence, while the rigging dripped with a deathwatch sound. Then Wiki said, "I've not a notion what you're talking about."

"The deed of sale. I've got it."

Wiki stared, too stunned for speech, and the whaling master's tone became defensive. "I got it when I went back into the store for the poncho. I reckoned I was the legal owner of the deed, so I asked him for it."

"Him? You mean Gomes?"

"Aye. The clerk."

"He gave it to you—just like that?"

"My name was on it! It proved that the schooner is mine!"

"He didn't make any objection?"

Captain Stackpole said angrily, "Yes, he did object. He was bloody difficult about it, as it happens. I had to show him my fist. And now you're wondering if I stabbed him."

Stackpole had certainly had the opportunity for murder, Wiki thought, remembering the time lapse before he had rejoined the gaucho party on the riverside path to the salt dunes. At the time, he hadn't paid much attention, because he had been watching Bernantio study the tracks.

He didn't have a chance to speak, however, because Stackpole carried on. "When I went back into the store my only intention was to buy that poncho, just the way I said I would after you told me that we were likely to be out all night. All the time, though, I was thinking about that bill of sale, because it proved that Adams really had purchased the *Grim Reaper* on my behalf—that I wasn't the fool you reckoned. So I thought I should have it, and told the clerk to give it to me. He argued, but he couldn't deny that my name was on it, and so he finally handed it over."

"Why didn't you tell me this earlier?"

"Once I realized that schooner was well and truly gone, I didn't think the deed of sale was all that important. Then, when we found the corpse of the clerk, I kept my mouth shut because I knew damn well that you'd jump to conclusions and arrest me."

"So that's why you didn't report to Captain Wilkes," Wiki realized. At last, he thought, he had found a reason for Stackpole's strange evasiveness.

"Once he realized I'd had both motive and opportunity for murder, he would've clapped me in the brig, for sure," Stackpole moodily confirmed.

"But it's obvious you didn't kill the clerk!"

Contrary as ever, the whaling master declined to look relieved. Instead, he blinked suspiciously, and demanded, "What makes you so sure?"

"Because the front door was locked and the key was in the clerk's pocket." His listener looked blank, so Wiki explained, "Dead men don't get up to lock doors."

Silence, broken only by the slow creak of the hull as the brigantine wallowed on the fog-swathed swell. Then Stackpole said with abrupt understanding, "So who locked the door after the clerk was dead?"

Wiki shrugged. "His killer, presumably."

"And he couldn't have used the clerk's key and then put it back in his pocket, because he had to lock the door behind him after he let himself out."

"Exactly."

"So he had his own key."

"Or had *found* a key. When we searched Adams's corpse, the pockets were empty, remember. It's logical that Adams had a key to the store, and the killer took it, along with everything else."

Stackpole paused, thinking this over, and then said reluctantly, "Are you sure we did a proper search?"

Wiki had had the same doubts. At the time, dark had been falling, and they had been too spooked by the sudden detachment of the grinning skull to heave the corpse right out of the trench. Despite its apparent good state of preservation, it had been too easy to imagine the entire skeleton breaking up if they lifted the body too roughly, so instead they had felt through his clothes.

Nevertheless, Wiki said firmly, "I'm sure of it, just as I'm certain that the man who murdered him took away all the contents of his pockets—including his key, which he used to lock the door behind him after the clerk was killed."

"So you reckon that whoever killed Adams killed the clerk, too?"

"It seems logical."

Another long silence. Then Stackpole said slowly, "I agree that it seems likely that whoever killed Adams found the key in his clothes, and pocketed it for future use. But instead of getting clear of the Río Negro while he had the chance, he waited around for quite a few days before he got around to breaking into the store and committing the second murder, which sounds kinda bizarre to me. Why didn't he go with the *Grim Reaper* when she sailed? What's your explanation for that? And why did he kill the clerk at all?"

"I assume he wanted to get hold of the deed of sale."

"Then I foiled him, didn't I," said the whaleman sardonically.

"You certainly did. Just like everyone else, including me," Wiki dryly returned, "he had no idea that you'd taken it off the clerk."

Stackpole had the grace to look sheepish, but his tone was as assertive as ever as he demanded, "And what about that other door—the outside door to the surgery that Ducatel opened?"

"It seems much more likely that the killer used the key to the front door."

"I meant, what if the killer had a key to the surgery already?"

Wiki was puzzled. "What are you trying to say?"

"That Ducatel looks like the prime suspect to me!"

Captain Stackpole's voice had risen, and Wiki touched his arm, noticing that Alf Seward had looked in their direction. More quietly, the whaling master went on, "We all know that Ducatel's on his beam ends, financially."

"Is he? I thought he'd done rather well out of marrying the daughter of a landowner. He looked prosperous enough to me."

"But he attended Captain Hallett at his deathbed, remember—and I reckon he was lying in his teeth when he said that Caleb Adams never came to the ranch. And I reckon that Adams was in on the plot, too."

"What plot?" said Wiki, more confused than ever.

"To seize the schooner, and get away with my thousand dollars! But in order to cover up the crime that quack of a surgeon had to steal that deed, and so he headed for the store and killed the clerk when he wouldn't hand it over."

"What about Adams? Surely you don't think Dr. Ducatel killed him?"

"Oh, Ducatel intended to double-cross him all along, and as you said, it's logical that the same man murdered both Adams and the clerk. Yup," said the whaleman, patently happy with his conclusions. "He lied to us about Adams goin' to the ranch, and then Hallett died—Ducatel might have had a hand in that, too, by thunder! And so the money and the schooner fell into his hands, only the schooner was up at the salt dunes. He followed Caleb Adams to the schooner, but for some reason Adams had headed to the Gualichú tree, and so he killed him there. It must have been a shock to find that Adams didn't have the deed on him, as Ducatel needed it to make the ownership of the schooner look legal, but finally he worked out that it must be somewhere at the store, and that's how the clerk got killed."

"But why kill the clerk at all?"

"What?"

"Ducatel had his own key to the store, and no one would have thought it curious if the doctor had been seen going into his surgery, even if he hadn't been there for a while. He could have easily searched for the deed when the clerk wasn't there—after dark, for instance."

"Mebbe he just plain wanted to get rid of him."

"Out of plain bad temper?" Wiki dryly queried.

"Why not?" The whaleman's tone was more aggressive than ever. "It sure looked to me as if someone hacked down the old man in a murderous rage."

It had looked like that to Wiki, too. He said, "I'd like to know how you got the idea that Ducatel and Adams were together in a plot to rob you."

"Of both my money and my schooner," Stackpole confirmed, nodding energetically.

"But the deed proves that the sale really happened. Caleb Adams could have been acting honestly."

"He was another innocent victim, you reckon?" The whaling master's tone was cynical.

"It's possible."

"Because of the deed of sale?"

"Aye." Wishing to end this pointless argument, Wiki said on a practical note, "Give it to me, and I'll get it to Captain Wilkes as soon as this fog lifts. It's lucky in a way that the wind died, as the *Vin* is still close by. You'll come with me?"

He expected Stackpole to shake his head, as without doubt he wouldn't be anxious to try to explain to the short-tempered expedition commodore why he had held the deed for so many days without telling anyone about it. Instead, however, the whaling master looked around, his expression back to being shifty.

Lowering his voice still further, he confided, "There's something very odd about that deed."

"Odd?" echoed Wiki.

"That's why I was making for the *Swallow* when this goddamned fog came down."

"The *Swallow*?"

"Aye. I wanted to see you, and consult. I took a while to notice it, and now, no matter how hard I think, I can't see an answer to the puzzle."

"What do you mean?"

"Take a look for yourself."

Glancing around again to make sure they weren't observed, the whaling master reached into the back pocket of his trousers, and pried out a folded document. He didn't bother to check it. Instead, he thrust it at Wiki.

It was the deed of sale. After he had unfolded it, Wiki looked at it for a long time. Adams's signature, like the script that filled the blank spaces on the form, was clear enough, but, just as remembered, the signature in the space for Hallett's name was a messy, indecipherable scrawl.

Losing patience, Stackpole prompted, "The date. And bear in mind that Captain Hallett passed away on Sunday, 13 January."

Wiki read the date on the deed of sale. Unlike the signature, it was perfectly clear: January 14, 1839. He looked at Stackpole in astonishment, and the whaling master nodded sagely back.

When he was supposed to have signed his schooner away, Captain Hallett had been cold in his grave for twenty-four hours.

Fourteen

January 31, 1839

Most unusually, Wiki did not wake with the ringing of eight bells at midnight, though he had fully intended to go up to deck and join his father as he took over at the start of the middle watch. He felt it was important to have a talk and try to settle their differences, and naturally had chosen a time when Mr. Seward could be guaranteed to be heading off for his bunk, but because he overslept it never happened.

As Wiki ruefully meditated later, he had spent too many months as a civilian with the expedition fleet, where he had no deck responsibilities. The lack of noise and activity had played its part as well, because though the brigantine was still rolling steadily they were going nowhere, and there were no sounds of orders being given. When he finally ran up the companionway stairs to the deck, the bell was ringing seven times—he had slept in as late as three-thirty in the morning.

The fog was as thick as ever. Captain Coffin was standing on the weather side of the poop, and didn't notice Wiki's arrival. The sailor assigned to the post of lookout on the foredeck droned in the time-old fashion, *"Al-l-l's w-e-l-l,"* but it did not feel to Wiki as if all were well, at all. The mist hung in dense curtains, clinging close to the surface of the dark sea, which heaved and shimmered, beset by heavy currents.

Wiki shinnied up the foremast, and had to go as far as the topgallant crosstrees before he could look over the fog heads. Against the graying sky to the northwest he could just discern the tips of masts, and realized that the *Peacock* and *Vincennes* lay much closer to the brigantine than he had imagined. Because of the strong landward current, the *Osprey* had drifted farther toward the fleet.

The situation was fraught with danger. The brigantine was still to oceanward of the estuary, so was lying directly between the big expedition ships and the open sea. If the long-threatened *pampero* arrived, Captain Wilkes would signal the captains to slip their cables and clear the land under a press of sail, and there was an awful likelihood that the ships would blunder into the unseen *Osprey*. No one would be keeping a lookout for her, being under the impression that the brigantine had made her departure long since.

Yet it was impossible to sail out of danger. Heaped clouds were boiling over the landward horizon, but the air was utterly still. The *Osprey* had her jib out, and all square sail set on the foremast, while the massive fore-and-aft mainsail was set on the aftermast, too. None of it was working, however, because the canvas sagged like wet laundry on a line.

Then, all at once, there was a flutter in the weather leech of the foretopsail. Wiki skidded back to deck in a hurry, and approached the quarterdeck.

Captain Coffin had seen it. He snapped at the boatswain, "Call all hands, then get in the royal."

Impelled by the boatswain's bellowed orders, seamen dashed out of the forecastle and ran to their stations. Halyards were slackened, and then the royal was hauled up to the yard with hearty pulling at clewlines and buntlines, until the canvas hung there in bags. Two of the cadets swung aloft to furl it by passing gaskets around it, tying it up tight to the spar.

Thunder rumbled, almost drowning out the sound of Mr. Seward's bootsteps as he hurriedly arrived on the afterdeck. Captain Coffin glanced at him, nodded, and said, "We'll get the t'gallant in, mister, and the tops'l after that."

The mate's responsive shouts triggered still more commotion. Seamen clambered up the shrouds, and spread out on the topgallant yard. Then they were bent far over the spar, feet braced wide apart on the footropes, grappling with the canvas, hauling it up by sheer force. Before they could finish the job, however, the squall arrived in a mighty blast, screaming like a banshee from the totally unexpected *southwest,* directly ahead, roaring upon them to attack the ship full-face.

Within instants the jib was gone, blown to ribbons, while the men on the yard let go of the topgallant, grabbing frantically instead for a secure hold. The released canvas instantly tore to fragments that flickered away on the gale like panicked birds. The heavy forecourse and deep topsail, which were still fully set, remained intact, however—which made the situation worse. Instead of breaking up they slammed back against the masts, taking the whole weight of the wind on their forward surfaces, and putting a gigantic strain on the rigging. The *Osprey* lurched, caught aback. Another great gust, and the brig was abruptly pelted with hard spots of rain.

Something had to be set forward to get the *Osprey* to pay her head off and bring her round. Wiki heard Mr. Seward roar, "Get the foretopmast stays'l on her—quick, for your lives!"

"Aye, sir!" It was a disembodied shout.

There were not enough hands on the foredeck to do the job. The mate led the dash forward, Captain Coffin close behind him, both slipping and stumbling as the brigantine bucked unhappily. The apprentice at the wheel, abruptly abandoned, cried desperately at their retreating backs, "She won't take no notice of the helm, sir; she won't respond!"

Well, of course she wouldn't, thought Wiki. The brig had been becalmed for hours, with no way on. Instead of joining his father and the mate, he ran to the afterdeck to stop the boy from struggling with the wheel. The rudder was designed to turn the ship by using the pressure of the water, but without forward or sternward impetus there was nothing for it to grip. Unless he could take advantage of the pressure of the gale on the sails that were blowing hard aback against the masts, they were at the mercy of the gathering storm.

There was another grave danger lurking in the fog. Wiki's mind was moving fast, picturing the ships of the fleet slipping their cables and flying off on the breast of the storm to get an offing well away from the land—while the invisible *Osprey* wallowed directly between them and the open sea. The sky slammed again as thunder bellowed right above their heads, and the wind lashed even harder. All about the decks and rigging the men snatched at handholds to steady themselves against the assault. When Wiki looked over his shoulder, the little gang led by Captain Coffin and his mate kept doggedly on, clambering onto the forecastle head one by one, only to be shoved back by a savage gust.

The poop was now manned only by the six cadets. Wiki took over the wheel, and snapped, "Get the mains'l in—now!" Six uncomprehending faces gaped dumbly. *"Now!"* he repeated, in a voice so remarkably like his father's that they ran to the sheets without stopping for questions. Dimly, he realized that they were used to him being the steersman already, because he had steered the whaleboat into the Río Negro, and so it was easier for them to obey orders given by the captain's son.

They hauled manfully, while he shouted at them. For a horrible moment it looked as if the upper spar would jam. Then, miraculously Captain Stackpole arrived, half dressed from his bed, joined by his six boat's crew, who streamed out of the steerage looking equally disheveled. The whaling master hauled up his trousers as he came, snapping his braces over his shoulders at the same instant that he snapped out an order to one of his men. The seaman darted up the shrouds, clambered onto the innermost end of the gaff, and jumped vigorously up and down to get it going.

Down came the gaff at the run, folding the sail on the boom as it went, and abruptly the mainmast was naked. Miraculously, the whaleman had jumped safely out of the way. There was a howl of rage from the forecastle head, but Wiki, at the wheel, ignored it.

His hands tested the spokes as the gale, still blowing from dead ahead, exerted its force on the two big square sails on the foremast. He felt the *Osprey* stagger, on the verge of luffing up into the wind. As he steadied the wheel, keeping the wind on the forward surfaces of the big sails, she began to gather way, instead—only sailing backward instead of forward, and achieving a quite remarkable speed.

There was a shriek of rage as someone on the bow discerned the stream of bubbles she left behind, and the gang realized what was happening. Wiki ignored it. Instead, he felt delighted with the old *Osprey*, because she steered as well in the reverse direction as most ships did going in the proper direction. Another furious yell from the foredeck—and then everyone silenced in utter horror as a tall ship materialized from the murk, a shockingly short distance in front of their retreating bow.

The *Vincennes*—under storm sail, so close that it seemed Mr. Seward, frozen on the forecastle head, could have tossed a biscuit on board of her. For a sickening moment she swerved straight toward the *Osprey*, as if determined to run her down. Then she righted, swung back the other way, and went thundering across their bows, her forefoot crashing down on the exact spot where the brigantine had been bare minutes before.

Her wash deluged the forecastle head, earning Wiki a shake of a fist in his direction. Then the gang resumed their battle with the foretopmast staysail, which snapped and fought like a wild beast as the wind found the tunnel of canvas and streamed into it. Inch by cautious inch, they began to haul. The head of the sail seemed to crawl along the stay. It seemed a long moment before a distant shout of triumph heralded that the sail was fully extended.

Wiki snapped a quick order to set the aftersail again. It was a hard, heavy job, but six lusty boys plus six brawny whalemen made short work of it, directed by Captain Stackpole, who chanted like a coasterman to keep rhythm as they hauled. Up the mast the gaff smoothly ran, horizontal to the deck at first, and then peaked up to an angle.

Captain Coffin was sprinting along the deck, lurching from side to side with the violent pitching, shouting as he came. Wiki didn't need the instructions. *Down* went the helm, the seamen on the foredeck eased off the sheets, and the brigantine flew up into the wind.

The square sails on the foremast shook and shivered, and then flapped violently, while the mainsail boom swung around. For a long, tense moment, the *Osprey* hung between conflicting forces. Would she fall off, and drift to leeward before they could seize control again? The brigantine was old, but gallant—she hardly hesitated. Round the foreyards came, the canvas bellied taut, and she was running forward, with plenty of searoom, and no ships to blunder into their path. Within moments, she had picked up a tearing pace. The wind was still terrific; the topgallant and the jib were ruined, but no one was gravely hurt, and there was no damage to the rigging.

Wiki, feeling pleased with his feat of saving the *Osprey* from certain doom, handed over the wheel to the cadet, who was still shaking visibly with excitement and fear. Then he saw that Mr. Seward was staring imperatively in his direction. With a jerk of one thumb the mate beckoned him over to the weather side of the afterdeck, and Wiki saw that his expression was taut with fury. It was at that moment that he realized that he had committed the unthinkable—he had taken charge of another man's ship without permission. In the navy, he probably would have been hanged.

Then he was forced to wait. The mate said nothing for a couple of moments, instead taking his pipe out of his jacket pocket and blowing through the stem several times to make sure it was clear, before filling the tiny bowl with slow, deliberate movements. As Wiki fought down the impulse to shift from one foot to the other, Mr. Seward lit one of the lucifer matches called "fusees," favored by seamen because they burned in the dampest wind, and puffed at the little flame until he had the pipe drawing to his satisfaction. The red light reflected on his taut, fine-boned face.

After the usual struggle to extinguish the match, the mate finally nailed Wiki with a pale green stare. With the same deliberation with which he had filled and lit his pipe, he embarked on a long, detailed opinion of Wiki's past and pedigree. It could have been amusing, Wiki meditated, considering that his father, standing above them on the poop, was listening to his son's ancestry being so brutally dissected. However, Captain Coffin kept silent, which was not at all unexpected. From his own experience, Wiki knew that it was impossible for a shipmaster to undermine an officer's authority by checking him in front of the crew, not to mention a crowd of visitors. Additionally, Wiki recognized the icy glint under his half-lowered eyelid, and knew that he was as furious as his mate.

Just as Mr. Seward ran out of imagination and words, to Wiki's surprise Captain Stackpole strolled up, his attitude relaxed. "Jehovah, that was close," he remarked. "I couldn't make up my mind if we was going to be crushed by some great ship, or go over on our beam ends with the next big gust. Caught aback, and damn near run afoul, by God! Either could have been the end of us, but somehow we eluded both. Was it luck that saved us?" he asked himself, and answered with a shake of the head. "No, by damn, I think it was uncommon fine seamanship."

He paused ruminatively, while everyone stared dumbstruck, the silence filled only by the creak of planking, the whine of the wind in the rigging, and the rushing sea. "Reminded me of a time I was first mate of a Brazil Banks whaler," he went on comfortably. "The old *Potosi,* it was, and Charley Griffing was the captain. Do you know him?" he inquired of Wiki. "Hails from Greenport, Long Island. Currently in command of the *Franklin,* or so I heard."

Wiki silently shook his head.

"Amazed I haven't told you this yarn before," Captain Stackpole went on, with every appearance of enjoying himself. "On account of it happened on this very same coast. We was forced to call into a miserable little Brazilian port, being low on fresh water, not to mention needing a doctor, the yellow fever having broken out in the foc'sle. A helluva anchorage to enter, the only entrance being a narrow channel with a reef on one side with an old wreck stuck to it, and a steep-to cliff on the other. Two miles long, that channel was, leading up to a nice little harbor with a wharf and a couple of sheds. Can't remember the name of the place, but maybe you know it?"

Again, Wiki shook his head.

"Well, we sailed halfway up that narrow channel with no incident. Then a tide-rip we didn't know about struck us of a sudden, and before we knew it we was set head-on for the reef. And, my God, we was going at quite a clip at the time, a brisk onshore wind being with us. I can still remember that wreck standing up out of the rocks and rising higher as we got closer, just like she was beckoning us to a similar doom. Tell the truth, my blood turns to ice just to think of it."

The whaling master paused, his eyes narrowed in a reflective squint, while no one about the deck said a word. Then he said, "The old man didn't turn a hair, simply hollered for us to let the lee braces rip and bring her aback—and damn, did we rush to it. I remember how those yards swung for the backstays like of their own accord. Then there was just a little hesitation, and the faintest jerk as the old *Potosi* gathered sternway. Backward we sailed, all the way out of that channel and into the open sea, in the most beautiful sternboard ever seen on that coast. They're still talking about it there, I warrant."

The cadets were mesmerized by the tale, Wiki saw. He glanced at the mate to see how he was taking it, expecting to see reinvigorated rage. However, Alf Seward's back was turned toward him, all his attention on Captain Coffin, whose face had gone blank. As Wiki watched, the mate lifted his hand in an eloquent little gesture of regret. Now that someone had pointed out that the crime was justified by the emergency, he was silently apologizing to Captain Coffin for having humiliated his son so publicly.

Something about the way that hand was raised . . . Wiki blinked, unable to believe what he was seeing. Belatedly, he realized that Stackpole was waiting for some kind of comment, and said mechanically, "So Captain Griffing saved his ship?"

"Aye. Piled her up on the rocks at the Falklands about four years after that," Captain Stackpole said cheerfully, "but he sure saved her at the time with that sternboard. And, because it saved our ship and our lives, I've been uncommon appreciative of that kind of seamanship, ever since. Remember that offer I made you to ship with me as second mate?" he inquired. "Well, I'll change it to first mate, by God, once I've got quit of the one I've got. What do you reckon about that?"

For a moment Wiki didn't respond, because he was still watching Mr. Seward, and thinking that he now knew exactly why the mate of the *Osprey* behaved the way he did, and why his father had been so unwelcoming, too. It was hard not to shake his head in disgust with himself that he had taken so long to see the obvious.

Then he realized that Captain Stackpole was waiting for an answer, and had to struggle to remember what the whaling master had said. "I think we have other matters to talk over," he managed at last.

"Then we'll have a little chat," Stackpole said heartily, leading him away.

The moment they were safely out of earshot, however, his expression changed, and he growled, "You had every excuse just now, your father having lost his head and abandoned his post, but I have to warn you, boy, that if you ever take over the quarterdeck of *my* ship without permission, I'll knock your head off your shoulders so quick you won't have time to know what's happening. Understood? Good. Now then, what do you reckon?"

Wiki took a deep breath. "I reckon we should get that deed of sale over to Captain Wilkes."

"The way the *Vincennes* was flying off to the open sea, *I* reckon we'll find the old *Trojan* first," said Stackpole, and guffawed.

It was a prediction that proved well off the mark. An hour later a sail was raised—but it was not the whaler *Trojan*. Instead, it was the New York sealer *Athenian*.

Fifteen

Wiki was one of the first on board the *Osprey* to spy the sealing brig, because he was on the topgallant yard helping to bend on a new sail, to replace the one that had torn to shreds. Captain Coffin had graciously assented when Captain Stackpole had offered his boat's crew to help out with the work, and Wiki had climbed aloft without bothering to ask permission. It wasn't an easy job, because the wind was still strong and gusty, and the brigantine was jolting about madly on the lumpy sea, but it made a very pleasant change, because the two Polynesian whalemen from Stackpole's boat's crew were on either side of him.

They were Tahitian, as Wiki had found out during the traditional self-introductions. One had a mane of black hair that any gaucho would have envied, while the other had the bushiest eyebrows Wiki had ever seen on an islander, and both were very young, not yet twenty. As usual, the ritual exchange of genealogies was succeeded by the new politeness of Oceania, which was an exchange of tales of how they came to be on board of American ships. Just like all the other islanders Wiki had encountered in port and at sea, these two lads had shipped on their first Yankee whaler for adventure and fun.

"'The thought came to me in Tahiti,'" the bushy-browed one confessed in a chant:

I shall sail away like a white man,
I shall paddle to some distant country,
I shall hunt in some amorous land.

The only difference from most was that after more than a year, the two Tahitians were still together. Even when one had been discharged sick, his comrade had proved staunch, and stayed with him. One day, they said, they would go home together, marry pretty wives, live with them at Matavai Bay, and boast about their adventures for the rest of their lives—but not yet. They were very interested in the exploring expedition, and asked if the fleet might call at Tahiti.

"Who knows?" said Wiki. Whatever plans Captain Wilkes might have for the Pacific was kept a secret from them all.

Now, they worked side by side on the lee arm of the yard, securing the new canvas sheet after it had been run up on buntlines, and the three were talking together in the Tahitian language—though for Wiki it was almost like talking in *te reo Maori*, because eight out of ten words were pretty much the same. They were also watching Mr. Seward, who was supervising the work from the bottom of the mast, and the Tahitians were laughing at Wiki because he had taken so long to discern what they had noticed right away. Then they were distracted, as all three pairs of quick Polynesian eyes glimpsed a little cloud of sail bearing down on them from the southeast.

By the time the new topgallant was set, the *Athenian* was plainly visible from the *Osprey*'s decks. The sealing brig was breasting the seas in businesslike fashion, under forecourse, single-reefed topsails, and double-reefed topgallants. Though the water dashed up from her bow, she was obviously not in any particular hurry, because when they signalized her the captain readily consented to haul aback so they could hold a conversation.

The brigantine ran down to her, and a massively built fellow with a huge black beard clambered onto the brig's poop, to exchange hearty hails with Captain Coffin. The distance and the wind made their words indistinct, but it was evident that he had heard and understood the invitation to come aboard, because once the brigantine came to a standstill downwind of his ship, the *Athenian* lowered a boat, which arrived with amazingly little fuss, considering the rugged conditions. Meantime, one of the *Osprey* boats had been hauled inboard and stowed upside down on the skids, leaving the davits free. Falls were dropped, the headsman hooked on, and the boat, with the brig's master still inside, was rapidly hoisted, while the oarsmen scrambled up the side of the *Osprey*.

They were rough-looking fellows, and didn't smell very wonderful either, being clad in half-cured sealskin suits. However, their young captain had done his best to look like a God-fearing Yankee, having shifted into his best broadcloth when the *Osprey* was raised, though the immense beard and his lashed-back thicket of black hair rather marred the effect. Jumping with a crash out of the boat and onto the deck, he shouted, "William Coffin, ahoy! Don't you know me, sir?"

"Jim Nash, by God!" cried Captain Coffin, striding up with his hand held out. "What the devil is a Stonington lad doing in charge of a New Yorker?"

Captain Stackpole arrived at that moment. The whaling master's expression darkened threateningly at the sight of the man who had left the *Grim Reaper* at El Carmen, and could be considered the source of his current woes, but he made no comment as introductions were made—because of the strong possibility that Captain Nash had been cheated, too, guessed Wiki.

Also, Captain Coffin, garrulous as ever, didn't give him a chance. "You do remember my son?" he asked Nash, urging them all down the stairs. "I brought him along on my visits to Stonington over his first few years in America, so I'm sure you've met before. How's your father, Jim? Have you heard from home? And how did you get to be in charge of a New York sealer?" he demanded.

"Happened by accident," Nash cheerfully answered this last as they arrived in the cabin. "And won't be master of her for much longer, neither, on account of the brig is up for sale," he elaborated, thumping onto a green cushion. Then he silenced, looking around the room with an awed expression.

The cat undulated up to him, and sniffed at his boots. Catching the scent of seal, she hissed like a snake, and shot into the pantry with her tail bunched up and her fur standing on end, which Jim Nash found very funny. Then he sobered as Captain Coffin demanded, "Why are you selling the *Athenian*? I heard great tales that you did uncommon well on the sealing ground," he went on, and glanced meaningfully at Captain Stackpole, whose brows were bunched together.

"That I did," Captain Nash agreed. For the first time, he seemed to notice the whaling master's aggressive look, and his expression became puzzled. He said rather defensively, "And selling the brig ain't my idea, but my owners' instructions, delivered to me by a Stonington sealer back in November, not long after he arrived on this coast."

Then the steward arrived with a pot of coffee, and a plate of cake, and Captain Nash immediately relaxed, attacking the repast as if he hadn't tasted civilized food and drink in months. At the same time, prompted by Captain Coffin's stream of questions, he gossiped about old Stonington, Connecticut, with his mouth full, while Wiki—who didn't recognize the sealing master at all, though most of the names mentioned were familiar—waited impatiently to insert a question, and Stackpole looked equally eager. However, his father forestalled them both by finally commanding, "Explain yourself, Jim."

The Stonington man brushed crumbs out of his beard, saying amiably, "Explain myself how?"

"Why are your owners selling the *Athenian*? There has to be a good reason they're so anxious to get quit of her! How many strokes does she leak?"

"Tight as a bottle, I promise," Nash denied in wounded tones. "She was in the Mediterranean trade, and was always treated handsome."

"So why did they take her out of the wine and raisin business, and send her to Patagonia a-sealing?"

"You know what New Yorkers are like!" the other exclaimed. "They heard gossip about a resurgence of sealing on this coast, and scented a profit thereby—but the profit didn't come as quick as they'd like, so even though our holds are packed full of pelts, they've lost interest in the trade. Do you feel in need of another ship, William?" he went on hopefully. "It's a rare opportunity that you'd be mad to miss. The *Athenian*'s younger than the *Osprey*, by many a mile. Honor-built in Stonington, just twelve years ago. One hundred forty-eight tons burthen, oak frames and straking, copper fastened throughout, very roomy, extremely handy, and a first-rate sea boat. Give her a coat of pitch and a few sheets of copper, and she'll get you to whatever outlandish lagoon you can name, and skim like a bird to Macao after that."

"Replace the *Osprey*? Not till she founders under me!" Captain Coffin snorted. Then he said, "How much?"

"Fifteen thousand, five hundred."

"*What!* You're a rogue, Jim. And you still haven't told us how you got to be the master of this pricey little craft."

Captain Nash meditatively pulled at his earlobe—and suddenly Wiki placed him. It was a characteristic little gesture that gave him away. Jim Nash had been seventeen when they'd met, and Wiki had been twelve, so they hadn't had much to do with each other. However, he remembered that Jim had been massively built even then. He also recollected that Jim Nash had saved a boy's life. When he'd heard frantic hollering in a thicket, he investigated, fortunately, because a gang of boys had been playing a rough game called slinging the monkey, and left their victim slung by his heels from the apex of a triangle of wood—with a slow fire burning underneath. If Jim hadn't happened by, the boy would have roasted to death. According to the legend, once he'd kicked out the fire and let the boy down, he'd got a few names out of him. Then he'd tracked down the culprits, and personally thrashed them within an inch of their lives.

"It must've been May 1836 when I shipped on board of the *Athenian*—but as first mate, not captain," he was saying. "I'd never commanded a ship in my life! Rowland Hallett was master—a fine man, he, and a fine mariner, too. We made the Río Negro in October, and when he got to El Carmen he found the schooner *Grim Reaper* up for sale, so he bought her to use as a tender."

"The *Grim Reaper*, huh?" barked Stackpole.

"Aye," said Nash. He waited, looking cautious again, but Stackpole kept silent, so he went on with his tale. "Captain Hallett filled her with provisions and salt, manned her with a gang of Indians and a couple of our sailors, and then took command of her himself—logged me as master of the *Athenian*! I'd have to check the logbook to be certain sure, but I've a strong feeling it was October 17, 1836—a memorial date, because I was so confounded surprised."

"And where did you sail after that?" Captain Stackpole said quickly.

"Aha," said Nash, and put his finger alongside his nose. "That's for me to know and not to tell. Let's just say we did just fine, even if it did take two years longer than the owners liked." He watched Captain Coffin pour three glasses of brandy, took one when it was handed out to him, watched Captain Stackpole take the second, and then looked at Wiki, who sipped coffee.

He exclaimed to Captain Coffin, "A son of *yours* is temperance?"

"He's doing his utmost to drink up my entire cargo of coffee, and put me in the parish poorhouse," Captain Coffin informed him.

Nash laughed, and then said, "You're carrying somethin' so ordinary as coffee? I imagined it would be tortoiseshell, or lacquerwood—somethin' exotic."

"In my personal hold," replied Captain Coffin, with a great show of dignity, "I am carrying a cargo more exotic than you could ever imagine."

"Then you better tell me what it is, since my imagination ain't up to the job."

"Natural specimens." The words were pronounced slowly and impressively.

"Natural—*what?*"

"Rocks and plants, and wondrous reptiles, and strange fish and snails, too. I've had the honor of being chartered by the U.S. Exploring Expedition to carry everything weird and wonderful they've collected so far to the States, to be put in museums where ignorant folks like you and me will congregate to marvel."

"Good God!" Jim Nash shook his head in wonder, without noticing that Wiki was going through a mighty struggle to keep from collapsing with laughter. "I heard that a discovery fleet was poking about these parts, but would never have thought that a man like you would have somethin' to do with it," he said. Then the Stonington man grinned and added, "Reptiles and snails and fish, huh? I bet they stink to high heaven."

Captain Coffin gave him a haughty look, and changed the subject. "Tell us more about that little schooner Captain Hallet bought," he said, while Captain Stackpole shifted forward on his cushion, and Wiki sat straight.

"She served us well, the *Grim Reaper* did," said Nash readily. "We first set up a camp on a Patagonian beach, and left a work gang there with most of the provisions and salt, then off we went to the beaches I refuse to name." And he winked at the whaling master, at ease now he had half of a glass of brandy inside him. "Once we arrived," he went on, "we used the schooner as a tender to get men and tools to the rookeries, and pelts and oil back. She could hold five thousand skins, and once we filled her holds she'd carry 'em to the camp, and leave 'em for the gang there to beam clear of fat, peg out, and dry. Then she would sail up the Río Negro to take on provisions and salt, and head back to the killing grounds. And so it went, until we had stockpiled enough furs to fill the holds of the *Athenian* for the passage home. Forty thousand," he concluded smugly.

"Forty *thousand*?" cried Captain Stackpole.

"That's what the *Athenian* is holding right now. It took us two years, but it'll fetch a nice little sum on the market. The owners are fools to sell, believe me."

So Ramón, son of Huinchan, had been confused when he had mentioned five thousand pelts, Wiki realized. The Indian had meant multiples of five thousand, and it made more sense now that he had puffed out his chest with pride.

He said curiously, "Who sold you the *Grim Reaper* in the first place?"

"I don't know the name of the original owner," Nash returned as cooperatively as ever, though he looked a little surprised that Wiki had so unexpectedly joined the conversation. "We bought her through an agent, who was the local storekeeper."

Stackpole interrupted, "Caleb Adams?"

"He was indeed Caleb Adams," agreed Jim Nash. "Do you know him?"

"I do indeed," Stackpole said grimly.

Wiki said, "We discovered his dead body, just the other day."

"What?" Nash's eyes widened. "*He's* dead, too?"

Stackpole blinked, and looked at Wiki, who cautiously asked, "Who else is dead?" Surely Nash didn't know about the clerk?

"Poor Rowland Hallett, that's who." Jim Nash hauled out a huge handkerchief, blinking hard. "He was bit by a bull seal, and his finger got infected. Then his hand went bad, and his arm started to go rotten, too. So we hurried him to El Carmen, and consulted a man what has the bloody sauce to call himself a surgeon."

"Ducatel," said Stackpole grimly.

"Aye, that's the name. He reassured us that he'd come right if we left him there to be doctored, but instead of making him better, he cut off his arm and killed him. When we got back to El Carmen to take poor Hallett back on board, it was to receive the dismal news that he had passed away the day before. On the Sabbath." With a loud trumpeting, Jim blew his nose, and said, "And Adams is dead, too?"

There was a pause, and then Wiki observed, "*He* didn't die of natural causes."

"What d'you mean?"

The whaling master answered: "Someone murdered him—and it's *his* job to find out who and why." He jabbed a thumb in Wiki's direction.

"*Murdered?* What the devil are you saying?" Nash looked at Captain Coffin, who was watching and listening quietly, and demanded, "What the hell is going on?"

"Wiki's a sheriff's deputy," said Captain Coffin. "He keeps himself busy solving murders. It's an odd kind of hobby, but he appears to like it."

"What do you need a sheriff on the *Osprey* for? How many murders do you get, for God's sake?"

"Not with me," said Captain Coffin hastily. "He's with the expedition."

"The same expedition what's given you the job of carrying the specimens?"

"That's the one."

"Well, it's a damned waste of taxpayers' money, in my honest opinion, and it don't surprise me that they have murders on board. Why don't you do your boy a favor? Buy the *Athenian* and put him in command."

"He's too busy finding murderers for that."

"You reckon? So how did he get involved in this case?"

Stackpole said, "I boarded the U.S. brig *Swallow* with an official complaint of piracy, found they had a sheriff on board, and took him upriver to investigate."

"Piracy?" said Nash blankly.

"Of the schooner *Grim Reaper*! The same schooner I arranged with Adams to buy from Hallett on my behalf!"

Captain Nash's eyes sharpened. Then he said cautiously, "Would you, by any chance, be S. R. Stackpole?"

"Samuel Rodman Stackpole," Captain Stackpole confirmed in a growl. "The damn poor fool who gave Adams a draft for one thousand dollars to buy her, and left him to find a gang of sealing hands, and stock her with provisions and salt. Eight days later, when I returned to pick up my purchase, Adams had disappeared, and the schooner was gone—pirated!"

"Some thieves killed Adams, and then got away with the *Grim Reaper*?" Jim Nash clicked his tongue and shook his head. "Oh dear, oh dear, poor Adams, robbed of a schooner he didn't even own. How did you find his corpse?"

Wiki said, "We were tracking the route he rode upriver from the store."

"He was lyin' there dead, huh?" Obviously, Jim was picturing a dried-out corpse lying by the side of the trail, because he went on, "You sure he was murdered? That he didn't die of thirst or somethin' like that? Men keel over real easy up the Río Negro, you know."

"He'd been knifed and then shot to death."

"Well, that sure sounds like murder, and a thorough job of it, too," the Stonington man admitted. "You got any theories about the killer?"

"The thief, of course," Stackpole interrupted. "Adams stole my money and my schooner, and then his killer stole both from him."

Nash exclaimed, "What the devil gave you the idea that Adams *stole* the money?"

"When we realized the deed of sale was forged, of course!"

"Forged?"

"It was signed the day after Captain Hallett died, and yet it was made out in his name!"

Nash looked puzzled, and then light dawned in his face. "That's because it was *Captain Hallett* who made arrangements with Adams to sell the schooner," he said.

Dead silence. Captain Coffin was sitting at his ease on the red settee, one arm stretched along the back, and the other hand holding his brandy glass. He was watching and listening with alert interest, but as before, he did not offer a word.

Wiki said, "Captain Hallett really *did* give Adams the job of selling her?"

"He did, indeed," Nash replied. "On January 6, the same day that we arrived up the Río Negro to hand him over to a doctor—which is why the deed is kinda confusing, I guess. Though Adams produced the form, nothing was signed, on account of Captain Hallett's arm made it impossible. He was in a real bad way, and we was in a hurry to entrust the poor fellow to that quack what pretends to practice medicine. Then we left him at the surgeon's ranch, and went back to the brig and sailed off to pick up the drying gang, along with their stockpile of pelts, leaving the *Grim Reaper* lying at anchor off El Carmen for the inspection of prospective purchasers. Got back on January 14, to hear the good news that the schooner had been sold—and the terrible tidings that we'd lost our captain. He'd expired just the day before, bless his departed soul. So I was the one what signed the deed of sale in his place."

Wiki echoed, "*You* signed it?"

"That I did, after checking all the details that Adams had filled in. And Adams signed it, too, on the buyer's behalf. S. R. Stackpole," Nash added, and looked at the whaling master, and said, "I guess that's you."

Stackpole groped in a back pocket, and hauled out the deed of sale. "That signature's yours?"

Jim Nash inspected the illegible scrawl, handed it back, and said, "It is."

"You don't write very well," reproved Wiki.

Ignoring this, Stackpole pursued, "And Adams gave you my draft on a Connecticut bank?"

"He did," Jim agreed.

"For a thousand dollars?"

"Aye." Jim Nash slapped the front of his jacket as if he had it stowed in a pocket, though he added complacently, "It's in the brig's strongbox, and the owners should be mighty gratified about that, too."

"I reckon they should," grimly agreed Captain Stackpole. "But they ain't goin' to know about it, are they—because you're going to give me my money back."

Jim Nash shook his head emphatically. "No, I ain't. You bought her fair and square, and I got documents to prove it—my receipt from Adams, and the affidavit you gave Adams appointing him your representative."

"But where's my bloody schooner?" Stackpole cried.

"I appreciate that you paid over the money and got nothing in return," Jim Nash said, and wagged his head in vast sympathy for a fellow shipmaster who'd been thoroughly diddled. "That really is too bad, but I don't know what I can do about it. What you have to do is report it to the authorities, who should pass on the news to a man-of-war. Mighty tough on pirates, is the U.S. Navy. Tell you what, though," he went on, illuminated by a great idea. "If you buy the *Athenian,* I'll strike a thousand dollars off the price, to make up for your loss. Couldn't be fairer than that, huh?"

Stackpole, very obviously, didn't think much of this generous offer. Wiki meditated that if looks could have killed, Jim Nash would have been felled to the deck.

After waiting in vain for a reply, Jim looked at Wiki, and said with lively interest, "So where did you find the corpse? At the salt dunes?"

"Inland, past the *salinas,*" said Wiki. "His killer had buried him, but not very well, so that the skull was exposed. The vultures led us to his grave."

Nash grimaced, demonstrating yet again that even hardened sealers had feelings. He said, "But why were you tracking Adams past the *salinas*?"

"We'd found that all the goods in the store had gone, and reckoned they'd been taken to provision the *Grim Reaper,* which I calculated was up at the salt dunes," Stackpole said.

"But that's ridiculous," said Nash. "Adams told me he was going to load the provisions after the schooner got back to El Carmen."

Wiki said, puzzled, "He *told* you he was going to load at El Carmen?"

"After he'd filled the salt bins," Nash agreed. "He was goin' to the salt dunes to fill with salt first, and then he was sailing back to load with provisions."

"He told you all this on the fourteenth, after you signed the deed?"

"Aye. And then I went up to the salt dunes with him."

"On horseback?"

"No, of course not," Jim Nash said. "On the schooner."

Wiki felt more bewildered than ever. He said, "But Ramón told me that there wasn't a captain on board when the *Grim Reaper* sailed upriver."

"Ramón?"

"The *capataz* of the Indian sealing gang that worked for Captain Hallett."

"My God, you do get around! Ramón had the makings of a fine sealing master—though, mind you, Hallett was very good with the Indians, treated 'em like Christians. He looked for the heart and soul of a man, and paid no notice of the color of his skin." Jim Nash hauled out his handkerchief again, partly because of renewed grief, and partly to hide embarrassment as he abruptly realized that what he'd said might not be the height of diplomacy, considering that Wiki was brown.

Wiki said tactfully, "The feeling was mutual—Ramón also said that Captain Hallett was a fair and just *caudillo* who worked as hard as his men."

"Aye, that he was." Again the sealer blew his nose. Then Nash went on in more practical tones, "So he told you there wasn't a captain on board the *Grim Reaper* when we sailed to the dunes? Well, the way that it was, Adams took the tiller for the run, and I sat at my ease. And Ramón knew I was captain of the *Athenian,* not the schooner, so what he said would've made sense to him, even if it didn't to you."

And Ramón had been derisive at the very idea of a *pulpero* like Adams being considered a captain. Nodding, Wiki changed the subject. "Why did you sail upriver with Adams?"

"I was doing him a favor," said Jim. "Just two of the seamen he'd hired turned up, and they was useless sogers, so I loaned a couple of good men to help him out."

Wiki exclaimed, "He'd hired *seamen*?"

"Adams shouldn't have done that," Stackpole protested. "I told him to find a sealing gang, but that I didn't need seamen. I was going to send over three hands from the *Trojan* to sail the schooner to the rookeries."

"Perhaps Adams hired them to get her up to the salt dunes and back to the pueblo, not to take her out to sea," Wiki suggested.

Nash looked doubtful, and said, "He gave me the strong impression he'd hired those two useless sogers for the whole of the sealing season."

Wiki asked, "But he hadn't found a gang to do the actual sealing?"

"Nope. He said he couldn't find Indians who were willing. Anyways, I helped out by loaning him two good seamen from the *Athenian* for the trip."

Wiki guessed, "Peter and Dick?"

Nash was astonished. "You truly are a sleuth! How d'you know their names?"

"Ramón told us," said Wiki.

"Ramón? Well, of course he knew Peter and Dick, on account of they sailed the schooner every time the gang was being ferried to a sealing beach."

Wiki nodded again, and said, "Tell me about the two so-called seamen Adams had hired."

"Portuguese," Nash replied succinctly. "Wore gaucho costumes, but spoke Portuguese. It was a crime to call 'em seamen, though I heard they had a fishing boat. Didn't seem to know one rope from another, though it could've been pure laziness. Adams was mighty wild about the third fellow, the sailing master what didn't turn up, because he would've shown 'em how to work, or so I gathered."

Stackpole cried, "I didn't tell him to hire a sailing master!"

Ignoring this, Wiki said urgently, "Did you hear the names of those Portuguese men?"

"Gomes—one name for both of 'em, on account of they was brothers."

Wiki paused, his thoughts racing. Then he said, "What happened after you moored the schooner at the dunes?"

"I'd brought three of the *Athenian* boats, which followed the schooner upriver, and we set to getting our pelts out of the schooner and into them."

Stackpole said bitterly, "Weren't you taking a risk, leaving valuable furs on board?"

"It was safe enough, we reckoned, and there wasn't all that many of them, just five hundred or so. We trusted Adams to make sure they wasn't stolen, and was right, because when we got back they were just the way we left 'em. Truth to tell, we figured that the sight of a few dozen hides would help a speculator make up his mind to buy," Nash candidly confessed, earning himself another black look.

Captain Coffin entered the conversation for the first time for a while, saying thoughtfully, "Wouldn't it have been easier to unload the skins while the schooner was moored off El Carmen?"

Just like the provisions, thought Wiki.

"It didn't make any difference to us," Jim Nash said, and shrugged. "It was all happening on the water, wherever."

"Did it take long?" Wiki asked.

"Nope. We started the moment the schooner was moored, and got the last into the boats by dark that same day. Slept on the schooner, sailed the boats down the river before dawn, and were at the estuary by sunup. That was the last I saw of the Río Negro—we took our departure as soon as we was all back on board the brig."

"This was on the fifteenth?"

"Aye."

"And Peter and Dick were with you?"

Nash's brows shot up. "Well, of course! I doubt they've ever jumped ship in their lives. They'll get a nice advance in Rio, after we've sold the brig, and a whole lot more money after they've worked their passage back to New York. Why forfeit all that by jumping ship in a godforsaken place like the Río Negro?"

"So you haven't lost any of your men?"

"None," confirmed Nash, and then went on, "We've decided Rio de Janeiro is the best place to put the *Athenian* up for sale. Would've been there before now, except for a couple of little whales."

Distracted, Wiki exclaimed, "Whales?"

"Aye. We had trypots on board, of course, and they topped up our seal-oil barrels nicely."

Wiki shook his head in awe, thinking he would never stop learning about Yankee opportunism, and then, because he wondered whether Adams had set off for the *salinas* before or after Jim Nash took his departure from the dunes, he asked, "Was Adams still on board of the schooner when you left?"

"Nope. He came on my boat as far as El Carmen. We dropped him off at the steps, and that's the last I ever saw of him."

Wiki sat up straight, because this gave an entirely new slant to the affair.

Captain Coffin said curiously, "Why did he want to get back to El Carmen?"

"He was in a passion, to tell the truth, on account of the nonappearance of that sailing master he'd hired. Once he found him, he was heading back upriver on horseback to collect the *Grim Reaper* and sail her down again to load the provisions—or so he said."

Wiki said slowly, "So he could have arrived back at the store to find the provisions gone."

"Well, if that was the case, it would've done nothin' to calm him down."

"Adams was angry by nature, or so I noticed," Stackpole remarked.

"Ain't that nothing but the truth!"

Surprised, Wiki asked, "You knew Adams well?"

"I should say I did," Jim replied with emphasis. "Sealed a couple of seasons with him, on my very first voyage."

Wiki exclaimed, *"Adams was a sealer?"*

"Didn't you know?" Nash looked surprised. "But that's why we gave him so much business, on account of I knew him so well."

Urgently, Wiki said, "What kind of man was he—what was Adams like?"

Jim thought a moment, and then said, "I liked him. He was a damn fine seaman, and even better at the sealing business. Entertaining, too—full of rousing yarns. Flashy sort of cove, had a lot of confidence in himself. Wore a sort of medal about his neck, a curious thing, one of those old Spanish coins with a cross on one side, and a three-masted ship on the other. What d'you call 'em—pieces of eight? The first seal he ever killed vomited it up in its death throes—must've swallowed it with some gravel when it scooped a fish off the bottom. It was gold, but he bored a hole in it and hung it round his neck, and reckoned it brought him luck."

Stackpole fished about in his pockets again, brought out a medal, and shoved it at Jim Nash. "This it?"

Nash took it, and inspected it. "Aye," he said, handing it back. "How did you get hold of it?"

"Cut it off the string that hung around the neck of his corpse."

Jim Nash grimaced. "So his luck deserted him in the end, poor old Caleb—though I reckon it was running out already. Sorry about that, because I respected the man. Taught me a lot, though you had to watch his temper. He'd fly into a murderous rage without a hint of warning, and even though he was a little chap, it was a good idea to get out of the way quick. He once even flew at *me* with his cudgel. I might've been just eighteen, but I was a lot bigger than him, and he learned not to try that again."

"Was he apt to bear a grudge?" inquired Captain Coffin.

"You can definitely say that. He bore no grudge ag'in me, because I beat him fair and square, but if he thought he'd been done wrong, he wouldn't rest till he got revenge. He was a good sealing man, though—could put away four hundred seals a day without straining himself overmuch, or even givin' himself a fright."

Wiki asked, "So why did he get out of sealing?"

"There was a brawl of some sort—but I don't know the details, on account of I wasn't there, it being a later voyage. Someone told me he left his ship in a hurry—in Montevideo, I think—and that was the last I heard of him for quite a few months. But when we arrived up the Río Negro in October 1836, there he was in charge of that store—told us he owned it, and that this was the life for him. It was a real surprise, I tell you—and very useful, too, considerin' we was doing business in those parts."

Stackpole said, "The first time I dealt with him, he seemed to be doing well."

"He was doing very well indeed. Within a couple of years, though, he was lookin' considerable poorer."

"I noticed that, too," said Stackpole.

"General de Rosas has deliberately ruined the economy of the Río Negro, according to a customs officer we met," said Wiki.

"That's what I heard, too," said Jim. "That quack of a surgeon, Ducatel, was particular' vociferous about it."

"I also heard that they're plotting revolution," Wiki went on.

"Well, I must say that don't surprise me."

"Did Adams ever talk about it?"

"Nope, he never mentioned anythin' along those lines. I don't reckon he was interested in politics, just in making money—and I got the strong impression he was badly lacking in that department. The agent's fee for selling the schooner would've come in mighty handy."

"Adams was after more than the fee," Stackpole growled. "That deed of sale might have been real, but all along he was planning to keep the schooner for himself."

"I find that hard to believe," said Nash, exhibiting loyalty to an old sealing mate. "Though he was certainly on his beam ends," he added thoughtfully.

Wiki asked, "Did he say anything about going back to sealing?"

"Well, now that you mention it, just before I gave him the job of selling the schooner, he did ask if we needed another hand on the *Athenian*. But of course I had to say no, what with the brig's owners orderin' us to put her on the block."

There was a shout on deck—Mr. Seward issuing orders to take in the new topgallant. They all looked up at the skylight, where a gust of wind abruptly rattled the panes. Jim drained his brandy and stood up. "Better run," he said.

They all crowded up the companionway, Captain Nash first, then Wiki, then Captain Stackpole, with Captain Coffin bringing up the rear. When Nash opened the door at the top it was to find the rain lashing down, and he stopped short, grimacing. Wiki could see his boat's crew waiting by the davits to lower his boat, once he was inside it. Their heads were pulled down between their shoulders as the wind gusted and the rain hissed. "Who wouldn't sell a farm to go to sea?" he rhetorically asked, and braced himself to run.

Wiki stopped him by gripping his arm, saying urgently, "Who

was the sailing master who didn't turn up? Did Adams mention his name?"

"Aye, but what the hell was it?" Nash stood and ruminated a moment, rain dripping off his nose, but then shook his head, made a dash for the boat, and jumped inside it. The davit falls rattled as his men eased off the ropes, and the boat lowered in jerks, so that his burly form disappeared bit by bit.

Just as his waist was at the level of the rail, light dawned in his face. He shouted, "I remember now—the name was Harden!"

Then, without another word, he was gone.

Sixteen

The commotion of taking in sail was short-lived. Within minutes the sky was patched with blue, the wind had moderated, the rain had stopped, and the reefs in the canvas were being let out. Wiki stood at the larboard rail with his hair whipping about his face as he watched the *Athenian* draw away to the north. Then he realized that Captain Stackpole had joined him. The whaling master was leaning on the rail staring moodily at the gray, heaving waves.

He looked at Wiki and said, "So Adams hired two seamen and a sailing master, contrary to my instructions. Why d'you reckon he did that?"

Wiki said nothing, instead thinking with astonishment that he missed Forsythe's pungent comments and flashes of insight, and that he would have given a great deal to talk with the southerner right now.

Tiring of waiting for an answer, Stackpole shifted, demanding harshly, "So when d'you reckon it was that Adams made up his mind to steal the schooner? After Nash had left, or before?"

"Jim Nash said that Adams asked him for a job on the *Athenian*, but he had to say no, as he had instructions to end the voyage and put the brig up for sale," Wiki finally replied. "When he offered the schooner to you, Adams knew that you intended to take her on a sealing voyage. Did he ask you whether you'd give him a job as your sealing master—or even one of your sealing gang?"

Stackpole shook his head.

"Then I think you have your answer."

The whaleman's expression was blank for a moment, and then grim. "He planned to steal her right from the start, and take her out sealing himself," he said, almost to himself. His voice rose as he bitterly demanded, "Why didn't he steal the money, too? That would've really made his day!"

Wiki shrugged. "If it had been cash money, it might have been different—though he would have had two lots of people chasing him up, Nash for his money, and you for your schooner. But a bank draft was too complicated. He would have had to get to a big town to cash it, with an increased chance of being caught. No, it was easier for him to hand over the draft when Nash signed the deed of sale."

Stackpole sighed deeply. "So that's it," he said. "Nash has his money, but I don't have my schooner. And there's not a bloody thing we can do about it."

"I don't agree," said Wiki.

His father had quietly joined them, Wiki saw. He leaned his back against the rail with his hands in his pockets and a quizzical look in his half-shut eye.

Stackpole, who hadn't noticed Captain Coffin's arrival, said, "What do you mean?"

"I think we should get back to the Río Negro."

"The devil we're not! I need to get back to the *Trojan*!"

Captain Coffin said to Wiki, "I assume you've got a good reason for saying that?"

Wiki nodded, remembering what Forsythe had exclaimed when he'd learned that the clerk had been killed: *"You reckon the storekeeper's killer missed the boat because he wanted to get hold of that bill of sale, but then hung around for seven or more days before he finally got around to knifing the clerk? . . . But the bloody schooner was gone!"*

As the southerner had said, it didn't make sense—which meant that the only logical reason for killing the clerk for the bill of sale was that . . .

Wiki said with perfect certainty, "The schooner's still up the river."

Stackpole exclaimed, "But you were so certain that she'd sailed!"

"I know," Wiki admitted, feeling rueful. Bernantio and his gauchos, silent and secretive by nature, had headed upriver at the gallop after leaving him and Stackpole at the dunes, he remembered. At the time, he'd assumed that they had given up the hunt, but he'd forgotten the famous stubbornness of the *rastreadores*. If they hadn't been distracted by frantic rumors of a French invasion, they would have found the schooner, he was sure, and knew now that he shouldn't have paid them off so fast.

He said, "She's hidden in the willow trees at one of the little river islands upriver of the salt dunes, most likely with her masts unstepped."

Stunned silence, during which Captain Coffin studied Wiki's face. Finally, he remarked, "Well, the wind's in our favor." Then he headed to the quarterdeck to issue orders to Mr. Seward.

Captain Stackpole was staring at Wiki with conflicting emotions chasing across his face—hope, followed by disbelief, and finally speculation. He said, "Did you change your mind because of something Nash said?"

Again, Wiki paused, remembering that Stackpole himself had remarked that once the schooner was gone, the deed of sale was no longer important, but said, "Jim did make it apparent that the killer didn't have a crew to get the schooner out to sea."

"But Adams had shipped two seamen and a sailing master! Against my instructions," Stackpole added moodily.

More evidence that Adams had planned all along to steal the *Grim Reaper,* Wiki thought. He said, "There were only the two Gomes fishermen on board the schooner, remember, and Nash didn't think much of them."

"But Adams was collecting the sailing master . . ."

Stackpole's voice faded as realization struck. "It was Harden!" he exclaimed. "And Harden's joined the expedition fleet!"

"I wonder why Adams hired him, in the first place?" Wiki asked. "Nash told us that Adams himself was a fine seaman. Did you know that he was a sailor?"

"I had no idea that he was either a sailor or a sealer—for me, he was just a trader. I only ever dealt with him at his store," Stackpole said. "So it was big news to me that he might be a fine seaman. However, though he would have taken command on the passage to the rookeries, he would then put someone else in charge of the schooner while she was lying off the sealing beaches. It was more important for Adams to be on shore to oversee the sealing gang, while whoever was looking after the schooner took care of sending men, provisions, and tools to the beach as needed, and stowing furs as they came on board."

"Is that the usual routine?" Wiki asked, interested.

"It's what Captain Hallett did—he put his first mate in charge of the *Athenian,* while Hallett himself acted as sealing master. As Ramón said, Peter and Dick were on board, and they would have looked after the *Grim Reaper* while Hallett was on the beach."

That made sense, Wiki thought. Nash had said that Adams was an even better sealer than a seaman, and he would have had to train whatever sealers he had been able to find, and supervise them after that.

"Anyway, it don't signify now," Stackpole said gloomily. "Adams is dead, Harden is with the fleet, and the Gomes brothers are back at their old trade of fishing. Even if we do find the schooner, God knows what kind of shape she'll be in."

Having issued orders to Mr. Seward, Wiki's father had gone to the companionway door, and was standing looking back at them with his hand on the latch. When Wiki walked across the deck to join him, Stackpole followed. Together, they went down the stairs, where the aroma of coffee and food rose to meet them.

They sat around the red and green horseshoe-shaped sofa again, and the steward brought over a tray of sliced breads, pickles, and salt meats, followed by a pot of steaming coffee and mugs. They hadn't had a meal at the dining table yet, Wiki noticed, and thought that it must be reserved for shoreside visitors. He didn't mind, because he much preferred to be informal.

Stackpole slurped coffee, chewed bread and meat, and then said, "I thought that Adams was disobeying my instructions, at first, but I guess he hired those seamen and that sailing master for himself."

"He tried to hire an Indian sealing gang, too," said Wiki.

The whaleman lifted his brows, evidently remembering the conversation with Ramón, because he snorted, and said, "Didn't have any luck, did he."

Wiki said, "I wonder a lot about Benjamin Harden. Why did Adams hire him as sailing master—and why did he take the job?" Again, Forsythe's words rang in his mind: *"If he's got such a grand mission for revolution, why would he want to leave the Río Negro?"*

His father said, "Presumably he's a competent navigator."

"That's why Captain Wilkes was so keen to ship him for the expedition," Wiki agreed. "What makes me curious is what he's been doing since he joined the fleet."

The brigantine gave a sudden lurch, and they heard an infuriated shout from above and a spatter as their wake splashed up the stern windows. Captain Coffin hurried up the companionway, but evidently it was just a lapse on the helmsman's part, because a moment later they heard his footsteps coming down.

As he came into the cabin he said to Wiki, "I've only seen Harden once, when he headed the boat that came to collect those two carpenters."

"That was only the second time I saw him myself," Wiki admitted. "The other time was when Captain Ringgold was desperate for a pilot to get the *Sea Gull* off the sandbank, and Harden miraculously appeared to offer his services."

"Miraculously?" his father echoed.

Wiki was beginning to wonder a lot about that, but he simply nodded.

"You seemed worried about his boat's crew," Captain Coffin remembered.

"They were five of the old sealers we rescued from their sinking ship about three months ago, and who were shipped with the fleet after that. The two carpenters they collected—Boyd and Folger—were two more of them."

"Who recruited those surly sogers? Wilkes?"

"Aye," said Wiki. "To take advantage of their experience in the Antarctic Ocean."

"What kind of experience?" Stackpole queried.

"They sailed with Captain Nathaniel Palmer."

Captain Stackpole looked baffled, but Captain Coffin's left eye opened as wide as the other, a sign of vast surprise. "Nat Palmer of Stonington?" he exclaimed. "But I know him! He's the man who discovered the continent of Antarctica, back in 1820!"

"Don't ever tell Captain Wilkes that—as he's quite determined to be the official discoverer," Wiki advised with a grin. "And another thing you mustn't mention is that the expedition is not the first United States discovering venture."

His father looked both startled and diverted. "It isn't?"

"Back in 1829 a set of Connecticut merchants put up the money for a three-ship fleet to survey the Antarctic. Because sealers know that ocean best, the crews were made up of sealing men, and the ships were sealing vessels, one of them commanded by Palmer. The venture was called the South Sea Fur Company and Exploring Expedition."

Stackpole said cynically, "And what was the priority, sealing or exploring?"

Wiki smiled. "The crews certainly thought that the real mission was to find new seal rookeries, so they could all make their eternal fortunes. However, the captains had different ideas, and set to surveying the ocean instead, which the crews didn't like at all. A few ringleaders talked mutiny, and a number refused duty. When Palmer made port in South America a whole lot more deserted, with the result that he was forced to abandon the voyage, being so short of hands."

Captain Coffin said, "And these sealers were among those who refused duty?"

"They were the original troublemakers," Wiki said.

"The ringleaders?" Stackpole exclaimed. "And yet Wilkes has shipped them for the exploring expedition?"

"Aye," said Wiki grimly.

"Damned if I'd want to ship men with that reputation. They made trouble yet?"

"They've not had the opportunity. They were deliberately spread about the ships so they could share their lore with as many men as possible. But now it seems that they've been gathered together again—as Harden's boat's crew."

"Harden," Captain Coffin repeated slowly. "Cocky sort of fellow, I thought."

"Río Negro scuttlebutt says he's a rebel against de Rosas," said Stackpole.

Wiki nodded, and told his father, "His full name is Benjamin Harden, according to his Protection Paper. Apparently he was put into the fort at Buenos Aires for attempted desertion, and was scooped up by one of the de Rosas press gangs. He went on patrol with the army for a while, but then mutinied, starting a riot in which a couple of men were killed. He was severely punished, so deserted, and now incites rebellion."

"How severely punished?"

"Twelve hundred lashes over three sessions, they say."

"My God."

"I don't believe it," said Wiki.

"Neither do I," said his father.

"I've heard that it's true," said Stackpole, confirming to Wiki that the gossip was general. "And it sounds to me as if Harden and these mutinous sealers you've been describing have a lot in common. He's determined to bring about the downfall of de Rosas, they say—so is there any chance that it's not just a coincidence, that he's collecting up the sealers for a purpose?"

"It's possible," said Wiki.

Then Stackpole abruptly shook his head. "Nope, I take that back. It just ain't possible that he knew about those sealers, so why would he search them out?"

Wiki said, "Perhaps he did know about them."

"What?"

"I told him myself." This time it was his own words that rang in Wiki's mind: *"There's a number of men set to jump ship and leave the expedition . . . If there was a sealing voyage in the offing, they'd probably kill to join it."*

Stackpole said with puzzlement, "When?"

"When I was talking to you, not long after we arrived in Adams's store. I'd asked you whether seamen ever jumped ship at the Río Negro, and you said that no sailor would ever desert in a place like El Carmen."

The whaling master stared, and then his mouth fell open as the memory came back. "That was when you told me about those old sealers who'd leave the fleet at the first opportunity!"

"Exactly," said Wiki.

"But the old clerk didn't know enough English to understand

what you were saying, so he couldn't have passed it on," Stackpole objected. Then more light dawned. "You reckon we was overheard?" he exclaimed with open horror.

"By someone who was hiding in the surgery," Wiki said. He remembered the clerk's edgy manner, and the way his gaze had flickered uneasily about, always coming to rest on the wall by the surgery door. He also remembered the sense of a human presence when they had entered the surgery after Ducatel had opened the outside door; he remembered how easily the key had turned in the oiled lock; he remembered the tidily folded blankets on the surgery bed.

"My God!" Stackpole swore. "That means he overheard me badger the clerk into handing over the bill of sale!"

"And the clerk was knifed in a murderous rage," Wiki somberly said.

"He killed him *because* he handed the bill over to me!"

"Probably very soon after you left," agreed Wiki.

Captain Coffin interrupted, saying, "You're still talking about Harden?"

Silence. Then Stackpole said heavily, "Aye, we're talking about Harden."

"Quite apart from the question of whether he murdered the clerk in a passion, why would a rebel join the fleet with the deliberate aim of recruiting sealers?"

Exactly, thought Wiki. Again, Forsythe's voice echoed in his head: *"If he's got such a grand mission for revolution, why would he want to leave the Río Negro?"*

Stackpole said, "That's a point! Harden's not a sealer! Why would he want to recruit a bunch of old sealers to the revolutionary cause?"

Captain Coffin said doubtfully, "They might have the right kind of expertise."

"Those old sealers don't have any skills except for sealing," Wiki argued, then admitted, "Though they can carry out basic sailors' duties, of course."

"Folger was a bo'sun and Boyd was his mate," Captain Coffin reminded him. His expression was as intent as it had been in the afterhouse of the *Vincennes*.

"I'm sure they have blacksmiths aplenty up the river. And the sealers certainly couldn't match the locals on horseback. They'd be nothing but a hindrance."

"Why horseback? What about the schooner?" his father suggested.

"That's a thought," said Wiki, with an approving grin.

Stackpole stared, and then light dawned in his face. He said, astounded, "You reckon those sealers were recruited as crew for the *Grim Reaper*?"

"Exactly," said Wiki, and nodded. "And that's why I want to get to the Río Negro. The sealers are probably ready to abscond with their boat first chance after the *Vin* gets back to the estuary, so I'd like to find the schooner first."

Silence, as they all listened to the scudding sounds as the *Osprey* fled west on the breast of the gale. Then the whaling master finally expressed the obvious: "Do you think Harden killed Adams, as well as the clerk?"

Wiki didn't answer. Instead, he looked at his father.

Captain Coffin was silent too, contemplating Wiki pensively. Then he remarked, "You said that a couple of men died during the riot that Harden incited. Who was the killer, do you know?"

"Harden," said Wiki. "According to the story I heard, that's the reason he was flogged."

The steward came in, and silently cleared the low table of the clutter of plates and leftovers. When he returned to the pantry with the loaded tray, the cat, who had been on Stackpole's knee snatching the tidbits he surreptitiously fed her, jumped down and optimistically followed, her tail as upright as a flagpole.

As soon as the door swung shut Captain Coffin observed to Wiki, "You said to Jim that when Adams returned to the store after being dropped at the El Carmen steps, he might've found it empty."

"My guess is that he *definitely* found it empty. The deed of sale was signed on the fourteenth, and the schooner was sailed to the dunes that same afternoon. Adams returned to El Carmen at dawn the next day—the fifteenth. His clerk, who'd been off work because of family illness, he said, got back that same day to find Adams gone, and the store emptied out."

"I wonder what time the clerk turned up?"

Wiki shrugged ruefully. It was something he'd forgotten to ask.

"We have to assume it was sometime in the morning," said his father. "Which means that the goods were packed out the previous evening."

"Exactly," said Wiki. "I imagine they brought in the horses as soon as the schooner was out of sight."

Another silence, and then Captain Coffin said, "Do you think Adams found Harden at the store—or in El Carmen at all?"

Wiki shook his head.

"I don't think so, either. I think Harden was the man who packed the goods upriver on the horses."

Wiki pointed out, "He would have needed help."

Both shipmasters looked at him expectantly, but he said nothing, and finally Stackpole said, "The clerk must've let them in. Whoever they was," he added pointedly.

"I'm sure he wasn't nearly as loyal to Adams as he pretended to be," agreed Wiki. He remembered the abundant stock of provisions at the Gomes house. "I expect he'd been stealing from the store for months, if not years."

Captain Coffin objected, "But wasn't he away from work at the time?"

"He swore to Stackpole and me that he'd been away from the store the week previous to the fifteenth," Wiki said. "But when Ducatel and

I went to the Gomes house, the women of his family insisted that he'd gone to work as usual."

"Jim Nash didn't say anything about a clerk being present when he signed the deed of sale."

"Gomes could have been out on an errand, or it might have been siesta. *Someone* had to let the thieves into the store, and the clerk is the obvious man."

Stackpole said alertly, "*Thieves?* You think the goods were stolen, and not just carried to the schooner in spite of Adams's instructions to the contrary?"

"I'm sure they were stolen."

Captain Coffin studied Wiki very shrewdly indeed, but instead of pursuing this, he asked, "So what happened after Adams arrived at the store to find it cleared out?"

Stackpole said at once, in ghoulish tones, "He tracked the horse train to the salt dunes—which sealed his death warrant. Adams asked what the hell he thought he was doing by taking his goods instead of waiting for the schooner to arrive at the pueblo, and they got into a fight. That's when Harden killed him."

He turned to Wiki, and demanded, "Don't that make sense?"

"I certainly agree that Adams trailed the horse train," Wiki allowed. "I even know he rode a horse that favored its left forefoot."

"Well, that's it, then. Adams was angry by nature. He started up a fight, and got killed, so Harden stole the schooner, too."

Wiki paused, and then said, "But don't you wonder why Harden—who was a confirmed revolutionary—would want a sealing schooner?"

Dead silence. Then Stackpole was struck with inspiration. "For a rebel transport!" he triumphantly exclaimed.

"Transport?" Captain Coffin echoed. "But where would he transport rebels?"

"According to the scuttlebutt I kept on hearing in El Carmen, he was arming the rebels, all set to lead them up to the Río de la Plata to do battle with de Rosas, and what easier way to get them there, than with the *Grim Reaper*?"

"I'm sure that would be a good use for the schooner—if you are right," Wiki allowed.

His father said shrewdly, "But you have more questions?"

"I do indeed," Wiki admitted.

"Such as?"

"If the killing was the outcome of a spontaneous fight, why was the corpse buried at a prominent landmark?" Again, remembered words rang in Wiki's mind, this time in Captain Wilkes's voice: *"That's a very strange place to bury a murdered man. It's as if the killer wanted him to be found."*

Stackpole said uncertainly, "Maybe that's where the fight happened."

Wiki shook his head. "Bernantio could find no signs of a struggle. The body was strapped to his horse, and carried there for a reason."

"But why was the head sticking out of the grave, if he wasn't killed in that same spot? You reckoned that the victim had jerked his head out of the salt in a last convulsion," Stackpole pointed out.

Wiki lifted his brows and said, "That's a very good question."

"And if he was buried after he was dead, why was there a shot in the middle of the forehead?"

"To open up the head to attract the vultures?" Wiki suggested. "They would have stripped it clean within a couple of hours."

Stackpole grimaced, and Wiki's father visibly shuddered, muttering, "I hate to picture the thoughts that roam about in your brain when you're standing midnight watches, my son." Wiki grinned, and his father guessed, "You're wondering if the head was left sticking out of the grave to make certain the body was found."

"You know me well," said Wiki. He paused, and then said, "I also wish that we'd lifted the body out of the trench and examined it properly."

Stackpole cried, "But why?"

"So we could check to see if the dead man had been severely flogged at some time in the past."

While the two shipmasters were staring at him with blank astonishment, a cry of *"Land ho!"* echoed down from the masthead above.

Wiki leaped off the sofa, and was ahead of the two captains as he sprinted up the companionway. Without stopping to ask permission of Mr. Seward, he jumped onto the bulwarks, and shinnied up the mainmast shrouds to have a look for himself.

The familiar outline of the sandhills, the headland, and the flagstaff lay ahead. Breakers driven by the onshore gale crashed high against the beach and the shoals, and the wind gusted unevenly, in the baffling way that it did in this region. There was not a sign of life on land and, to Wiki's regret, no hint of sails on the sea.

He skidded back to deck, approached his father, and said, "Once we're anchored, can I have a boat and five good men to go upriver? Well armed," he added.

"We're using my boat and my boat's crew!" snapped Captain Stackpole, arriving beside him. "And I'm damn well coming, too!"

Captain Coffin merely nodded, being preoccupied in bringing the *Osprey* to a mooring. With the onshore gale filling her sails, she was scudding toward her old anchorage at rather too smart a pace, considering that they were on a lee shore where there was a danger of being blown into the shoals by a sudden gust. The *Osprey* luffed, coming up into the wind, and he said to the mate, "Strip her down to fores'l, foretopmast stays'l, and mains'l, mister, and don't lose any time about it."

Mr. Seward nodded, and hurried forward to supervise, shouting orders as he went. Apprentices tailed onto lines and seamen clambered aloft. Within minutes, with the energetic help of the six whaleboat crew, the royal, topgallant, and topsail were tied up to their yards. Then it was time to furl the jib, which meant that two hands had to crawl out onto the bowsprit. Wiki supposed that he shouldn't be surprised when Mr. Seward went out himself, followed by one of the cadets, and after that everything happened too fast for anyone to think.

Just as the mate arrived at the outer jibstay, an unexpected gust veered sharply from the north, heeling the brigantine over at the same time that a billow rose as high as her bow. Captain Coffin shouted, the apprentice at the wheel lost his head, and the *Osprey* flew up into the wind. The end of the bowsprit dug into the wave, and when it came up again Mr. Seward was gone.

Sprinting forward, Wiki saw the mate's head bob up and hit against the jibstay. Then Mr. Seward went straight down, trailed by a thin stream of blood. Because he was barefooted, and didn't have to pause to kick off his boots, Wiki was the first to dive over the rail.

Icy cold water closed about his head and gurgled in his ears. Then he was back on the surface, blinking salt out of his eyes. Dimly, he heard concerted screaming, and glimpsed fingers pointing forward to where Mr. Seward had sunk. Wiki kicked hard, struck out for the bow, and arrowed down.

Locating the senseless form by a stream of bubbles, he reached out and grabbed a leg. At the touch, the mate regained consciousness, and instantly panicked. Twisting up and around, he snatched at Wiki's hair. If it had been its original length, he would have drowned them both, but the sodden ringlets slipped out of his grip with an excruciating tug. Then Mr. Seward had him in a stranglehold around the neck. Without compunction, Wiki hit him so hard that he would have done some damage if the blow hadn't been cushioned by the water. The mate flopped again. As Wiki disentangled himself, he realized that the two Tahitians had joined him in the water. Between the three of them, they got the unconscious form back to the ship.

Captain Coffin, along with just about all the crew, was leaning anxiously over the rail. Wiki clambered up the side, slithered over the gangway, and then reached down to take Mr. Seward from the two Polynesians. Once he had him on deck, he stood, heaved Mr. Seward's senseless form over one shoulder, and set off for the mate's stateroom.

His father pursued him to the companionway door, his expression panic-stricken. He exclaimed, "What are you doing?"

"He's alive—don't fret," Wiki grunted, without looking back. "I'll get him to his berth and into dry clothes. The steward can dress his head."

Numbly, Captain Coffin opened the door. Then they were both on the companionway. Wiki crouched as he stepped down, to avoid knocking Mr. Seward's head on the beams. The mate's stateroom was sternward of the two rooms that had been allotted to him and Captain Stackpole. Wiki headed in that direction, saying over his free shoulder, "I'd be obliged if you'd open his door for me, before you go back to the deck."

"*I'll* attend to Mr. Seward," his father said very firmly.

Wiki let out a grunt of derision. "And leave Captain Stackpole in charge of your ship?" He could hear the foresail flogging against the braces.

His father looked around rather wildly. "But—"

"It's all *right*," Wiki snapped, and then said more gently, "I know."

"I haven't a notion what—"

"I know that Mr. Seward is a woman."

Dead silence. Then his father numbly opened the door of the stateroom, and Wiki tipped Mr. Seward, still unconscious, onto the neatly made berth.

"I knew that *you* would guess it," Captain Coffin growled.

Wiki smiled, because he had already worked out why his father had been so flustered and angry about receiving his son on board his ship. As Captain Coffin was acutely aware, in the Pacific it was natural to distinguish sex by mannerisms, stance, and movement, and not by what a person wore. The two Tahitians had realized that Alf Seward was a woman the instant they'd clapped eyes on him; because

Wiki was becoming more American with every month of the discovery voyage, he had taken a little longer.

He repeated, "Go up to deck."

"But it isn't proper for you—"

"Oh, for God's sake," said Wiki. It was hard not to laugh. "Your secret is safe with me," he promised, forbearing to mention the Tahitians. "Go and look after your ship."

Still muttering to himself, his father headed back up the companionway. Just as he disappeared, the steward arrived at the stateroom door, looking anxious. Wiki sent him off for towels, and then threw blankets over the slack form, having no desire whatsoever to see Mr. Seward in the flesh. Reaching under the blankets, he yanked off the seaboots that had almost drowned them both, and then sodden trousers and drawers. A similar foray at the head of the bed got rid of the equally saturated shirt, which joined the pile of wet discarded clothing on the floor.

The towels arrived, and Wiki sent the steward off again for hot tea and brandy. By the time Mr. Seward was dried off, still under the blankets, he was blinking awake. They looked at each other, but not a word was said.

Then, as Wiki produced a clean frock shirt, there was a shout from above to hail a sail in sight. Mr. Seward straightened up, huddling the blankets around his chilled body as he pulled the shirt on, looking a great deal more alert. Then his top half was decent. Abandoning him to the steward's medicating, Wiki ran pell-mell up to deck, and sprang up the mainmast.

He had been so confident that the expedition fleet had been raised that it was a shock to see that the ocean to the east, south, and north was still empty. It took a confused moment for him to turn and scan the landward side—and there he saw the two masts of a schooner coming out of the river estuary.

The *Grim Reaper*, making for the open sea.

Seventeen

In a flash, Wiki realized what had happened—that the Río Negro pilot and the seven sealers must have escaped upriver during the fog. They had spent the interval re-rigging the schooner, and now, under the impression that the expedition fleet had left the Río Negro for good, were escaping out to sea.

With amazing speed and agility, Captain Stackpole had joined him in the hamper. "My God, my God," he cried. " 'Tis my schooner—and she's bloody well getting away!"

Wiki had already seen sails sprout, and realized that there was no chance for the *Osprey* to get under way fast enough to intercept. Then Captain Stackpole hollered out again, in utter stupefaction. Instead of heading for the horizon, the *Grim Reaper* came around, and tacked directly for them.

"What the hell are they doing?" the whaleman cried.

The two Tahitians, in the foremast rigging, understood at once, and hollered out a warning that was so urgent they forgot to use English.

The *Osprey*, her sails dowsed, was on the verge of dropping anchor. She had no way on, but was wallowing up and down instead, leaning over with the force of the wind and tide on her hull. If the sturdy little schooner rammed her, she was done. With a great hole in her lee side, she would fill at once, and sink like a stone.

Closer the schooner beat toward them, all her canvas spread, while shouts of horrified realization burst out on the decks below, accompanied by Captain Coffin's roared orders to make sail. Then the *Grim Reaper* was less than two hundred yards away. Within cannon shot, Wiki bemusedly thought—and as if in response he saw a puff of smoke, and heard the flat distinctive thud of a gun being fired directly at them. *My God! Not only have they rerigged the schooner, but they have armed her, as well!*

A ragged splash of water spurted up twenty yards from their lee bow. Captain Coffin was yelling like a maniac, issuing a stream of orders—not only for the topsail to be loosed, but for the *Osprey*'s own armament to be hoisted up from the hold. The equally frantic boatswain whistled and roared as he sorted excited men into parties.

Wiki scrambled down to deck, ran forward, and clambered up the foremast so fast he was the first to join the Tahitians on the yard. Frantically, gaskets were cast away, and the topsail unfolded in a series of rattles, while the schooner beat closer, closer. The canvas billowed and flogged, and then was sheeted home by hands on deck. Wiki, with the other topmen, clambered upward to attend to the topgallant.

Again the *Grim Reaper* fired, a shot that was rapidly followed by another. Two puffs of smoke, and two echoless thuds. The hail of shot was briefly visible against the sky, but again it fell short. Then at last the topgallant sail was set and drawing. Wiki skidded down a backstay, running headlong for the helm.

Another double thud, another double puff from the *Grim Reaper*. Every man on the brigantine's deck hunched his head between his shoulders as the projectiles screamed through the rigging. It was grapeshot, Wiki's mind told him, just as a halyard fell apart with a thud and a crack. The breeze was gusting hard, but still the schooner beat doggedly upwind toward her prey.

A shout of rage—from Mr. Seward, who was rushing out of the companionway door, a bandage around his head. Luckily, he had remembered to pull on trousers. He shook a fist at the oncoming schooner, started a man up the rigging to splice the broken rope, then sprinted forward to supervise the setting of the head sails.

Wiki arrived at the wheel just as the jib wriggled up the stay and gusted into a long triangle. The apprentice at the helm, shaking with fright and excitement, seemed glad to hand it over. When he looked at his father, Captain Coffin was fully engaged in hassling the men who were swaying something long and heavy out of the hold. To Wiki's amazement, it was a nine-pounder cannon. Cases of muskets and grenades were coming up, too. He had not a notion that Salem traders were so well armed.

The brigantine was starting to pay her head off. Wiki could feel her coming to life under his feet. Then the brigantine had way on, and was sailing on the breast of the gale—directly toward the schooner, which was still beating upwind to meet them. It was high time to tack off and escape.

"Ready about!" Captain Coffin roared, two feet from Wiki's ear.

"Stations!" bawled Mr. Seward on the foredeck.

"Hard down the wheel!" Captain Coffin shouted at Wiki, seemingly unaware that his son was the helmsman. Then, to Mr. Seward: "Lee-oh!"

"Aye, sir!" The foresheet was let go, the head sheets were released, and with the pressure off the foremast canvas the *Osprey* flew up into the gusting gale. The weather leeches of the square sails shook and shivered with a violent rattling sound. The brigantine slowed, losing just about all the momentum she had so painfully gained, her bow pointed to the eye of the wind.

The foremast yards swung crazily until they were hard against the backstays, the sails crashing and banging, and men yelling like demons as they hauled. It was a precarious moment. If she missed stays now, she would fall off, and drift down upon the menacing schooner. However, the jaunty old girl answered at once—Wiki would never have guessed that such an antique vessel could be so handy on her helm. The boom swung and the big mainsail filled, and the foreyards were dragged round by chanting men. About the *Osprey* came, as neat as a goose backpaddling water.

The schooner had gained ground while the brigantine was going through the maneuver. Looking over his shoulder, Wiki saw her yaw, and realized she was preparing to get off another shot. A flat bang, and another stream of balls through rigging. More ropes parted, the topgallant sagged, and a row of holes popped into the taut canvas of the topsail. Wiki fought with the helm as the brigantine lost her precariously gained way.

Captain Stackpole, who had taken over the job of running repairs without being asked, hollered at his boat's crew, who sprang aloft to splice the broken cordage, braving another hail of shot. Then, miraculously, the firing paused. When Wiki looked over his shoulder again, the *Grim Reaper* was back on course, making up ground and then gaining perceptibly.

The gap was reduced to one hundred yards, then ninety. Another double hail of shot, and bangs and twangs as the rigging of the *Osprey* absorbed more damage. Captain Coffin swore, "What's wrong with you men? Are you all stuffed with cotton wadding?"

No one answered, because the sailors were far too busy. One party, headed by the carpenter, was preparing the gun. Men hooked on stout ropes, a side tackle to each side of the carriage, and a train-tackle leading to a ringbolt in the deck at the rear. A strong breeching, long enough to allow the cannon to recoil after every shot, but short enough to prevent it from breaking loose, was secured to the brig's hull by two ringbolts and looped to a knob at the back end of the gun.

It was going to take far too long, Wiki thought nervously, with another quick backward look at the schooner. At last the *Osprey* was matching her speed, so that the ninety-yard gap between the two vessels wasn't diminishing. However, she was well in range of those fiendishly efficient swivel guns, which let off another double fusillade at that very moment. A cry, and a man tumbled out of the lee shrouds. Miraculously, he landed safely on hands and feet, but blood was running down one arm. A snapped order from Captain Coffin, and the wounded man was hurried down the companionway by a shipmate.

At last the cannon was set for loading. The carpenter, who also acted as gun captain, cried orders in rapid succession. The cartridge, a flannel bag filled with powder, was rammed down the muzzle, then the nine-pound iron ball, followed by a wad.

"Man side-tackle falls, run out!"

With a grumble the snout of the cannon was shoved through the space in the stern quarter rail. The carpenter crouched over the sights, and barked a stream of orders to his crew, who were grunting and laboring with crowbars and handspikes. At last he was satisfied. Back he stood, shouting, "Fire!"

A huge bang, and the afterdeck was shrouded in stinging smoke. Everyone peered through it to see where the shot had fallen, but it was impossible to tell. They had overshot, Wiki thought. The schooner sailed on in hot chase, with no sign of damage, closing the gap by another ten yards, so that he could clearly see the two swivel guns firing in her bows. More shot whistled through the rigging, but without hitting a single rope or sheet of canvas. Obviously, the gunners hadn't allowed for the narrowing distance, and had aimed too high, but it was an unnervingly close escape.

Managing by a huge effort of will to ignore what was happening elsewhere, the carpenter ordered the gun readied for loading again. Wiki was still wet through from his plunge in the sea, and was shaking with both cold and excitement, so that his teeth chattered as he said to him, "D-dismantling sh-shot."

The carpenter stood straight, turned, and stared at him as if something had crawled out of a knothole in the deck. "I beg your pardon, Mr. Coffin?"

"Dismantling shot," Wiki said more clearly. "Like the b-bolas. Three chains—each about th-three feet long—j-joined together at a common center, and then rolled into a b-ball."

"But what use is that?" the carpenter cried.

"The three chains spread out when they are fired. If you aim high enough, they will wrap around masts and rigging and wrench them to pieces."

"You want me to aim at the bloody *rigging*?" the carpenter exclaimed in utter disbelief, and then repeated himself in more seemly fashion, having noticed that Captain Coffin was listening. "My personal ambition, Mr. Coffin," he said, "is to hole her 'twixt wind and water, and send her to the bottom afore she do the same to us."

"But it would be nice if Captain Stackpole were able to repair her after he g-gets her b-back," Wiki argued, still shivering. "And he can't do that if she is lying on the b-bottom with large holes in her hull."

"The schooner belongs to Cap'n Stackpole?" the carpenter exclaimed.

"Aye, sir," said Wiki, watching the leading edge of the topgallant sail and adjusting the helm.

"He's right!" Captain Coffin cried, all animation. "Mr. Seward—a party to assemble dismantling shot, if you please!"

The mate arrived, green eyes slitted as he looked Wiki up and down. "You're wet through, Mr. Coffin," he growled. "What do you want to do—catch your death of cold? Get below and change at once!"

"Aye, sir," said Wiki, wondering why the whole world didn't immediately discern that Mr. Seward was a woman, and obediently handed over the wheel. When he arrived below, the steward was bandaging the hurt man's arm, and judging by the stream of oaths from the victim, the seaman was going to survive to tell the tale. The invective halted a moment as another fusillade tore through rope, canvas, and air abovedecks, but then resumed as vigorously as before.

Wiki's fingers were so numb that it seemed to take forever to drag off his wet, clinging clothes, and scramble into clean, dry ones. When he finally made it to deck, a quick backward look saw the schooner in the same place. To his mystification, two apprentices were filling grenade shells with flour, each one finished off with a fuzee.

More comprehensibly, three more cadets were cutting chain into three-foot lengths, while a fourth shackled them together in groups of three. The first of these, rolled into a ball, was handed to the carpenter, who was dancing with impatience, and down the throat of the gun it went, to join the cartridge of gunpowder. So swiftly did he aim, Wiki shied involuntarily when the gun went off, as he hadn't heard the command to fire. Then, as the chains spread out and whirled through the air, he jumped with fright again, because the ghastly device emitted a sound he'd never heard before, like the screaming of the condemned in the lowest level of hell.

Everyone about the decks looked equally stunned at the sheer violence of the noise. Even more incredibly, it wailed its way through the rigging of the schooner without effect. The *Grim Reaper* didn't even shy in fright, instead veering to take advantage of a gust from the north which brought her even closer.

Seventy yards, then fifty. To Wiki's surprise, he saw a man on the schooner jump onto the weather bow, brace himself, and then swing an arm as if throwing a ball. He glimpsed the flying missile, and then a grenade thumped onto the deck of the brigantine, and bounced. The boatswain, who was closest, frantically kicked, and the grenade jumped over the lee rail, fizzing as it went.

"Dear God!" cried Captain Coffin. If the grenade had burst, the brigantine would have been quickly reduced to a mute patch of charred wreckage—and it was obvious that the men on the schooner would have made sure that none of the *Osprey* men who survived the explosion would still be alive to tell the tale.

Another grenade was hurled, then another. Both fell harmlessly into the water, but it was horribly evident that many more were on the way. Captain Coffin roared, "Give me the man with the strongest arm! Someone to put grenades of our own on board that bastard!"

Wiki's teeth had stopped chattering, but he was numb with amazement. They were going to retaliate with grenades armed with *flour*? He couldn't believe it. Nevertheless, he managed to shout at his father, "The whalemen! Harpooners!"

Miraculously, Captain Stackpole had heard him—and understood, too. He snapped out two names, and two brawny-shouldered whalemen came running to the poop. Each was handed a flour grenade with the fuzee lit and burning steadily. Each took up the famous harpooner stance, one foot braced behind, the forward leg bent so the knee was tucked firmly against the bulwarks beneath the taffrail. Each brought his grenade-loaded arm back.

"Fire!" cried the carpenter, intoxicated with battle. Both men swung with the power of experienced harpooners, and smoothly released. Wiki distinctly saw the two grenades fly over the space between the two ships, and land on the schooner's deck.

There was a double thump as the two grenades blew up simultaneously—and the *Grim Reaper* was cloaked in a billowing white cloud, which sparked weirdly as individual particles of flour caught fire and exploded. Blinded and startled, the schooner fell off the wind, and sagged away in their wake.

"*Now* for dismantling shot!" cried Captain Coffin. The two topmasts of the *Grim Reaper*, sticking up out of the great white pastrylike puff, made a perfect target. The gun crew worked like demons, and another devil's invention howled over the widening gap, while Wiki darted up the mast of the brigantine for a better view.

The aim was a little low, but the result was just as effective. Wiki heard the bang as the spring stay was cut, and then a distant clatter as the mainmast collapsed—and the *Grim Reaper* turned broadside to the gale.

Within moments, impelled by the twin forces of wind and tide on her hull, she was sagging directly for the deadly shoals and certain doom, while Captain Stackpole's roars of pain and fury at the imminent loss of his property echoed from the foredeck of the *Osprey*. The cloud of flour was thinning, and Wiki could glimpse figures on her deck frantically clearing away the raffle of ropes and spars to try to straighten her up.

Then, from his vantage point aloft, he saw a figure struggle out onto the bowsprit of the schooner. A moment later, a scrap of canvas began to wriggle up a stay that was still, miraculously, secured to what was left of her foremast. He could hear puzzled comments from the decks of the *Osprey*, and then abruptly realized what was happening.

At the same moment, Captain Stackpole yelled, "She's trying to set a sail to pay her head off!"

It was magnificent seamanship, and Wiki felt a pang that the man behind the gallant action should be nothing better than a murdering pirate. As the thin triangle of canvas blew taut the *Grim Reaper* straightened up, and it became obvious that whoever was in charge was steering head-on to the beach. The breakers pounded high but, as Wiki knew well, the bottom there was free of rocks. Then the schooner was in the surf, surrounded by spray and flying spume—and the *Grim Reaper* grounded with a crash.

The remnants of her masts jumped out of her with the jolt, but the bowsprit remained in place, sticking out over the sand. Eight figures scrambled out onto it, and ran in single file to safety. Wiki watched them jump down to the beach, dash to the cliff, and begin to climb. High above, the flagstaff poked a finger at the pale sky—and by the flagpole were two horsemen, their ponchos lifting and falling in the wind. Onward the eight men climbed, onward, while the riders watched and waited, unmoving. Wiki narrowed his eyes, indefinably reminded of the sketch Titian Peale had made of the gauchos roping the buck, then realized that it was because the far-off horsemen were carrying rifles.

At last the climbers had reached the top of the cliff—and the nearer horseman raised his weapon and aimed. His movements were careful and precise as he selected his target. Wiki thought he heard a shot, though perhaps he imagined it, because of the distance. One of the escaping figures threw up his arms, and fell, tumbling down the precipice. The other seven men paused, then ran more frantically than ever. Seconds later they had disappeared, leaving their fallen comrade at the bottom of the cliff.

With the consummate skill of experienced whalemen, Stackpole's boat's crew put their boat down on the water while the *Osprey* was still under way. Scrambling down to deck at a headlong pace, Wiki had to take a running jump to get into the boat before they had pulled out of range. Captain Stackpole grinned tightly as Wiki landed in the stern sheets, and then barked out an order. The crew hauled mightily at their oars, and the boat scudded swiftly through the water.

The grounded schooner made an easy landmark, standing upright in the surf, dismasted but otherwise apparently entire. Wiki saw Captain Stackpole's head turn as he scrutinized the state of his property, but he said nothing, and the whaleboat surged on for the beach. With a long crunch of gravel, the boat grounded, sending a wash up the sand that surged and foamed almost as far as the fallen man.

Four oarsmen leaped out and held the whaleboat still, while Wiki and Stackpole jumped out into the surf. Looking up, Wiki caught another glimpse of the two horsemen at the edge of the precipice, still watching. Then he ran toward the sprawled body at the foot of the cliff.

The man was lying partly on his stomach and partly on one side, his head resting in the crook of an upturned arm. His bloodied shirt had torn, exposing part of his smooth back, and the pistol stuck in his belt. Wiki turned the body fully over onto its back. It flopped awkwardly, because of the jumble of broken bones inside the skin. The shielding arm fell away from the unmarked face just as the whaling master arrived.

Stackpole cried, *"That's Caleb Adams!"*

Wiki straightened, brushing dirt off his palms as he looked down at the body of the man he had known as Benjamin Harden. Adams's eyes were shut, and there was sand in his reddish beard and the creases of his face. The front of his shirt was scarlet with blood that leaked from a shot hole in the upper left side of his chest, but Wiki reckoned it was the fall that had killed him.

He looked at Stackpole and said dryly, "No mistaken identity this time?"

"I'd know him anywhere, even with those whiskers." Captain Stackpole's tone held utter certainty. Then he blinked. "So the other body—the body buried at the foot of the Gualichú tree . . . ?"

"Harden's," said Wiki. When he turned to look at the *Osprey*, the brigantine was dowsing her sails and dropping anchor. His father had lowered a boat, which was pulling for the schooner.

He looked back at Stackpole. "If we had taken him out of the grave, we would have seen the scars on his back from that flogging. Otherwise, it was natural to identify the remains as Adams's corpse, just the way Adams planned when he buried Harden that way. The body was wearing the right clothes, and the right medal hung round the neck. The skull was picked clean, so the face was gone."

"Dear God," said Stackpole, and shook his head in rueful disgust.

"Adams probably also planned on whoever blundered over the skull being too spooked to heave the corpse right out of the grave," Wiki reassured him.

But Stackpole wasn't even listening. Instead he said, as if to himself, "So Caleb Adams murdered Harden, not the other way around."

"And stole his Protection Paper," Wiki agreed.

The whaling master abruptly paid attention. "So he could impersonate him?"

"Aye." Wiki remembered how Adams had furtively checked the riverbank before he had accosted Ringgold; he remembered the confident flourish with which Harden's Protection Paper had been produced. His audacity had been astounding, but the masquerade had worked.

"Dear God," said Stackpole again. Then he said to Wiki in an accusing kind of voice, "You're not even a bit surprised that this is Adams."

Wiki shook his head. "It just didn't make sense that a revolutionary would recruit sealers for the rebel cause," he said. "The instant I realized that Adams was a professional sealer, it was easy to work out what really happened."

Stackpole's face wrinkled in the shadow of his hat while he thought this over. Then he shifted from boot to boot, and said, "So it was Adams who was hiding in the surgery while you and I was talking?"

Wiki shrugged. "It was his store," he pointed out. The trader had slunk back to home territory like a dog to its den. "He probably moved in there right after the schooner was safely hidden."

The whaling master squinted at him. "The two Gomes brothers would've had to help him to hide the schooner."

"There's no reason why they wouldn't," Wiki said. "While they could have guessed that he was stealing the schooner, they didn't know that he was a murderer, as well as a thief—and were used to obeying him, anyway. Their father had worked for him for at least two years, remember. Remember Adams's temper? He probably had them all intimidated."

"So that's why the clerk kept quiet about his boss hiding in the surgery," Stackpole guessed, and added grimly, "And got knifed for his trouble."

They both turned as Captain Coffin's boat arrived in the surf. He'd left men on the wreck, Wiki saw, because there were still several figures clambering all over it. His father was smiling as he trudged toward them, and then his face suddenly went stiff with alarm, and he shouted, "Look out!"

Wiki whirled. Adams's eyes were open. Wiki saw the pistol

aimed in one bloodied hand, and jumped for it. The pistol went off an instant after his bare foot slammed down on the upraised wrist, clamping it to the sand. The explosion was deafening, followed by a loud whine and the slam of a ricochet. When Wiki kicked the pistol away the clunk as it hit rock seemed faint by comparison.

Stackpole cried, "My God, he's still alive!"

Not for long, Wiki thought. Adams was staring at him with such ferocity that the nape of his neck crawled, but there was agony in the storekeeper's face as well, and his eyes were beginning to glaze.

Stackpole didn't seem to notice that death was so close. Instead, he shouted furiously at Adams, "Why did you steal the *Grim Reaper* from me? All you needed was to ask for a goddamn berth—I would've made you sealing master!"

Adams didn't speak. Instead he turned his head and spat. It obviously hurt, and the phlegm was thick with blood, but the contempt was unmistakable.

The whaling master took an abrupt step backward, looking shaken. He said to Wiki, "He stole my schooner, he cheated me—yet I dealt with him, I *trusted* him! And he killed the man he'd hired as sailing master! Why would he *do* that?"

Wiki was silent a moment, thinking that the more interesting question was why Harden had agreed to ship as sailing master in the first place. Was it because he had plans for the moment when the schooner, with the storekeeper on board, disappeared upriver?

He said to his father, "What's the schooner's condition like?"

Captain Coffin's expression became surprised at the unexpected question, but he said matter-of-factly, "She'll float off with the next high tide."

Stackpole cried, "She's undamaged?"

"Tight as a bottle, and floats like one, too," Captain Coffin assured him. "All she needs is new masts and rerigging. She didn't ground hard, because she's not heavy enough—there's hardly anything inside her, apart from ballast and salt."

Wiki nodded. Not only did he remember the way the *Grim Reaper* had yawed every time the swivels had fired, but this was what he had expected.

"Not much in the way of provisions?" he checked.

"Hardly anything at all," replied his father.

Wiki looked down at Adams. "You got back to the store to find that Harden had stolen all your provisions," he stated. "He'd brought in a party with plenty of horses, and they had packed out your entire stock, and carried it to the caves."

"For his goddamned revolution!"

They all flinched at the tortured fury in Adams's unexpected shout. His broken body spasmed with remembered rage. He was glaring at Wiki, apparently unaware of the thick gout of blood that bubbled out of his mouth.

Wiki continued, "You pursued them, but by the time you caught up with Harden all your goods had vanished, along with the horses and the rebels."

Adams's head jerked in a grotesque affirmative. Then he swore in the same harsh, loud voice, *"But I made the bastard pay, by God!"*

He had knifed him in a blind rage—just as he had later killed the clerk. Wiki said, "You found him alone at the *salinas*?"

Adams jerked again, but though he tried to speak, nothing but a dreadful croak came out. A second great glob of blood poured out of the twisted mouth, and then the madly staring eyes glazed over forever.

The silence was broken by a distant shout. Wiki roused himself, and took several backward steps to look up at the horsemen, who were still waiting and watching at the edge of the cliff.

The shout had been a question. Wiki called out an affirmative, and received a brief message in reply.

Captain Coffin said curiously, "Is that Bernantio and one of his men?"

"Gauchos don't carry guns. And didn't you hear him call out in Portuguese, not Spanish?"

Captain Coffin shook his head. "What did he ask?"

"He asked if Adams was dead."

"Ah." A nod, and then Captain Coffin asked, "What did he say then?"

"He said, *The storekeeper killed my father,*" Wiki translated. However, he had to repeat himself, because the words were drowned out by the distant thud of hooves as the Gomes brothers wheeled their steeds and galloped away.

Epilogue

February 3, 1839

When the cutter drew up to the tall side of the flagship *Vincennes,* seven men were being punished for the crime of attempted desertion. The awful sounds of a ritual flogging echoed down to the water.

The seven sealers had been easily hunted down—because Bernantio and his gauchos had materialized on the riverbank landing of the estuary, and gracefully offered their services to the officer in charge of the search party. Wiki, though delighted to become reaquainted with the *rastreadores,* had surveyed them rather cynically as he translated. Not only did he think that Bernantio had had a good idea of the whereabouts of the *Grim Reaper*'s hiding place all along, but, remembering how the *rastreador* had shown no interest at all in the worn tracks that had led from the riverside path to the rebels' caves, he had a strong suspicion Bernantio had known who had stolen the provisions, too. However, life was hard on the pampas and the steppe, and Wiki held no grudge, even when Bernantio gave him a conspiratorial grin as he received the fee for turning in the runaways after they had been hunted down and lassoed.

Back on the *Vincennes,* the sealers had each been condemned to forty-eight lashes—though without the court-martial that should have preceded such an extreme punishment—and so the flogging was protracted. Forsythe motioned his men to still the boat with their oars, and they waited for the thuds and screams to finish. For Wiki, the interval seemed endless, and even Forsythe shifted about uneasily.

"They should've let 'em go, and bloody good riddance," he muttered.

Wiki couldn't have agreed more. The seven sealers had been trouble from the start, and now they had a hurt to fuel their grievances. However, he said nothing. Forsythe's cuttersmen, all proper tarry sailors with a wealth of sea experience, were equally silent, studying the progress of the rerigging of the schooner, now afloat and swarming with Stackpole's men, instead of betraying their thoughts.

Then Forsythe, just like several times before, said smugly, "So it was because of things what I pointed out that you figured Harden was the murdered man."

The southerner had listened with riveted attention to the story, asked many questions, and been both unsurprised and complacent when informed that his comments had provided vital clues. *"You reckon the storekeeper's killer missed the boat because he wanted to get hold of that bill of sale . . . But the bloody schooner was gone! . . . If he's got such a grand mission for revolution, why would he want to leave the Río Negro?"*

Forsythe was coming to regard himself as quite a sleuth, which boded ill for the future, thought Wiki. However he smiled as he agreed, "That's right."

"Next time there's a murder, you'll listen real bloody careful to what I say, I reckon."

"Heaven forfend there is one," Wiki prayed.

The last man had been flogged, and the decks above vibrated to the sounds of marching feet as the crew was dismissed. The cutter pulled over to the side of the ship, and an oarsman held a rope to steady the boat while Wiki scrambled onto the ladder. When he stepped over the gangway, a bucket of water was being tossed over the foot of the grating to wash away the blood.

To Wiki's surprise, his father was standing near the portico of the afterhouse, talking with Lawrence J. Smith. He had a folio of documents under his arm, so Wiki deduced that he had come on board to receive the last of the scientific reports before taking his departure for Philadephia. As soon as their eyes met, Captain Coffin abandoned the conversation, and walked toward him.

"Bloody awful way of doing things," he declaimed before he even arrived, without bothering to lower his voice. "Men must be punished, but the punishment should come hot on the heels of the crime, and not with this ghastly ceremony."

"So why were you here to view it?" asked Wiki.

"Got trapped. By the time Wilkes had stopped handing on instructions, it was time for him to superintend the damnable business. I spent the time in the saloon, but at least the coffee was good."

"Which is entirely due to your business acumen," Wiki said with amusement. The coffee had been dreadful before Captain Coffin had sold those sacks of coffee beans to the purser of the fleet.

To his surprise, his father drew him over to the lee rail, and looked around to make sure they weren't overheard. Then he said in a low voice, "Leave this goddamned expedition—join us on the *Osprey*."

Wiki smiled, realizing the sacrifice this had cost his father, but shook his head.

"Why not?" his father said aggressively. "I want you to sail with me."

"Mr. Seward wouldn't like it."

"Fiddlesticks. He might take a while to get used to you being privy to his secret, but he'll soon get over that. He's . . ." Captain Coffin looked around again, then lowered his voice still further. "He has good reasons for being the way he is," he muttered in Wiki's ear. "He was married very young to the captain of a small coasting brig, and helped him with the work just like a man would, but the master was drowned after just a few years—a tragic affair—and Alf found it impossible to adjust to landlife again. Loves the sea with a passion. No family to tie him down, so he embarked on his deception. Spent the next few years traipsing from ship to ship—not so different from you, my boy!—because he had to get out in a hurry whenever someone was on the verge of guessing his sex. Then he made that pierhead jump onto the *Osprey*."

Captain Coffin paused at last, and Wiki said curiously, "How long did it take you to guess the truth?"

To his surprise, his father laughed. "I didn't! Eight months after he shipped he came to me and revealed all, much to my astonishment. He said he'd only ever lasted six months before being uncovered, in the past, and the suspense was killing him, so he wanted to get it over and done with."

Wiki shook his head. He wondered how his father could have been so dense.

Reading his mind, Captain Coffin said wryly, "I talk too much, Wiki. I enjoy telling my yarns so much that I don't pay enough attention to my audience. I guess the only time I really looked at him was when I was giving him orders—or consulting about ship affairs."

"You were keeping different watches," Wiki reassured him, and then asked, "When he fessed up, you came to an arrangement?"

"Exactly," said Captain Coffin with satisfaction. "And it has worked out first-rate. He suits me—he handles the crew like a real officer, and he's a capital seaman, too. He's kind enough to be patient with the cadets, but makes sure they don't carry on like beasts. He's good company, too—has a fine tenor voice, dances the best jig in the ship, and plays the fiddle like a Gypsy."

"Good God," said Wiki. He was perfectly astonished by this recital of virtues.

"And as you know, he cherishes the barky as if she were his own.

You saw how shipshape he keeps her! Though he might be as prickly as a crab, he *suits* me," Captain Coffin repeated. "You'll enjoy life on the *Osprey*, once Alf gets used to you."

"But what would I do to fill in the time?"

"You keep on telling me I need a second mate."

"Which is most certainly so," Wiki agreed. "Your little secret shouldn't stop you from hiring someone else, though," he recommended with a grin. "Tell Mr. Seward to dress him down the way he dressed me down after I made that sternboard, and he won't feel a single doubt that your mate is a man, and a real tough one, too."

His father had the grace to look embarrassed, but was obstinate enough to try another tack. "Jim Nash's suggestion wasn't such a bad idea, you know," he said. "That brig of his is sure to be much less seaworthy than he pretends she is, but I could buy a smart vessel and put you in command. There are advantages to sailing as a fleet—I could use your vessel as a tender in the Fijis!"

"Excellent idea," Wiki said warmly. "But Mr. Seward is the fellow you should put in charge of a second ship."

Captain Coffin looked shocked to the core. He cast another furtive glance around, and hissed, "*Put a woman in command?* You must be out of your mind! Would women be allowed to command voyaging canoes?" he demanded.

"No, of course not." It was Wiki's turn to be taken aback.

"Well, then?" said his father triumphantly.

"Because Polynesians navigate with their testicles." Wiki was serious: the voyagers had three aids to navigation—the stars, the flight paths of migrating birds, and the currents, and the best way to gauge the flow of the current was by sitting on a thwart.

"Jesus Christ!" his father exclaimed, stunned yet again. "Don't *ever* say that in polite company."

Wiki laughed, and then pursued his argument. "In the isolation of the aftercabin, Mr. Seward's secret would never be discovered," he guaranteed. Because of his time as an officer on whaleships, along with more recent experience with Captain Wilkes, Wiki was acutely aware of the loneliness of the man in command at sea, and knew perfectly well that George had gone to great lengths to persuade him to ship on the *Swallow* just so he'd have an old friend for company on the long voyage about the globe.

"Dear God, what a notion," Captain Coffin muttered, but there was a thoughtful glint in his half-hidden eye. Then he cocked that eye at Wiki, and warned, "We weigh anchor and get under way the moment I get back on board."

Wiki felt the wind on his cheek—a fresh gale, fair for the northward voyage. He said, "You'll have a short passage, with luck." The expedition fleet, by contrast, would have to beat against the wind to get south to Cape Horn.

"This is your last chance!" his father barked.

Wiki said gently, "If I leave the expedition now, I'll spend the rest of my life wondering what I've missed."

Then, for the first time ever, he embraced his father in the Maori fashion. Drawing him close by the shoulders, he pressed his nose against his, and stood still with his eyes shut, softly breathing in his father's air, forehead touching forehead.

When Captain Coffin drew away, his eyes were glistening. "Well, then," he said gruffly, and clapped Wiki on the shoulder, and strode over to the gangway without looking back.

For a long moment Wiki stood watching the rakishly elegant figure retreat, wondering where he would be when he met his father again. Then he remembered his appointment with Captain Wilkes, and turned back to the portico of the afterhouse. He nodded as the marine on sentry saluted, then followed the ramrod back and marching boots down the wide corridor to the chartroom.

There was a single preoccupied grunt when the sentry knocked on the door, so Wiki hoped to find Captain Wilkes alone. However, Lawrence J. Smith was with him, more smug than ever with his recent promotion. Wiki knew that the men and his fellow officers despised him, and that it was commonly believed that his elevation was entirely due to the fact that he was the captain's toady. However, Lieutenant Smith was far too thick-skinned to allow anything like that to spoil his self-satisfaction.

"Wiremu," he greeted.

Instead of replying, Wiki turned to Captain Wilkes, who was holding Wiki's written report of the murder investigation, and looking immensely pleased with himself. "So I was right when I guessed that the murdered man had been deliberately buried at a prominent landmark," he said.

"That's a very strange place to bury a murdered man. It's as if the killer wanted him to be found." "Aye, sir," said Wiki.

"Quite the sleuth, aren't I?" the commodore of the expedition joked. "If we should experience another murder—which the good Lord forbid—I could give you a run for your money, eh?"

"I do believe you could, sir," said Wiki.

"That horseman who shot Adams? He was one of the murdered clerk's sons?"

Wiki nodded. "I'd seen both of them before—though not in the flesh," he elaborated, and told him about the armed horsemen Mr. Peale had sketched in the background of his study of the gauchos.

"Good Lord," said Captain Wilkes. He was fascinated.

"They must have been stalking Adams ever since we discovered their father's body and informed the family. Adams had managed to escape first to the *Sea Gull,* and then to the expedition fleet, but risked being ambushed when he went upriver to retrieve the *Grim Reaper.* However, instead of chasing the schooner in their fishing boat, the Gomes brothers followed on horseback—which means that if the *Osprey* had not engaged the *Grim Reaper* in combat, Adams would have got away."

"I have already congratulated Captain Coffin on his gallant action," Captain Wilkes said sharply. His brow darkened, a sign that the interview with Wiki's father had been the usual contentious one.

Wiki nodded without expression, at a loss to know what to say. He shifted restlessly, hoping it was time to return to the *Swallow*.

Instead of dismissing him, however, Captain Wilkes went on meditatively, "So you had a profitable time up the Río Negro."

"I beg your pardon, sir?"

"It gratifies me to learn that you worked well with some of the other scientifics of the expedition. With his talents for art and observation, Naturalist Peale assisted your mission to some small degree, it seems. And Philologist Hale is an eminently worthy young man, don't you agree?"

"Aye, sir," said Wiki, forbearing to mention that Horatio Hale held views about the origin of his people that were decidedly at odds with his own, and that he found Mr. Peale both hostile and condescending.

"It's a relationship I would like to foster. We'll be weighing anchor within two hours, so you'll oblige me by removing to the *Peacock* without delay."

Wiki involuntarily exclaimed, *"What!"*

"You heard me," Captain Wilkes said in testy tones. "I'm shifting you to the *Peacock*. Mr. Smith made the suggestion, and I think it's a first-class idea."

Wiki thought, *Oh God*. When he looked at Lieutenant Smith he could see that his prim little mouth was pouted in a knowing smile, and there was cold dislike in his prominent eyes. He turned back to Captain Wilkes, protesting, "But how do Mr. Hale and Mr. Peale feel about it? Has anyone consulted with them?"

Captain Wilkes flushed. "I don't have to consult with anyone, sir! Mr. Hale has already indicated to Mr. Smith that he would like to tap your knowledge of Pacific languages at leisure, and, as Mr. Smith also points out, you should benefit greatly from Mr. Peale's vast experience. And, anyway, it's damn well time you associated with your fellow scientifics, instead of the sailors of the *Swallow*!"

"But—" cried Wiki.

"I want no further argument," Captain Wilkes snapped. "Get out, and bloody well follow orders for once!"

"Aye, sir," said Wiki bleakly—for how could he tell Captain Wilkes that Hale didn't consider him a fellow scientific at all, regarding him instead as a curiosity? Or that there was a New Zealand Maori on board the *Peacock* who would seize the first opportunity to kill him, for no other reason than that their tribes were deadly enemies? He felt utterly desperate, but was helpless to do anything about it.

Out on deck the wind was frisking up. Clouds scudded high in the sky, and seabirds screamed as they whirled high around the masts where men were casting off gaskets to release sail. When Wiki looked out over the gray heave of the sea, the *Osprey* was already a distant silhouette, like a fleeting moth on the horizon.

Background Reading

Chappell, David A. *Double Ghosts: Oceanian Voyagers on Euroamerican Ships*. Armonk, New York, and London, England: M. E. Sharpe, 1997.

Darwin, Charles. Beagle *Diary*. Edited by Richard Darwin Keynes. Cambridge, UK: Cambridge University Press, 1988.

Graham, R. B. Cunninghame. *South American Sketches*. Edited by John Walker. Norman, Ok.: University of Oklahoma Press, 1978.

———. *Tales of Horsemen*. Edinburgh: Canongate Publishing, 1981.

Hale, Horatio. *Ethnography and Philology*. 1846. Reprint, Upper Saddle River, N.J.: Gregg Press, 1968.

Harland, John. *Seamanship in the Age of Sail*. London: Conway Maritime Press, 1984.

Paine, Ralph D. *The Ships and Sailors of Old Salem*. London: Heath Cranton, 1924.

Poesch, Jessie J. *Titian Ramsey Peale, 1799–1885, and His Journals of the Wilkes Expedition*. Philadelphia, Pa.: American Philosophical Society, 1961.

Reynolds, William. *The Private Journal of William Reynolds: United States Exploring Expedition, 1838–1842*. Edited by Nathaniel Philbrick and Thomas Philbrick. New York: Penguin, 2004.

———. *Voyage to the Southern Ocean: The Letters of Lieutenant William Reynolds from the U.S. Exploring Expedition, 1838–1842*. Edited by Anne Hoffman Cleaver and E. Jeffrey Stann. Annapolis, Md.: Naval Institute Press, 1988.

Tily, James C. *The Uniforms of the United States Navy*. New York: Thomas Yoseloff, 1964.

Viola, Herman J., and Carolyn Margolis, eds. *Magnificent Voyagers: The U.S. Exploring Expedition, 1838–1842*. Washington, D.C.: Smithsonian Institution, 1985.

Wilkes, Charles. *Autobiography of Rear Admiral Charles Wilkes, U.S. Navy 1798–1877*. Edited by William James Morgan, David B. Tyler, Joye L. Leonhart, Mary F. Loughlin. Washington, D.C.: Naval History Division, 1978.

———. *Narrative of the United States Exploring Expedition*. 5 vols. 1844. Reprint, Upper Saddle River, N.J.: Gregg Press, 1970.